Karen Robards

Loving Julia

CENTER POINT PUBLISHING
THORNDIKE, MAINE

This Center Point Large Print edition
is published in the year 2002 by arrangement with
Warner Books, Inc.

The text of this Large Print edition is unabridged.
In other aspects, this book may vary from the original edition.
Printed in Thailand. Set in 16-point
Times New Roman type by Bill Coskrey.

ISBN 1-58547-145-3

Library of Congress Cataloging-in-Publication Data

Robards, Karen.
    Loving Julia / Karen Robards.
      p. cm.
    ISBN 1-58547-145-3 (lib. bdg. : alk. paper)
    1. Large type books. I. Title.

PS3568.O196 L68 2002
813'.54--dc21

                                              2001028982

To
my mother-in-law,
Frances Sigler,
her children,
Anthony, Suzanne, Jerry,
Carl, Nancy, Pam, and Betty, and
their families.
And, as always,
to Doug and Peter.

I

OU, Jool, get yer arse movin' and do as yer bid! Now! Or, by God, I'll. . . ."

A swipe with a brutishly thick forearm finished the threat. Jewel Combs ducked the blow with the agility of long practice. The rush of air as it just missed her head blew long tendrils of her inky black hair upward in its wake. She was not one whit bothered by the violence. Getting hit was nothing new to her; if a day had passed since her birth some sixteen years before when someone had not hit her for something, she could not remember it. Dodging blows—or taking them if she wasn't fast enough on her feet—was a fact of life for her and all those like her: the ragged, dirty urchins who had no home but London's filthy back streets.

In fact, she was luckier than most, and she knew it. She had a family, of a sort. Jem Meeks was meaner than a gutter rat and almost as ugly with his thin, cadaverous face and long beak of a nose, but if you did as you were bid he saw to it that you had a place to lay your head nights and a crust of bread with a bit of meat to sup on. And he kept you safe. No one bothered you if you were one of Jem Meeks' band of pickpockets, hawkers, and petty thieves.

"I'm goin', I'm goin', ya ol' cod's head!" Jewel muttered tartly. Reaching behind her, she yanked tight and tied the laces of her most prized possession—a new dress salvaged from the castoffs of some down and out theater company.

At that time of night the loft was nearly deserted; the assorted characters who resided there practiced their vocations after dark. Besides her and Jem, there was only Ol'

7

Bates (whose lay was pretending to be blind drunk until some cove bent over him to rifle his pockets, and then robbing the surprised cove instead), and Nat the Tinker (so called because he would carry the finest of the watches and gewgaws he lifted under his coat, and offer them for sale to passersby on the street when the need for drink was in him). Ol' Bates was sick, as he had been often lately what with the damp all around, and Nat was sleeping off a drunk.

Jewel stepped carefully over Nat's snoring form, which lay sprawled across one of the half dozen or so beds made of old sacks that covered one section of the floor of the huge, drafty loft. Reaching the exit, she ducked her head to get through the low door. The stairs twisting downward were broken and rickety, blackened by the fire that had left the warehouse unusable and prey to squatters like themselves. But Jewel took them with the surefootedness of a young goat, carefully holding her skirts clear of her feet to keep her precious dress safe. A large rat skittered down ahead of her, staying close to the wall. Its long naked tail left a trail in the heavy layer of soot and dirt. Jewel barely noticed it. Like blows, rats were a part of her life.

Behind her, Jem clumped more cautiously. The thud, thud of his heavy boots echoed the gradually accelerating thumping of her heart. She wasn't afraid, not Jewel, but she didn't much care for this new lay he'd come up with. But, as Jem said, times were hard in this year of our Lord 1841, what with them so-called Corn Laws doing in the gentry so that they weren't near as plump in the pocket as they used to be. And with the winter as bad as it had been, and the nobs just now starting to trickle back to town, why, things were in a sad way.

Jewel was an expert ticker hunter (tickers being watches and hunting them being, in a manner of speaking, what she did), trained by the best pickpocket around, as Jem claimed he had been before he had gotten hit with the rheumatiz. But when there was nothing in the purses of those she robbed even artistry such as hers was of little value. None of them had been having much luck lately, not even Corey the Chaser. His lay was jumping out in front of gentlemen's rigs and then rolling away at the last possible moment, screaming so that the victim would think him injured and offer him something—generally a pound note—to keep him from raising too much fuss about being run down. As Jem said, "Ya gotta do wot ya gotta do," and to eat they had had to come up with some new lays. If Jewel didn't like the one he had chosen for her, well, she could do it or get out.

Her one consolation was that the new game had required the acquisition of the fine looking dress she now wore. Jewel clutched the crimson silk skirt and jumped down the remaining four steps so as not to have to wade through the pile of offal that someone had dumped on them. Landing lightly, she tugged at her tight bodice and tucked in between her breasts a torn edge of the black lace that adorned it, trying not to notice the pumping of blood in the veins of her neck, or the sweat that dampened her palms. She had loathed this lay from the first, when Jem had assured her it was a one time thing. But that first time had netted them a tidy sum, and Jem was never one to pass by a source of easy money. If her stomach wasn't strong enough to stand the sight of a little blood, well, then, her stomach shouldn't be so damned weak livered. Or so Jem said.

The worst part was that they needed Mick for this lay.

She hated Mick, really hated him. He liked the new lay, liked the violence and the blood, she could tell he did. Mick was short and stocky with oily dark hair, a broad pock-marked face and little gleaming black eyes that glistened like cockroaches whenever they rested on Jewel. And he had thick, meaty hands—about a dozen pair of them, which he could never keep to himself. So far, she had managed to fend off anything more than the occasional grab, but she knew that she had Jem more than her own physical prowess to thank for that. Of course, if ever the day came when she refused to do what Jem asked, well, she would have to make damned sure that day never came. For a chit with no one to look after her, London's slums were a dangerous place. Jewel figured she would last about one day before she fell victim to one of the area's many predators. Then she would be lucky to end up, alive, in a whorehouse.

Her hand was outstretched to touch the crazily leaning door that led onto the street when it suddenly swung open. She had no time to step back before she was pulled against a thick chest and imprisoned by bearishly strong arms.

"Eh, Jewel me dear, waitin' fer me, were ya? That's awright, I like me wenches eager." Mick squeezed her tight while a slow grin exposed teeth that were already beginning to turn brown around the edges from rot.

"I tole ya to be 'ome early. Ya knew we was goin' out ternight." Jem's irritable grumble came from behind Jewel. She jerked angrily against Mick's hold, feeling safe with Jem at hand.

"Ah, Jemmy, I'm 'ere, ain't I? An' I'm ready fer work."

Despite her struggles, Mick hugged Jewel even tighter as he spoke, rubbing his crotch against her in a way that made her want to throw up. His man-thing was hard and swollen and it hurt as he pressed it into her flesh. She shoved him fruitlessly. She might have grown up wild, but she was a good girl that way. Her ma, whom Jewel could just barely remember, had told her always to keep herself to herself, and Jewel always had. There might come a time when she had to trade her body for food and shelter, but that time hadn't come yet. If it did, well then, she would do what she had to do. But she sure as hell wasn't goin' to let Mick toss her on her backside for free in the meantime.

"Yer gettin' some real nice little titties on ya, Jewely," Mick whispered in her ear as he rubbed himself against her again.

Jewel clenched her teeth in revulsion. She *hated* Mick. . . . What she would really like to do was stick a knife in his middle. But since she didn't have a knife on her she made do with the next best thing. Catching a fold of the flesh in the soft area near his armpit, she twisted it between her thumb and forefinger as viciously as she could. Mick yelped and jumped back, helped by a mighty shove from Jewel.

"Ya keep them filthy 'ands an' that filthy mind offa me, Mick Parkins, or I'll slit yer throat for ya some fine night whilst you lay sleepin'," she hissed, glaring at him ferociously before stomping on through the door. Behind her, she heard Jem's bark of laughter.

"Better watch yerself, me bucko, or she'll be carvin' ya up for fish bait," Jem advised with a chuckle.

"She'll sing a different tune one o' these days, the little bitch, mark me words," Mick growled.

Jewel tried to ignore the little shiver of fear that ran up

her spine at the threat. Mick was getting bolder with her all the time, and one day soon she feared that even the threat of Jem's retaliation would not be enough to keep him off her.

"C'mon, let's get goin'. We ain't got all night." Jem was walking beside her now, and Jewel put the threat of Mick aside for the moment. Mick came up close behind her, as she didn't resent his nearness. Now they were merely partners in crime, all three intent on the job they had to do.

Even at noontime the narrow cobbled street was shadowed by the dilapidated buildings of timber and brick covered with dingy, peeling mortar that leaned one against the other, blocking out the sun. Now, as Big Ben boomed the strokes of two A.M. in the distance, the street was as dark as the inside of an unlit cellar. There was a sputtering streetlamp on the far corner, but its light came nowhere near the middle of the street where the three of them walked, Jem and Mick in shabby frieze coats and slouch hats pulled low, and Jewel in her red silk dress with her hair twisted up into as close as she could come to a fashionable knot.

Thick fog rolling in off the Thames shrouded everything, making the air heavy and damp and depositing slimy particles on Jewel's hair and skin. She shivered at the cold, glancing resentfully at her companions. *They* wore coats while she had to be next door to naked to attract the pigeon. But then, feeling cold was nothing new to her. She didn't know why it was bothering her so much lately. Maybe she was getting old. . . .

The smell from the nearby river and the overflowing gutters underfoot was enough to knock the uninitiated right off their feet. Jewel, sucking in the stink along with the fog, barely noticed it. Just as she barely noticed the drunks lying in the gutter, or the shadowy forms lurking in doorways or skulking along the labyrinth of connecting streets through which they passed. Like the rats, the cold, and the stink they were a part of life in the slums of Whitechapel.

"Ye'll do jest fine, Jool-girl."

Jem, clearly sensing her nervousness with that strange sixth sense of his, clapped a hand on her bare shoulder as he spoke. Jewel jumped at the unexpected touch, but the large warm hand steadied her as it propelled her toward the cross street where the streetlamps sputtered fuzzily through the fog-muffled darkness. It was almost time. . . .

She rubbed her arms, left bare by the short puffed sleeves of the low cut dress, wishing vainly for the warmth of summer as she did so. It was mild for early March despite the fog. But it was still much too cold for her fashionable bodice. Her work clothes, she thought with a grimace, and rubbed her arms again.

They reached the lamplit street, and with a final encouraging squeeze of her shoulder Jem pushed Jewel out into the light while he and Mick ducked into a nearby alley. It was her job to walk along the street, with Jem and Mick following in the shadows, until she found a pigeon. Then she had to lure him in, and she hated it. In her usual lay, she had respect. She worked the shoppers haggling at street markets in her own territory, where she was well-known amongst the street people. There, her friends would cover for her if things went wrong. What made the new lay so dangerous was that they were operating outside their usual territory; tonight Jem had decided that they would work the area near Covent Garden, hoping to catch a cit or a toff heading home from a night on the town with his pockets well lined and his wits befuddled by drink. They planned to relieve their victim of all his valuables instead of just his ticker or his purse, and if the pigeon was plump enough they wouldn't have to work again for several days.

Jewel had to admit that a single hit with this lay brought in considerably more than she usually managed to pinch in as much as a week on her own. The pigeon was chosen with care, and Jem and Mick were thorough, stripping the man of every single valuable, from the occasional fur lined cloak to the more common fat purse, ornate gold watches on heavy chains, profusions of rings, fobs and seals, silver hip flasks, small painted miniatures of family members framed in gold (it was amazin' what some folks carried on their persons!) to sometimes even his clothes and shoes, if they were grand enough and if Jem felt they might fetch a good price resold. Yes, it was certainly quicker prigging the whole man rather than just lifting the items from his pockets, but it was more dangerous, too. In this lay, the three of them came face to face with their victims. They could be identified with ease.

Along the cobblestone street other females moved, some with their heads down and covered with shawls to denote their modesty, some lurching along as they lovingly swilled the contents of stone jugs, some decked out in tawdry finery and on the prowl—as was Jewel.

Two men, well-to-do cits by their clothes, were walking along the street together, steady on their feet and sober of countenance. Not very good prospects, Jewel thought, forcing herself to concentrate on the business at hand. The sooner she played her part, the sooner it would be over with.

Ahead of her, a whore in a floss-trimmed dress so faded that it was difficult to tell if it had once been blue or green approached the men, smiling so that her few teeth showed and thrusting her body forward so that they could get a better look at her ample—and nearly bare—bosom.

"Wanna 'ave some fun, gents?" she whined, her coy smile not masking the avarice in her eyes. One of the men looked at her with some interest, but the other pulled him away.

"Don't be daft, George, she's likely got the pox," snorted the second. Then to the whore he added, "Get on away from us, or I'll have the watch on you!"

The woman snarled, her face contorting with malice, and let loose with a stream of profanity that made the men's cheeks redden. Her language didn't bother Jewel at all. Jewel had heard as bad or worse all her life, and was capable of doing a sight better herself when the occasion called for it. The only thing that bothered her was that the two men were now hurrying away. They hadn't been good prospects together, but would have been perfect if the whore had managed to separate them. But she hadn't, and now the area was deserted except for street people.

"Damn it, Jool, get your arse walkin'. We can't stand around 'ere all bloody night!"

The hissed admonition from Mick caused Jewel to grit her teeth. She wasn't his bloody doxy, to be ordered around as he chose! But she forced herself to relax, and concentrate. The sooner she found a pigeon for the plucking, the sooner this night would be over, and she would be safe in her warm pallet under the eaves.

" 'Ey, Jool, you takin' up whorin'? Whisht I was a skirt,

so I could fall back on sommit like that! Lord God, light as the gentry's pockets are lately, I be like to starve to death!"

The half admiring, half envious voice of the old man behind her made Jewel start. You be as jumpy as a parson with a whore, she scolded herself as she turned to grin at him. Willy Tilden was an inch or so shorter than her own medium height, and he was even thinner than she was. If not for the web of wrinkles that lined his face, he would have looked like a boy. But he was nearly sixty, they said, and he was one of the best, a master pickpocket. He had recognized Jewel's talent early on, and gave her the respect one professional accorded another. Jewel admired him, but she was also wary of him. Another of Willy's lays was the providing of females to Mother Miranda, the notorious abbess. Jewel had no wish to end up lining Willy's pockets by being sold off like a parcel to that one.

"Not too likely, Willy," Jewel responded. Her tone held the respect an apprentice owes a master, and the old man grinned at her before moving on. She didn't like the idea that word would soon be out on the streets that Jewel Combs had turned whore, but there was nothing she could do about it.

" 'Ist, ya bleedin' wantwit, keep yer mind about ya! 'Ere comes a ripe 'un."

Jem's near shout of a whisper came from a recessed doorway some few feet behind Jewel. Jewel looked up quickly to see a young man, a toff by the evidence of his fancy wine coat and tan breeches. He was staggering down the street and she was amazed that she had not noticed him some ten minutes earlier. He was singing "God Save the Queen" at the top of his lungs; the sound echoed off the narrow buildings to provide its own ringing chorus. From his singing, to say nothing of the way he stopped to lean a hand against a storefront for support from time to time, it was clear that he was extremely well to live. Jewel's eyes gleamed as he passed beneath a streetlight, and she saw that he was very young, not yet twenty, she guessed. An easy pigeon to pluck, she thought with relief. Mick should have no excuse to rough him up at all.

The old whore in the faded dress perked up and started toward the yodeling newcomer. A furious mutter from behind her reminded Jewel that she had better make a move fast. As drunk as this young toff was, he was unlikely to be discriminating in his appraisal of female flesh.

"Sorry, ducks, but this gent be mine," Jewel said as she overtook the old whore. Sidling up to the gentleman, she slid a hand caressingly up his velvet sleeve, giving the other woman an ungentle shove with her hips at the same time.

"I saw 'im first!" the whore screeched as she recovered from her sideways totter, glaring at Jewel, who glared back. Both were prepared to fight for their prize like hungry mongrels, if need be.

"This is-is most flattering, ladies, but b-believe me, there is no need," the gentleman interrupted, his eyes blinking as he focused on first one then the other of them. Jewel was ready to swear that he could not differentiate between them. He was really magnificently dog-bitten; the odor of rum hung about him like the old whore's cheap perfume.

Jewel glared at the other woman, who was trying to edge back into contention, then smiled at the young gentleman with exaggerated sweetness, thrusting her chest forward provocatively. He was not to know that her ripe looking curves had been greatly enhanced by the old rags she had thrust down into the too full bosom of her dress to fill it out and force her own small breasts upward. From above, all a gentleman could see was creamy, ripe looking flesh.

"Listen, you bitch, that's my fella!" The old whore, enraged by Jewel's success in fixing the gentleman's attention at last, gave the younger girl a hearty shove. Jewel staggered, keeping herself upright by her hold on the gentleman's coat—he staggered with her—then swung on the other woman, her lips parted in a vicious snarl.

"Get on away from 'ere, ya scraggy ol' witch, afore I knock yer block off! Ya 'ear me, now?"

"I tell ya, 'e's mine!"

The battle was about to begin in earnest when the gentleman stepped between them, shaking his head with regret. Under the gaslight Jewel noticed with the tiny part of her mind that was not focused on her rival that his hair was very blond. . . .

"Ladies, I beg you, do not fight over me. I find you both very, very fetching, but, uh, well, to be quite frank, tonight I fear I am not quite . . . quite myself. To be perfectly plain with you, I do not . . . do not think I am . . . capable of the feat you require. So sorry, ladies."

With a lopsided grin he bowed in the general direction of the lamppost and started to lurch away. Desperate, Jewel grabbed at his arm. She could not let him get away now.

"Wait! I, uh, seein' as yer so 'andsome an' all, I'll give it ter ya real cheap. Yer sure ter my taste, guvnor." She smiled at him and rolled her eyes in the way that she had seen the whores do. He smiled back at her, and for a moment she thought she had him. Then he shook his head.

"You're a pretty wench, I think. I can't quite see properly at the moment. Are you hard up for cash? If so, I'll be glad to make you a little . . . a little loan. . . ." With that he reached into his pocket and pulled out a purse that bulged at the seams. Jewel's eyes bulged nearly as much as he opened it, and peeled off a couple of notes from the pile to tuck into her bodice. Hardly feeling his fingers brushing her flesh, she could not tear her eyes from the thick roll of notes remaining in the purse. It must contain hundreds of pounds—a fat pigeon indeed, and she was losing him!

"I'm 'ard up too, sir," whined the whore, and if looks could kill the older woman would have been stretched out dead at Jewel's feet. She was sure she could get him to at least walk with her a little way—far enough to where Jem and Mick could drag him into an alley—if only the old bitch would go away!

The toff tucked some notes into the crack between the other woman's fat breasts, smiled seraphically at the pair of them, and again started to lurch away. Down the street a ways, a ramshackle tavern belched forth a quartet of shabby revelers; joining arms, they staggered off in the opposite direction. The toff followed happily in their wake, and Jewel ground her teeth. Then, with a single seething glance at her rival, she would have gone after the toff, but the older woman stopped her with a hand on her arm.

"We need to 'ave us a little chat, lovey," she purred menacingly, her grime encrusted nails digging into the soft flesh of Jewel's upper arm. Jewel turned, feeling the roots of her hair tighten with temper. Hissing like an enraged cat, she started to give the woman the roundhouse punch she had been asking for. But the sound of the toff's voice, high pitched with drunken indignation, jolted her attention back to him.

"You. Just what do you think you're doing?" The young gentleman was protesting in vain at being force-marched down the street between Jem and Mick. The three were nearly of a height, but their burliness and rough clothes overwhelmed his slender, fashionably dressed person.

"I say now, this isn't quite-quite cricket!" He was struggling, but the effort was wasted. Jewel watched in consternation as Mick wrapped his burly arms around the toff in a bone crushing hug, lifted him from his feet, and bore him back into the sheltering darkness of a narrow alley.

"Let me go, ya ol' windbag," Jewel hissed at the whore, who was gaping at the now empty alley entrance. When the woman was slow to obey, Jewel shoved her so hard that she stumbled backward and, tripping over a loose cobblestone, sat down hard in the gutter that was running over with filth.

The woman howled as she struggled to her feet, but Jewel scarcely spared her a glance. She picked up her voluminous skirt in both hands and sped down the street. Even before she reached the alley, she heard the sickening thud of blows and the groans of someone in pain. By the time she rounded the corner into the narrow, shadow filled darkness, the toff was lying on his back behind a heap of garbage while Jem wrestled his purse away from him. Despite, or perhaps because of, his drunken state, the young man was determined to hang onto his purse. He and Jem engaged in a fruitless tug of war until Mick settled the matter by aiming a vicious kick to the toff's ribs. The gentleman cried out, doubling up as Jem quickly stuffed the purse into the capacious pockets of his coat. Then Jem ran his hands over the still groaning, writhing victim, quickly extracting his watch, fobs and other gewgaws and storing them in his pockets alongside the purse.

"C'mon, c'mon, the two of ya!" He gestured to them to follow him, then scuttled furtively away without waiting for either one of them. Jewel, watching Mick gloat over the moaning, curled up man on the ground, seeing the blood that was the same color as her dress drip from the toff's battered face to speckle the cobblestones, felt her stomach heave. There had been no need for such brutality; as drunk as he was, they should have been able to take this pigeon's purse with no trouble at all.

"Bloody thieving bastards!" the toff groaned.

To Jewel's horror he came up off the pavement, lunging upward with his clenched fist leading the way. He caught Mick square on the nose; Mick groaned and jumped back, while the toff's momentum sent him staggering off balance against the brick wall of the alley. Blood spurting from his nose, Mick jumped toward the toff, who was trying to get away on unsteady legs. Jewel saw the glint of a knife in Mick's hand as it plunged toward the other man's back.

"Stop!" Jewel screamed, running toward the fused pair. But even as she reached them Mick stepped back. The knife in his fist was red to the hilt with blood. Dark crimson welled from a slit in the gentleman's claret coat; his hands clawed against the smoke darkened brick as he sank down slowly, so slowly, to lie on his side on the cobblestones.

"You've done for 'im, ya bloody idiot!" Jewel screeched as she knelt beside the man, staring at his inert body with horror.

Mick glared at her for a moment, then bent down to wipe

the bloody knife on the tail of his victim's coat. He straightened, sliding the knife inside his coat before turning those hard black eyes on Jewel.

"You'd best keep yer tongue between yer teeth about this if ya know wot's good fer ya."

Jewel nodded jerkily, knowing that Mick wouldn't hesitate to use his knife on her if he even suspected she might peach on him.

Mick grunted, apparently satisfied with her response. "C'mon then, let's get the 'ell away from 'ere. The watch'll be along soon."

Before she could even get to her feet, he was walking rapidly away. As Jewel stared after him, he began to run.

She was just about to follow him when the man at her feet groaned. Looking down, she saw that he was moving his arm. So he was not dead—yet. But if he did die, what Mick had done would be murder. And she and Jem were involved up to their necks. Damn Mick anyway! He'd be the death of them all!

Jewel blanched as she recalled the exact penalty for murder. Oh, God, she didn't want to die after watching her intestines being burned before her eyes! Would she be considered responsible for the toff's death, though she had not wielded the knife? She thought of their lay, and her mouth went dry. Sure she would. She had lured the pigeon . . . Then the toff groaned again.

She couldn't just leave him. Cursing, uttering every foul word she had ever heard under her breath, she dropped to her knees beside him. His eyes opened for a second.

"Call the watch," he muttered before his eyes closed again. Jewel shuddered. The watch might come along at any moment. They might even have heard the fight. If she saw them coming, she could run, knowing that he would not be left to die on the street alone. But all hell would break loose if the toff was found bloody and dying on the street. If he died, it would be murder. If he didn't, he could identify them all.

Jewel's blood ran cold. She had to do something fast. Wetting her dry lips, she caught the collar of the toff's fancy coat in both hands, and heaved. He was senseless as she began to drag him away, scant inches at a time, his passage marked by a trail of blood. For all his slender build, he was heavy, and again Jewel considered leaving him and running away like Mick and Jem. But surely it was better, whether he should die or live, to have him do so off the street and out of sight.

II

Two days later Jewel stood at the foot of a rusty iron bedstead, chewing on her lower lip as she watched Father Simon, the old priest who roamed the back slums of Whitechapel in search of souls to save, administer the last rites to the fair haired boy who lay as one already dead. Pale as a wax figure, dark rings circling sunken eyes, breath rattling stertorously through colorless lips, he no longer looked like a toff. He looked about sixteen, and Jewel's eyes burned as she watched the ritual movements of the priest.

Death was nothing new to her; she had seen it before, from the time she held the cold and still corpse of her mother, dead of the wasting disease and too much drink, in her seven-year-old arms, to her present day frequent encounters with old winos curled in the gutters in death as they were in life. But this—this healthy young man for whose dying she had to shoulder some share of blame— was different. Though she had schooled herself to care nothing about him, she found that despite everything her heart was not yet that callous.

The flat they were in belonged to Willy Tilden. She had brought the toff to it because it was close, and because she had thought Willy might dare to go against Jem and help her. If Willy hadn't agreed to shelter her, she didn't know what she would have done. She was grateful he had, although she had no doubt that Willy would eventually expect to be paid. He had been eyeing her sort of funny for the last two days, and it didn't take a genius to figure out what was in his mind. To Willy, it probably seemed like the most natural thing in the world for her to pay for putting him out of his bed by putting herself in it. That was a problem she would have to deal with once the toff was gone.

At first she had thought that she herself could return to the warehouse as soon as the toff passed over. But in the hours and days since she had dragged him off the street, she had come to realize that returning to Jem's fold after this might not be the wisest thing she had ever done: She was a witness to what would be murder when the young man died, and Mick wouldn't like knowing that there was someone who could testify against him if he was ever brought before Old Bailey. Mick was bound to be sweating now, wondering what had become of her and the toff. He was probably lying low, keeping off the streets in case the

Bow Street runners were already searching for him, as they would have been if Jewel had been taken by the watch and had peached. Knowing Mick, she could not be sure that he was not thinking of another murder—hers. And maybe Jem was, too. You never knew about Jem. But she did know that she was a threat to their safety, and they didn't like any kind of threat. And the knowledge scared her.

So she had stayed in Willy Tilden's one room flat, stuck with a dying toff who had succeeded in almost making her cry for the first time in years. Father Simon, who had had some experience with wounds as a young corpsman at Waterloo some twenty-seven years before, said it wouldn't be long now. Probably in less than a day the young man would be dead. And Jewel would be left with no money, no home to go back to, no friends she could trust. She would have to disappear—only she hadn't quite figured out where she was going to go. The City was a bleak, unwelcoming place when one had no money and no friends.

The toff groaned, which he had been doing intermittently since she had wrested him out of his coat and boots, bandaged him up and put him to bed. His eyes opened, and he peered blindly around the room. Both of his eyes were swollen almost shut from Mick's blows, and a deep bruise purpled the right side of his jaw. Except for the blood stained makeshift bandage she had contrived for him from one of Willy's shirts, he was naked to the waist. His skin, except for a faint sprinkling of fair hairs, was nearly as white and soft as her own. Clearly he had been pampered and indulged all his life.

As Jewel watched him now, he kicked fretfully at the thin, grimy blanket covering him, muttered something, and closed his eyes again. He had been out of his mind ever since he had lost consciousness right after the stabbing. But Father Simon didn't know that the toff had been rambling deliriously off and on for two days, so he leaned over, the boy, saying, "Yes, my son?" There was no response from the toff, as Jewel had foreseen. She shook her head, and moved to the side of the bed to touch the priest on his black-clad arm.

" 'E can't 'ear ya, Father."

"No." The priest sighed, turning to look at her out of red-rimmed eyes. The bottle was Father Simon's vice, and the effects of it showed in the old man's florid complexion and bloodshot eyes. But his hands as they administered the sacraments were steady, and when he was not blathering on about hellfire and damnation he could be kind.

"Who is he? Has he a family to be notified?"

"I—I don' know," Jewel answered nervously, looking down at the patient as he tossed upon the bed. "Like I tole ya, I, uh, I foun' 'im like this, jest lyin' in the street. I-I couldn' jest leave 'im. But 'e ain't got no purse . . . uh, not that I was lookin' for it, mind, 'cept for somethin' to iden-tify him with."

Father Simon snorted. "Robbed, no doubt. Well, someone will come looking for him most likely. He's one of the nobs, or I miss my guess." His eyes narrowed on Jewel thoughtfully. "Mighty Christian of you, to take care of him like this."

Jewel shrugged, taking care not to meet the priest's eyes. "I tole ya, I jest couldn' leave 'im lay."

"Hmmm." Jewel wasn't sure what that meant, and she thought it safer not to ask. But Father Simon continued.

"Word's out that you've left Jemmy. Word's out he's looking for you."

"Is 'e?" Jewel looked at the priest now, wide-eyed. What she saw there made her relax a little. He seemed to be concerned for her, and she remembered that he had always seemed to like her. But she remembered, too, that things ain't always what they seem. She wasn't sure just what his lay was, but she was sure that she wasn't going to go all soft and weepy and pour out her troubles to him. If he knew, he could go to the Bow Street runners—or even Jem or Mick—and give her up. And then where would she be? But before she could frame a reasonable reply, the toff groaned again, and the priest turned back to him.

"Who the devil are you?" The toff spoke in a barely audible whisper, staring straight at the priest as he did so. His pale blue eyes looked awake and aware despite the pain that filled them. Father Simon, to whom the words were addressed, replied softly with the information that he was a priest.

"What happened? Where am I?" There seemed no doubt that the toff had regained his senses at last. Jewel moved around to the other side of the bed, eyes wide and heart knocking against her ribs. Would he remember her? Would he guess the role she had played in what had happened to him?

The toff's eyes swung to her. Jewel's own golden eyes met the pale blue stare, and locked. He seemed to be trying to remember. . . . She prayed frantically that he would again be overcome by unconsciousness as his eyes slid over her disheveled black hair, her pale face, and then down to her too slender body, still clad in the low cut red silk dress.

Then his eyes came back up to hers again.

"Ah, yes," he said, still in that hoarse whisper. "I do remember you. The persistent who—, uh, young lady I met on the street just before I was attacked by those bloody brigands. You've been taking care of me, haven't you?"

Wordlessly Jewel nodded. He didn't seem to connect her to his attackers—yet. Already his eyes were clouding. He looked as if he would fade out of consciousness at any moment.

"What is your name? Do you have any family that we can notify?" The urgency of Father Simon's voice seemed to bring the young man to himself once more.

"Name's Stratham. Timothy Stratham." He smiled faintly, a bitter stretching of his mouth. "As to family, believe me, they don't want to hear anything about me."

"Nonsense, my son. Of course they want to know what has become of you. They are probably worried half out of their minds right now."

The glazed look was coming back into the toff's eyes. "You don't know . . . my family," he whispered. Then, "Stay with me, Father." And he closed his eyes.

Father Simon did stay. Except for a few short periods, he watched with Jewel far into the night. Willy looked in briefly, seemed displeased to find the toff still alive and in his bed, and left again with a sour sniff. Father Simon looked at Jewel after he had gone. She was curled up in a sitting position on the cold board floor, a blanket wrapped around her shoulders against the damp and chill. A tiny fire sputtered fitfully on the hearth, but it was not enough to add more than a smidgeon of warmth or cheer to the grim surroundings.

"You are in trouble, my child?" The priest had not spoken for nearly an hour. Jewel jumped before the sense of the words sank in and she stared at him out of wide, distrustful eyes.

"Wot's yer meanin', Father?"

He sighed. "Come, Jewel, I am your friend. Can't you trust me? I will help you, if I can."

Jewel snorted. "Oh, yeah, out o' the bloomin' kindness of yer 'eart. Wot's in it fer yerself, Father, if ya was to 'elp me?"

Father Simon shook his head sadly. In the near darkness his bald pate shone with the reflected light of the fire. His eyes looked blurred and rheumy, but his voice was gentle.

"Must everyone want something in return for a kindness, Jewel?"

"Most do," she replied with a shrug.

Father Simon sighed again, but before he could reply the toff began to mutter distractedly, tossing and turning in the bed. Jewel rose with some difficulty, her bones aching from her uncomfortable vigil on the cold floor. She crossed to the bedside to offer her patient some water. Anything to end the priest's talk, she thought as she slipped a hand behind the man's head and slid a spoonful of water between his parched lips. He choked, coughing. His skin was burning hot beneath her hand.

Suddenly, his hand came up to catch hers. Jewel jumped, spilling what few drops remained of the water down his cheek, and looked down into pale blue eyes that were once again foggy but aware. For a moment he looked as if he couldn't quite place her.

"Ah, yes, the whore," he muttered. Jewel stiffened, letting his head fall back on the nearly flat pillow.

"I ain't no whore," she said angrily, glaring down at him. Father Simon came to stand beside her.

"Indeed, she's not. She has been caring for you since you were attacked, you know."

The toff—Timothy—grimaced, a weak and barely discernible gesture.

"Sorry. I didn't mean to offend." He moved his head as if to clear it, but the motion must have hurt because he stopped and groaned. "You must . . . let me pay you for your trouble." His eyes clouded, then cleared again. "Oh, that's right, I was robbed, was I not? Did they get . . . everything?"

Wordlessly Jewel nodded. Timothy closed his eyes. "Damn! I had more than four hundred pounds in that purse! Just after quarter day, you know! I was in . . . high gear." His head moved with impotent anger against the pillows. "Sorry again. I guess I . . . owe you. But don't worry. Everybody knows that Timothy Stratham always, always pays his debts."

He started to cough then. He hadn't coughed before, and Jewel and Father Simon looked at each other with alarm as the spasms racked him. When the attack was over, he lay without moving, looking so white and drawn that Jewel thought for an instant that he had died in that moment. But his pale eyes opened again, resting wearily on her before moving on to the priest.

"Am I going . . . to die, Father?"

Father Simon pursed his lips, and reached to pick up the white, almost womanish hand that lay so limply atop the grimy blanket.

"Yes, my son, I fear so. But like everything, it is in God's hands."

Timothy's lips made a weak attempt at a smile. "My family always said that I'd come to a bad end." He closed his eyes for a long moment, and the priest seemed nervous that the boy would slip into unconsciousness again.

"Won't you tell us where to reach your family, my son? I'm sure that any estrangement between you was not meant to withstand your finding yourself in such dire straits."

Timothy's mouth twisted again in that pathetic smile, but his blue eyes remained closed. "You don't know my family, Father," he repeated. "They have been trying to be rid of me for years. They will be relieved, if nothing more, when I am gone."

"They should be contacted. . . ."

Timothy moved his head impatiently, then grimaced with pain. "Very well, Father, I will furnish you with their direction. If you will first do something for me." He opened his eyes and fixed them on Jewel with an expression she could not decipher.

"Anything within my power, my son."

"Is it within your power to wed me to this young lady, Father?"

Jewel blinked, staring down at the toff as if she suspected he might have sunk back into delirium without their having noticed. Father Simon cleared his throat.

"Why should you wish to do that, Timothy?"

Timothy's burning eyes shifted to the priest. "When I turn twenty-five, in four years time, I come into an inheritance from my mother. A very substantial inheritance. It would keep this young lady in comfort for the rest of her life. If I die without an heir, the cousin who is my guardian will merely add my modest fortune to his own much greater one. I would rather this young lady—what is your name, by the way?" he added impatiently to Jewel. She told him, and he went on. "I would rather Jewel here have my money in payment for her kindness than see it go to my cousin. He is a cold bastard—begging your pardon, Father—and besides, he has no need of it."

Father Simon was silent for a moment. Jewel was, too. They both stared down at the pale face that appeared perfectly serious and perfectly sane. But of course he could not be. His offer of marriage had to be the product of delirium. Didn't it? Did he really have money—and would he, could he, be serious about marrying her and leaving it to her when he died? To have enough money for good food and warm clothes and a room all to herself with a big, blazing fire every night if she wished—to never be hungry or cold again . . . or afraid . . . Jewel felt dizzy from the very thought of it.

"Jewel?" Father Simon murmured at last. "It would be a . . . solution for you."

Jewel stared at him for a moment without speaking. Her thoughts were churning so fast she felt dizzy.

"Well?" the toff demanded irritably, his voice weaker than it had been before. "Will you or won't you? I can't see any reason for you to refuse."

"Be a bleedin' fool to, wouldn't I?" Jewel answered slowly, still not trusting the possibility. There had to be some catch to this; the toff couldn't be just going to hand over money to her.

"Make the arrangements, Father. Quickly, please." Timothy closed his eyes on that last. As quickly as that he was asleep. Father Simon looked at Jewel again.

"I'll have to see about a special license."

Jewel nodded, still staring down at the unconscious form of the boy in the bed. He would be her husband. Every nerve in her body shrank from the idea. But of course he would never be her husband in anything but name. He was dying. She would not have to put up with the reality of a man who owned her as he might own a dog, and use her worse—as man after man had used her mother. She forced the thought from her consciousness.

"I'll be back as quickly as I can."

Jewel nodded in reply to the priest's soft statement, but remained by Timothy's bedside, staring down at him blankly long after Father Simon had gone. She felt very calm, almost unnaturally so. If the toff lasted until Father Simon got back, she would go through the ceremony required to make her his wife, be he delirious or crazed or what. Be a bleedin' fool if she didn't, she told herself again, and settled down with a blanket on the floor to wait.

I I I

RAIN fell in icy sheets that had long since soaked through the thin shawl that Jewel had wrapped around her red silk dress. She was soaked to the skin, with long strands of her black hair straggling down from the fancy upsweep that had looked so elegant in the glass when she had fixed it to lie in freezing, dripping rat's tails against her bare white neck. Her grand red velvet hat with its perky ostrich plume—which, like the shawl, she had "borrowed" from a friend—tilted soggily over one eye, its wide brim allowing a torrent of water to stream down a scant inch in front of her reddened nose.

But still she stood on the edge of the small triangular park like a foolish gawk, staring up wide-eyed at the imposing stone facade of the mansion on Grosvenor Square. She had been standing there for nearly three hours, heedless of the occasional splashing carriage or hurrying maidservant, all the while trying to work up the courage to march to that massive oak door and make use of the gleaming brass knocker. It was formed in the shape of a lion's head, and for some reason, that made the knot in her stomach twist even tighter. Even the bloomin' knocker was grand.

But she belonged to that house now. Or so she had been telling herself for the past week, ever since Timothy had died. She had married him, all legal so Father Simon said at the time. Timothy had told her to come to this address with the proof of their marriage after he was gone. He had told her to present their marriage lines to the Earl of Moorland, whom he claimed was his guardian, with his compliments. So Jewel had decided to try her luck. The worst they could do to her was throw her out on her arse, right?

After Timothy had passed over, only hours after they were wed, Jewel had been considerably shaken. In fact, although it shamed her to admit it, she had shed more than a few tears. Father Simon had put his arm around her shoulders, and Jewel had had to stifle an urge to collapse sobbing against his chest. But instead she had lifted her chin and pulled away to stand alone. As she had always been alone. . . . Father Simon had told her not to worry, that he would see to everything, including the body. Jewel had not waited around to see what happened next. There were too many problems—Willy for one, and what might happen when Timothy's family was notified to claim his body. It seemed likely they would send a runner to investigate, and she wasn't having truck with no runner.

Thoroughly unnerved, she had instinctively melted into the streets. For a week she had scavenged for food in the alleys behind Kensington Palace, taking care to stay out of her old neighborhood. At night she had cadged pallet space from an old friend of her mother's, an ex-opera dancer turned whore named Cilla. But staying with Cilla meant trying not to listen when the woman brought her customers home with her. Jewel had hidden beneath her blanket on the floor, feeling sick at the sound of a man's earthy groans and the wildly creaking bedsprings.

Then, last night, when she had slipped from Cilla's flat rather than listen to another bout of creaking springs, she had seen Mick. And he had seen her. She had started to run, on instinct, and he had chased her through the tangle of dark alleys, the look in his eyes confirming her very worst nightmares. Terrified, knowing with terrible certainty how little her life was worth if Mick should catch her, she had fled to Father Simon's small house after giving Mick the slip at last. But the scrawny old woman who answered the door in response to her frantic pounding said that Father Simon was "indisposed" and couldn't be disturbed. Jewel had known that meant drunk. Of course, she hadn't really expected to be rescued that easily, had she? Life wasn't like that.

With a proud stiffening of her spine, Jewel had turned

from the priest's door even as the woman had closed it in her face. There was no help for her here—or anywhere. She was on her own, just as she had been nearly all her life. It was up to Jewel to take care of Jewel.

She had to get right away, she knew, where Mick and Jem could never find her. What better place was there to hide out than a mansion in the fancy part of town? Anyway, it was time she found out if Timothy's claim of being cousin to an earl was air or truth. She had been squeamish to put it to the touch before, but now she felt that the choice had been taken out of her hands. So she had slunk back to Cilla's flat around noontime when she knew the other woman would be sound asleep, and the street people who might be willing to give her up to Mick for a farthing or so would be in their daytime hidey-holes. She had cleaned herself up as quietly as she could to the tune of Cilla's resonant snores. Then she had taken her courage and her marriage lines—as well as Cilla's Norwich silk shawl and best bonnet—and gone to present herself in Grosvenor Square, the most posh address in the city. To her new cousin. A bloomin' belted earl, if Timothy had been telling the truth. And what his worship would make of Mistress Timothy Stratham, there was no telling.

The knot in her stomach twisted again. Cor, she was goin' to lose the measly bit of bread that had been her dinner if she wasn't careful. How could she, Jewel Combs, go up those curving white marble steps to that elegant front door and ask for a bleedin' earl? They would likely spit on her. The notion stiffened her spine. Jewel looked up at the imposing facade of the three-storied brick structure and felt her throat go dry. Surely she was not afraid of a *house?* It was getting dark, the rain had settled to a cold drizzle, and her growling stomach reminded her that she had not eaten at all that day. Looking around at the nearly deserted park, Jewel knew that she had to do it *now*. She had to make herself known to the people inside that house—to the earl. But knocking on that door with the brass lion's head growling at her was going to be the hardest thing she had ever done in her life.

"They be people jest like me, even that bloody earl," she told herself with determination. Then, before she could change her mind, she clutched the beaded and spangled reticule—another "loan" from Cilla—that held her marriage lines and stepped into the road. Her foot immediately sank into a puddle that was calf deep, immersing her whole foot and the hem of her dress in icy water.

"Bloody 'ell!" Jewel muttered under her breath. Annoyed color mounted in her cheeks as she hitched up her skirts and stomped across the cobbled road and up the rain slickened steps. Some impression she was going to make, her grand hat drooping like a soused whore's, her silk dress so wet it was clinging to her like was indecent, and her nose running from the wet and cold.

"Them that's inside be no better than me," she said aloud, then sniffed mightily to give herself courage as she let the knocker fall. The resounding boom was louder than she had expected, but despite the sudden quiver in her knees—it was bloody cold, whose knees wouldn't shake like jelly?—she stood her ground, chin up, expression determined. When the door swung open, a black-clad personage with a dignity to rival God's stood staring down at her with an expression of disbelief.

"Y-e-s?"

"Yer lordship?"

The personage's nostrils distended. "Certainly not."

"I got somethin' to show the Earl o' Moorland." Despite her best efforts to be ladylike, the personage was looking at her like she had just crawled out from under a rock.

"Indeed. I am afraid that his lordship is not at home. Good day."

And before Jewel could say anything more, the door was shut resoundingly in her face.

"Well, bloody 'ell!" She stared at the closed door for a fulminating instant as indignation began to simmer. Bloody rude bugger, he was! Lifting the knocker's handle, she let it fall again. It hit the lion squarely in the nose with a resounding boom. This time the door opened only a few inches.

"Get away from here, you, or I'll have the watch called." The personage was frowning down his long nose at her.

"I tell ya, I got somethin' to show the earl!"

"And I tell you that the earl is not at home."

"Well, then, when will 'e be 'ome?"

"Never, for the likes of you. Now, be off!"

And he closed the door again. Jewel clenched her jaw, and banged the lion's head with such force that the handle bounced.

The magnificent personage jerked open the door this time and practically hissed at her. "Will you go away?"

Dander up, Jewel scowled ferociously back at him. "Yer bloody rude, did ya know that? I ask ya a civil question, and . . ."

"George, have Rudy run for the watch." The personage

spoke with icy control over his shoulder, before turning back to Jewel with a glacial glare. "You heard, girl? You'd best be gone, or it will be the worse for you."

"Yer the one t'will be the worse for, ya slimy fat slug," Jewel spat.

The door was closing in her face again. Bloody insufferable idiot! She had a right to her say just like anyone else! Furious, she threw herself against the swirls of intricately carved oak.

The personage, obviously not expecting a direct attack, was caught by surprise. The door swung open, Jewel stumbled into a great hall ablaze with candles, her feet slipping and sliding on the highly polished marble floor before coming to rest on a creamy carpet patterned with peach flowers. Her wet feet made dirty marks on the pristine wool and she quickly stepped back onto the marble, her eyes wide as she looked around her at the soaring entryway.

"Here now, you little slut, get out of here! George, lend a hand here!" The personage came up behind her, grabbing her by her upper arm.

"Ya take yer damned hands offa me, ya bloody old fart!" Jewel screeched, scrambling to regain her balance as the man swung her around. He thrust her toward the door, which another, younger man in an equally magnificent suit held open. Jewel felt herself being propelled over the slippery floor, then drew back her foot and kicked the personage in the shin with all her might.

"Bitch!" he yelled, dropping his hold on her arm and dancing on one leg. "You'll pay for this, you little . . . Henry, Thomas!"

He was obviously summoning reinforcements. He

snatched at Jewel, but caught only her shawl, which he regarded with horror and immediately dropped to lie in a soggy puddle on the floor. Meanwhile, Jewel darted away, her wet feet sliding on the marble so that she had to save herself from failing by catching the curved arm of an elegant gilt chair. She took refuge behind it as two other finely dressed men ran into the hall from different directions.

"Get her!" the personage directed, and the four men converged on the chair. Shifting from foot to foot so as to be ready for whatever mayhem ensued, she glared at them over the chair's striped silk back. The personage was limping slightly as he closed in on her, arms outstretched like a wrestler coming at his opponent. Jewel smiled grimly at the sight; she had always been one to enjoy a good mill.

"Come on then, buckos, and I'll 'ave meself a piece of each of ya!" The cockiness of her words matched the gleam in her eyes. Not for nothing had she grown up in the slums of Whitechapel. She would give them a fight they'd not soon forget . . .

"I assume that you can explain this, uh, comedy, Smathers?"

The drawled words dropped like icicles from above. Their effect on the four men was galvanizing. They snapped instantaneously to attention, eyes wide with apprehension as they turned collectively to look up at a lean blond gentleman clad in impeccable black evening clothes.

He stood near the top of the elegant staircase that curved down into the hall, one hand on the highly polished balustrade as he surveyed the scene below with cold detachment. But his apparent disinterest was not shared by the equally blonde beauty standing one step above him.

"Really, Sebastian, just look at the hall! There's water everywhere! Smathers. . . . Oh, lud, Sebastian, he has a-a-a *trollop* in here!"

"I ain't no trull!" Jewel interjected, belligerence flashing in her eyes as she glared at the pair on the stairs.

"Sebastian, she spoke to me! A female of that stamp! Oh, lud, I fear I am going to faint!"

"Don't be ridiculous, Caroline. Even you could not faint merely because a common wench spoke to you."

The words, uttered in the iciest voice Jewel had ever heard, were withering. The blonde woman's eyes flickered once, and then she folded her lips together and was silent. But as twin flags of color rose in her cheeks, she glared at all those in the hall who had witnessed her discomfiture and Jewel knew who would pay for her embarrassment.

"Well, Smathers?" The blond gentleman regarded the little group below with cold distaste. The only apparent change in his expression was a slight lifting of his eyebrows. Jewel was surprised to see that the small gesture caused Smathers, the magnificent personage, to sweat.

"I'm very sorry for the commotion, your lordship. This . . . female," his eyes flamed for a second on Jewel, "forced her way in. I was just going to have the footmen throw her out."

"That seems to be the proper course of action," the gentleman said. Apparently losing interest now that all was on its way to being resolved, he turned back to Caroline and offered her the support of his arm. "Continue with it."

"Yes, your lordship." There was relief and grim satisfaction in Smathers' voice, and vengeance in the look he turned on Jewel. He and the three footmen moved toward her purposefully.

Jewel waited until they were close before shoving the chair toward them with all her might. Its carved feet screeched over the marble floor, caught on the edge of the carpet, and overturned with a crash. Smathers swore and grabbed for Jewel, but she had already darted between the two footmen, and was dodging behind a small table decorated with a ridiculously large blue and white vase filled with cream-colored roses.

"Oh, lud, have a care for the vase! It's a Meissen!" The screech came from Caroline, who had only managed to descend one stair on the gentleman's arm. Her blue eyes, large with horror, were on the vase, which tottered dangerously on its stand. Jewel, seized by an inspiration, snatched up the vase and held it high over her head.

"C'mon, then," she said to her pursuers with relish. "An' I'll smash this thing to smithereens."

Smathers and the footmen stopped in their tracks, their eyes darting fearfully from the uplifted vase to Jewel's determined face to the horrified one of the lady above.

"Really, Sebastian, can't you do something? This is dreadful! Suppose our guests arrive early, and chance to see this—this disgraceful display?"

"Your guests, my dear—not ours. Nevertheless, you have a point. Gossip is so wearying, is it not?" The gentleness of his words in no way robbed them of their bite. Caroline colored furiously.

"You would know far more about that than I, my lord," she flared, then immediately looked frightened. "I didn't mean . . ."

"I know precisely what you meant, Caroline." The

boredom was back in his voice. He turned his attention to the tableau in the hallway. "Smathers, I had not noticed how you had aged. How remiss of me! Removing a scrawny brat who should not have been allowed to enter in the first place would at one time not have been beyond your capabilities. If you wish to retire, you have only to tell me. I will arrange for a pension to be paid you."

"No, no, my lord," Smathers gasped, his eyes slits of fury as they darted toward Jewel. "I . . ."

"And who ya be callin' a scrawny brat?" Jewel interrupted furiously, her eyes flashing up at the gentleman on the stairs. "I be just as good as you, you . . . you man-milliner!"

In tune to the concerted gasp of the assemblage, the gentleman's eyes focused on Jewel. His eyebrows rose again as he surveyed her from head to toe with slow deliberation. Despite her seething indignation, she had to fight an urge to squirm beneath that dispassionate regard.

"Shut your mouth, you little twit! That be the Earl of Moorland you're addressing!" This horrified hiss came from a footman. Jewel lowered the vase fractionally, her eyes widening with interest as she stared at the gentleman on the stairs. The Earl of Moorland, was he? He didn't look like no earl. He should have been bigger, older, with a leonine head and rugged features. This man was blond, lean and blindingly beautiful, with the flawlessly molded face of one of the Lord's archangels. He was far too beautiful to be a man, let alone an earl. Jewel glared at him just to reinforce her own immunity to his attraction.

"If ya be the earl, then ya be the very gent I've got business with," she declared, moving from behind the table.

Just in case, she kept a hold on the vase and a wary eye out for any sudden movement by Smathers or the others.

"*You* have business with *me?*" the earl asked ever so gently. "Somehow I doubt it."

"Oh, do ya? Well, I got somethin' to be delivered with Mr. Timothy Stratham's compliments to the Earl o' Moorland, if that's really who ya be. I must say, ya don't look much like no earl." Jewel regarded the outrageously handsome man on the stairs with stark suspicion.

"Really, Sebastian, can't you make her leave? The guests will be arriving. . . ."

"Why don't you go back upstairs and have Hanks pin up your hair again, Caroline? The left side is falling a bit, I fancy." He didn't even look at her as he said it, but something in his tone caused the lady to whiten.

"You are cruel, Sebastian," she whispered, and with that breathy murmur she turned and disappeared into the upstairs hallway.

When she was gone, the earl turned his attention to the scene below him. "Smathers, I am very disappointed in the way you have handled this. I will not require your further assistance, I believe. And the rest of you may resume your usual duties as well."

Smathers' face became an impassive mask. He bowed, muttered, "Yes, my lord," and shooing two of the footmen before him, vanished into the nether regions of the house. The third footman assumed a statue-like position at the foot of the stairs. From the expression on his face, he was now deaf and blind to all proceedings.

"So you have something for the Earl of Moorland from Timothy Stratham, do you?" the earl said slowly as he descended the stairs. "You may accompany me. George, something to wrap around this creature, if you please. She seems to be dripping all over the floor."

"I ain't no creature, and there be no need to turn up yer fancy nose jest because a body's wet," Jewel said resentfully as the footman vanished to do his master's bidding. "It be rainin' outside, in case ya ain't stuck yer nose out all day. Anybody'd be wet if they'd stood out in it, includin' your bleedin' lordship."

"How colorfully you express yourself," the earl murmured, and Jewel had to squash an urge to hurl the vase right at that too beautiful face.

Then the footman came back carrying a towel and a blanket, and at the earl's nod offered them to Jewel. Figuring it was now safe to put down the vase, she did so, and accepted the articles with poor grace. The earl was already walking away from her down a hall that led toward the back of the house. She trailed him until he stopped outside a closed door, while the expressionless footman followed her.

"Kindly wrap the towel around your hair and the blanket around your body, if you please. I object to having puddles of water formed in my office."

That cool, disinterested voice aroused the most violent emotions in Jewel's breast. She wanted to do something outrageous, to shriek and claw and scream. But she didn't. Something about the elegant, upright carriage, the lean, powerful body in its immaculate black evening clothes, the icy blue eyes and perfectly carved features discouraged her.

"At once, if you please."

Jewel glared at him. He looked back at her out of eyes as

blue as the sky on a cloudless summer day. His hair, a silvery gold that most women would have killed for, gleamed angelically in the candlelight. His brow was high and broad beneath the shining crown of hair; his nose was straight and elegant, his mouth finely chiseled with the lower lip slightly fuller than the upper. His cheekbones were high, his jaw square, and his skin tone was a fair golden bronze. Without a doubt, he was the most handsome man Jewel had ever seen in her life. Far too handsome to inspire fear—and yet there was something about his stance, about the expression in those celestial eyes, that discouraged her from arguing further. In a sort of compromise with the urgings of her more belligerent side, Jewel sniffed expressively before wrapping the blanket around her body. Its warmth was comforting, although she knew her comfort had been the last thing on his mind.

"George will take your, er, hat."

Jewel looked up sharply, glaring at him again. But discretion triumphed, and she removed the sodden hat and handed it to the footman who, in response to a dismissive signal from the earl, bore it away.

With as much dignity as she could muster, she wrapped the towel around her head like a turban and walked through the door the earl held for her into a book-lined study. A fire had been lit in the hearth, and a lamp glowed on a massive wood desk. A wine-colored leather chair had been pulled up behind the desk, and a matching chair faced it. Against the far wall rested a wine and gold striped velvet settee. Mounted firearms decorated the walls, and over the fireplace was a huge painting depicting a hunting scene in greens and golds and scarlets.

All this Jewel saw in the instant before she sat in the chair facing the desk. And it dazzled her into momentary speechlessness. So much care and warmth and comfort for one man. It was almost a crime.

"Now, please state your business."

Jewel found herself uncharacteristically at a loss for words. She fumbled in the beaded reticule at her wrist and produced her marriage lines, which she handed to him. He accepted the document as silently as she passed it over. Only the faintest wrinkling of his brow betrayed his feelings as he scanned the few lines that made her legally Mrs. Timothy Stratham. Then he looked up, his blue eyes colder than ever as they ran over her as if he were just now seeing her for the first time.

"If you will forgive me for saying so, you're remarkably poorly dressed for an adventuress."

Jewel blinked. Whatever reaction she had been expecting, it was not this. "Wot?"

"My God, you even butcher the Queen's English. And you are trying to convince me that my lately deceased cousin—who was many unpleasant things, but one hopes, not quite run mad!—married you?"

"If Timothy Stratham be yer cousin, then that's right, 'e did."

The earl was silent for a moment, the coldness deepening in his eyes. When finally he spoke, his voice was as chilling as his expression. "Tell me, what type of background breeds a vulture such as you, who would prey on the family of a young man not a week in his grave? You look rather young for that kind of game, so it stands to reason that someone has hired you. Come, admit it, and let's have done with this farce. You might as well because you won't get so much as a farthing out of me."

"Timothy did 'ave a proper funeral, then?" Jewel's voice was subdued. The idea of that sweet-faced young man lying in a cold dark grave was sobering, even in the light of the earl's insults.

The earl's eyes narrowed again. "I suggest again that you admit the lie and have done. Do you know that what you are attempting is called fraud, and is punished by many years' imprisonment in Newgate?"

Jewel swallowed, her eyes widening as the threat went home. Newgate was more frightening than hellfire to London's street people.

"But it be true! Timothy Stratham *did* marry me, and tol' me ter bring me marriage lines to the Earl o' Moorland, who ya claim to be! 'e said, 'It'll be one in the eye for ole Seb,' and 'e laughed."

The earl's beautiful face tightened as if he were struggling to deny some unwanted emotion. Then just as suddenly, it emptied of everything save cool detachment. He leaned back in his chair, his eyes never leaving Jewel. "You begin to interest me. Suppose you tell me this remarkable tale from beginning to end—the truth, mind!"

Jewel straightened indignantly. "I'm not no liar!"

"We'll see, won't we?" The earl regarded her affronted face without any apparent contrition. "Now tell me your tale if you please. Unless you want to be thrown out on your ear, of course."

"By ya and wot army?" Jewel muttered to herself. But when the earl looked at her in that daunting way of his, she launched hastily into a somewhat censored account of how she came to be married to Timothy Stratham. In her version of events, she was merely a passerby who happened to see the poor injured man on the street and rendered him assistance. As she finished her account with Father Simon's name and direction, she saw that the earl's eyebrows were once again lifted slightly, and bit her lip. Had she somehow let slip something she shouldn't?

"So you cared for him as he lay dying," the earl mused when she had finished. He still leaned slightly back in his chair, but his eyes as they met hers were keen. "And you took advantage of my cousin's weakness on his death bed to persuade him to marry you. Is that not how it happened?"

"N-No!" Jewel stuttered with relief that this was the area of her tale he was choosing to question. In this part of what had happened, she was completely innocent. "Timothy said 'e wanted ter give me a reward for takin' care of 'im, but the robbers 'ad took all 'is money and 'e said 'e would marry me instead. 'E said that that way I'd be took care of fer the rest of me life."

"Oh, he did, did he?" The earl's eyes narrowed. He was just about to go on when the study door opened with scarcely more than a ceremonial knock.

"Sebastian, Caroline tells me that you refuse to join our guests. That is quite in keeping with your usual churlish behavior, but this time I must insist. Lord Portmouth is among them and he is your godfather, you know. You cannot be so rude as to slight him."

"Oh, but I can, mama. You of all people should know that." The earl smiled at the slight, imperious woman who stood in the doorway regarding him coldly. Her manner was so like his that Jewel would have known who she was even if he had not addressed her as "mama." She had the same build as he, the same porcelain-perfect features, even the same coloring—although age had turned her hair a distinguished shade of silver and fine lines marred the flawless surface of her skin. Dressed in a high-necked, long-sleeved black silk dress that was ornamented only by a gleaming onyx brooch at the base of her throat, she was still as arrestingly attractive as her son. Only her voice, with its edge of petulant dissatisfaction, differed markedly from his.

"Really, Sebastian, just because you are the subject of some unsavory gossip over Elizabeth's death is no reason to make a social outcast of yourself. Or are you worried that someone might ask about that backward child of yours? You should be used to that by now—My heavens, what in the world is *that?*"

Jewel had twisted in her chair to better see the speaker as this exchange took place, and her movement caught the lady's attention. She stared at Jewel with repugnance, and Jewel returned her look with interest. Despite the earl's icy manner and insults, Jewel felt herself instinctively siding with him in what she sensed was an ongoing battle with his icicle of a mother.

"Prepare yourself for a shock, mama," the earl said with a slight, malicious twist of his lips. "This is the newest addition to our happy family. Timothy's widow, to be precise. Uh, Jewel, you may make your curtsy to your new cousin, my mother, the Dowager Countess of Moorland."

"Sebastian, I have had enough of your childish tricks, and so I warn you! If you think to palm me off with some Banbury story. . . . !"

"Oh, it's quite true, mama, I assure you. I have the marriage lines right here." The earl sounded as if he were enjoying himself. Jewel, far from following his admonition to curtsy to his mama, was glaring at the lady.

"Sebastian, if this is another of your attempts to annoy me . . ."

"Not at all, mama. You may see for yourself if you wish."

He proffered the marriage lines. With carefully controlled movements the countess crossed the room and took the document from his hand. As she read it, her face creased in the same slight frown that had marred the earl's features earlier.

"And are you going to let this—this creature pull the wool over your eyes with this? It is not worth the paper it is printed on."

"Who d' ya think . . ." Jewel started indignantly, but was silenced by the earl's quick frown and uplifted hand.

"Be silent," he said, scarcely sparing her a look. Much to her own surprise, Jewel obeyed him.

"Strangely enough," he continued, "I believe the document is genuine." His mother glared at him. He smiled blandly back at her.

"Even if she did somehow coerce Timothy into marrying her, we have only to turn her away, and it won't matter. Who would listen to her with him dead—and besides, we have her marriage lines." A cunning look came into the countess' eyes as she regarded Jewel, who sat stiff and resentful in her chair. "Very foolish of you to hand over the paper, girl. Without this, what proof do you have?"

"Why, mama, what other proof does she need if I am prepared to accept her as Timothy's relic?"

The countess made a low, choked sound as she stared at

her son. "You cannot. Sebastian, you are doing this merely to persecute me. Oh, why was I cursed with such an unnatural son?"

"Bad luck, wasn't it, that I didn't die instead of Edward? Well, such is the way of things."

"Sebastian, you can't . . ."

"Oh, but I can," he said softly, his eyes never leaving her face. "And I am. And, dearest mama, there is absolutely nothing you can do about it."

The countess glared at him. Jewel could have sworn the woman's eyes were filled with hate. But surely no mother could actually hate her own flesh and blood?

"If you go through with this, you will rue the day, I promise you," the countess said in a low choked voice. Turning, she fixed her eyes on Jewel. "And if you think that you will ever be accepted by this family, let alone anyone else—"

"But I mean to see to that, too, mama," the earl purred.

And at that, the countess turned on her heel and stalked from the room, slamming the door behind her.

I V

HE earl's eyes returned to rest almost ruefully on Jewel. "Well, girl, I hope you are equal to this because now we're for it. I mean to see to it that you become worthy of us." He smiled faintly. "It will be a challenge, won't it, rather like turning a sow's ear into a silk purse? I wonder if it can be done."

"Yer bloody insultin', did ya know that? Who ya callin' a sow's ear? I'm a person, I am, jes' as good as ya, or that highfalutin' ma of yers." This insult on top of all the others was too much for her temper. Jewel sprang from the chair and stood glaring at the earl, her hands clenched in fists at her side. The blanket slipped, giving him an unrestricted view of her attire—and the body it covered. Jewel felt his eyes on her, and shivered. There was only the most detached kind of interest in his look, as if she were a tarnished piece of brass he was wondering whether it would be worth the effort to have shined up. But still it made her aware of herself as a woman in a way she had never been before.

"That dress is an abomination," he said as his eyes ran over the soaked red silk. Jewel looked down at the gown that she still thought looked mighty fine despite its wetting as he continued. "It's something a whore would wear. Are you . . . Well, I suppose it doesn't matter now."

"No, I ain't no 'ore!" Jewel bellowed, taking a hasty step forward as her fists came up to waist level. She wasn't taking any more insults, earl or no earl!

"Sit down," he said, the words barely audible. Something about his eyes gave them more force than her loudest shriek. Jewel surprised herself again by obediently sitting, but saved face by glaring at him even more fiercely than before.

"The first thing you will learn is to moderate your voice when you speak. I will not be shouted at. Is that clear?" Those blue eyes met hers, and instead of celestial heavens the color reminded Jewel of cold blue steel. She scowled, opened her mouth for a sassy reply, met those eyes again, and muttered, "Ayeh."

He sighed. "I assume that is an affirmative. In future,

when addressing me, you will say 'Yes, my lord,' or 'No, my lord.' Can you remember that, do you think?"

"I ain't a bleedin' idiot."

Jewel's resentful murmur brought a brisk "Excellent!" in reply. The earl got to his feet, and while she watched him with some trepidation moved with sinewy grace around the desk to tower over her as he sat in the chair. Looking up at him, she felt suddenly very small, and she didn't like the sensation at all. When his hand came out, catching her under the chin, she flinched. His skin was so warm—just feeling his hand on her made her go all shivery inside. Cor, he was a very good-looking gentleman. . . .

But such thoughts did her no good at all, she told herself even as her hand shot out to knock his away. Before she could make contact he caught her by the wrist, imprisoning her hand in midair. His fingers were surprisingly strong, she noticed with a return of the shivery feeling. They tightened their grip and her eyes widened as she stared up at him. It occurred to her that this too beautiful lord could break her arm with no trouble at all, like snapping a sparrow's bone.

"I'm not going to hurt you," he said, and Jewel realized with a quick flush of embarrassment that he must have felt her shiver. She was thankful he had misinterpreted it. "I just want to look at you. All right?"

This first evidence that he regarded her as something other than an object to be ordered about mollified Jewel somewhat. She gave a jerky nod. He released her wrist, and turned her face up again so that the lamplight shone directly on it. His free hand caught the towel, pulling it from her head so that her hair fell from what remained of its pins to straggle in a damp, midnight black rat's nest to her waist.

His eyes raked the mess, then moved over the high cheek-boned, pointy chinned face. Jewel knew that she was no beauty, but still she resented the almost clinical detachment with which he assessed and then dismissed each individual feature: high broad forehead partly hidden under the tangled mass of hair, thick brows as black as her hair winging upward at the edges so that they seemed to take flight at her temples, black-lashed eyes the color of amber set deep and with a faint slant at the edges, a small straight nose unbecomingly reddened, parchment pale skin that was chapped and roughened by exposure to the elements stretching taut over hollowed, hungry cheeks, and a full-lipped mouth that lacked color. Jem had often said that she looked like a little gypsy, but still it was galling to be less than pretty in the eyes of this haughty lord who was so dazzingly beautiful himself.

"Open your mouth," he said. Jewel blinked at him, and tried to jerk her chin free. Once again those long fingered hands proved surprisingly strong.

"I ain't a bleedin' 'orse!"

"No one said you were. Now open your mouth."

Sulkily Jewel obeyed. There was something about him that made a body feel that she was better off to do as he said. Not that she was afraid of him, mind.

His eyes ran over her small teeth, which were relatively even and strong. He nodded once, and Jewel took that for permission to close her mouth. She did so, looking him over from head to toe with open provocation just so he would know she was not totally cowed. But he didn't seem one whit disturbed by her close inspection; on the contrary, it was she who was bothered. Seen so close, it was apparent that the lean, broad shouldered frame beneath the impeccable evening clothes was impressively muscular. Jewel hadn't realized it before, but now she became aware that she liked leanly muscled men. His physique didn't repulse her as had, say, Mick's burly form.

"Stand up."

"Wot?" His command caught her by surprise, and she frowned. He repeated it with a cool lack of emphasis, and stepped back from her, allowing her sufficient room to obey. Jewel, to her own surprise, stood without further question, looking at him warily. The blanket drooped from her shoulder, and he reached out to remove it altogether, throwing it aside as though it might be unclean.

"I ain't got the pox, if that be wot's worryin' ya."

"You relieve my mind." His voice was as tranquil as if they were discussing the weather. Jewel ground her teeth. This fine earl would drive her to drink within a week, she thought—or maybe even to murder him. The thought made her smile.

"How old are you?" he demanded abruptly, his eyes narrowed as he watched the change a smile brought to her face.

"Sixteen, or thereabouts, I think. How old ya be?"

It was deliberate impertinence, and Jewel did not really expect him to answer, but he did without apparent rancor.

"Thirty-one."

Exactly fifteen years old older than herself, Jewel calculated as his eyes ran over her again. Old enough so that he was a full grown man, not a clumsy boy.

"You're way too thin, but I suppose that's only to be expected and can be remedied. We will hope that your figure will improve as your diet does."

His eyes turned critically to her small breasts, clearly revealed even to the tiny upright nipples by the damp silk that clung to her. His gaze rested there for an instant before moving down over her tiny waist and boyish hips. The only undergarment she ever wore was a pair of drawers, and with her dress as wet as it was, every curve and hollow of her shape was revealed to him. Looking down at herself, Jewel felt a sense of shame that her body wasn't more lushly female. But she told herself that it was just as well. He was very handsome, too handsome. And when he ordered her to do something in that voice of his she couldn't seem to do anything but obey him. It was uncanny, the effect he had on her. She didn't like it, not one little bit. It was time she started to show that she had a mind of her own again.

"Seen enough?" she asked pertly as his eyes returned to her face at last. She was surprised to find that, standing, she still had to tilt her head back to look into those celestial eyes. She had not realized that he was so tall.

The sight of those beautiful eyes frowning down into her own unexpectedly flustered her, and she took a step backwards, ending up with the backs of her knees pressed closely against the seat of her chair.

His eyebrows rose faintly at her action, and his eyes narrowed on her face. Feeling herself blush, Jewel prayed that he would not be able to guess the unsettling feelings he stirred in her body.

"You'll never be a diamond of the first water, but I suppose you can be rigged out to be presentable enough. You'll have to learn to speak, to dress, to conduct yourself like a lady. I'll have to hire you a governess, I suppose. Some elderly female, perhaps." His eyes gleamed brightly blue with calculation as they ran over her again. His impersonal regard when she was so intensely aware of him was maddening.

" 'Old your 'orses a minute, 'ere. Suppose I don' wan' ter be turned into a bleedin' lady? I don' 'ave to do wot ya tell me, ya know. I can jes' take wot's comin' ter me and leave."

He smiled then, a slow sweet smile that made Jewel tingle from the top of her head to the soles of her feet. There was something about that smile that made her feel the way she had felt once when she had been to an exhibition at Astley's Amphitheater and seen a snake curl around its handler's neck.

"Let's get something clear between us, my girl. You will do just exactly as I tell you. If you do not, if you do not obey me precisely in everything, then I will turn you back out into the streets without a second thought. Your marriage lines, as my mother so thoughtfully pointed out, are not worth the paper they are written on unless I choose to acknowledge them. If I do not choose to accept them and you, what will you do? Hire a barrister and press a suit against the estate? You'd be laughed out of court with your whore's cant—even supposing you could find a barrister willing to take your case. With my sponsorship, however, you will be well fed, which from the looks of you is something you've never been, well clothed, housed, and educated far above your station. You will have my cousin's name, and in four years time, on what would have been his twenty-fifth birthday, his not inconsiderable competence to call your own. But make no mistake, my girl. In return for all this you will do as I say without question. If you wish to go, you have only to say so now. But once you agree, there will be no turning back. In return for the future I hold out to you, you will obey me in all things. It is your choice. Think well before you make it. Once made, there will be no going back."

Jewel looked at the earl, her eyes narrowed to a dull golden gleam in the lamplight. Then she looked around at the leather chairs, the books that lined the walls, the luxurious carpet beneath her feet, the paintings on the wall. A fire blazed cheerfully in the hearth, making the room toasty warm. The entire house was undoubtedly warm—here, in this mansion, warmth was not a luxury but something that was taken for granted, like air to breathe. She would have plenty of food to eat, and a warm, dry bed to sleep in free of bugs or the possibility of other, less welcome intruders, clean, whole clothes—and she would be safe. She would be a fool not to agree with any conditions he set on that. Then she thought of something, and frowned darkly.

"There be jes' one thing."

"And what is that?"

"I won't be—do nothin' bad wit' ya!" She blurted it out, her voice belligerent, her eyes gleaming with golden challenge.

His eyes widened slightly, and he stared at her for a moment. A muscle at the corner of his mouth twitched. He looked to be on the verge of laughing, which she sensed was a rare thing for him. Contrarily, the knowledge that he found her assertion amusing nettled her. It was humbling to discover that he thought her *so* lacking in attraction.

"My dear girl, you may put aside any fears that you may

be harboring. I assure you, I have absolutely no designs on your person. You are as safe with me as you would be with your own father or brother. If you have either."

"I ain't got no family a-tall." Her answer was muttered. The sudden shame that rose in her at the admission surprised her. Being the daughter of a woman who had had to whore for a living had never bothered Jewel particularly before. But now, in the face of this man, it did.

"You are more fortunate than I then," he responded dryly, lifting an eyebrow at her. "Well, do we have a bargain or don't we?"

Jewel nodded. "We got a deal."

He smiled then, a faint curving of his lips. "Very wise of you. You've given up little to gain much. I will have Mrs. Masters prepare a room for you. After she shows you to it, a bath will be sent up to you. Oblige me by making full use of it. Tomorrow I travel to the country. I think the best thing will be for you to accompany me. Your education will prosper better away from town where there are fewer eyes to see and tongues to wag. I leave at first light, so be ready. One of the maids will wake you in time."

He crossed to the side of the room and tugged on a tasseled rope while Jewel watched him with some trepidation. She would not have been at all surprised to see little horned gremlins descend out of the ceiling at his signal. It was somehow in keeping with her notion that she had just sold her soul to the devil.

"Your name, what was it again?" He was looking at her with the merest suggestion of a frown.

"Jewel. Jewel Combs."

"My lord," he prompted.

"My lord," she echoed, feeling foolish, and he nodded.

"Jewel Stratham, don't you mean, since you have married my cousin Stratham?"

Jewel was startled to realize that she hadn't even thought about that. But, yes, she realized now, her name—and so much else—had been changed forever. "Jewel Stratham, then. My lord."

He nodded again, showing approval that she had remembered the correct way to address him.

"Jewel is not, I think, fitting for the role of my cousin's relic. It reminds one—quite irresistibly!—of the stratum which you will no longer occupy. I think you shall be called Julia. Similar enough so that you should have no problems answering to it, but still the name of a lady."

"But—" Jewel started to protest this disposal of her name as if it were no more than a dirty rag, but caught his eye in time to remember her promise to obey him in all things. She looked around her again at the warmth and luxury of the room, thought of the sumptuous dinner that was certain to be provided for her shortly, and bit her tongue. He could call her Henry the Eighth if he wanted, if she could eat good.

"Are we agreed? Jewel Combs is now Mrs. Julia Stratham?" His eyes were on her, measuring her compliance. Jewel nodded.

"Ayeh. My lord," she added as those eyebrows went up. He smiled at her.

"I can see that you're a clever girl, Julia. We should get on very well. Ah, yes, Mrs. Masters." He turned his attention to the plump middle aged lady who presented herself after a brief knock in the doorway. "This is Mr. Timothy's widow. She requires a room—the gold one, I think—a bath, and a meal. Also, some nightclothes, and, uh, some suitable garments for travel on the morrow. Oh, and you may address her as Miss Julia. She is to be quite one of the family."

"Mr. Timothy's wife, my lord?" Mrs. Masters' voice was squeaky with disbelief as her eyes ran over the new Mrs. Julia Stratham.

Jewel stiffened, conscious of the picture she must present with the still wet red gown clinging to every slim curve, the pale flesh of her breasts peeking out above the bodice, and her eyes shadowed with exhaustion and hunger. Mrs. Masters looked scornful, affronted, and offended in turn—until her rheumy blue eyes met the celestial ones of her master. Then all expression was quickly wiped from her face. Jewel's sizzling temper subsided. There was no need for her to say anything to put the snooty creature in her place when the earl's silence was so eloquent.

"Yes, Mrs. Masters. Didn't I just say so?" He turned to Jewel, who looked at him as a drowning man might a life line. "Go with Mrs. Masters. She will provide all that you require. I will see you in the morning."

"Please follow me, Miss Julia." Mrs. Masters turned to go. Her tone was stiffly correct, but Jewel knew that her dislike of having to treat courteously one whom she had instantly dismissed as a guttersnipe or worse was fairly choking her.

The earl made a gesture indicating that Jewel should follow the housekeeper. With a final sideways look at the beautiful masculine face, which suddenly struck her as being a port in a storm of dislike, and a determined straightening of her shoulders, she did.

V

HEN the girl had gone, Sebastian Peyton, eighth Earl of Moorland, moved back to the chair behind his desk and sat down, feeling suddenly weary. Automatically his hand reached for the mother-of-pearl cigar box that held the thin brown cheroots that were one of his numerous vices. Extracting one and lighting it, he inhaled the aromatic smoke with pleasure. He was engaged to meet a trio of cronies for dinner and a night of activities that would no doubt add to their unsavory reputations as scions of noble families whose scandalous careers put them outside the social pale. But for once his heart was not in it.

He leaned back in the chair, closed his eyes, and put the cheroot between his lips, savoring it. Life held too few pleasures, he thought bleakly. It was a cold and barren business with only small things like his cheroots, a good glass of brandy, or maybe a particularly ravishing high flyer to provide leavening. Which was probably why he hadn't sent the brass-faced little chit about her business. He was bored, deadly bored, and she looked like she might provide some amusing moments. Added to which, admitting her to the family had annoyed his mother mightily, and he enjoyed annoying his mother. It paid her back in small measure for all those years when she had ignored him.

Funny how life worked out when you thought about it. Edward, his sainted brother who had been the darling of his mother's heart and would have been the earl now if he had lived, had been dead these past ten years. And he himself had been widowed for what would be two years next month. And now Timothy, too, was gone.

Sebastian had never cared greatly for the lad, whose mother had spoiled him rotten just as Sebastian's mother, sister to Timothy's mother, had spoiled Edward. But he had been very young to die.

"Here's one in the eye for old Seb." Sebastian could imagine how the thought had cheered the dying youth. Timothy had deeply resented his cousin because Sebastian had refused to pay another farthing of his monstrous gambling debts, or to finance his taste for expensive light-skirts, or to advance him any sums over and above the allowance which came to him each quarter. In addition, he had rung a rare peal over Timothy's head the last time the boy had come begging to him, and recommended that he find honest employment if he could not support himself on the funds that were available to him. It was an object lesson designed to put a damper on Timothy's rackety ways before the boy came into his adequate but not enormous principal and promptly ran through every last shilling of it. But Timothy had been furious, and had stormed out of the house in high dudgeon. That had been some six months ago, and as Timothy had his own bachelor lodgings Sebastian had not seen him since.

But there was one thing that Sebastian could do for Timothy, and he had already set the wheels in motion to do it: He could see that the boy's killer was hanged from the highest tree at Tyburn. Already he had a pair of Bow Street runners on the job. Now that Mistress Jewel Combs—no, Julia Stratham, how could he have forgotten?—had turned up they would have far more to go on than they had before. The girl's story had enough holes in it to drive a carriage through, but he was sure somewhere in her web of lies lay the truth.

He opened his eyes and reached for pen and paper, scribbling a brief note, then sanding the missive, folding, and sealing it. He got to his feet, moving over to the bell pull and tugging it impatiently. When Smathers answered his summons, he handed the butler the note.

"Have this taken around to Bow Street if you please. At once."

"Yes, my lord." Smathers bowed himself out, and Sebastian stared at the closed door for an instant. He found himself hoping that the stupid little chit had not been the one who had knifed Timothy. For all her vulgarity she was scarcely more than a child, and a hungry, frightened one at that. It would sit ill with him to have her hanged.

Sentimental nonsense, he told himself harshly. Moving abruptly toward the door, he decided he would go out after all.

V I

tell ya, I will not do it!" Jewel glared at the assembled trio of women who were regarding her with varying degrees of exasperated contempt.

"The master said you were to have a bath, Miss Julia, and a bath you shall have." Mrs. Masters advanced on Jewel with a martial light in her eye. Jewel, an equally battle ready gleam in her own eyes, crouched slightly and raised her clenched fists into fighting position.

"C'mon, then, ya fat sow," she hissed. "I'll dump ya and yer gang in this contraption if ya like, but that's as near as

I'll come ter it! And ya may take those words as 'oly writ because I mean wot I say!"

Mrs. Masters stopped in her tracks, glaring at Jewel as she seemed to think better of her plan to strip the girl and place her in the steaming porcelain tub by main force. Behind her one of the young maids put a hand over her mouth to stifle a giggle. The other one merely watched goggle-eyed.

"Very well then, Miss Julia, I will see to it that the master is informed of your wishes," Mrs. Masters said stiffly, a light that promised retribution in her eyes. With a martial nod of her head and a swish of her ample black skirts, Mrs. Masters swept from the room, leaving the two maids to follow.

The door closed with awful gentleness behind the three of them. Jewel slowly allowed herself to relax. Mrs. Masters' threat of going to the earl was an empty one, she guessed. The housekeeper would not dare bother her master about such a matter. Even if she did, Jewel thought, it would make no difference. The earl could have no notion of the dreadful thing that that woman expected her to do in the guise of carrying out his orders.

A peremptory knock at the door made Jewel start. She whirled to face it just as it swung open. To her horror she found herself looking at the earl. He wore a fine topcoat of soft dark wool and a white silk scarf around his neck. Obviously he had just been about to go out. He entered without waiting for her permission to do so, moving with a deceptively lazy stride, his eyes narrowed as they ran over her person. Jewel took an instinctive step backwards at the coldness of his look, knowing from her short experience of him that it meant trouble. As she sternly tried to control her quailing insides, she caught just a glimpse of a smirking Mrs. Masters in the hallway outside before the earl gently closed the door in her face.

"Wot do ya want?" Jewel was apprehensive, but the words came out sounding belligerent. The earl, crossing to stand in front of the finely wrought white marble fireplace in which blazed a luxurious fire, merely looked at her over his shoulder for a moment without answering. Jewel felt herself wilting under that chilling gaze.

"I thought we had agreed that you were to do as I bade you?"

Jewel nodded once.

"Well then, did I not instruct you that you were to bathe?"

Jewel's chin came up at that. Here, she thought, she was on strong ground. "Ayeh, ya did, and I like ter 'ave a bath as well as the next one. And I *would,* but not in that!" Her hand came out to point in a gesture of loathing at the steaming tub that sat innocently in front of the fire. The earl looked at the tub, then his eyebrows rose ever so slightly.

"Is something amiss with it?"

Jewel almost choked. "I can't 'ave a bath in that!"

"Why ever not? That is what it is for, you know."

"Because they tell me I'm ter get right down inside it! Get me whole body wet! I'll die of the bloody ague, I will." Her eyes narrowed on him suddenly. "Is that wot ya want? Ter murder me, so that you'll not 'ave to worry about me bein' married to yer cousin?"

"You are becoming very boring, you know. Of course I don't wish to murder you! The matter comes down to this: You agreed to obey me without question, I have instructed you to bathe, and you refuse. For the final time, you may either do as I bid you or you may leave my house. It is entirely up to you."

Jewel met those cold blue eyes, and felt anxiety knot like a wet rope in her chest. It was clear that he meant what he said. Yes, she was worried about the ills that complete immersion could cause—everyone knew that they were many and serious—but there was another problem, one that she hated to divulge to a man. Especially this one.

"I—I can't," she muttered wretchedly, her eyes on the carpet. She couldn't do as he asked and she couldn't tell him why. She just couldn't. . . . His eyebrows rose again, and he turned toward the door.

"Very well then, I will tell Smathers to retrieve your hat and shawl and show you out. We shan't meet again, so I will bid you farewell."

He was walking toward the door as he spoke, his black-clad shoulders very broad and formidable from the rear. Jewel stared at that unyielding back, hesitated, bit her lip, and spoke.

"Ya don' unnerstan'," she cried, and he cast her a look over his shoulder, one eyebrow lifted questioningly.

"What is it I don't understand?"

"They want me ter—ter get naked! In front of them! I can't do it, and I won't! Not even if it means I 'ave to leave 'ere!" The shame of having to tell him made her avert her blushing face.

The earl turned slowly to face her, his expression disbelieving as his eyes ran up and down her slender body.

"You object to undressing before other females?"

"Before—before anybody!" Jewel blurted, her eyes as

they swung back to him blazing gold. The earl's eyes were expressionless as they met hers.

"So the little guttersnipe is modest, is she?" he said softly, as though to himself. "Well, well." His voice hardened. "If this is an act designed to impress me with your virtue, you needn't bother. I could care less if you have whored for half of England in your short span of years. What interests me is what you will do from today on."

"I never did nothin' like that! I keep tellin' ya, I ain't no 'ore!"

The earl looked at her for a long moment, then nodded. "Very well then, the problem is easily solved. You may bathe in privacy if you wish. I will instruct Mrs. Masters." He turned away again, one hand on the intricately carved gilt doorknob that had caused Jewel to marvel when she had first touched it. Then he looked back at her. "I rely on you to do a thorough job. To, uh, get right down inside there." His nod at the tub told her to what he was referring as he repeated her own words to her.

"I will. I promise." The color was receding from her face now. Funny, but she no longer felt embarrassed.

"My lord," he prompted, and as she echoed him he turned and left her alone, closing the door behind him.

She could hear him speaking softly to the housekeeper in the hallway. Although she waited some minutes to see what would happen next, nothing did. As she had already guessed, the earl's word was law in the house.

After a long time she began slowly undressing in front of the fire. Naked, she approached the tub with trepidation. It was, she found as she slid first a toe and then a leg and then her whole body into the water, not unpleasant at all. She sat there gingerly for a few minutes, waiting to see what effect the water would have on her skin, but when nothing happened, she succumbed to the lure of the sweet smelling little cakes of soap. Picking one up, she sniffed. Roses! They grew masses of them at Kensington Palace in the summer, and she had often stopped to admire their lush beauty and heady perfume. Now she could anoint her whole body with the scent. Slowly she began to lather her hands, her face, the rest of her. The sensation was heavenly, and by the time she had washed her hair and climbed out of the tub—leaving the water gray with grime and her skin surprisingly white—she had decided that an all-over bath was not a bad thing at all. O' course, she could still come down with the ague. . . .

V I I

HE next morning Jewel was dressed and standing in the grand entryway with an impassive footman in attendance for a good quarter-hour before the earl came downstairs. Even on so brief an acquaintance she sensed that it would be unwise to keep him waiting. He would undoubtedly leave without sparing her a second thought, and she found she hated the thought of that.

The black wool dress she wore beneath a matching pelisse was whole and clean, but with its high neck and its long tight sleeves it was as ugly as any garment she had ever seen. And it was miles too big, hanging around her slender frame like a gunny sack around a twig. Added to that, it itched. Jewel scratched her midriff resentfully as she thought about it. After seeing the garment, she would have worn her red silk again if it had been anywhere to be found. But upon asking a maid, she had been told that the most beautiful dress she had ever owned in her life had been taken and burned.

When the earl finally put in an appearance, he was clad in a tan ankle length coat with many capes on the shoulders that made him appear much broader than he had the night before. Beneath it, she caught just a glimpse of a plain black coat, a white, intricately tied cravat, and biscuit colored breeches. The heels of his gleaming white-topped boots echoed against the polished wood of the stairs as he descended. Watching him, she was struck again by how gorgeous he was. Last night, in her dreams, he had figured as the devil. Looking at him, today, she was again reminded of a statue she had seen of one of the Lord's archangels. There was no flaw to be found in that smooth countenance at all. The molding of forehead, cheekbones, chin, the set of the heavenly blue eyes beneath slanting ash-brown brows, the carving of the long, straight nose and neither too full nor too thin lips were perfection itself. Surely even Gabriel himself had not been so beauteous to look upon. Just the sight of him as he walked toward her was enough to make Jewel's toes curl in her too big shoes, and she chided herself impatiently for her folly. He was not interested in her, nor likely to be, she told herself. But still, a niggling voice inside her head answered back, a cat can look at a king.

A stray sunbeam slanted in through the carved glass semicircle over the door to touch on his hair, bringing it to shining, gilded life. The effect was uncanny, almost as though a halo encircled his head. Jewel stared, and as she stared he looked down and met her eyes.

"Good morning, Julia," he said tranquilly as he stepped into the entryway, nodding once to Smathers, who came hurrying to hand him his hat and gloves. To Jewel's surprise Smathers was now as courteously correct with her as he was with the earl. Just as though she had never forced her way into his house or kicked him on his shin, he also handed her a hat and gloves. The gloves were black as was the hideous bonnet. After one look of utter repulsion, she resignedly pulled on the gloves and set the bonnet on her head, tying the ribbons in a crooked bow.

"The carriage is outside, my lord."

"Thank you, Smathers. Come, Julia." He walked by her, settling the slouch hat on his head and pulling on his gloves as he did so. Jewel followed, feeling a little like a stray dog.

Outside the sun was just beginning to peep over the trees in the park opposite, lending a yellow glow to the retreating blanket of fog. The rain had stopped, but puddles lay on the cobbled street, and the air was frigid. Fat flakes of soot drifted down from smoke rising from chimney pots all around the square. The few individuals who were about so early—servants mostly—were well wrapped against the cold. A stooped little man bundled up to his eyebrows in a long coat and knit scarves pushed a handcart down the street. The noise of the cart's wooden wheels against the cobblestones all but drowned out his monotonous cries of "Milk, maids! Here's milk!" A liveried groom walked a team of matched bays up and down in front of the house, hurrying over when he saw the earl.

"Mornin', my lord. They be in fine fettle today."

"That's as well, Jenkins, because I hope to make good time. The air of London sits ill with me of late."

"Aye, my lord." The groom sounded knowing as the earl paused at the single step leading into the open carriage. He held out a hand to her, clearly intending to help her up. Jewel, as unaccustomed to such courtesies as she was to riding in a carriage at all, hesitated briefly before taking his hand. Her heart pounded, and this time it wasn't from the earl's touch; she was nervous about riding in such a rackety looking vehicle. But she would die rather than reveal her fear to him. Setting her teeth, she settled herself into the seat without a word.

The earl stepped briskly into the carriage after her, and called, "Let 'em go, Jenkins!"

The curricle lurched forward, nearly unseating Jewel, who was not prepared for such a sudden start. She regained her balance with an angry mutter just as the groom leaped nimbly up behind them, to stand woodenfaced at the rear. Jewel felt his curiosity about her, but the earl had made no attempt to enlighten him as to her identity. Apparently servants were entitled to know only what their masters wished. . . . At the realization that she was, in the earl's eyes at least, of even lower status than a servant, a hot rush of damaged pride surged through her veins. Which was just as well because it helped her to stay warm for nearly an hour, during which time not a single word was spoken by the earl. The groom and she were equally silent, not wanting— or daring?—to impinge on "my lord's" mood. As another hour crept forward, and Jewel grew steadily colder and less comfortable with her precarious perch on the slippery leather seat, the silence began to irk her.

"Would it be too much fer ya ter tell me where we be goin'?" If more than a trace of sarcasm laced her voice, the earl, looking down at her as if he had forgotten her existence seemed oblivious to it.

"To the country," he said briefly. Jewel's lip curled.

"T'anks," she said, and there was no hiding the sarcasm this time. But he still gave no sign of noticing. Glaring at him, she scratched her midriff for what must have been the hundredth time that morning. This time he looked at her with an impatient frown.

"What the devil are you scratching about? Surely you don't have fleas!"

This unfair attack sent Jewel's temper flaring.

"Listen, yer 'igh-and-mightiness, I agreed ter do wot ya say, but that don't mean ya got the right ter insult me!" Clutching the side of the curricle with one hand to steady herself as they hit a series of particularly bad ruts, Jewel glowered at him. The earl looked down at her in some surprise, rather as if a piece of wood had talked back to him.

"I beg your pardon. But perhaps you could explain to me why you keep, uh, tugging at the waist of that dress?"

"Because it bloody well itches!" His apology had not improved her temper one iota. She still glowered at him, and he, damn him, had the gall to look amused.

"Yes, I assumed that. But, er, why?"

" 'Ow should I know? It's yer bleedin' dress!"

His eyes narrowed thoughtfully, and he transferred the reins to one hand before reaching to lightly prod the material of her skirt. Jewel, glaring, twitched her skirt out of his reach, then had to grab the side of the curricle again to keep from being jounced from her seat.

"What are you wearing underneath it?"

Jewel stared at him. "My drawers, what else?" Surprisingly, making such a statement before the great "my lord" did not embarrass her at all, but she suddenly remembered the listening ears of the groom behind them and colored to the roots of her hair. The earl's lips twitched.

"Is that, er, all?"

"I don' think this be a fittin' subject for us ter discuss," she said primly, feeling proud of her new dignity. His lips twitched again, and then he grinned. Jewel, looking up at him as he laughed, was amazed at the transformation it wrought. He looked young, carefree, handsome, charming. She stared, dazzled. Then she frowned fiercely at him as she realized that he was laughing at *her.*

"I believe that in addition to drawers a young lady generally wears a chemise, stays, and several petticoats beneath her outer garment. The material of the dress is not designed to directly touch the skin. This dress in particular seems to be of wool; no doubt that explains your, er, itching."

Jewel glared at him, fiercely resenting the grin that still lurked around his mouth. Handsome or not, earl or not, he didn't have the right to laugh at her: But even as she scowled, she reached automatically to scratch her itching belly, catching herself just in time.

"I know that," she muttered, angry and embarrassed at the same time. "Wot do ya think I am, an ignoramus? I jes' didn't 'appen to 'ave my underclothes wit' me."

"Of course you didn't. Mrs. Masters should have seen that you were provided with the proper garments. No doubt she overlooked the necessity."

"No doubt," Jewel said sourly, thinking that Mrs. Masters had probably put out the scratchy wool dress and nothing else on purpose. But the soothing tone of the earl's voice insensibly made her feel a trifle better. Jewel said nothing, but her hand made another abortive movement to relieve the discomfort of the scratchy dress. The earl's lips twitched, and her temper heated all over again.

"Please feel free," he murmured, and grinned. Jewel glared at him, and with a heroic exercise of will managed not to scratch.

The rest of the journey passed in almost total silence. The earl, apparently caught up in his own thoughts, said nothing as he drove with more speed than care over muddy rutted roads. Jenkins blew a blast on a shrill horn whenever they approached a toll, and that was the only sound he made. Jewel herself, growing colder by the moment and exercising enormous self-control in the matter of her itchy dress, contributed a series of sniffs.

The day warmed only slightly as it passed into afternoon, and she was freezing. Frowning direly, she wrapped her arms around her body to provide what meager warmth they could, but before long she realized the cold was the least of her problems. The carriage lurched and jolted horribly as the earl raced them on. Jewel pressed herself back against the cold seat, feeling more and more seasick with each passing minute. She shut her eyes as the curricle drove on, jolting through the ruts with complete disregard for her increasing misery. If it did not stop soon, she realized, she was going to be sick.

Finally she was. All over the natty leather inside of the curricle, and the earl's highly polished black boots.

"Good God!" said the earl as he reined in his horses. When she had finished retching, and sat leaning weakly back against the seat with her eyes closed, she heard him say, "Hold 'em for me, Jenkins." Then she felt the warmth of his hand beneath her chin. She only wished she could wrap that warmth around all of her. She was so sick, and so cold, and so bloody miserable.

"Why didn't you tell me you were feeling unwell, you foolish chit?" The earl sounded only a trifle testy, which against all reason had the effect of sending Jewel's temper soaring.

"If ya 'ad the sense of a bloody goat, ya would have known it! Not bein' a sailin' man, I'm not accustomed ter 'avin' my insides shook about like they was caught in a 'urricane on the 'igh seas!" She opened her eyes and glared at him. Behind her, Jenkins gave a brief cough that might have been a muffled laugh.

"I'll thank you to watch your tongue, my girl," the earl responded, his eyes narrowing on her face.

"Pish and tosh," Jewel said rudely, and closed her eyes again. At this point she didn't care about offending the earl. She didn't care about whistling a home and food and care down the wind. All she cared about was letting this impossible, arrogant man know that she was not quite a nothing, to be subjected to horrible discomforts as though she didn't matter at all.

"My lord," he said quite calmly as though he was merely instructing her again in the correct form of address. She had half-expected him to respond to her rudeness with anger. But instead she heard the creak of springs as he climbed out of the carriage, then to her surprise felt his hands beneath her armpits. Opening her eyes wide, she stared at him as he lifted her down.

"See to the carriage, would you, Jenkins?" he threw over his shoulder as he pulled her arm beneath his so that it was pressed close to the hard warmth of his body. He urged her to walk back the way they had come. Jewel did, feeling stronger as she gulped in the cold air and felt the solid ground beneath her feet.

"Sorry about yer boots. My lord," she surprised herself by muttering. Then he smiled, that warm charming smile that lit up his eyes. She stared, dazzled by the impact of it at close range. He was too beautiful to smile—what it did for that gorgeous face was unfair.

"They'll clean," he said, and fished in the pocket of his coat for a silver flask.

"Drink this," he said, handing it to her, and Jewel obeyed. The straight scotch burned going down, but the effect was warming and she took another long swallow.

"Enough, or we'll have you drunk." He took the flask from her, regarding her with cold eyes that she found almost comforting because they were familiar. "If you are fond of the bottle, you'll have to learn to do without. Ladies do not drink hard liquor."

"Ya shouldn've give it ter me if ya dinna wan' me ter drink it," Jewel retorted, and was rewarded by an easing of his expression. He didn't smile again, but he no longer looked so cold.

"Touch . If you think you can bear up now, we should be getting on. I dislike spending nights on the road."

"I dislike riding," Jewel muttered, but was not surprised to be escorted back to the now cleaned carriage and lifted aboard. He was a moment or so behind her, and Jewel took perverse pleasure from watching his high-and-mighty lordship wipe his stained boots on what few tufts of grass remained in the mud. Then he jumped up beside her, reclaimed the reins from a pokerfaced Jenkins, and clucked to the horses. The carriage lurched forward again. With a low moan Jewel clutched the side of the curricle and resigned herself to enduring more hours of misery.

By the time dusk fell, Jewel was resigned to death. In fact, she longed for it. She had never been so physically miserable in all her life. She prayed for a crash, for the earl to suffer a heart attack, anything that would cause them to stop. But still the benighted vehicle lurched and jolted and jerked on and on through the freezing wind of an approaching winter's night.

They entered Norfolk, and after a while rattled through the little village of Bishop's Lynn. Jewel felt too ill to do more than notice the spires of the two churches situated on the opposite ends of the town. Then they seemed to be drawing close to the sea because Jewel heard a faint roaring that she had at first thought was in her own head, and then decided was the sound of waves breaking on the shore. The idea would have excited her if she hadn't felt so ill. She had never seen the sea.

"Are we nearly there?" she was finally compelled to ask as her body seemed frozen through, and her stomach threatened to turn itself inside out again, though it was now quite empty.

"Not nearly. We are there," the earl responded briefly, pointing ahead with his whip. And thus, silhouetted against the backdrop of a darkening sky, did Jewel get her first glimpse of the house that she would learn was called White Friars.

VIII

FTER the misery of the journey Jewel was briefly cheered when the enormous pile of gray rock that the earl indicated was their destination appeared against the mountain of charcoal clouds that shrouded the horizon. At last, she thought, a bloody end to this 'ellish rockin', and before it rained again, too. Maybe her luck was changing for the better.

But that was before the curricle bowled down the avenue and Jewel got her first good look at the house. It was composed of three wings in the shape of a rectangle with the bottom bar missing. The driveway closely followed the shape of the house, forming a semicircle so that one could drive up to the front entry and away from the house again without ever turning around. Dozens upon dozens of mullioned windows stared down at the driveway, their arched shape embellished by elaborate carvings of gargoyles that seemed to be laughing gleefully at the folly of those who approached.

The house itself exuded a presence. As ridiculous as the thought was, it seemed to brood; its shadow, barely distinguishable from the deepening gloom of falling night, nevertheless fell over the curricle with a chill dampness that sent a shiver running up Jewel's spine. Curiously, in the whole massive place only three windows were lit. Two, high up in the center wing, seemed to stare down on the approaching curricle like unblinking eyes.

Jewel chided herself for her folly, but all the common sense of which she was capable did not help. The house looked colder and more desolate than the night it would shelter them from.

The massive door swung open before the curricle came to a stop. A swarm of servants carrying lanterns descended the steps. The earl, who had perceptibly tensed as soon as the house was in view, reined in, jumped down from the curricle, and curtly told Jenkins to go to the horses' heads. Then he turned to look up at Jewel, who still sat in the curricle, staring wide-eyed at the house.

"Get down," he said, his voice terse.

"Eh, it be uncommon grand, but it gives me the willies," she breathed before she could stop herself.

He drew in a sharp breath. "It's only a house."

Then she looked at him. The light from the lanterns cast an orange glow over his features, making him look far more devil than angel. His gilt hair seemed to flame. A devil master for a devil house, she thought, and shivered.

"Get down," he said again, and she had the feeling he was forcing the words between his teeth.

For the benefit of the expressionless servants, she thought, he held up a hand to help her alight. With one more look at that bleakly forbidding face, she placed her hand on his, and was struck once again by the warmth of his skin that penetrated even through their gloves. Then she was standing beside him, trying not to look as ill at ease as she felt. The swarming servants didn't help. She felt them looking at her curiously.

"Hello, Johnson. How have things been?" The earl addressed this low toned question to a tall, majestic, completely bald figure in a severe black suit. Jewel had now seen enough of the way a gentleman's establishment was run to guess that he was the butler.

"Not so good, my lord. Miss Chloe—well, not so good." The man's voice was as low as his master's, and he sounded troubled.

The earl looked suddenly more glacially remote than Jewel had thought was humanly possible.

"This is Mr. Timothy's widow," he said brusquely, ignoring the butler's last comment completely. "Miss Julia. She'll be making her home here for a while. She requires a maid, a bath, and some clothes for sleeping and for the morrow. And dinner on a tray in her room."

"Yes, my lord." Johnson seemed not the least offended by the earl's coldness. His spaniel-brown eyes ran over Jewel with interest. She tried not to show how self-conscious she felt under that expert assessment. After all, there was no way he could tell just by looking that the clothes she wore were not her own, or that the meal the earl's household had provided for her the previous night had been the most she had consumed at one time in her entire life. Her true station in life was not stamped on her forehead, was it?

"Bring a bottle of scotch to the library, Johnson," the earl said, turning away.

"And dinner, my lord?" The butler's question was quiet, but the earl rounded on him like a tiger flicked with a lash.

"Just the scotch, Johnson." The icy voice was nowhere near as cold as the glacial glint in his eyes. The butler bowed his acquiescence. Then, without another word to anyone, he turned, striding up the steps and into the house. Jewel stared after him, trying hard not to feel abandoned. From the almost approachable companion he had been during their journey, he had turned in an instant to the cold, remote, heartless noble she had at first thought him. Bloody rude bugger he was, even for an earl, she told herself.

"This way, Miss Julia." Johnson stepped back and gestured toward the house, obviously waiting for her to precede him. Jewel did, gathering up her skirts in hands that felt clumsy and walking slowly up the dozen or so shallow stone steps that time and generations of aristocratic feet had hollowed out slightly in the middle. With a sense of unreality she took in the carvings of gargoyles and angels, lutes and garlands of roses that formed a great arch of stone around the massive oak door. The door itself was decorated with finely wrought iron. Jewel stared at it and beyond into a great stone hall hung with tapestries where a black uniformed maid was lighting dozens of candles. Jewel felt her stomach turn over as she took in the soaring ceiling festooned with swirls and flourishes, the elaborate staircase that wound its way up one side of the hall, the huge unlit chandelier suspended above flower strewn carpets and gilt chairs and ebony tables. The grandeur of the place overwhelmed her with the feeling that she did not belong. The lowliest mongrel dog born and bred on the estate had more right here than she did. Then she stiffened her spine. She did, too, belong. She had a piece of paper in her possession that gave her as much right here as any of them. More, in fact; she was not a servant but a member of the family.

Holding that thought firmly in mind, she made it inside the arched entryway with scarcely any hesitation at all. She then found herself confronted by a small plump woman clad head to toe in black bombazine. Neat wings of white hair were smoothed back on either side of her head beneath a ruffled white cap to form a bun at her nape. She had sharp black eyes that seemed to see right through Jewel. Surrounding her eyes and mouth was a wreath of wrinkles that Jewel guessed came from smiling. As far as appearances were concerned, this was a hale and hearty country woman who looked as if she should be someone's grandmother.

"Good evening, miss." The woman smiled a warm welcome, then looked over Jewel's head at Johnson with concern in her eyes. "His lordship?" Johnson shook his head with a frown, and the smile faded from the woman's face as she returned her attention to Jewel.

"This is Mrs. Johnson, the housekeeper and my missus." Johnson made the introduction. "Miss Julia is Mr. Timothy's widow. My lord has brought her home to live."

"Mr. Timothy's widow!" Without the earl's chastening presence, this particular servant apparently felt free to show her surprise. Her eyes ran over Jewel again, her expression keen. But she kept to herself whatever thoughts may have occurred to her as she took in Jewel's thin form, the too large black dress, the black hair mussed from the journey and once again falling from its upsweep so that wispy tendrils straggled around a too white, too thin face.

"You look fagged to death, Miss! I always had a kindness for Mr. Timothy, a nice lad, that. Pity about him dying so tragic. But enough of that! I'll show you upstairs myself, the green room I think, it has a nice view. Johnson, you tell Emily to organize a bath for Miss Julia. She can maid Miss until her own maid arrives." She peered over Jewel's shoulder. "I'm right in assuming your maid is not with you, Miss Julia? Will she be coming in the coach with his lordship's valet? He always arrives a day or so after his lordship with all his lordship's things."

"I don' 'ave no maid," Jewel said, looking the smaller woman right in the eyes.

"I see," said Mrs. Johnson, taken aback at the unexpected Cockney accent that rolled out of the mouth of her new mistress. Johnson looked shocked as well. But something in Jewel's expression must have warned them that they would be better off making no comment.

"Come then, Miss Julia, and I'll take you up," Mrs. Johnson said briskly. She led the way toward the wide staircase that curved upward at the end of the great hall. As they walked toward it, Jewel saw a delicate iron railing surrounding what appeared to be a balcony halfway up the stone wall.

"The minstrel's gallery," said Mrs. Johnson, noticing her look. "They used to use it whenever there was a ball here. But since Miss Elizabeth's passing . . ." She broke off, shaking her head. "Well, you don't want to hear me rattle on." She continued the climb to the second floor in what Jewel guessed was uncharacteristic silence.

The room Jewel was shown to was lovely. It was huge by her standards with green and white vine-patterned wallpaper and simple white curtains shading the two floor to ceiling windows. A delicate four-poster bed dominated one wall while a matching armoire and dressing table stood against another. A green, white, and pink floral carpet lay on the polished oak floor beside the bed. Another carpet lay in front of the white marble fireplace that was so pristine that it obviously hadn't been used in many a day.

Mrs. Johnson, noting the absence of a fire, called down to a servant below. In just a few minutes a young girl in a black uniform entered carrying an armload of wood. This she piled into the fireplace, and in short order a flame was flicking at the logs. Another black-uniformed young girl appeared before the first one had finished, and Mrs. Johnson introduced her as Emily. She was small with a round rosy face and merry brown eyes. Her hair was scraped back beneath a white mob cap, but from the single curl that peeped out, Jewel saw that it was a warm brown color.

Emily curtsied to Jewel, then stood with her hands clasped before her, staring down at the floor as Mrs. Johnson explained to her that she would be serving as Miss Julia's maid until a real lady's maid could be engaged for her. Then, with a smile at Jewel and a stern look for Emily, who was still staring at the floor, Mrs. Johnson dismissed the girl.

"You may start your duties on the morrow, Emily," the housekeeper said. "I will do for Miss Julia tonight."

"Yes, ma'am," Emily replied in a shy voice, and with another curtsy took herself off. Mrs. Johnson then turned to Jewel.

"She's a good girl, Miss Julia, just a little overwhelmed at this elevation in her station. But if she doesn't please, you have only to tell me and we'll find someone else. Until his lordship engages a proper lady's maid for you, that is." After a sweeping glance around the room, Mrs. Johnson said, "If you would like, Miss Julia, I will have a bath sent up. Oh, and your dinner, of course. Unless you would prefer to eat downstairs in the dining room?"

"N-no. T'anks. Uh, Mrs. Johnson, I think I'll 'ave that bath tomorrer, if yer don' mind. Could I jest 'ave my supper tonight? Up 'ere?"

"Certainly, Miss Julia, whatever you wish. I'll tell Emily that you prefer to bathe in the mornings then, shall I?"

The truth was that Jewel preferred not to bathe at all, at least not in the way the gentry apparently did it, naked and immersed in water up to her neck. She had rather enjoyed her experience with the rose soap the night before, but it was not something she cared to repeat too often. The chances of contracting the ague went up considerably, she thought, the more one took such foolhardy chances. In any case, tonight all she wanted to do was eat and crawl into that supremely comfortable looking bed.

"Shall I help you undress, Miss Julia?" Mrs. Johnson moved toward her as she spoke. Startled, Jewel took a step backward.

"No, no, Mrs. Johnson, I c'n take off me own clothes. T'anks."

"Very well, Miss Julia. I will have Emily bring up appropriate night attire, as you didn't bring your baggage with you." Jewel nodded assent to this. "Will that be all then, Miss Julia?"

Jewel nodded, and Mrs. Johnson turned toward the door. Then with her hand on the knob she stopped and looked over her shoulder.

"Uh, Miss Julia." She hesitated, frowning. "If you should hear . . . sounds in the night, please don't be frightened. Miss Chloe suffers from nightmares, and sometimes she screams. She's in this wing, so if she does you will surely hear her."

Jewel's hand paused in the act of unbuttoning her pelisse. She stared at the housekeeper. "Who be Miss Chloe?"

"Miss Chloe is his lordship's daughter."

" 'Is daughter!" Of course, the earl's mother had said something about a backward child, Jewel recalled. She found the notion that he was married and a father oddly unsettling. She added slowly. "Be 'is wife 'ere, too?"

"Lady Moorland is dead," Mrs. Johnson said, her cheerful face suddenly stern. And then before Jewel could question her further she left the room, closing the door quietly behind her.

I X

IVE days later Jewel was still waiting to be roused from her slumber by the terrified screams of a little girl. But so far it hadn't happened. Instead, she had difficulty sleeping because of the profound quiet; all her life she had been used to the noise and bustle of the city around her as she slept.

From her bedroom window the morning after she had arrived she had seen a little girl surely no more than six years old go for a walk with an older woman whom Jewel assumed was her nursemaid. The child had looked small and fine-boned with the earl's gilded hair streaming down her back from beneath a velvet cap. She was dressed in a stylish claret velvet coat that made her look like a miniature of a fashionable lady.

But what struck Jewel most about the child was how very unchildlike she seemed. She didn't laugh, or run, or shout as a little girl might be expected to do when she reached the freedom of the outdoors. She merely walked along in silence, her hand in her nursemaid's, looking neither to the left nor the right until the pair rounded a privet hedge and disappeared from sight. Jewel stared after them for a moment, then shrugged. The earl's daughter was none of her concern. No more than the earl was.

She had not seen him at all since the day they arrived. When she had asked for him timidly the first morning, she had been told by a pokerfaced Johnson that he was "out." And "out" or "busy" he had remained until finally she stopped asking. Once she had gotten a glimpse of him riding from the stables as if the hounds of hell were on his heels, but other than that she had not set eyes on him, and his apparent lack of interest in her well-being both angered and, oddly, hurt her.

He had left instructions that she was to be provided with a wardrobe, and the first morning a seamstress had arrived at the house. She had proceeded to push and pull Jewel until she was ready to scream.

But the first of her new dresses was to arrive that very day. Jewel, though she hated to admit it, was excited. In her whole life she had never had a dress made especially for her. Jewel was sure the dresses would be beautiful; anything would be an improvement on the scratchy black wool. Although she now wore some of the proper underclothes—she flatly refused to wear stays, they made her feel like she couldn't breathe—the dress still itched. Only now she knew enough to only scratch when she was alone.

Except for the seamstress Jewel had seen no one from outside the house. She passed the time exploring the house and grounds, trying her best to stay out of everyone's way. There was a veritable army of servants: stillroom maids and laundry maids, parlor maids and upstairs maids, footmen and under-footmen, gardeners and under-gardeners, in addition to Chloe's nursemaid, Leister, the earl's valet, and Johnson and Mrs. Johnson. Each one of them curtsied every time they saw her, which made Jewel extremely uncomfortable. She had no idea how to acknowledge such a salutation. Should she curtsy back, or smile, or say thanks, or ignore the whole business? Confused as she was, she took the latter course and then wondered if that was why the servants never spoke to her. Or perhaps they weren't supposed to speak to her?

Being one of the gentry was more complicated than she had ever guessed. Even eating was an ordeal. After one try at eating a meal in the grand dining room, alone at a table vast enough to seat fifty people, she had vowed never to repeat the experience. Two footmen had served her meal while Johnson supervised. There was enough food to feed at least ten people, and the table was awash with glittering crystal, silver, and china, most of which Jewel hadn't the least notion what to do with.

Ever since, she had been eating from a tray in her room. But she was getting tired of having no one to talk to. Certainly being rich was not quite as much fun as she had expected. She was lonely, ill at ease, and felt more and more like a fish out of water. For the first time in her life she was at leisure, and she decided she had never been so well to pass and yet so heartily bored in her life.

So when Emily knocked on the door of her room after luncheon on the fifth day with the announcement that her new clothes had arrived, Jewel welcomed the diversion with open arms. For such a vast order—it was not every day that someone asked Miss Soames to provide them with a complete wardrobe—the seamstress had come again herself instead of having the garments sent as was her custom.

"Here you are, Mrs. Stratham. And I hope you enjoy them," Miss Soames said, as she prepared to leave, having seen the items into Emily's hands. The maid, excited by prospect of her lady's having a real wardrobe at last, was already opening the boxes and laying the contents out on the bed. Out came white linen petticoats, white silk chemises, white lawn nightgowns, white silk and cotton stockings, garters, stays, and then dress after dress in unrelieved black. Emily's face fell and Jewel's eyes widened.

"But miss, they be all black!" Jewel protested faintly to Miss Soames.

The seamstress' eyebrows rose as her eyes ran over Jewel with condescension. "But of course they are, my dear Mrs. Stratham. On his lordship's orders. He led me to understand you recently lost your husband."

"Oh. Oh, ayeh, me 'usband," Jewel mumbled, having almost forgotten that she had been married, let alone widowed. She had seen fat shopkeepers' wives walking about in black dresses after their husbands had died, but they were old women, married a long time. But *she* couldn't dress in black for the rest of her life! And considering the quantity of garments the earl had had made up for her, he was apparently expecting her to do just that.

"Wait right 'ere, would ya? I 'ave to go 'ave a l'il talk wit' somebody." Jewel's eyes gleamed with determination as she marched from the room in search of the earl. Dressing in black for the next half century for a husband she had scarcely known was ridiculous.

"May I help you, Miss Julia?" One of the footmen—or under-footmen, she could never tell—materialized out of the shadows beneath the stairs as she stepped down into the grand hall.

"I be lookin' for 'is lordship," she announced, staring right into his eyes as if daring him to put a rub in her way.

"His lordship is in the library, I believe, Miss Julia."

"And where'd that be?"

"On the first floor of the north wing. But, Miss Julia, he gave specific orders that he is not to be disturbed."

"Well, bully for 'im," Jewel muttered as she marched in the direction of the north wing. Her earlier exploration of the house paid off, as she easily found her way through the labyrinthian corridors to the one door on the first floor that was always closed. Hardly pausing to draw a deep breath, she rapped her knuckles sharply on the polished oak door.

"Who is it?" the earl answered, irritation plain in his voice.

"It be me, Jewel—uh, Julia, yer lordship," Jewel answered. After a slight pause she heard a distinct, "Go away." Her temper heated. Just because he was an all-powerful earl didn't mean he could dismiss her as if she were nothing! The light of battle flared in her eyes as she turned the knob and opened the door.

He was sprawled in a big wing chair before the fire, one booted foot resting on a footstool while the other was planted solidly on the rug. A glass holding an amber liquid was in one hand while a bottle containing more rested on a table at his elbow. A long thin cigar lay in a gold dish on the same table, a white drift of smoke rising lazily from it. On the footstool an open book lay face down. He was in shirt-sleeves, without coat or cravat, and wore buckskin trousers instead of the breeches she had expected. The fire gleamed brightly off the silver-gilt of his hair, but left his face in shadow. Jewel could only see the gleam of his eyes as they ran over her slowly from head to toe.

"Do you know, I had almost forgotten about you? If you were to take yourself off again, I might succeed completely." His voice was slightly slurred, and if not actively hostile was certainly not welcoming. Jewel's chin came up, and she took a couple of steps into the room.

"Do come in," he said ironically.

She ignored that, too, advancing determinedly until she stood beside the stool where that one booted foot still rested. He sat without moving, looking up at her through narrowed eyes that Jewel could see now were more than a little bloodshot.

"You be holed up in 'ere drinkin'!" The discovery that he was at least a trifle bosky surprised her, or she would never have said it out loud.

"What the bloody hell business is it of yours?" he growled. As she watched he deliberately lifted the glass to his lips and drained the contents, then poured himself another.

His tone more than his words angered her.

"It ain't me bizness a-tall, if ya wan' ter get soused," she agreed cordially, and his eyes glinted at her for an instant before shifting to his glass.

"Damned right, it isn't," he muttered, and took another long swallow.

Watching him, Jewel thought that he didn't look much like the complete to a shade lord whose acquaintance she had made in London. This man was just as handsome, but it was a surly, mussed handsomeness instead of the sartorial perfection she had thought characteristic of him. His hair was disordered, his cheeks showed a trace of stubble, and his white shirt was faintly crumpled. All in all, Jewel thought that she could like this man better than the other— if looks were everything. In this state he was not nearly so intimidating; at least, accustomed as she was to loud, abusive, imbibing males, she didn't find him so.

"Did you want something?" He was looking at her again. In the shock of finding him like this, she had nearly forgotten her errand.

"Them new dresses ya got me, they be all black!" she accused, her grievance resurfacing with a vengeance.

"So, what of it?" It was clear from his tone that he had lost what tiny vestige of interest he might once have felt in her reason for barging in on his privacy.

Jewel glared at him. "If ya 'ad asked me afore ya went ter orderin' 'em, I'd 'ave tole ya that I don' like black. I wan' ter tell Miss Soames to make 'em over again, in colors."

He made a negative gesture with his head. "Impossible. In case you have forgotten, you're a widow now. You're in mourning."

"So are ya if Timothy be yer cousin, but I don' see ya goin' aroun' all in black," Jewel flared.

"What I choose to do and what I choose for you to do are two different things," he said, looking up at her with hooded eyes. "The correct period of mourning for a young widow is one year. During that time you will observe all outward conventions of respect for your deceased husband, including dressing exclusively in black. Do I make myself clear?"

Jewel stared at him, her lips tightening. His eyes met hers just as she was about to explode. Their expression checked her outburst as effectively as a splash of cold water. She scowled at him as he continued to regard her with cold blue eyes and faintly lifted brows. Finally, she nodded reluctantly.

"Yes, my lord," he prompted, speaking to his glass.

"Yes, my lord," she repeated, hands clenching as she turned to go. She would like to tell him what he could do with his "my lords," but she didn't quite dare.

"Wait," he said, and she turned back to look at him.

"I had really almost forgotten your existence," he said, sounding as if the words were meant more for himself than her. He looked up at her, his eyes sharpening. "But now that you've reminded me, something really must be done about your atrocious accent. And your manners. I will have Johnson engage a governess for you as soon as possible, certainly no later than the end of the week. Then you may begin to learn to speak and behave like a civilized human being."

Jewel bristled. Maybe she didn't talk as fancy as he did, but at least she didn't insult him with every breath she uttered.

"Ya got ter be the rudest man I've ever met," she said through her teeth, and turned to leave him again. This time he stopped her with a snap of his fingers. Thoroughly affronted—she was not a dog!—Jewel turned to glare at him.

"My lord," he corrected softly. Jewel ground her teeth.

"My lord," she managed, seething, and was turning to go for the third time when the portrait over the mantel caught her eye. It was a beautiful thing done in pastels, showing a slender young woman with soft fair hair seated in a chair, her white skirts billowing around her. Leaning against her knee was a small girl of perhaps three years with long, silver-gilt curls and sky blue eyes. The child was beautiful while the woman was merely pretty. But there was such love in the woman's quiet face as she gazed at the child that Jewel was touched by it.

"My daughter, Chloe, and my wife Elizabeth," the earl said tonelessly, following her gaze. "It was completed about a year before her death."

"I 'ad 'eard yer wife 'ad passed over." After seeing the portrait Jewel felt genuine pity for him. "I'm sorry fer yer loss."

The earl laughed, the sound surprisingly harsh. "The servants have been talking, have they?" He took a long swallow from his glass. "And did they tell you that I killed her?"

Jewel froze, staring at him. Then her eyes lifted to the portrait again. That sweet lady. . . .

He surged abruptly to his feet, hurling the glass from him so that it shattered against the stones of the fireplace. Jewel jumped back, unnerved by the unexpected violence of his action. He glowered at her.

"Get out of here," he growled, and when Jewel could only stand staring at him, his eyes flamed at her like blue fires from the depths of hell.

"Go on, get out of my sight!" He took a step toward her, his fists clenched, his eyes threatening more violence. The spell broken, Jewel turned and fled.

X

HE next morning Jewel could stand it no longer. She had to know the truth behind the earl's words. Had he killed his wife? Perhaps she had died in childbirth, and he felt responsible? It was useless to speculate. Undoubtedly the servants knew; she already was beginning to realize that servants knew everything that went on in a household. Something she couldn't quite put into words niggled over gossiping about the earl with those who were paid to serve him, but she couldn't help it. She had to know.

"Emily," Jewel began tentatively the next morning when the girl entered her bedroom carrying a breakfast tray of steaming chocolate and crusty rolls. (Surprising how easy it had been to get used to such luxuries as three delicious meals a day and more if she wanted them without having to lift a finger.)

"Yes, Miss Julia?" Emily set the tray down on the round table near the window. Jewel, clad in a white silk wrapper, seated herself in a wing chair pulled up to the table and prepared to eat. Emily shook the napkin out into her lap and poured the chocolate while Jewel buttered a warm roll and bit into it with relish.

"I 'eard somethin' the other day that made me wonder," Jewel began mendaciously around a mouthful of roll. Looking up at Emily, who stood motionless as she waited to hear what her mistress would say, she shook her head impatiently. "Oh, sit, won't ya? This is bloomin' ridiculous."

Emily's round spaniel eyes grew even rounder. "Oh, no,

Miss Julia, I couldn't! 'Twouldn't be proper!"

Jewel sighed. Servants had stringent notions of what was proper and what was not. For instance, Emily considered it proper for a lady to bathe every evening before she retired for the night—a full bath, stark naked, immersed in steaming water to her neck. After a week or so of useless protest Jewel was almost resigned to it now. She was even getting used to the girl's silent comings and goings while she dressed or undressed. And she knew that Emily thought it was proper for a lady's maid to actually assist the lady into and out of her clothing. Jewel hadn't yet come to that, but with Emily's silent persistence she guessed it was just a matter of time before she did.

"At least 'ave a bit ter eat," Jewel murmured, defeated, but Emily declined again.

"Thank you kindly, Miss Julia, but if Mrs. Johnson ever found out I was eatin' with the family I could lose my place."

Jewel gave up and got on with the matter at hand. "Do ya know 'ow the earl's wife died?"

Emily's eyes widened again, and she looked nervously to the right and left as though afraid someone might be listening.

"She—she fell." The answer was whispered. Jewel took a healthy bite of a butter-encrusted roll and eyed her maid speculatively as she chewed.

"I know there be more to it than that. I wan' ya ter tell me."

Emily moistened her lips. "She, Lady Moorland, went for a walk one morning. Usually she took Miss Chloe with her, but it was nippy out that day. Nearly two years ago it was, in the early spring, like now. Miss Chloe had a bit of a sniffle so she left her in. Miss Caroline was here—she was Lady Moorland's cousin, you know. It was real funny because Miss Caroline was married into the family first, to his lordship's older brother, and she would have been Lady Moorland if Master Edward had lived, but he died and so Miss Elizabeth became milady. Anyway, Miss Caroline usually walked with milady when Miss Chloe stayed in, but on that particular morning the Dowager Countess, who was visiting to try to wheedle some more money out of his lordship, sent her in to the village on an errand. So milady went out alone for her walk, and she never came back. Not alive, that is."

Emily stopped. "So 'ow'd she die?" Jewel demanded impatiently, a roll suspended in her hand as she forgot to take a bite of it.

"There's an old monastery over by the Wash, a ruin really, and milady used to like to walk there. The day she died, they said she climbed up into the tower where the bell used to be. Somehow she . . . fell." Emily stopped again, looking frightened. The girl's very fear told Jewel that there was more to the story than this.

"Tell me ever'thin', Emily, please. If she died in a fall, why would the—would anyone say 'is lordship killed 'er?"

Emily looked absolutely wretched. "Oh, Miss Julia, I really shouldn't be talkin' about this. We've been told never to talk about it."

"Who told you that?"

"Mrs. Johnson. She said that she wasn't havin' no gossip about the master in this house."

"What gossip, Emily?" demanded Jewel, maddened.

"Some said—some said his lordship threw milady off that tower."

Jewel stared at Emily for a long moment. "Why would anyone say that? Was 'e with 'er when she fell?"

Emily shook her head. "No, miss. At least he wasn't with her when milady left the house. But when they were courtin' they used to meet in that old ruin, milady bein' from the neighborhood. And his lordship . . . well, he and milady had their problems."

"That don't mean 'e killed 'er." Jewel was strangely indignant to think that the earl's obvious pain was based on so flimsy a premise.

"No." Emily was beginning to warm to her subject. "But there were other things. The doctor said milady hadn't landed as she would have if she'd just fallen. She was too far out, like she'd been pushed. And she was on her back, not her stomach. And one of the tenant's boys said that he'd seen somebody—he thought it was his lordship because he'd seen that blond hair real plain—go into the monastery with milady that day. And everyone knew that his lordship and milady had problems. They had a way of lookin' at each other that'd give you the shivers. Like they hated each other. I once heard milady say to him that he weren't no kind of a father, and his lordship said back that that made them a good pair because she weren't no kind of a wife. They didn't talk to each other for weeks and weeks, and his lordship went up to London. He came back just a week or so before milady died, and they must have had a real bad row because milady wouldn't even stay in the same room with his lordship. Don't none of us know what all the trouble was about, and I don't guess anyone but his lordship ever will. And I wish anyone good luck gettin' anything out of *him*."

Emily shook her head for emphasis. Jewel stared at her, forgetting even to eat in her fascination with what she had heard. Had the earl killed his wife? Of course not! Like a lot of other people apparently had, she was letting her imagination take threads of gossip and rumors and weave them into whole cloth. The evidence she had heard against the earl was flimsy in the extreme.

"Was 'is lordship charged with murder?" Jewel's mind boggled at the image of the aristocratic earl brought up before Old Bailey. Emily shook her head.

"There wasn't enough evidence to bring a formal charge, they said. First, the boy who claimed he saw his lordship go into the church with milady was only eight years old. The magistrate at the inquest said that no jury would convict a man based on the testimony of a boy that age. And he said, just because a man and his wife had problems doesn't make the man guilty of murder. And then there was the friar." Emily paused importantly.

"What friar?" Jewel demanded as Emily had clearly intended she should.

"That's just it. There wasn't no friar. No real friar, that is. People say he's the ghost of Friar Benedict, one of the white friars who lived in the old monastery more than three hundred years ago. He's supposed to have been mortal enemies with the first earl, who was awarded all the land that used to belong to the monastery by Queen Elizabeth. Friar Benedict refused to leave the monastery when the first earl ordered them all out, and the earl ended up having him hung. And this house was built on the very spot where it happened. From that time on, the white friar has appeared to the people hereabouts whenever one of the Peyton family is about to die. They say that he comes to take his enemies with him into death. It's been going on for almost three hundred years now without fail. Some people saw the white friar out at the old monastery before Master Edward was killed in that hunting accident, and some saw him before the old lord died. And some, including Martin, the first footman, saw him before milady died. Right here in this house, Miss Julia." Emily paused, wide-eyed, obviously pleasurably frightened by her own story.

"So what do the so-called white friar 'ave to do with 'is lordship not killin' 'is wife?"

Emily, who had leaned closer and rested her hands on the small table during her telling of the legend, straightened. "The magistrate, he said he didn't believe in no ghost friar. He said if so many people saw him, then it was because somebody was dressing up like him. And until somebody could prove who was dressing up in a white robe and flitting around the old ruins and this house—his lordship could account for his whereabouts almost every time the friar appeared, though he said he was out riding alone when milady died—then he was danged if he was going to charge anybody with murder. So he said milady's death was a misadventure. It made milady's dad real mad, and he would never speak to his lordship after that. A lot of people think he's the one who started saying that his lordship murdered milady. But old Mr. Tynesdale died last year, and a lot of the talk died with him. Though everybody remembers, of course."

Jewel bit into the long spared roll, a frown fixed between

her brows as she absorbed all she had been told. The part about the ghost of the white friar gave her the willies, but she could not by any stretch of the imagination picture the earl dressed up in a white monk's robe and running around the neighborhood in it. It was such a ridiculous notion that she immediately felt better. Of course he had not done such a thing, nor had he thrown his wife off a tower. It was too silly to even contemplate.

"Shall I help you dress, Miss Julia?"

While Jewel had been thinking, Emily had put out her clothes for the day. The question was asked in a hopeful tone, but Jewel had no hesitation about shaking her head.

"I c'n manage, t'anks." Then as Emily, looking disappointed, started to leave the room, Jewel called her back.

"Which way is that monastery, Emily?"

"You don't want to go there, Miss Julia! It's . . ."

"I jest wan' ter look at it. Admire the ruin, so to speak."

Emily looked skeptical, but she gave Jewel directions. Jewel dismissed her with another word of thanks, and got dressed. In less than half an hour she was walking over the heath toward the Wash.

The heath was still damp with dew, releasing a sweet, spicy fragrance every time her skirt brushed against a sturdy green bush. Thick clumps of rhododendron in colors ranging from deepest crimson to pink to white grew wild alongside the path that had been worn smooth by generations of wandering feet. Pine plantations rose against the horizon to the west, while to the east the ground dropped away to form the rocky cliffs that looked out over the Wash.

Jewel walked along the path at the cliffs' edge, marveling at the fresh salt scent of the sea and the spectacular beauty of the waves breaking over the jagged rocks below. Gulls and terns wheeled in the bright blue sky overhead, adding their shrill cries to the roar of the sea. To a girl who had never before been outside of London, the magnificence of so much open space and natural beauty was dazzling.

After perhaps twenty minutes of brisk walking, Jewel saw the old monastery. The two-story stone structure was blackened with age and covered with vines and moss. Obviously the Wash had moved inland considerably since it had been built because the monastery was perched right on the edge of the cliffs, its far wall long since tumbled down into the sea. Only the three-story bell tower remained intact on that far side, owing its survival no doubt to the fact that it rested on a small jut of rock.

Jewel felt a cold little finger trace its way down her spine as she reflected that the arched opening that must once have housed a large bell was the one from which Elizabeth fell to her death. Jewel shivered as she walked around the side of the ruin, stepping over the jagged piles of stones that had fallen from the relatively intact inland wall. There was an aura of cold about the place that had nothing to do with the temperature.

Behind the monastery, close again to the encroaching cliffs, was a tiny cemetery. There were only a few stones left to mark the graves, but Jewel guessed that many more must have been lost to time. The shadow of the bell tower slanted across the graves, and Jewel shivered again. The place both repelled and fascinated her.

Jewel had meant only to look at the ruin, but when she saw a small arched opening in the wall, she could not resist the impulse to go inside. Clambering over a pile of moss covered stones, she stood in the doorway looking around. Clearly this room had once been a chapel. The remains of arched windows opened both inland and toward the sea, and in the top of one remained a few shards of ruby glass. The sun slanting down through the glass cast a bright red beam toward an arched recess cut in the rough stone of an interior wall. From its location behind where the altar must once have been, she guessed it had once held a statue, probably of Jesus or Mother Mary.

The thought of centuries-dead monks kneeling in prayer in this chapel was faintly eerie, but worse was the realization that Elizabeth must have passed through this very room many times during her short life as a girl to explore, as a young lady to meet Sebastian, and as a woman to meet her death. It was a chilling thought, and Jewel was about to withdraw to the beckoning warmth of the sun when she heard the sound of someone crying. She stiffened, listening intently. The sound was muffled, barely audible, but it was unmistakable nevertheless: someone—or something—was sobbing its heart out.

Jewel felt the hairs rise on the back of her neck. The sound came from somewhere above, and for an awful moment she had a vision of Elizabeth's shade weeping in the bell tower from whence she had fallen to her death. But she dismissed the thought as ridiculous, of course, there was definitely someone up there, and whoever was up there was crying.

Drawn irresistably forward, Jewel walked through a little door beside the arched recess and found herself inside the tower itself. Steps carved into the stone wound upwards. Jewel hesitated, her every instinct urging her to run outside into the sunlight, but the sound of the crying pulled her. It came unmistakably from the embrasure where the bell had once been, and it was as heartrending as before. Whoever was up there was hurt to the depths of her soul.

Jewel couldn't help it. She had to know if it was Elizabeth's ghost she heard, or a live, distressed lady. Because the sounds were unmistakably female. As she wound her way up, careful not to slip on the worn, moss covered steps, she felt her nerves creep into a hard knot in her belly.

A warm golden glow seemed to emanate from the bell room above. Jewel stared up wide-eyed at the bright light that spilled through what had once been a trap-door and was now merely a hole in the stone floor, wondering with a kind of fascinated horror if this was some kind of ghostly manifestation. Even as her heart began to climb into her throat, she realized that the glow was caused by sunlight streaming through the open embrasures through which the bell had once swung.

The crying was louder, more distinct. Jewel once again got the impression of heartrending grief. Then she cautiously thrust her head through the opening to see the sunlight glinting brightly off a small gilded head.

Chloe. It was Chloe who was huddled on the floor, curled into a fetal position with her head buried against her knees. The claret velvet cloak was wrapped around her like a blanket, and her small body shook with the force of her sobs.

Jewel felt her heart clench. The sight of the little girl crying in this place where her mother had died wrenched her soul. Quietly she pulled herself through the opening, then moved to crouch beside the sobbing child.

"Chloe," she said softly, her hand moving to touch the little girl's bright hair.

The child's head whipped up, her eyes huge and teary, dazzled by the sun for a moment as she blinked at Jewel. There was an expression of such wild joy on her small face that Jewel immediately realized that for a brief moment Chloe thought that it was her mother kneeling down beside her. Then the child's eyes narrowed against the sun, and her mouth contorted. She leapt to her feet, letting out an infuriated cry. When Jewel tried to catch her, to hold her and comfort her, she shoved her with such force that Jewel sat down hard on her behind.

"Chloe, wait!"

But it was too late. Before Jewel could even get to her feet, the little girl had vanished through the trap-door. Jewel could hear the quick patter of her slippered feet on the stairs as she ran away.

X I

As the earl had threatened, a governess was engaged within the week. Mrs. Thomas was a middle-aged widow with a straight back and a long nose, and in no time at all she was looking down it at Jewel.

She had just been dismissed as governess to the daughters of a prosperous landowner in the neighboring county, not because of any fault of hers, Johnson said, but because the girls were now old enough to make a governess unnecessary. According to the registry office that had recommended her, Mrs. Thomas was all that could be desired: she was an impoverished gentlewoman, daughter of a country parson, with a wealth of experience in schooling young ladies. In addition, she had a reputation for not putting up with any nonsense from her charges. She seemed, Johnson told the earl, like the ideal person to have charge of Jewel's education.

All of this Jewel had from Johnson. Although she had seen the earl on horseback twice from her window, she had not spoken to him since that disastrous conversation in the library. Like Chloe he seemed more a ghost than a tangible presence in the house.

Mrs. Thomas was given a room near the rear of the north wing, adjoining what used to be the schoolroom. Evidently Chloe was judged not yet ready for an education because it was obvious that the room had not been used in at least twenty years. But after Mrs. Johnson had set the maids to washing the walls and the floor and polishing the furniture, Mrs. Thomas allowed with a sniff that it would "do." And thus did Jewel begin the unexpectedly arduous process of becoming a lady.

"Really, Miss Julia, ladies do not hunch over when they walk. Neither do they stride about like a man! Keep your back straight, and take small, gliding steps. Gliding, gliding! No, not like that! Like this!"

Over the next two weeks Mrs. Thomas ordered boards strapped to Jewel's back during the hours she was in the schoolroom to teach her to sit, stand, and walk with a graceful posture. Whenever Jewel moved about the room, she was first supposed to place a book on her head. If the book fell off, she had to put it in place again and again until she could walk the entire circumference of the room without dislodging it. There were lessons in elocution that involved saying "h" into candles; there were lessons in manners and movements and dress. These lessons were repeated over and over and over until Jewel felt like screaming, or murdering Mrs. Thomas, or committing suicide by jumping out the schoolroom window herself.

Finally, after a particularly arduous session, Jewel rebelled. Mrs. Thomas had ordered her to bed without any dinner as if she were a naughty child simply because Jewel's table manners failed to please. Red-faced with fury at having her dinner literally snatched from beneath her nose, Jewel's eyes flamed as she slowly rose from the table, fists clenched at her sides. This was the final straw! The old Gorgon had pushed her too far, and Jewel meant to respond with a roundhouse right that would knock that priggish lady flat on her back.

Mrs. Thomas must have read Jewel's violent intentions in her eyes because her own steely gray ones widened to the circumference of saucers. She held up a hand as if to ward Jewel off while backing from the schoolroom with more speed than dignity. Once safely in the hallway her hand dropped, and she glared at Jewel with outrage.

"His lordship will hear of this!" she threatened before turning on her heel with such dispatch that her skirts swirled about her skinny shanks as she marched down the hall.

Seething, Jewel hurled a pithy epithet in the woman's wake. But then she was left to face the probable consequences of her action. The old biddy would undoubtedly run straight to the great "my lord" with her tale. Jewel remembered how the earl looked when he was angry, the icy stare that seemed to freeze its victim to the spot, the soft, silky voice that was more rending than razor-sharp steel. She also remembered his violence in the library, the furious flaming of his eyes as he hurled his glass at the fire and growled at her to get out. The memory made her shiver.

"Ter bloody 'ell with 'im. Ter bloody 'ell with 'em all!" Jewel said aloud, her chin lifting. She immediately felt better. There she was, the old Jewel with her fighting spirit that this fancy house with its fancy ways had nearly managed to suppress. She didn't have to take the kind of abuse she'd been getting from anyone, not even on the orders of a bleedin' earl. Who was he anyway to be so special? Nobody, that's who. Just because he had been born into a family that had been around for a few centuries didn't make him any better than she was. Take away his la-de-da family and his lah-de-da money and his lah-de-da ways and put him out on the street where she'd been raised, and he'd be as helpless as a newborn infant.

The picture of the haughty earl at the mercy of the denizens of the streets made her feel slightly better. She didn't like feeling afraid of anyone, and as much as she hated to admit it the great "my-lord" scared her more than a little. The realization fired her anger to new heights. Jewel Combs had never been afraid of anything in her life! She had never had to be because she could take care of herself. But this new person that she was becoming, this Julia Stratham, was afraid all the time. She feared the contempt of the servants, from the lowliest groom to the lordly Johnson; she feared Mrs. Thomas because of her position as stand-in for the earl; she even feared the simplest acts of her new life like eating and walking and talking. She feared that whatever she did she would make a fool of herself, and that everyone would laugh. The idea, which she had never consciously admitted before, made her so furious that she wanted to spit. She did, a full round blob of spittle that landed plop on the highly polished floor, then felt slightly ashamed of herself as she stared at it. But only slightly. The rest of her felt pleased to be back in her old skin.

"I don't belong 'ere!"

The thought sprang full grown to her mind. Even as Jewel turned it over she realized how suffocated she had felt, starting from almost the very first night when the earl had bedazzled her into that tub of steaming water. Everything she had done since had been at his behest and not her own, she realized, and she had not enjoyed a bit of it. Except for the food, she amended hastily. But even the fact of having ample food for the first time in her life wasn't worth turning herself into another creature entirely.

She could leave. There were no shackles on her wrists, no manacles linking her legs. She could walk out of here just as free as the air and not look back. She could be the Jewel she had always been, and to hell with this foolishness about becoming a lady. All she had ever intended was to get Timothy's leavings, which were hers by right, but the earl had both blackmailed and bedazzled her until she had felt herself helplessly caught in the web of his power.

But she was not helpless, and she was not caught. She could leave—if she was willing to face the threat of Mick, the uncertainty of being out on the streets again, the prospect of hunger and homelessness and having to live by her trade which could end with her swinging on the gibbet if she were caught. Was she willing to give up the security that had sounded so attractive to her when the earl had first made her his proposition? Or was she going to let herself be bought by three square meals a day and a roof over her head? Jewel's back stiffened, and she walked determinedly out the door of the schoolroom. She had been meek Julia Stratham long enough. Jewel Combs was back, and about time, too!

If she took a small portion of what was hers by right and by law, she would never have to fear anything again. Jewel's eyes narrowed as she considered the thought. The earl would never miss a few gewgaws, and for her they would mean the difference between living in some comfort and going back empty-handed to the streets. It wasn't even stealing, Jewel told herself—not that she had anything against stealing, of course. The earl was holding Timothy's property, which was rightfully hers as his widow.

Once in her room Jewel started pulling on as many of her dresses as she could force one over the other. They were ugly crow's dresses, true, but they were made of the finest materials and would last her a good long while. By the time she had struggled into number five, having had to leave the last two unbuttoned, she was about as graceful in her movements as an overstuffed sausage. Before she became Julia Stratham she had had fewer dresses during her entire lifetime, so she gave up trying to squeeze into any more. But she decided to take the wool cloak, too. It was nice and warm and she would have to walk until she could get a ride.

Should she walk along the roads? she wondered as she hurriedly ripped the coverlet from her bed and stripped the elegantly embroidered case from her pillow to carry the rest of her booty. Or should she skulk through the fields for fear that the great my-lord would come after her? She doubted that he would go to so much trouble on her behalf, but just to make certain she decided to stick to the fields for a while. When he learned of the mementos she was taking, he was going to be furious. Even if he didn't come after her himself he could have her arrested for theft. Would he do such a thing, knowing that the sentence could be anything from transportation to death? Jewel pictured that cold handsome face with the icy blue eyes, and shivered. Yes, she thought, he very likely would.

It occurred to her then that she could not just walk out the front door in high dudgeon, lugging a pillowcase of valuables with her. Her anger had blinded her to the fact that such a course of action could only lead to the servants restraining her, and then bringing her before the earl. The thought made her shiver.

Her best choice, she decided, was to wait until the household was abed before making her escape. As the dinner hour was already past, she wouldn't have too long to wait. Yes, waiting was the wisest course, even if it meant she might have to endure an unpleasant interview with his lordship in the meantime if Mrs. Thomas' complaint moved him enough. But as she thought about it Jewel decided that the earl was unlikely to disturb himself at this time of an evening because of her. She would probably be ordered to present herself to him in the morning.

In the meantime, she crossed to the door, threw the bolt, then hastily divested herself of the extra clothes. Every instinct she possessed warned her that no one, positively no one, must know what she intended to do. She must behave as though this was just another evening. Emily would be coming soon to turn down the bed, and see if she could help her mistress into her nightclothes, which she still persisted in trying to do. Much as she hated to do it, Jewel neatly hung the dresses back in the wardrobe. She stuffed the pillow back inside its case and smoothed the coverlet over all, and sat down in one of the chairs near the window to wait.

By the time the clock had struck one in the morning Jewel was ready. Hours before she had dismissed Emily, and then sat and listened as the house had gradually grown silent. For the past two hours she hadn't heard a sound to indicate that anyone was still up and about. Of course, the earl slept in another wing, so she had no way of telling if he had gone to bed. But, believing that at such a late hour he surely must have, she struggled back into the five dresses and grabbed the pillowcase. Cautiously edging open her door and peeking around it, Jewel was relieved to see that the hallway was deserted. She stepped out, easing the door shut behind her. Moving with as much silent stealth as she could manage with five sets of skirts hampering her, she gave a little prayer of thanks that hers was the closest bedroom to the stairs. She crept down them into the great hall, which was dark with shadows. As she had thought, the house was deserted and still as death.

She went first to the kitchen, where she turned an entire silver service with all its fancy little forks and knives and spoons into her pillowcase. The silver rattled noisily, and she shook her head at herself. She was already losing her touch. Not too long ago, she could have lifted the whole lot in the presence of a roomful of people with none of them hearing a thing.

Spurred now by a rising sense of excitement (it was good

to be herself again, going about the business she knew best!), Jewel went back down the passageway to the dining room. There she added a fine set of silver napkin holders, a gold tray, and a lovely pair of miniatures in ornate gold frames to her collection. She eyed a silver soup tureen with some regret, knowing it was too large for her rapidly filling pillowcase. Making a hurried tour of the other downstairs rooms, she appropriated an intricately wrought gold filigree music box, a collection of antique snuffboxes, a silver duck decanter, and a pleasantly heavy gold cigar case among other smaller objects. By that time her pillowcase had grown so heavy that it was all she could do to carry it two-handed, so she decided that she had enough. Wrestling her burden until it lay over one shoulder like St. Nicholas' pack, she held onto it with both hands as she headed toward the front door.

Grabbing the knob, she found it was locked. Cursing under her breath, she let the bundle slide to the floor so that her hands were free to work the bolt. It was heavy, and she had to struggle to pull it up. When finally it gave, it was with a protesting groan that made her wince. In the hushed silence of the house it sounded as loud as a shriek.

But apparently no one heard. Jewel hastily jockeyed her loot into position again over her shoulder, and nudged the door open with her foot. The cool air felt good, as over-heated as she was from her exertions and over-dressed state. As she passed through the door, she noticed a ray of moonlight that fell on a pair of crossed swords adorning the wall to the right. They were beautiful things of finely wrought gold and silver. Jewel couldn't resist.

She lowered her bundle with a swift look around to make

sure that she was still alone, then ran to get a chair so that she could reach the swords. She was panting with exertion as she stood on the woven rush seat reaching for her prize. Only by standing on tiptoe and stretching could she just manage to close her hand around one solid gold hilt. The cool, smooth feel of the precious metal brought a delighted smile to her face as she lifted it away from its moorings.

"Reluctant as I am to spoil your fun, I am afraid that I must draw the line at those swords. They have been in my family for generations."

The soft, slightly drawled voice with its edge of ice hit Jewel with all the force of a lightning bolt. She whirled, dropping the sword as if it had suddenly turned red-hot, and barely saved herself from falling off the chair by clutching its back as it teetered.

"Blimey!" she gasped above the echoing clatter of metal bouncing on the stone floor. She was too horrified to do anything but gape at him. Her worst fear had become reality; she was face to face with the earl himself.

Despite the lateness of the hour he had obviously not yet been to bed. The smell of brandy reached her nostrils, and she knew the reason, she decided with an inward sniff. He was still wearing the white shirt and tan breeches that he had worn all day, if the creases that marred them both were anything to go by. A faint shadow darkened his jaw, and his eyes gleamed brightly blue in the flickering light of the candle he carried. He was, as he had been every time she had ever seen him, maddeningly handsome. Still she stared at him with as much horror as if he had been the most grotesque monster on the face of the earth.

At her expression of utter terror, he smiled. It was not a

pretty smile. Then he walked forward until he stood directly in front of where she perched on top of the chair, and held up a hand to her.

"Get down."

Clinging to the chairback, Jewel stared down at that hand as if it were a poisonous reptile. The earth would end before she would put hers into it—how had he known what she was about? Was he in league with the devil? He looked like the devil with those icy eyes boring through her skin.

"I said get down." This time the tone of his voice made her shiver. She put her small, suddenly cold hand in his much larger, warmer one, and allowed him to assist her to alight. But then she was standing much too close to him. She backed a pace, then another, and felt marginally safer.

"Once a thief, always a thief, I see." His voice was conversational as his eyes moved from the sword that had fallen partly under the chair to the bulging pillowcase that lay full in the path of bright moonlight streaming in through the half-open door. Jewel hung her head guiltily, then snapped it up again. She was not going to let him intimidate her again! She was not!

"I'm takin' only wot belongs ter me. An' jes' a little o' it, too."

The earl looked at her. The expression on his face was hard to read in the shifting shadows, but there was no mistaking the predatory gleam in the blue eyes.

"Suppose you explain that extraordinary remark."

The silky voice made her shiver, but Jewel was determined to stand up to him this time. She was herself again, and Jewel Combs didn't take no guff from nobody!

"Ya owe me wotever it be that Timothy left. This," she

indicated the pillowcase and the sword with a sweeping gesture, "ain't nothin' compared to that. So don't ya be accusin' me o' stealin', yer lordship. I ain't namin' no names, but we both know who's really done that!"

Those blue eyes narrowed until they were mere slits glittering in the darkness. Watching them with the fascination of a bird for a snake, Jewel swallowed.

"I would be very careful of what accusations I throw about if I were you. You could find yourself in some deep trouble. Even deeper than you are already."

"I ain't in no trouble!"

"Aren't you?" There was that frightening smile again. He moved so suddenly that Jewel jumped, stepping away from her and picking up the pillowcase in one hand as though it weighed nothing at all as he closed the door with the other. Jewel listened with a sinking feeling as he shot the bolt home again. She was trapped.

"Suppose I were to send for the local constable? With this preponderance of evidence," he shook the pillowcase so that the contents rattled noisily, "I have little doubt that you would be taken up as a thief."

"Ya wouldn't!"

"Why not? We had a bargain, remember. I gave you a chance to back out of it in London, which you refused to take. I told you then that you wouldn't get another."

"I don't want nothin' ter do with yer bargain. Seems ter me that ya left a few things out when ya tole me about it. Like torture."

"Torture!" he sounded surprised. As he looked at her sulky face glaring up at him through the darkness, Jewel could almost swear she saw the glimmer of a smile.

"Explain yourself, if you please."

"That ole witch makes me talk at candles 'till I nearly singe my eyelashes off, and bend my knees until they ache, and straps a bleedin' board to my back, and now she won't even let me eat! If that ain't torture, I don' know what yer call it."

He was silent for a moment after this diatribe, looking at her indignant face. He set the pillowcase down on the floor at his feet, and his arms crossed over his chest. Still he looked at her.

"Ah, yes, I remember now. The estimable woman engaged to educate you. What did you say her name was? Mrs. Thomas? She did express a desire to have speech with me this evening. I was unfortunately unable to accommodate her. Now I begin to wonder what I missed."

So he hadn't talked to Mrs. Thomas? That gave her the chance to get her grievances in first.

"She stole my dinner right from under my nose, and—"

He raised a hand. "Wait a minute. Mrs. Thomas stole your dinner? Why should she do that? Are we not feeding her? I shall have to speak to Mrs. Johnson."

Jewel looked at him with a great deal of resentment. Him and his jokes! "She said I eat like a pig. And I do not! I—"

Again that upraised hand silenced her. "So your governess was attempting to teach you table manners, is that it?"

"She 'ad no right to take my dinner! I was 'ungry!"

"And were no doubt eating like a pig." The earl's voice was dry. Jewel was about to protest vehemently, but he silenced her with a shake of his head.

"So Mrs. Thomas took your dinner. And I assume you

protested. It is to be hoped that you did not physically assault the poor lady?" At his questioning tone Jewel felt slightly guilty.

"Not . . . exactly."

"And what does that mean?"

"I just kind o' looked at 'er, and she backed out o' the room and took off down the 'all like a mouse wot's seen a cat." Jewel chuckled, remembering. "Eh, it were a sight to see."

"So you frightened her."

"She 'ad it comin'."

The earl looked suddenly stern. "And so will you have it coming if I hear of such an incident again. Is that understood? I am prepared to overlook this little comedy tonight, but there is to be no repetition of it or the next time I will not be so forgiving. If you feel your governess is too harsh, you have only to apply to me. But you really must not terrify the poor woman."

"I 'ate 'er!"

"I don't imagine she's overfond of you either, you impossible brat. But she's been hired to turn you into a lady, and you're to let her do it. Is that clear?"

"No." The sulky word was muttered under her breath. Jewel was not quite foolish enough to defy him loudly. But he heard anyway.

"What was that?"

A sense of desperation mingled with outrage in Jewel's breast. He was taking her over again, turning her into that namby-pamby female who was afraid of her own shadow. If she knuckled under to him, she soon wouldn't be Jewel any longer. She would be right back in that schoolroom, no better off than she had been before.

"Yer takin' away who I am!" she burst out.

"I beg your pardon?"

"Jewel Combs. I ain't 'er no more."

The earl's eyebrows lifted. "Do you want to be?" he asked. While she gaped at him he took her elbow and turned her in the direction of the stairs. "Jewel Combs was a little street rat with no future but poverty and want. Julia Stratham has a home and a family, and will never be without creature comforts for as long as she lives. I know who I'd rather be." Jewel looked at him over her shoulder for a moment, much struck by what he had said. Julia Stratham had a family? Who—him? Was he actually meaning to classify himself as her family?

"Now go to bed, and let's have an end to this nonsense," he ordered, giving her a little push with his hand in the small of her back.

Jewel obediently moved in the direction of the stairs. Climbing them, feeling his eyes on her back, she knew her decision had already been made. As soon as the earl had appeared in the hall, it had been made. She would not try to run away again. She was thoroughly caught once more.

From then on she and Mrs. Thomas existed in a state of uneasy truce. Jewel never again gave her trouble, and genuinely tried to absorb the lessons the older woman had to teach. And Mrs. Thomas taught well. Jewel learned after much repetition which piece of silverware went with which course at dinner, and became reasonably adept at handling various eating implements. She learned to accept a cup of tea and sip it without slurping or spilling. She learned to serve tea to others while just taking quick peeks to see what her hands were doing. She painfully memorized Mrs. Thomas' hard and fast rules about who curtsied to whom and when (she had blundered into the correct behavior by not acknowledging a servant's curtsy in any way.) And, of course, she learned the correct attire for a lady in the morning, afternoon, and evening.

All these lessons were hard, but the worst was learning to talk. According to Mrs. Thomas, the mangled syllables that emerged from Jewel's mouth could hardly be termed speech. But for the life of her, Jewel could not seem to twist her tongue enough to produce the accents of a lady. Mrs. Thomas had her practicing more "h"s in front of candles, the flames of which would waver if she said the letter correctly. At first, Mrs. Thomas had ordered her to read aloud, on the theory that Jewel was bound to absorb some of the printed words' elegance of expression. Only after much shamed roundaboutation on Jewel's part did she admit she could not read. So then with all the grim determination Wellington must have employed at Waterloo, Mrs. Thomas set herself to teaching her the tricks of written language. Jewel was forced to spend hours every morning, board strapped to her back and book resting on her head as she laboriously sounded the words of one of Mrs. Radcliffe's lurid novels into a candle resting on the mantel.

The daily arrival of luncheon brought a much welcomed respite, but in the afternoon the hated board was strapped on again as she practiced social graces such as curtsying. One must dip so far for a duchess, so far for a lady, and to the floor with head bowed for the Queen. (Fat chance of ever meeting her, Jewel sneered as she did this over and over.) There were occasions when one extended a hand for a gentleman to bow over, or more rarely kiss. Sometimes a polite inclination of the head was all that was required.

Jewel had to learn the rudiments of making polite conversation. Suitable topics seemed to be limited to the weather and various other inanities like "How *kind* you are, my lord," in response to a compliment, and "These cakes are just *delicious,*" in praise of a refreshment.

There were so many rules, Jewel was surprised that anyone ever remembered them all. Her respect for the gentry, particularly poor put upon females, increased a hundredfold. What they had to know just to talk to one another! The tortures they had to endure just to walk across a room and sit down! If she had known before what she knew now, she might have told his high and mighty lordship to take his silky tongue and choke on it when they had entered into their devil's bargain all those days ago.

One afternoon three weeks after her return to the fold, Jewel was sulkily engaged in practicing her curtsys, board strapped to her back, book balanced precariously on her head. It was a gorgeous spring day outside with the sun shining and the sky a bright beckoning blue. Jewel would have given much to be outdoors. But Mrs. Thomas felt that too much fresh air was harmful to young ladies' complexions, so Jewel had escaped the house only a handful of times since that lady's advent. Staring longingly at the slice of blue sky she could see through the window, she followed Mrs. Thomas' direction and sank into a medium-low curtsy suitable for greeting an elderly, socially important dowager. Hated black skirts held at the correct angle by stiff wristed hands, head rigid so as not to dislodge the despised book, Jewel sank carefully into what she privately called the pigeon squat.

The sound of a single pair of hands applauding from somewhere behind her caused her head to jerk around. Her feet got tangled up in her skirt, the board prevented her from regaining her balance, the book slid from her head with a resounding crash, and she ended up sitting down smack on her bottom on the hard plank floor.

"Bloody 'ell," she muttered, rubbing the injured part of her anatomy before she remembered that a lady was not even supposed to be aware that she possessed an arse, much less touch it. Struggling into a sitting position as Mrs. Thomas exclaimed, "Really, Miss Julia!" Jewel ignored the flustered governess in favor of glaring at the earl, who had caused the whole thing by clapping.

He was standing in the doorway, one broad shoulder resting against the door jamb, his arms crossed over his chest, his eyebrows raised in that superior look she hated as he took in her undignified sprawl. With the sunlight streaming through the window to touch his gilded hair and his eyes glinting as blue as the sky outside, he was as breathtakingly handsome as ever.

Jewel acknowledged the fact reluctantly. It annoyed her to admit that just the sight of him made her heart beat faster. What caused an even stranger, painful emotion was the very fact of how clear it was that she had no similar effect on him. He was looking at her in much the same way an organ grinder's audience watches the performing monkey. Her glare turned into a glower as she took in that look. To her fury, her new expression seemed to amuse him more than ever. He was laughing at her, the superior swine! For something that was all his fault! An earl should know that it was civil to at least tap on the door before scaring a body half out of her wits. Jewel scowled fiercely at him as she internally expanded on this grievance. After all her weeks of practice and the marked improvements that even Mrs. Thomas grudgingly admitted, it was just like him to come upon her and put her immediately at a disadvantage. Well, he'd soon see that she was no longer someone to be made mock of!

"Good afternoon, my lord," she said in a nearly flawless upper class accent. She wiped the scowl from her face and raised her eyebrows haughtily, in imitation of his own expression.

"Good afternoon, Julia," he replied gravely, as though he had fully expected her to greet him in such a way.

Nettled at his lack of astonishment over her progress, Jewel resolved to impress him further. Looking toward the window, she saw the dazzling sunshine outside and remembered that the weather was always a proper topic of conversation.

"Lovely weather we're having, isn't it?" She wasn't positive, but she thought she saw his lips twitch. Her scowl came rushing back.

"It certainly is." His reply was perfectly serious and polite.

Jewel relaxed a little. Perhaps he was not laughing at her. After all, she was talking just as she had been taught. It must be only her imagination that made her think that she was amusing him.

"Oh, my lord, have you come to check on our progress?" Mrs. Thomas dropped a hasty curtsy, which she must have forgotten in the stress of Jewel's embarrassing downfall.

"We've made a great deal of headway, as you can, ummm, see." Then, in an aside to Jewel, she added in a sugary voice, "Why don't you get up off the floor, dear, and curtsy properly to his lordship?"

Jewel, who had almost forgotten that she was sitting in an undignified sprawl on the floor, flushed. But she found the matter of getting up quite difficult. The board on her back made it impossible for her to lean forward, and therefore to rise. Struggling vainly to find enough leverage to get her feet beneath her, Jewel could not. She flopped about like a fish out of water, her eyes flying to the earl, whom she was *sure* was laughing at her.

Indeed, one corner of his mouth had twisted up in the beginning of a grin, and those celestial eyes twinkled. Humiliated, Jewel felt her temper begin to heat as she had to turn over onto her stomach before clambering awkwardly to her feet.

"I'd like to see yer 'igh-and-mightiness try gettin' up with this 'ere contraption on yer back!" she spat in her best Cockney voice as she stood at last. Mrs. Thomas moaned despairingly. The earl's half-grin widened into a real one.

"My lord," he murmured provokingly.

Jewel's eyes blazed. If the book had still been sitting on her head she would have thrown it straight at that gorgeous face. As it was, she had to content herself with clenching her fists and gritting her teeth. He had a positive knack for riling her, he did!

"My lord," she gritted with what dignity she could muster.

Mrs. Thomas, after a grimly chastening look at her bristling charge, smiled at the earl. "What can we show you, my lord?" she simpered. "Miss Julia has exhibited enormous improvement in all areas."

"Has she?" the earl's tone expressed his skepticism. His eyes swept over Jewel again, and her temper boiled over at the amusement in them. She would show him!

"Indeed I have, my lord." Her mastery of the "h" sound pleased her enormously. Feeling vindicated, she unclenched her fists and smiled smugly at him. "Notwithstanding my faux pas of a few moments ago, I am quite the lady now."

"Are you indeed?" He came into the room, sounding suitably impressed. Jewel noticed absently how well his chocolate coat molded his broad shoulders, and how very muscular his legs looked in buff breeches. To think she had once dismissed him contemptuously as a man-milliner! He was many obnoxious things, but she no longer had any doubts at all about his masculinity. He might be beautiful to look upon, but he was certainly all man.

"I'm pleased, of course, to hear you say so," he continued smoothly, choosing a chair at the cluttered schoolroom table. "I feel that I must point out, however, that the correct pronunciation of that very elegant French expression you just used is not 'fox paws.' "

"We, uh, we do have a teeny little problem with our French," Mrs. Thomas stuttered, throwing a sidelong glare at Jewel.

"That's all right. A few weeks ago she couldn't even speak English, let alone French."

"I could too speak English!" Maddened, Jewel let her accent slip again as she speared his lordship with a look of pure venom.

"Indeed." His tone was dry. With a hasty, alarmed glance at her smouldering charge, Mrs. Thomas said quickly, "Do your curtsy again, Miss Julia. This time, to—to Lady Soames."

Jewel, feeling very much like a freak in a circus sideshow, nearly rebelled. But she realized that a display of temper on her part would only amuse him more. With what dignity she could muster, she grasped her skirt in her hands and bent her knees, dipping only moderately. The board kept her posture militarily erect, but she herself was responsible for the haughty lift of her chin and the graceful extension of her arms. Watching, the earl looked suddenly arrested, as if he were seeing something he hadn't expected.

"Very nice," he said when she stood again. The wryness she had come to associate with him was absent from his voice.

Mrs. Thomas, flushed with triumph, put Jewel through her paces. With two spots of indignant color high in her cheeks, Jewel dipped in curtsy after curtsy, just like, she thought, a performing dog. Spurred on by the earl's watching eyes, she was better by far than she had ever been before with only Mrs. Thomas for an audience. When that lady trumpeted ecstatically, "And now, to the Queen!" Jewel sank down in a deep obeisance that was flawless in execution.

"We may make something of you yet," the earl said when she straightened and stood regarding him with transparent satisfaction. The patronizing words brought an angry sparkle to her eyes, but before she could ruin the impression she had made with another outburst of Cockney temper, Mrs. Thomas interrupted.

"Now that his lordship is here, perhaps he would like to take tea with us. So that he may evaluate your progress in that area, Miss Julia."

"Thank you for the invitation," the earl replied smoothly, his eyes never leaving Jewel's flushed face. "But I prefer that Miss Julia join me for dinner tonight."

"Oh yes, certainly, my lord. That would certainly be an excellent test of her abilities."

"Yes, it will, won't it?" The earl got lazily to his feet, smiling at Jewel with a charm that she disliked. Why should he be putting on that smarmy look for her? It made her think of apples and serpents. . . . She frowned after him as he moved toward the door. She was still frowning as he looked back to tell her, "I will see you in the gold salon at seven for an aperitif before dinner."

Only after he was gone did she remember that he hadn't even bothered to wait for her acceptance. Takin' it for granted that she would come running when he called. She didn't like that notion one bit.

XII

T was just before seven when Jewel, flushed and excited but also faintly recalcitrant, presented herself in the gold salon.

Emily and Mrs. Thomas together had outdone themselves in their efforts to remake both her outer and inner selves. While Jewel had sat at her dressing table, eyes watering at the sharp yanks Emily inflicted on her while trying to force her hair into a style that was "all the crack," Mrs. Thomas had stood beside her, lecturing Jewel on what eating implement to use with what course, how to sit, what to talk about and what not to talk about, and all the various other intricacies of polite behavior. By the time the woman had finished, Jewel's first inclination was to go into the salon and do every outrageous thing she could think of.

But the thought of the earl's amusement if she should do any such thing was deterrent enough. She would go down to the salon and act like a lady if it killed her. Which, she thought as Emily helped her into the whaleboned corset that both Emily and Mrs. Thomas had insisted had to be worn on this occasion, it was very likely to do. She was practically gasping for breath as Emily threw three separate white petticoats over her head and fastened them, and Mrs. Thomas helped with the black silk gown that was different only in material from the one Jewel had worn earlier in the day. Upon finally noticing Jewel's distress, both Mrs. Thomas and Emily assured her that she was hardly laced at all. The corset was so loose that it could practically fall off her, Mrs. Thomas exclaimed. And I be a chimney sweep, Jewel muttered to herself, but she found that breathing really did grow easier as she got used to the constriction.

The question of why the earl had asked her to join him for dinner when he had never voluntarily paid attention to her presence in the house before drifted continually at the edges of her mind. To her knowledge he himself never ate in the dining room. According to gossip repeated by Emily, Johnson always served the earl his dinner on a tray in the library. More often than not, Emily reported, the meal was barely touched, but great inroads were made on the brandy. Oh well, it was his lordship's business and not for the likes of them to question, Emily always concluded. While Jewel was not quite sure she agreed with that, she could find no answer for the question that troubled her. As Emily draped a black silk shawl with a foot long fringe over her shoulders, and Mrs. Thomas filled her ears with a barrage of last minute instructions, Jewel dismissed the matter, at least temporarily, from her mind.

The earl was not in the salon when Jewel entered it. She paused uncertainly in the doorway, not sure what a lady should do under the circumstances. Such an eventuality had not been covered even by the very thorough Mrs. Thomas. Her first inclination was to hightail it back to her room and forget the whole thing, but that was a cowardly thing to do and she was no coward. After assuring herself that the earl was definitely not lurking behind a curtain, she wandered aimlessly around the room, admiring the lovely things that graced it.

Gold watered silk covered the walls and draped the tall windows while the carpet was white with an intricate pattern of gold birds and green vines. The furnishings were Egyptian in style, with the satinwood legs and arms of the chairs and settee carved into tiny sphinxes. Jewel was particularly fascinated by an enormous carved wood crocodile fitted out with a green velvet cushion on its back, obviously intended for use as a footstool. The thing was so lifelike she would have feared sitting on it, and she stared at it amazed.

"Admiring Hercules, are you?" The familiar drawling voice came from behind her. Taken by surprise and feeling instinctively guilty as though she had no business in this room or even in this house, Jewel whirled around, clapping her hands behind her back.

The earl stood in the doorway, looking impossibly elegant in black evening clothes, the white linen of his shirt and cravat gleaming in the soft glow of the dozens of candles that illuminated the room. The same candlelight brought his hair to shimmering silver-gilt life. Jewel stared at it, thinking that the halo effect it gave was positively uncanny. Beneath it, his smooth-shaven face with its flawless features was so handsome as to be almost unreal. And those eyes, those sky blue eyes that looked as if they should belong to Gabriel himself, were fixed on her with an expression that made her shiver, though the room was warm.

" 'Er, Hercules?" she repeated uneasily, not quite sure what to make of the way his eyes were moving over her.

He had assured her in the beginning that he had no designs on her person, but she had since been informed by Emily that both before and after milady's death he had been very much in the petticoat line. Not that he did anything here, where his own daughter was in residence, but the gossip that came down from London was something else altogether! He was quite the rake, Emily had reported with hushed fascination, with ladies of every sort falling all over themselves, some hoping to become the next Countess of Moorland and some just hoping to enjoy the earl's favor for a while.

Looking at him, Jewel could well believe the rumors. On the strength of his looks alone she would have believed that he had to beat the females away with a stick. But he was rich and well born to boot—he had everything. Then Jewel remembered his dead wife and the daughter he apparently never saw though they lived in the same house, and took that back. Even the Earl of Moorland did not have everything.

"Hercules is what I call that monstrosity of a crocodile," the earl was saying, and Jewel returned her gaze to the object in question.

"If you think it is a monstrosity, then why have it?" she asked, speaking with great care so as not to lose the proper accent.

"I like it," he said, smiling charmingly. That glinting smile threw Jewel's thought processes off again. She stared up at him, quite forgetting what she had been going to say. Blimey, he was a smashin' lookin' man.

"I asked you if you would care for a drink before dinner." His eyebrows were slightly raised as he repeated the question. Jewel hastily got a hold on herself.

"Just a small sherry please," she answered as she had been taught, mentally scolding herself. If his looks were going to addle her this much, she was better off not looking at him at all. With a decided nod she averted her eyes. Her gaze landed on the painting of demons writhing in hellfire that adorned the wall over the fireplace. The horror of it made her eyes widen.

"Wot's that?" In her surprise her accent slipped and she never even noticed. The earl, coming up beside her and handing her a small glass of sherry, looked at her revolted face instead of the painting.

"That is Dante's Inferno," he said with a slight smile. "A madman's version of hell. Don't you care for it?"

"It's 'orrible," she said with conviction, then flushed as she realized what she had said. "I mean, I think it is quite terrifying, don't you?"

He laughed. "I liked your original version better. The truth by all means."

She shifted her attention from the painting to his face, turning scarlet as she realized that she had forgotten her role so early in their encounter. She wanted to impress him. Why? The answer to that was such a jumble in her head that she couldn't make head nor tail of it.

Those heavenly blue eyes narrowed as they ran over her from the tip of her elegantly (and painfully!) coiffed head to what he could see of her tiny kid slippers. Jewel knew that she had changed a great deal since coming to live at White Friars. Her skin was smooth, soft, and very white now. Her black hair shone with health and care. She had gained weight from her greedy consumption of all the sumptuous food, and while still slender, her shape had developed soft curves where a woman was supposed to have them. Her hands, which had never before seen any attention, were creamed and cared for by Emily each day, and were now as soft and white as her face. She was clean and she smelled nice, both from the rose scented soap with which she bathed nightly and from the rose petal sachets Emily tucked in with her undergarments. She had no need to feel uncomfortable in the face of the earl's scrutiny—but she did.

"I'm glad to see that you left the board back in the schoolroom," he said.

Expecting praise, or at least some comment on the remarkable improvement she knew had been wrought in her appearance, his comment nettled her. Her temper sparked, and almost before she could stop it a Cockney insult rose to the tip of her tongue. But she bit it back. Her head lifted, and she looked at him with only a faint spark at the backs of her golden eyes to betray her annoyance.

"It didn't go with this dress, you see," she said sweetly, as if she were to the manor born. He laughed again, looking surprised.

"Very good," he answered. "I almost begin to have hopes for you."

What Jewel would have replied to that was lost as Johnson announced dinner.

They dined in state with five courses and as many wines. Jewel was seated at the earl's right, and in the face of his constant scrutiny she had to concentrate fiercely not to lose track of what implements to use and what glasses to drink from. But she was a pattern-card of perfection if she had to say so herself. She carefully ran her soup spoon from the front to the rear of the bowl before delicately sipping the subtly spiced chicken broth from the side, not the tip. When the footman brought the main course—a capon in wine sauce—Jewel took the heavy silver fork in one hand and an even heavier knife in the other, managed to cut a dainty piece off the slippery fowl, and transfer it to her mouth without spilling so much as a drop. Pardonably proud of herself, she looked up to find that the earl was looking amused again.

"What are you laughing at?" she demanded with careful restraint when the earl had been served and the footman had moved discreetly out of earshot.

"Was I laughing?" the earl asked innocently. "I was not aware of it."

"You were laughing at me," Jewel charged, concentrating on holding onto her newly acquired accent. Her careful enunciation dampened the ire of the words, but her eyes as they sparked at him said what her tone did not. It was impossible, she found, to argue with the earl and attempt to cut her chicken at the same time. So she carefully replaced her eating implements on her plate and glared at him.

"You are mistaken," he said serenely as he took another bite of the capon. *He* had no trouble eating and talking at the same time, she noticed with resentment. "If I was laughing, it was at myself. I really didn't think it could be done, you know."

"What didn't you think could be done?" Mystified, Jewel stopped thinking about her dinner altogether and concentrated instead on his cryptic words and on maintaining her ladylike accent.

"I didn't think the sow's ear really could be turned into a silk purse."

Sputtering with temper, she abandoned her accent in favor of defending herself.

"Who you callin' a—"

He held up one long slim finger. Seething, Jewel nevertheless swallowed the rest of her diatribe.

"I was wrong," he said quietly. Jewel stared at him, still suspicious that he was insulting her in some way.

"What does that mean?" she recovered her accent along with some of her temper.

"In the short time you have been in this house, you have become a very lovely lady, indeed."

He lifted his glass to her, and smiled. She misliked the look in those blue eyes. Men were men, be they staggeringly handsome gentlemen or ordinary blokes. And she had seen that look in too many men's eyes to mistake it.

"If you're trying to turn me up sweet, you're wasting

your time," she told him bluntly, hanging on to her accent with an effort.

He shook his head, laughing a little. "What a suspicious mind you have! No, I am not trying to turn you up sweet. I meant what I said."

Still she looked at him suspiciously. His face was as bland as a baby's, his eyes sunnily clear as they met hers.

"Thank you," she said finally, still sounding a trifle wary.

"My lord," he prompted. Then, before she could even repeat the words, he resumed eating his meal and signaled that she should do the same. Evidently he realized her difficulty in eating and conversing at the same time because he confined himself to remarks requiring for the most part a simple yes or no answer until dessert was cleared away and they left the table.

"Shall we repair to the music room?" he asked, coming up behind her as she hesitated in the doorway of the dining room, not sure about what to do next. Mrs. Thomas' instructions had only covered the meal itself, not afterwards.

"All . . . right," Jewel said, trying not to feel nervous as he took her hand in his and placed it in the crook of his arm. Surely it was proper for him to walk her from the dining room in this way; after all, he was an earl, he must know how things were done.

But Jewel felt the heat of that arm all the way through the black superfine of his coat; the hardness of his muscles against her palm started a shivery feeling inside her that made her warier of herself than of him. *Him* she knew how to deal with; her own reactions were something else entirely. She was burningly aware of him so close beside her, her skirt brushing his legs as they walked, the whole of his right side close enough to warm her body. She looked up at him uncertainly, finding it unnerving to have to tilt her head back so far. He was much taller than she had at first supposed; the top of her head was not quite as high as his chin.

"Would you care for some music?"

"M-music?" She was so unsettled by his nearness that she had not even realized that they had reached the music room, so called because of the grand piano that dominated the portion of the chamber in front of the long windows.

"Yes, music," he repeated, looking over his shoulder and adding to Johnson, who followed with a silver tea service, "Just set that on the table. Miss Julia and I will serve ourselves."

"Yes, my lord."

Jewel thought that Johnson sounded even stiffer than usual as he complied. Almost as if the butler disapproved of something—but what? Jewel realized that the earl still held her arm pressed against his body, and hastily pulled away. Johnson, face impassive, bowed and left the room, closing the door behind him.

Jewel found herself alone with the earl, and she felt very uneasy suddenly. Perhaps it was the gleam in his eyes as they looked at her that gave her pause. She didn't like the way his lids half-dropped to conceal it. If he got out of line, was it permissible to slap an earl's face? If she could even bring herself to, she thought, and went hot all over as she imagined those chiseled lips on hers. . . .

"Why don't you pour the tea, and bring mine over to the piano? If you care for music, I will endeavor to provide it."

"You can play that thing?" In her surprise Jewel forgot her nervousness. She looked from him to the graceful instrument and back again.

"Certainly I can. You will be able to, too, before we're done with you. Part of your education."

Before Jewel could comment, he sat upon the piano bench, settling his fingers lightly over the keys. With his attention completely diverted from her, she was able to relax and concentrate on pouring the tea. Seating herself on the gold brocade settee, she concentrated on filling the delicate china cups. Only after they were properly full did Jewel even hear the music. It was pleasant to listen to, she thought as she carefully carried both cups toward the piano. A real nice, tinklin' tune.

"Ah, thank you, Julia." He stopped playing and accepted his cup, swiveling sideways on the bench to look up at her. His eyes seemed to take an inordinately long time to reach her face. With any other man she would instantly have known what to make of that long perusal, but with him . . . maybe she was just imagining the way he was looking at her because she wanted him to admire her as much as she did him.

"Sit down here, have your tea, and tell me how you like learning to be a lady."

"I don't like it at all, my lord," she said tartly, sitting beside him in the space he had made for her on the bench. It occurred to her that the words had come out perfectly without her even having to think about what to say or how to say it, almost like talk did when she was just Jewel. She was so surprised that she quite failed to be flustered at the earl's nearness, or note the droop of his lids as he stared down at the front of her bodice where her newly full breasts swelled tautly against the black silk.

"I said that quite well, didn't I?" She beamed up at him with innocent pleasure, totally failing to notice how slowly he lifted his eyes to meet hers.

"Very well indeed." The velvety texture of his voice as his eyes focused on the movement of her lips went right over her head in her excitement. Jewel smiled up at him with genuine delight, and his eyes widened slightly at the sudden blaze of beauty that completed her transformation in his mind from scrawny, grubby little waif to desirable woman.

"Maybe I do like learning to be a lady," she added cautiously, considering. "I like having lots of food to eat, and being warm and clean, and having nice clothes to wear—even if they are all black." This was accompanied by a mock reproachful glance up at him. He was watching her with lazy attention, Jewel saw, and felt warmed by this evidence of interest in her words. "I don't like all them, uh, the things Mrs. Thomas makes me do. I hate having that board strapped to my back—it hurts! And I hate doing curtsies over and over almost as much as I hate talking into candles all the time." Jewel realized what she had said and flashed him that radiant smile again. "But I do like talking properly when I'm doing it. I didn't leave off a single 'h' just now!"

"I applaud you," he murmured, his eyes never leaving her face as he took a meditative sip of tea. "But you do seem to have trouble remembering to address me as 'my lord'."

Her eyes twinkled saucily. "That's because I never think of you as my lord."

"Indeed?" Those surprisingly dark eyebrows lifted again, but for some reason the expression didn't anger her this time. "And what do you think of me as, if I dare to ask?"

She grinned, showing a definitely unladylike amount of small white teeth and a bewitching dimple in the newly plump contours of her right cheek.

"Now that would be telling." Jewel laughed up at him, feeling suddenly gay. If she had been thinking, she might have been inclined to wonder if her unaccustomed comfort in the earl's presence might not have something to do with the glasses of wine she had consumed with her dinner. Indeed, she had drunk rather more than she had eaten because drinking did not require nearly as much skill as eating did. In the length of time it took her to chase, capture, and properly subdue her capon alone, she had easily swallowed three whole glasses of wine.

"Something rude, no doubt." The earl's answering smile was somewhat speculative, but Jewel smiled saucily back at him. She really felt very happy sitting beside him while he smiled down at her with those devastating blue eyes.

"No doubt," she echoed in a beguiling voice, her eyes blinking into his. She felt as if she could drown in their cerulean depths. . . .

His hand came up to stroke lightly down the side of her soft cheek. Jewel felt that small touch like a thunderbolt right down to her toes. Her eyes stared into his, and she felt as if she were melting helplessly.

"My lord," he murmured, his eyes moving over her face like a caress.

"I always forget that part." Her voice was plaintive, and a faint frown puckered her forehead. He reached up to smooth out the wrinkle with the same finger that had feathered her cheek. Jewel's lips parted under the impact of that soft caressing touch.

"Never mind." His voice was as caressing as his fingers. "I propose that we dispense with the formalities altogether. You may call me Sebastian."

Jewel stared at him, feeling warmly befuddled. So close, his skin had the texture of soft grainless leather. It was naturally fair, but had been tanned to a light golden brown by the amount of time he spent outdoors, and was shades darker than her creamy whiteness. Beneath the halo of gleaming silver-gilt hair, his eyes with their surprisingly dark brows and lashes were as blue as the summer sky. His nose was straight, his mouth elegantly carved, his cheeks and chin finely drawn but indisputably masculine. Jewel vaguely recalled dismissing him as no more than a man-milliner at their first encounter. Now that she had become acquainted with the broad-shouldered, hard-muscled strength of him, she realized that the beauty of his face was mere camouflage for a very masculine male. In fact, looking at him now, she was reminded irresistibly of the old tale of the wolf in sheep's clothing.

"Old Seb," she murmured, remembering how Timothy had described him. Funny, she could hardly remember what Timothy had looked like, except that he had been fair, like a less vivid copy of Sebastian. Sebastian, whose eyes had darkened even as his hand tightened on her face. She felt the warmth and heat and strength of his fingers against the softness of her skin, and shivered responsively. She liked having him touch her. Her eyes were a molten gold in the candlelight as she looked up at him. "You weren't quite what I was expecting."

"Ah yes, Timothy," he said negligently, his eyes inspecting the face he had turned up to his with minute attention. "The boy had more taste than I ever credited him with."

"Thank you." She pinkened with delight at the compliment, and smiled dreamily up at him, turning her face against his subtly stroking fingers in much the same way as might a cat being rubbed.

"Sebastian."

"What?" His voice was softly caressing as he looked down into her dreamy-eyed face.

Jewel shook her head. "Nothing."

"Just Sebastian?" He was leaning closer now, murmuring to her so that Jewel could feel the whisper of his breath on her mouth. She stared into the dazzling beauty of his face, and wanted to die of pure bliss. She thought that never in her life had she been so happy. It was pure heaven to be sitting so close to him, with his fingers stroking softly over her cheek now, and his other arm sliding around her, supporting her on the backless bench. What a gentleman he was, she thought with a tender curve of her lips, to consider her comfort so thoughtfully.

"You are really very lovely." The words were drawled almost against her lips. He was close, so close that all she had to do was lift her mouth just the tiniest fraction and he would be kissing her. The idea of him kissing her made her senses go haywire. She wanted him to, oh, she wanted him to, she would die if he didn't . . . The quivering started deep in her belly and worked its way down her thighs and up to her breasts, causing an aching, pulsing feeling that was like nothing she had ever known. Like a sleep walker, she leaned forward to close the final hair's distance between them.

Her lips brushed his, and then he was kissing her, kissing her with a soft intensity that left her dazed and clinging to him. She couldn't get enough of his mouth. . . .

Her arms were around his neck, her mouth trembling under his. When she felt his tongue stroke over her lips, then slide gently between them to run over the smooth surface of her teeth, her breath stopped. She thought she would die with the wonder of it.

His mouth was withdrawn just the tiniest degree, and she tightened her arms in protest.

"Open your mouth, Julia," he whispered, and because he asked her to she did. Then he was kissing her again, his tongue sliding inside her mouth to claim its sweetness, and she was drowning in the wonder of it. Her last thought before she went under completely was to wonder if all men knew how to kiss like this. . . .

His mouth was withdrawn to nuzzle against the side of her face, trailing its way over her cheek to her neck and then up to her ear. She clung to his shoulders, her head limp on her neck as she allowed him to kiss her as he would. His arms pulled her closer, so that her breasts were pressed hard against his chest. Jewel loved the sensation of her softness against his strength, and her head began to whirl even more.

Then his lips pressed against the soft hollow behind her ear, and his tongue found the ear itself, gently tracing the delicate whorls. It tickled, just a bit, and the sensation made Jewel giggle. He stiffened at the foolish little sound, and the supporting arm was withdrawn from around her so suddenly that she nearly toppled backward off the bench. He had to catch her arm to prevent her fall. Then he hauled her upright again with a very ungentle hand on her arm.

"Sebastian!" She almost wailed a protest, her eyes huge as they blinked up at him. She felt as if she had been in a daze, and he had suddenly awakened her.

"How much wine did you have with dinner?" He was glaring at her, and the words were uttered through his teeth. Jewel stared up at him, bewildered by the sudden change in him.

"W-wot?"

"Obviously too much." He sounded thoroughly disgusted. Standing abruptly, he pulled her to her feet.

Jewel, surprised by his rough handling, was equally surprised to find that her knees would not support her. She sagged, and he caught her with an arm around her waist.

"Damn it to hell," he muttered, swinging her up into his arms. Jewel, not expecting the sudden change in her elevation, felt her head swim alarmingly. She clung to him, her hands clutching the rough silk of his hair as it curled into his nape, her eyes helplessly appealing as they sought his.

"Don't you want to kiss me anymore?" she whispered humbly. His eyes blazed into hers for an instant, and then his mouth tightened into a thin straight line.

"I'm a swine, but not that big a swine," he muttered. "I do draw the line at making love to inebriated little girls."

Before she could say anything else, he strode with her from the room. Jewel was vaguely conscious of Johnson's astonished face as Sebastian carried her through the great hall and up the stairs without uttering another word.

"I feel . . . funny." Jewel mouthed the words as the world

started to twirl around her. Her face must have whitened because he glared fiercely down at her.

"Don't you dare get sick," he warned through gritted teeth.

Jewel, head lolling back against a surprisingly comfortable broad chest, barely heard him. She felt as if she were spinning round and round in increasingly fast circles. He was striding along the south wing's upstairs hallway, making short work of the distance between the landing and her room. Jewel felt herself growing dizzier and dizzier as he made turn after turn after turn. . . .

Just as he reached the door to her room her stomach gave up the fight. He barely managed to tilt her away from him before she lost her dinner all over the woven wool runner that covered the floor.

"God damn it anyway," he said bitterly, looking at his spattered boots. He set her on her feet, supporting her with one amazingly strong arm as she sagged limply against him and he fumbled for the doorknob. Then he was opening the door and picking her up again. Jewel kept her eyes tightly closed as he shouldered through the door with her limp in his arms. She couldn't bear to see the disgust that she knew must be plain on his face.

"My lord . . . !"

"What has happened?"

The anxious voices belonged to Emily and Mrs. Thomas, who had of course been waiting up for her. Jewel's head swam alarmingly, but it cleared enough for her to recognize how deeply she had disgraced herself, again. Oh no, she moaned inwardly, keeping her eyes closed tight and wishing she was dead as she was descended upon by the exclaiming pair of women.

"Miss Julia became ill at dinner," Sebastian gritted in response to their alarmed inquiries as he dumped Jewel unceremoniously into the middle of her bed. He dropped her from such a height that she bounced, and immediately her stomach lurched again. Moaning, she rolled onto her stomach, burying her head in the pillows.

"Oh, my poor lady," she heard Emily say sympathetically, while Mrs. Thomas' less charitable mutterings did not quite manage to drown out the sound of boots retreating or the sharp closing of the door as Sebastian left.

X I I I

OU have disgraced me, utterly disgraced me! How I shall ever manage to hold up my head in his lordship's presence again . . . !"

Jewel had been listening to Mrs. Thomas' harangue throughout the morning and now into the afternoon. Her head still felt as if someone was pounding on it with a hammer, her stomach churned at the mere idea of food, and there was a foul taste in her mouth that nothing seemed able to eliminate. But her physical miseries were as nothing compared to the shame she felt. How would she ever face Sebastian—but even the memory of how she came to be calling him that made her wince. She had behaved like the veriest trollop.

Mrs. Thomas' shrill berating voice distracted Jewel from her thoughts, for which she wasn't altogether sorry. So far, she had listened to the governess' continuous scolding with a large amount of humility. To be perfectly honest, she agreed one hundred per cent with nearly every word the woman said. She had disgraced herself, and she supposed she had disgraced Mrs. Thomas as well. She would have even more trouble than Mrs. Thomas in holding up her head in Sebastian's presence. Everything that had transpired after dinner last night was slightly hazy in her mind, but not hazy enough to allow her to forget the most vital part of what had occurred. She had kissed Sebastian, kissed him passionately, and had wanted to go on kissing him forever and ever and ever. Even now, despite the shame that made her want to crawl away and just die, the mere memory of that kiss could send a shaft of flame shooting through her body.

Of course, she had had too much to drink, but that was no excuse for the way she had behaved. And she couldn't blame it all on Sebastian, either. He was a man, and men were subject to strong compulsions of the flesh. Everyone knew that. But she was a woman, a lady (or at least she was trying to be) and it had been her place to stop what had occurred. She hadn't even tried. Then, to make her humiliation complete, she had nearly passed out and Sebastian had had to carry her up to bed, for which she had repaid him by emptying the contents of her stomach on his immaculate boots once again. She moaned inwardly, remembering. How would she ever be able to face him again?

"Oh, shut yer mouth, ya old bag o' wind!" Jewel hadn't meant to say it aloud, but Mrs. Thomas' constant yammering was driving her out of her mind. The lady puffed up, uttered an outraged *"Well,"* and marched out of the schoolroom with a sniff.

"I know when I am fighting a losing battle!" Mrs.

Thomas threw over her shoulder as she went through the door. "A lady you'll never be!"

The door slammed behind her with a force that made Jewel moan and cradle her head in her hands. She was still sitting that way a good twenty minutes later, fully occupied in wishing herself dead, when the door opened again. Sure that it was Mrs. Thomas returned to scold her some more, Jewel sought to head off the coming tirade by saying wearily, "I apologize, all right?"

"It is quite all right with me, but not, I fear, with your esteemed mentor." There was no doubt that the silken syllables belonged to Sebastian. Jewel's head popped up, and she stared at him in horror while scarlet color suffused her face.

"My-my lord." Hardly knowing what she was doing, responding to some dimly felt inner wish to convince him that she *had* learned some of the lessons of a lady, she jumped to her feet and essayed a clumsy curtsy. Her knees seemed unwilling to cooperate, and for a moment she feared that she would finish her humiliation by toppling over. But she managed to right herself, and stood staring miserably at the snowy folds of his cravat. Not for anything on earth could she have forced herself to meet his eyes.

"What an interesting color your face is," he observed after a moment of silence. "Bright red mixed with sort of a caterpillar green is not exactly, er, becoming, but it is certainly unusual."

Jewel's eyes flew to his face. She was amusing him to no end, no doubt, although his mouth looked perfectly grave. His mouth! She was staring at it and he was watching her! Her face went redder than it had been before, and her eyes dropped to his cravat again.

"I owe you an apology for my behavior last night, my lord," she managed, praying that the stiffness of her voice would mask her deep sense of shame. She wanted to salvage whatever tiny scraps of dignity that she could from the debacle.

"Let's forget it, shall we?" he said abruptly. Jewel risked a look at him, surprised by the sudden roughness in his voice. "I was at fault as much as you. I should have kept a closer account of the amount of wine you were drinking. In future, you are to limit yourself to a single glass."

"Yes, my lord," Jewel whispered, his temperance when she had expected furious condemnation making her feel even worse. She felt ashamed tears forming in her eyes and blinked rapidly to disperse them. If she broke down now and cried in front of him, she would have to throw herself off the nearest cliff.

"I thought we agreed that you were to call me Sebastian."

He was standing just inside the door, still speaking in the same rough tone as he toyed with the riding crop he carried in one hand. He was dressed in an old tweed coat and a pair of suede pantaloons that had worn places about the knees. It was infuriating that even in such a shabby riding outfit he still managed to look elegant. Something to do with his build, she decided as her eyes went from the broad shoulders and lean torso to the narrow hips and hard muscled legs before she realized what she was doing and hastily averted her gaze.

She was miserably conscious of how dreadful she herself must look, with her eyes mud-brown today instead of golden and red-rimmed to boot, her complexion wan instead of creamily pale, and her hair drawn back off her face in a knot so tight (she suspected that the hairstyle was Emily's subtle version of punishment) that it tugged at her scalp and made her headache worse. In a high necked dress of black kerseymore she felt as drab and colorless as a candlemoth in the presence of a monarch butterfly.

"If you wish." Her voice was low. He looked at her in silence for a long moment, his lips compressing as she refused to meet his eyes. The riding crop flicked once, twice through his fingers, then abruptly slapped against the leather of his boot. Jewel started, and her eyes flew automatically to meet his.

"You look like death warmed over. I suggest you sit down before you fall down."

Jewel was so glad to do as he suggested that she didn't even resent being told how horrible she looked. Sinking into the chair she had vacated upon his entrance, she looked up at him again. He was really being very nice about the whole thing, not berating her for behaving like a light-skirt. And not saying a word about her losing her dinner all over him again. She tried offering him a tentative, tremulous smile, but just the facial movements required to form one caused such a pain to shoot through her head that she groaned, and had to lean forward and rest her forehead on the table.

"That bad, is it?" He sounded suddenly, hatefully amused. "Don't worry, I know just the thing to make you feel better."

She felt rather than saw him step out into the hall. His bellowed "Leister!" made her wince. There followed a low conversation, and he returned to the schoolroom. A few minutes later a dapper little man whom Jewel recognized as Sebastian's valet arrived holding a tray upon which rested a bottle of amber spirits, another bottle of some sort of spice, an egg cup (of all things), a glass, and a spoon.

"My special remedy, my lord," Leister said, carefully not looking at Jewel as Sebastian moved to take the tray from him. Sebastian dismissed him with a word of thanks and closed the door before turning back into the room with his burden.

"What's that for?" Her voice was suspicious.

He set the tray on the table and started mixing right before her eyes. First a splash of liquour, then the egg, then a dash of spice were put into the glass. He then stirred the revolting mixture vigorously before holding the glass out to her. Jewel stared at the frothy concoction with unconcealed repugnance.

"I ain't drinkin' that," she stated with utter conviction and a complete loss of her carefully cultivated accent.

"Don't be tiresome if you please. The hair of the dog that bit you is the best cure in the world for what ails you right now. And Leister has added his own modest refinements to an age old remedy. Drink this down, and in a little while I guarantee you'll feel much better."

He was looking amused again, and Jewel scowled at him. It was surprising how thoroughly he had managed to set her at ease when not a quarter of an hour ago she had just wanted to die.

" 'Course you should know."

He smiled seraphically, holding out the glass again. "Don't be sarcastic, Julia, it doesn't become you. Come, if you won't drink it under your own steam, I shall be forced to employ drastic measures."

"Like wot?" She was not going to drink that—that disgusting mess. She could feel her stomach heaving at the mere thought of it. He could not make her—could he? Her scowl darkened. The unconscionable swine probably could.

"I can always hold your nose, and when you open your mouth to breathe pour it down your throat."

"Ya wouldn' dare!"

He smiled in reply, holding out the glass to her. Julia, frowning fiercely, knew when she was defeated.

"Bully!" She muttered the word under her breath, taking the glass from him with a fearsome glare. He said nothing, merely folding his arms on his chest as he waited. She scowled again, first at him and then at the awful mixture. Finally, with a dreadful grimace she picked the glass up and bolted the contents. As the slimy mess went down her throat she gagged, and for an awful moment she thought she was going to compound her humiliation of the night before by throwing up again. But this time, if she did, he deserved it, she thought—and in her anger the mixture made it down to her stomach unrejected. Her head swam for a moment, but then it cleared and she knew that the horrible concoction was going to stay down.

"Very good." He sounded like a parent praising a wayward child. Jewel felt too awful to even scowl at him any more. Instead she groaned, and rested her head against the table again. To her fury he actually chuckled.

"You'll feel better soon, I promise. I suggest you spend the rest of the day in your bed. Tomorrow morning I'll see you in the library at nine sharp."

She looked up at that. "In the library?" She was confused. Why could he possibly want to see her in the library so early in the morning?

He paused on his way to the door. "Oh, did I forget to mention it? The estimable Mrs. Thomas just gave notice. She, uh, no longer feels capable of teaching you. Until a replacement can be found, I propose to assume the role of your instructor."

"You?" Words failed Jewel. The haughty Earl of Moorland teach a little guttersnipe—his words!—to be a lady? The idea was laughable, if she wasn't afraid he was serious.

"Why not? I thought it might prove amusing." And with that he went out the door, pausing to say over his shoulder, "I'll send your maid to you. She can help you to bed."

X I V

URING the rest of that spring and summer, Jewel Combs gradually all but disappeared. Her place was slowly, painfully, but in the end thoroughly taken by Julia Stratham, who was (nearly) every inch a lady.

Under Sebastian's implacable guidance Jewel even began to think of herself as Julia. In the mornings when she sat before her dressing table mirror while Emily brushed her hair, it was Julia she saw looking back at her: Julia with the smooth white skin and soft pink mouth, Julia with the slanting black eyebrows (expertly shaped now so that they gave her appearance a touch of the exotic instead of being merely bushy) above golden eyes to which health and happiness had added a vibrant sparkle, Julia with the thick glossy hair the color of ebony, Julia with the feminine curves that filled out the hated black dresses so that they really didn't look so drab after all. It was Julia who read the books Sebastian gave her and gravely discussed them with him later; it was Julia who curtsied and pirouetted for his approval; it was Julia who listened attentively to all he could tell her about the ways of the world he had inhabited since birth. It was Julia who learned to look on Sebastian as the family she had never had; friend, father, brother, and mentor all rolled into one gorgeously wrapped package, an omnipotent being who could make her laugh with a wry lift of his eyebrows, or explode her still hasty temper with a teasing remark. It was Julia whom he could reduce to shamed silence with no more than a frosty look, and it was Julia who strictly monitored her behavior so that it would please him. Because she wanted to please him badly. Sebastian had become far and away the most important person in her life.

Julia was good for Sebastian, too. The servants remarked on it to her, each in his or her own different way. Mrs. Johnson said with her customary bluntness that she had never seen the master so uncharacteristically good-humored. Johnson smiled the first smile Julia had ever seen crease his face as he said that he would be canceling that standing order for quarterly shipments of French brandy that he had placed with the neighborhood supplier. The last order they had got in was still practically untouched, the first time in years it had lasted so long. Leister hummed snatches of popular songs as he went about his duties; such lightmindedness (according to Mrs. Johnson) was unheard of in the proper gentleman's gentleman. Emily reported that the kitchen was agog at the length of time the earl had remained at White Friars. Usually he just stayed for a few weeks, and then he was off again to the Lord only knew where.

To Julia, lost in the halcyon glow of a burgeoning happiness, Sebastian was transformed by infinitesimal degrees from someone of whom she had to beware to the most marvelous being in the world. He bossed her, of course, and scolded her when he felt she needed it, which was frequently, but underneath it he treated her with a careless affection that was manna to her love starved soul. In return she nearly worshipped him, and he blossomed under the admiration that shone from her eyes. Like herself, she thought, he was hungry for love.

He was tireless in working to transform her into the lady he wished her to be, imparting to her much more than the fundamental tenets of gentility. From him she learned intangibles such as the usefulness of icy silence and a steady stare in the face of an impertinence, or the value of a haughtily raised eyebrow when it came to depressing pretensions. Not that he ever told her these tricks in so many words, but he used them himself with great success. And Julia almost unconsciously absorbed Sebastian's mannerisms like a sponge.

Much against her will, he even taught her to ride. Julia had quickly learned that saying no to Sebastian was of about as much use as spitting into the wind. Without much more persuasion than a single cool look he managed to get her into a riding habit and upon the back of an enormous beast named Bess.

Despite Sebastian's assurances that the creature would not hurt so much as a fly, Julia was terrified. Every time the horse's ears twitched she was sure she would be treated to a rampaging ride over the heath that would very likely end in her death. She wanted to scream, to cry, to throw herself from the animal's back and hug the ground, refusing ever again to leave it. But in the face of Sebastian's calm instructions as to how to sit and hold the reins, she didn't quite dare. Instead, miserably, she released her death grip on the horse's mane and took the reins in her shaking hands. She even managed to stay on while Sebastian led the animal around the paddock, though she did grab the front of the saddle for balance—but only when Sebastian was not looking.

When at last he pronounced the lesson concluded and reached for her, she slid into his arms like a homing pigeon to its nest. He had to support her into the house because her knees were shaking so badly that they wouldn't bear her weight. But Julia didn't care. She leaned against Sebastian's sheltering body, greedily absorbing his warmth and strength, her face wreathed in smiles. She had done it, she had learned to ride a horse and pleased Sebastian, and she was enormously proud of herself—until he casually mentioned that they would repeat the lesson the next day.

At that she protested. She could not, would not go through that ordeal again. But she did. Day after disastrous day, until at last even Sebastian had to admit defeat: despite all his efforts, she could just barely manage to stay aboard when the horse walked. If it moved into a faster gait—such as, God forbid, a slow trot—she was finished. With the best will in the world, she slid from the saddle every time to land in a disheveled heap on the ground. Finally even Sebastian had had to concede; Julia Stratham would never be a rider.

With considerably more success he taught her to dance, counting off the measures with imperturbable patience as she awkwardly stepped all over his feet. His tight hold on her waist and the closeness of the hard warmth of his body made her tingle from head to toe, and she quite enjoyed these lessons. If every once in a while she had a sneaking memory of the shattering quality of his kisses when her gaze chanced on his mouth or his body brushed too closely against hers, he seemed to have no such recollection. His attitude toward her verged on the avuncular, and it nettled Julia from time to time. But then she would tell herself that it was just as well; Sebastian could never be such a good friend if he were constantly trying to be her lover. And by now his friendship had become as necessary to her as the air she breathed.

Once she got over being embarrassed about treading on his polished boots, going into his arms for their dance session became the highlight of her day. She loved being held so close to him, loved being cradled in his arms. Once she wondered with a little quiver of surprise if she was so vulnerable to physical closeness because she had been deprived of it as a child. Even when her mother had been alive, she had had very little time for Jewel. But the unpleasantness of her past was behind her now. She was no longer Jewel but Julia, and when Sebastian held her in his arms she was the happiest creature in the world.

As they danced he would hum the lilting tunes in a surprisingly melodious voice, while at the same time admonishing her not to watch her feet or count the steps out loud. After she finally succeeded in complying with both these instructions at once, he waltzed her out of the music room, whirling her in his arms down the length of the great hall until she was laughing and breathless. He pronounced himself marginally satisfied. She was a very graceful dancer indeed, and if she would just learn not to *look* as if she were counting off the steps under her breath she would be an asset to any ballroom.

It seemed as though half the staff stopped what they were doing to watch this impromptu performance. Julia, laughing merrily as she leaned against the wall trying to catch her breath, thought she had never seen so many smiles at White Friars since she had arrived there. Up on the minstrel's gallery, from behind the shelter of an enormous tapestry, Julia caught a glimpse of the one spectator who was more important than all the rest put together: Chloe. Her small pale face pressed to the railings, she stared down at the commotion below, easily identified because of her size and her silver-gilt hair. But before Julia could bring Chloe's presence to Sebastian's attention, the child vanished. And looking at Sebastian's laughing face, she decided that no purpose would be served by reminding him of his daughter and her estrangement from him.

This was the one area he steadfastly refused to discuss with her. As she had become comfortable with his seeming fondness for her, and grown relatively certain that some misplaced word of hers would not cause his friendship to be withdrawn, Julia, with what she considered praiseworthy tact, urged him to interest himself in his only child. After all, Chloe was only six years old, and she needed her father more than ever since her mother's passing. As an orphan herself, Julia could well understand the desolation Chloe must be suffering.

Sebastian steadfastly refused to discuss the subject. He coldly thanked her for her concern, but told her he would appreciate her more if she put his private affairs from her mind. In saying all this, he was so much the icily distant earl she had first met that she feared to bring up the subject again.

But she could not banish it from her mind. Julia could not reconcile his indifference toward his daughter with what she had come to know of him. With her he was patient and tolerant, a charming companion and knowledgeable mentor. Why should he turn so reticent when faced with the daughter who was his own mirror image?

Impromptu picnics were one of the best parts of that summer. Julia thought that some of her happiest times were when Sebastian drove her in a small trap he kept about the place—they tacitly agreed that Julia would not have to ride one of the despised horses—to some picturesque spot where they dined on the excellent lunch provided by Henri the cook. Afterwards they would lie about on the grass, and drowse and talk. During one such occasion Julia regretted aloud that Chloe could not be a part of these expeditions. Sebastian sat up abruptly, a displeased frown settling over his face.

"She is better off with her nanny," he said sharply. Julia, with one look at his tightening face, said no more. His aversion to his daughter's company seemed inexplicable, but there was nothing she could do to change it without bringing his wrath down upon herself.

Still, she kept her eye out for the child, and was rewarded by finally getting a chance to make her acquaintance formally one bright day in early September. Sebastian had gone riding, and Julia was perforce at loose ends. She decided to go for a walk and encountered Chloe and her nursemaid taking their exercise near the lane.

"Good afternoon." Julia smiled at the nanny, who was tightly clasping her charge's small hand in her own.

"Good afternoon, miss." The nanny's name was June Belkerson, Julia remembered as the woman returned her smile a little stiffly. Julia transferred her attention to Chloe, whose head continued to be stubbornly averted. Clad in a dainty white frock sprigged with flowers the exact shade of her eyes, with her silver-gilt hair tied with a blue ribbon and left to tumble in loose curls down her back, Chloe was as beautiful a child as Sebastian was a man. It was incomprehensible that he could not feel intense pride in so lovely a daughter. Chloe steadfastly refused to look up, so Julia crouched down before her and tried to meet her eyes.

"Good afternoon, Chloe. Do you remember me?" The child made absolutely no response either by word or the slightest change of expression. The lovely little face, so perfect a miniature of Sebastian's, might have been made of porcelain for all the emotion it showed.

"She doesn't talk, miss." Miss Belkerson sounded impatient. Julia, surprised, glanced up.

"Why ever not?"

Miss Belkerson shrugged. "She hasn't said a word ever since I've been here, which is close on to two years now. Doctors have been to see her, and say there's nothing wrong with her. She just won't talk. Because of her mother maybe, they say. A trauma resulting from the loss of her mother."

"Perhaps she doesn't have anything to say." Julia didn't

know if she were more appalled at the idea of a child bearing so much grief that she could not speak or by the insensitivity of discussing the subject in front of her. With a pointed look at Miss Belkerson, whose plump, placid face looked kindly but none too intelligent, she added, "I presume she can hear?"

"She can hear all right. She minds real good, most of the time. But she's got this thing for running off, so I got to keep my eye on her real close. Drives me crazy sometimes, trying to find her. But so far she's come to no harm, and I can't watch her twenty-four hours in a day even if I wanted to."

Julia looked down at Chloe again without replying. The little girl was staring into the distance, giving no indication that she had heard so much as a syllable of the adults' conversation.

"I'd like us to be friends, Chloe," Julia said softly, crouching down to the child's eye level again. There was no reply, and after a moment Julia straightened.

"She's always like that, miss. But she heard you. Well, if you'll excuse us, it's time for Miss Chloe's nap. She always naps after our walk."

"Certainly." Julia watched as Miss Belkerson led Chloe away. What she had learned made her ache with pity for the child. How could Sebastian be such a monster as not to love her? It was so unlike what she had come to know of him.

Later that day, when dinner was done and she had joined Sebastian in the library as was now their custom, Julia's mind was still preoccupied with Chloe. Sebastian had to concern himself with the poor mite, and she seemed to be the only one who might be able to push him to do it.

"Sebastian," she began hesitantly as she sipped her tea and looked at him over the chessboard between them. He was determined to teach her the game, telling her that it would greatly improve her mind. Never mind that his efforts were not proving very successful; he refused to abandon the attempt. Several nights a week he set up the chessboard and spent the evening growing increasingly exasperated as Julia either could not or would not learn to play.

"That rook cannot move in that direction," he said grittily as she sat admiring the way his hair gleamed in the lamplight. Julia, who had forgotten that she even held the piece in her hand, absently moved it to a square in the opposite direction.

"For God's sake, you can't move it there either! Julia, for an intelligent young woman, you are remarkably stupid about chess."

Julia's head came up at that. "Well, my lord, you are remarkably stupid about some things, too." She glared at him over the chessboard, and he returned her look with the icy lift of his brows that he knew annoyed her beyond anything.

"Indeed?"

As he grew colder, she invariably grew hotter. She was positively sputtering now, forgetting in her surge of temper that she had meant to introduce the subject of Chloe tactfully. Diplomacy was wasted on him anyway, she told herself as the words tumbled off her tongue.

"Yes, indeed! And do you want to know one of the many things you are remarkably stupid about?"

"I am sure you are about to enlighten me."

"Your daughter! Yes, Chloe! She's a lovely little girl and she's only six years old and she's lost her mother. How can you be so unfeeling as to deny her her father too?"

His eyes had chilled over until they resembled frozen blue lakes. "As I've told you repeatedly, I refuse to discuss the subject." That meant that he was really angry, as Julia had learned from experience. Far from frightening her into caution, the knowledge fanned the flames of her own temper.

"She's your daughter, for goodness' sake. Your own flesh and blood! How can you be so cruel to her? She's just a child, and she needs your love. Why you are selfishly withholding it is totally beyond me."

"You are right. My reasons are beyond you. Beyond anything you can imagine, and I refuse to discuss them."

His eyes were blazing with an icy blue light that made them glitter like diamonds in the glow of the lamps. His words were as frozen as his eyes. He was very much the earl suddenly, despite the fact that he wore only a shirt and waistcoat and breeches as was his habit in these after dinner hours. Even without his coat and cravat, he looked every inch the aristocrat, but Julia refused to be cowed. She was no longer Jewel Combs, ignorant guttersnipe. She was Julia Stratham, his creation maybe but also his equal and his friend. She sincerely cared about his well-being and that of his daughter, and that gave her the right to probe into an area that he obviously preferred be left alone.

But perhaps she should try another approach. Direct confrontation was very rarely, if ever, successful with Sebastian, as she had learned by painful trial and error. Perhaps she could reason with him, make him see the error of his ways. She took a deep breath.

"Sebastian, don't you love Chloe?"

"I refuse to discuss this subject."

"She needs you, Sebastian. You are her father, after all. Do you know she has screaming nightmares at night? Do you know that she runs away from her nursemaid sometimes and disappears for hours? Do you know where she goes when she runs away? I do, Sebastian."

"Stop it, Julia!" He jumped to his feet, overturning the chessboard in his agitation. All the pieces went flying and the board clattered to the floor. His fists clenched and unclenched at his sides as he stood glaring down at her. A vein throbbed angrily in his neck, and a deep tide of red suffused his face. He looked murderous suddenly, and Julia had a fleeting picture of Elizabeth's sweet face. Was that why he could not face his daughter? She immediately banished the suspicion, but that it had appeared at all galvanized her. There had to be another reason for his avoidance of Chloe. There had to be.

"She goes to the old monastery, right up into the bell tower. I found her there one day, all huddled up on the floor crying her eyes out for her mother. When I spoke to her, I think she thought for a minute I was Elizabeth's ghost. Poor little mite, the look on her face broke my heart! And you think she doesn't need you, Sebastian? She does. You are her father, and she needs your love."

"May God damn you to hell."

His voice was so quiet that for a moment Julia was sure she must have misheard. But the look in his eyes told her that she had not. He looked like a man enduring the torment of hellfire. The expression terrified her, but after only an instant he turned and with long jerky strides left the room.

"Sebastian!" Julia jumped to her feet and went after him, but stopped in the doorway, defeated. As furious as he was, he would not want to listen to another word she had to say. She would wait for him to regain his self-control, and then maybe they could talk again. She was determined not to let the subject alone.

She stayed in the library for a while, glancing idly through book after book without really seeing a single word printed in any of them, trying not to look at the picture of Elizabeth and Chloe at all. Something about that picture affected her profoundly, and she was sure that it must affect Sebastian. Why did he keep it in the room where he spent most of his time? There was no answer, and there were many. But she didn't know which was the right one, and she refused to speculate any further. The Sebastian she had come to know was not the kind of man who would murder his wife. But then he was not the kind of man who would neglect a young child, his own child, either. So there was no answer for her in that. She could only go by her gut instinct that told her that Sebastian was not guilty of murdering Elizabeth. The case against him was just a web of gossip and innuendo.

Finally acknowledging that he would not be returning to the library that night, Julia went to bed. A sleepy Emily helped her off with her clothes and into her nightgown, and then Julia sent her off to bed and crawled beneath the covers herself. In the pitch darkness it was possible to imagine all kinds of hellish reasons for Sebastian's violent aversion to his daughter. But she resolutely refused to consider the most persuasive of those: guilt. There could be any number of other explanations. Perhaps he was a man who simply did not like children. Or perhaps Chloe wasn't really his child. That explanation would make sense if she had never seen Chloe. But Sebastian's mark was upon the child, much too obvious for anyone to ever deny.

It seemed like she had just fallen asleep when she heard the screams. Over the months she had lived at White Friars, she had become accustomed to the sounds of Chloe's occasional nightmares. They never lasted long, and lately she had been sleeping through them as just another sound of the night. But tonight they were frenzied, high pitched and terrified—and they did not stop. Perhaps something had happened to the child—or the nursemaid?

Julia did not stop to speculate further. Jumping out of bed, she caught up her white silk wrapper, threw it around herself and hurried from the room. Chloe's chamber was farther along the same corridor, just beyond the place where it veered into the west wing. As Julia rounded the bend, a spluttering candle in hand, she had to fight an impulse to clap her hands to her ears to block out the shrill echoing shrieks. A score of servants in their nightclothes were before her, she saw, gathered around the open doorway to Chloe's room. Elbowing her way to the front, she stopped short at the scene before her.

Chloe, silver-gilt hair in childish plaits that tumbled over the front of her prim, flower-print nightgown, was backed into the far corner of her room. Her face was as ghostly white as the finest English china, and her hands were held out in front of her as if to ward something off. Ceaseless piercing screams poured one on top of the other from her throat despite the frantic shushing of Miss Belkerson, who was trying without success to comfort the child, and Mrs. Johnson, who was hovering uselessly on Chloe's other side. Chloe's blue eyes were as saucer-wide as her mouth, and fixed with an expression of abject terror on Sebastian, who stood towering over her, his face as white as hers.

"Please, Miss Chloe, please. . . ." Miss Belkerson was muttering disjointedly, her eyes darting with agonized entreaty from Chloe to Sebastian and back again.

Mrs. Johnson was made of sterner stuff. Pointing the candle she carried at Sebastian, she said, "if you'll leave us, my lord, I'm sure Miss Belkerson will get her quieted down. I'm sorry to have to say it, and you can dismiss me for it if you wish, but you should never have come in here, not even if the little lass was sleeping. Now you've likely scared her out of what little wits she has left. It was not well done of you, my lord, if you'll pardon me for saying so."

Miss Belkerson, looking distraught as she tried to push down Chloe's outstretched arms, nodded once as if in agreement, then caught herself and cast another frightened glance up at Sebastian. He stood as white and motionless as if he had been carved from stone. Suddenly he pivoted, moving like a man just awakened from a nightmare, and walked from the room.

As soon as he was out of Chloe's sight the screams lessened in intensity. Julia, hand pressed to her mouth, watched as Chloe subsided into a sobbing heap in Miss Belkerson's arms. Poor child, poor child. . . . But poor Sebastian, too. He had looked as if he had suffered a death blow. Something was terribly wrong between him and his daughter, but whatever it was, he deserved compassion, too. She turned suddenly, lifting the skirts of her wrapper and nightgown, and practically flew from the room. She did not want him to be alone after this.

"Sebastian." She caught up to him at last in the great hall, and reached for his shirt-clad arm. He turned on her with such an expression of fury that she shrank back.

"Are you satisfied now?" he demanded savagely. "I told you to keep your nose out of things you know nothing about, but you just had to stick it in, didn't you? Do you see now why I avoid my daughter? The merest sight of me terrifies her into a screaming frenzy!"

He bit off the last words with such anger that Julia took another step backwards. He noted her retreat, acknowledged it with a bitter, sardonic smile, and turned his back on her without another word. Watching him as he strode away, Julia knew that she had to go after him, to offer what comfort she could. Whatever he was, whatever he had done, to her he was still Sebastian, her Sebastian. She owed him her loyalty if nothing else.

"The master's in a bad way, Miss Julia." Johnson had appeared in the hall behind her in time to hear that last savage exchange and had also been present in the gathering of servants outside Chloe's room.

"I know, Johnson." Julia smiled briefly, abstractedly, at the butler's concerned face. Taking her courage in her hands, she turned to follow Sebastian to his last refuge, the library.

XV

AUSING momentarily at the closed door, she took a deep breath and entered without knocking. The fire that was lit against the increasingly chill nights provided the only light in the room, and it had died down to a few smoldering embers. By the faint orange glow she could see him standing with his back to her, head thrown back as he drained the contents of a glass. He immediately poured out more brandy, and cursed as the bottle ran dry before the glass was full.

"Shall I have Johnson bring more brandy?" Julia spoke quietly as she closed the door behind her. He swung around snarling, his hand clenched around the glass as if he were thinking about hurling it at her head.

"Get out of here."

"Sebastian, I'm sorry. I didn't understand." She stayed near the door, unmoving, trying to read his expression through the shifting shadows.

"You still don't understand. It's not your business to understand. So get the hell out of here and leave me alone. I wish you'd done it in the first place."

He turned away from her, lifting the glass to his lips and tossing back the contents in a single gulp. He moved jerkily to one of the two big wing chairs facing the fire and sat down in it, his long legs sprawling out before him.

"Ring for more brandy. Then go." His voice was scarcely more than a rough murmur as he stared into the fire. Julia hesitated, then crossed to the bell pull. When Johnson tapped discreetly on the door, she opened it and sent him for more brandy. But when he left, she stayed, hovering near the door so that Sebastian would not remember her presence and order her to leave again. When Johnson reappeared with the brandy and two glasses she took the tray from him with a brief reassuring nod in answer to his anxious look. Sebastian might not know or care, but despite his usual autocratic manner the servants were fond of him.

Julia carried the tray to a small table near Sebastian's elbow, and he roused himself enough to look at her as she poured out a glass for him. From the wild red-rimmed glitter of his eyes and his uncoordinated movements, Sebastian had already had far too much to drink. She didn't know how well he held his liquor, but she had seen enough men drinking to know that shortly he would be extremely well to live indeed.

"I thought I told you to go away." He sounded more tired than angry now.

"Yes, you did. Here, take this." She handed him the glass, then poured a half measure into the other glass. With the bottle in one hand and the half-full glass in the other, she sank to her knees beside his chair, curling her legs up beneath her.

"You drinking too?" A sideways glance took in her half-full glass. "Planning on keeping me company, are you? I assure you, I'll do much better alone."

He took a long swallow from his glass, and then another, then returned his attention to the fire. Julia, watching him, felt her heart swell with pity. He looked so—so alone. She moved a little so that her shoulder was just touching the long hard stretch of his thigh. He needed someone now very much, she thought.

"Softhearted little thing, aren't you?" He must have felt her unspoken sympathy because his eyes veered toward her with an ugly sneer in their depths. "First Timothy, now me. Why don't you go find some stray kittens or something to waste your sympathy on?"

Julia looked up at him, guessing that he was lashing out at her because of his own desperate pain, and not knowing how to respond. He needed to talk, she knew, needed to pour out the hurt festering inside like pus in a wound. But she did not know the words to touch the place where he had held it so long buried. Anything she said was liable to turn him once again into a raging, mindless beast.

"Damn it, quit looking at me like I'm some dumb, hurt animal." His sudden snarl made her jump. Her eyes had been fixed on his face, she realized, and hastily she dropped them to the fire. She could feel his hostile gaze on her averted cheek. After a moment she looked back at him, helplessly drawn.

"Sebastian, you need to talk about whatever it is that's wrong with Chloe." She didn't know how else to say it, and hoped her gentle tone would blunt the sharp edge of his anger.

He said nothing for a long moment while she looked up at him with huge golden eyes, her black hair loose and cascading down over the thin white silk of her wrapper. In the soft glow of the dying fire he looked more devil than angel, she thought.

"So you think I need to talk, do you?" The words were drawled in a gritty undertone quite unlike anything she had ever heard from him. A hard smile played about his mouth, twisting the elegantly carved lips into a satyr's grimace before disappearing to leave them grimly straight. "Talk's not what I need." He laughed, the sound harsh. His eyes glittered with a strange hot light as they moved over her.

Julia felt her heartbeat quicken as his eyes touched on her body, which he must know was naked beneath the flimsy covering of her nightclothes. If any other man had looked at her like that, she would have been frightened. But despite everything, she was not afraid of Sebastian.

"Tell me about Chloe, Sebastian." Her quiet voice brought his eyes up from their insulting appraisal of her bosom as it swelled against the thin silk wrapper. He stared at her for a moment, his expression ugly.

"I'm tired of talking," he said in a thick gutteral voice. Then before she had any inkling of his intention, he let his glass fall with a dull thud and slosh of splashing brandy and reached for her. Her own glass fell too as his hands closed over her upper arms, dragging her up so that she was half-lying across his lap.

"Sebastian!" Shocked by the unexpectedness of his action, her eyes were huge golden pools staring up into the narrowed, glittering slits of his. His face was flushed with drink and something else. His mouth was twisted into a sneering half-smile. A vein pumped visibly just above the open collar of his shirt, and his hands were vice-tight on her arms.

"You're hurting me," she whispered, wincing with pain as his fingers tightened until they were digging deep into her soft flesh. He smiled, a tigerish smile that made her eyes widen. This was not Sebastian, not her Sebastian. This was a violent, brutal stranger.

"Good. I want to hurt you."

The gutteral mutter was not his voice. Julia writhed, trying to pull her arms free of his paralyzing grip. Suddenly this man was frightening her. The icy mask was gone, shattered into a thousand pieces. In its place was a tortured, twisted mortal man in pain himself and capable of inflicting pain.

"I'll enjoy hurting you." And then he dragged her up so that her head was pressed back against the crimson velvet squab of the chair. She was sitting on his lap, her legs bared to the knees by nightclothes that twisted across them, her eyes huge as he stared into them with that travesty of a smile twisting his lips. Staring helplessly back into those icy blue depths she thought she knew how the victim of a cobra must feel: mesmerized, incapable of any kind of movement. Although her legs were free, it never occurred to her to kick him; although she could have struggled and fought and screamed, that never occurred to her either. She just lay back against the velvet chair and returned him look for look with a kind of dreamlike fascination while he grew hard and heavy beneath her and his breathing quickened.

"Don't, Sebastian." Her voice was a husky, pleading murmur. It was the only protest she made as he leaned toward her, his eyes fixed on hers as his lips sought her mouth. A twisted grimace of a smile was his only response, and then his lips were on hers, not harshly, as she had expected, but soft, the merest whisper of a caress against her own. His mouth felt so warm, so right. At its touch a hot rush of feeling shot through her veins, and she moaned suddenly as all the exquisite memories of the last time he had kissed her came flooding back. Her eyes closed, and her arms came up to twine around his neck with the strength of the damned.

"Julia," she heard him mutter, but she was beyond speech herself, beyond anything but this molten spiraling urgency to kiss and touch and caress.

His mouth opened over hers, his tongue tracing the outline of her lips before urgently demanding entrance. She opened her mouth for him, opened it wide and welcomed him, driven by a need so fierce that she was shaking with it. She could never have enough . . . His mouth was hot and hard and hungry as it took hers with an urgency that had her mewling tiny sounds of ecstasy. His hands were moving over her, as hot and hard as his mouth, touching her in places where she had never been touched, lingering over her breasts until her nipples ached with tension and she cried out and arched her back. His hands roamed further, molding her waist and thighs and the secret feminine nest where her legs joined.

She was on fire for him, incapable of speech or thought or anything but this hot liquid feeling, melting in his arms, his to do with as he pleased. Somehow they slid from the chair to the floor and she was lying on her back on the rug, the scent of spilt brandy and man heady in her nostrils, the shadowy beauty of him looming over her as he bared her body by pulling her nightclothes up to form a bunchy twisted line above her breasts, which ached and throbbed with need. His hands found the soft swelling shapes, cupping their pale roundness while his fingers stroked over the pebble-hardness of her nipples. Julia thought she would die with the pleasure-pain of it.

And still he was kissing her. Ravenous kisses that made her head spin and her senses reel, fiery kisses that awakened in her an answering fire, wonderful kisses, magical kisses, making her feel things she had never imagined she could feel.

He was lying on her now, heavy and solid, crushing her into the carpet so that she could almost feel each separate fiber as it imprinted itself into her spine. The smooth texture of his buckskins chafed at her legs, while the linen of his shirt was rough against her breasts and his buttons cut into her soft skin. She clutched his back, nails digging into the solid flesh beneath the shirt, reveling in the strength of his muscles. And then suddenly it occurred to her to want to feel his skin against hers.

She moaned, tugging at his shirt until it came free of his trousers and then burrowing her hands up beneath the soft linen to touch his flesh. Smooth, hot flesh over rippling muscles, slick with sweat. She ran her hands up over his back to his shoulder blades, nails lightly scoring his skin, her breath coming in fast little pants as he took her mouth.

"Christ."

She barely heard the word, muttered as he shifted, doing something with his clothes. Moaning, she pulled him back to feel something hard and hot and naked pulsing against her thigh. His mouth claimed hers once again in a swift searing kiss, and then his head was moving lower, tracing a path across her face to her neck and then over the soft rise of an arching breast. He took the nipple in his mouth and she gasped. It was like nothing she had ever felt before, wonderful, marvelous, trailers of fire shooting down into her belly and thighs. He suckled her like a babe and she responded with soft little cries, her fingers on the back of his head, reveling in the soft silkiness of his hair as she pressed his face to her. His hands were moving too, stroking over her belly and the tops of her thighs before finding their way to the thick nest of black curls and stroking there too. She stiffened as he first touched her there, but his hard fingers were gentle as they slid between her legs, leaving liquid fire wherever they touched.

"Sebastian, oh, Sebastian." She was moaning his name without even being aware she did so as he did the most unbelievable things to her with his fingers, touching her in ways she had never dreamt of, rubbing and caressing and holding her until her legs spread wide for him and she was writhing with pleasure. When finally she felt one finger work its way inside her, she could stand it no more. She cried out, stiffening, arching, and then he was groaning as his finger was removed and replaced with that hot naked male part of him that had been pressed so tightly against her thigh.

He thrust himself inside her, forcing himself in, pushing so that she feared she must split in two, and she didn't care. She clung to him, head thrown back, eyes closed, as he possessed her, slowly at first, and then as she arched mindlessly against him harder and faster, his hands gripping her bottom as he held her still for his taking. She cried out at last, sobbing, her nails raking fiercely over his back as he thrust into her again and again, hurting her, but at the same time filling her with a fiery ecstasy that made the pain a small price to pay. She heard the hoarse gasp of his breathing, and answered it with her own. She felt his sweat drip onto her body to sizzle at the heat of her bare skin. She tasted the salt tang of his skin, smelled the musky scent of man, saw the gleam of taut, sweating back muscles as they flexed in the firelight. Then he was moving faster and faster, harder and harder, taking her with him, forcing her to writhe and cling and cry out as she tried to escape this fiery torment.

"Sebastian!" She moaned his name again as her hands slid down over his back to clutch at his steel-muscled buttocks. He cried out as she dug her nails into his hard flesh, and then drove into her with a force that sent her whirling, lost in a haze of smoke and fire and darkness. She felt him stiffen, shuddering, and then a cataclysmic ecstasy seized her and spun her away into a dark mindless void.

X V I

A long time later, Julia's eyes fluttered open to the sound of stertorous snoring. First she blinked groggily. Then she became aware of a crushing weight sprawled across her, bearing her down into the carpet. Finally she grew conscious of several things at once: first, she was naked from just below the shoulders down; second, the snoring dead weight was Sebastian, and from the ear shattering quality of his breathing he was fathoms deep asleep; and third, she had just become his woman in the most primitive sense. Remembering what he had done to her and how it had made her feel, she felt fiery red color steal into her cheeks. Moving carefully so as not to waken him, she lifted her hand to touch his hair. That beautiful silver-gilt hair . . .

There was a soreness between her thighs, and the sensitive skin of her breasts tingled and ached. She had given up without a murmur of protest the prize she had always defended so valiantly in the face of such overwhelming odds. Remembering Mick, Willy Tilden, and the others before them who had wanted to do the man-woman thing with her, and remembering the way she had kicked and bit and fought to keep them off her when the occasion warranted it, she was amazed as she realized that she hadn't even tried to defend herself against Sebastian. She could have fought him off, if she would have. Probably she would have needed to do no more than icily demand to be unhanded. Instead she had responded with a fierce ardor that had made the prize of her virginity merely an obstacle to be gotten out of the way.

Her body quivered even now as she remembered how he had kissed her, and touched and caressed and possessed her—Sebastian! Her own Sebastian, the most beautiful man she had ever seen in her life, who had once been as far above her touch as the stars, had made her his. For the first time in her life she belonged to someone, and what a someone: Sebastian.

His snores assaulted her ears, and she smiled, her hand coming up again to stroke the bright hair. What had happened had been unbelievable, both in the act itself and in how it had made her feel, but she did not regret it. No, she did not regret it in the least. Not with Sebastian.

Now she was his woman, and he would belong to her forever and ever. Would he marry her? Her mouth curved with amusement as she tried to imagine herself as the Countess of Moorland. Little Jewel Combs a countess? No, she corrected herself fiercely, not Jewel Combs, never Jewel Combs. The eighth Earl of Moorland could never marry Jewel Combs. But Julia Stratham—now that was a different person altogether. She was suddenly fiercely glad for the lessons and training that had made her a lady. For Sebastian. Her lips twitched suddenly as she considered how Sebastian had drummed one boring bit of knowledge after another into her head. The whole time he had been making her worthy of him, and he hadn't even known it. But now, as he had said himself, Julia Stratham was a very lovely lady indeed, and a fit mate to spend life at his side.

Gradually she noticed that the fire had died to a heap of glowing ashes. The parts of her body that were not covered by his were cold, and all of her was uncomfortable. Her back ached and her legs were falling asleep and her neck was stretched into the most awkward position imaginable to accommodate his bright head wedged into the curve between neck and shoulder. She was glad she had awakened first, glad that she had had those few moments to get her thoughts in order. But now it was time for him to awaken too. Those blue eyes would open and meet hers and he would smile—what would he say? Julia suddenly blushed. She felt deliciously shy and uncertain, like a bashful child.

"Sebastian." Tentatively she nudged the hard-muscled arm that sprawled across her middle. He was still wearing his shirt, and she had to fight an urge to run her hand over the linen covered muscle. Remembering the feel of those muscles, she blushed again. Becoming one with a man, this man, had been like nothing she had ever imagined. The mere memory was enough to take her breath away.

He didn't move, didn't by so much as a gasp or a twitch acknowledge her. Julia tried again, nudging him harder this time. When that didn't work, she caught hold of the shoulder nearest her and gave it a good shake. The steady snores continued unabated, and Julia remembered the amount of brandy he had consumed. He had been the next thing to foxed. . . . He would probably sleep for hours, and nothing she did was going to wake him up. Just as well, she decided after a moment. She must look a mess with her clothing twisted about her body and her hair mussed into a mass of tangles that straggled down to her waist. When he saw her next, she wanted to be beautiful, and every inch a lady. Picturing how he would see her if he awoke now suddenly horrified her.

Getting out from under him was quite a trick, but by dint of much wriggling and shoving she managed it. When she was on her feet at last, tugging her clothes down and smoothing them, he lay on his back on the floor, eyes closed and mouth slightly open as he snored with abandon. Even like that, when most men would have looked at best slightly repulsive and at worst obscene, *he* was beautiful. The silver-gilt hair was wildly disordered, but disorder became him. The shadow of a surprisingly dark stubble had appeared to darken his cheeks and chin, but that became him, too. He was still fully dressed, she discovered, even to his boots. But his shirt was twisted around his waist so that an inch or two of pale skin stretched taut over ridged muscle was visible. She was fascinated to see a faint line of dark gold hairs trail downwards. His pantaloons were unbuttoned. As Julia absorbed that fact and its import, she felt hot color wash up over her neck and quickly averted her eyes. Even after having been so intimate with him, she was still ignorant of his body and its functions. She supposed that she would soon learn, just as she had learned everything else about being a lady. Sebastian's lady.

She hated to leave him to spend the night on the floor, but there was no way she was going to be able to shift him by herself. And she blushed again at the very thought of asking Johnson or Leister to come and put their master to bed. They would guess what had happened at a glance.

A light rug had been left folded on the back of one of the chairs to ward off the occasional chill, and Julia compromised by spreading that over him. There were no pillows that she could see, but the coat he had discarded earlier was thrown casually over yet another chair. Catching the garment up, she held it in her hands for a moment and pictured it covering broad shoulders and muscular arms. Then she folded it with scant regard for the delicate fabric and placed it beneath his head. He snored on without so much as the flicker of a surprisingly long eyelash as she positioned his head on the makeshift pillow. Julia stood up, looking down at him for a long moment with a faint smile on her face. When she had first made the acquaintance of the elegant, arrogant Earl of Moorland, she had never in the furthest reaches of her imagination dreamed that in the course of a few short months she would see him like this.

Still smiling, she blew him a kiss and let herself out of the room. Already she was tingling in anticipation of the morrow; she would be Sebastian's love as well as his friend. . . .

She woke late the next morning. The sun was shining through the open curtains, which Julia knew meant that Emily had been in the room. She stretched luxuriously against the pillows, glad to be alone. She felt marvelously, wonderfully alive. Even the faint ache between her thighs felt good to her. Because of Sebastian. It was proof that she belonged to Sebastian.

A creak of the door hinges heralded Emily's return. Julia sat up in bed, shaking her head to clear the last traces of sleep from it, and smiled at her maid.

"Good morning, Miss Julia," Emily said composedly as she saw that her mistress was awake at last. "Shall I bring your chocolate now?"

"Yes, please, Emily. Oh, and I'd like a bath this morning, please." Julia was already climbing out of bed and crossing to the window to look out at the sun sparkling off the thin crust of frost that had covered the ground during the night. It was the first frost of the season, and it made her faintly sad to see it. Already summer was over, and fall was here.

Pulling the folds of the wrapper closer about her (not the one she had worn the night before) she turned back into the room to find that Emily had disappeared again. When the girl returned moments later with her breakfast of chocolate and rolls, Julia was surprised to find herself ravenous. Because of all the unaccustomed exercise of the night before, she thought with an inward giggle, and fell upon the meal with relish.

The bath was readied while she ate. She dismissed Emily for the first time in months, finding that she was newly shy about anyone seeing her nakedness after the events of the night. Sebastian, in making her body his, had changed it into something entirely new, something that she was not even totally familiar with herself. Besides, her native practicality warned, there might be some mark upon her skin that would betray her new state. It felt as though there should be—she was full of aches in the most unexpected places, she discovered as she climbed into the tub and washed herself vigorously from head to toe. Rubbing the rose scented soap that she had come to love into her hair, wanting the strands to be shining and sweet smelling for Sebastian, she hummed one of the gay little dance tunes that he had taught her, pausing from time to time to smile tenderly as she recalled dancing in his arms. If she had known then how wonderful it would feel to be utterly his, they would never have gotten any dancing done at all. The idea set her to giggling again. She giggled and blushed and soaped her arms and legs and wondered how he would like the scent of roses. At the idea that she would certainly find out, she blushed and dreamed some more.

Last night she had washed the physical signs from her body in the cold water left in the washstand before she had gone to bed. At the first sight of her virgin's blood staining her legs and her clothes, she had been a little dismayed. Had he hurt her in some way? But after a life spent in the gutters of London, there was little she had not been exposed to. She had seen young girls sold to old madames to be used for the pleasure of men, and wondered at the high prices they brought until it was crudely explained to her that they were new merchandise and thus highly valued by clients. So Julia knew about virgins and virginity, and after a brief moment's pause had sponged the blood away without fearing she was injured or dying as so many young girls did. She had put on a fresh nightgown and hidden the ruined nightgown and wrapper, then climbed into bed to think dreamily of Sebastian until at last she fell asleep.

Her bath water having grown cold, Julia returned her thoughts to practical matters and stepped out of the tub.

Wrapping her hair and her body in towels, she padded to the wardrobe. Today she would choose what she would wear, something that would make her look her most beautiful for Sebastian.

"You look wonderful, miss," Emily said with sincerity some time later as she styled Julia's hair. Julia sat at her dressing table looking into the mirror.

"Thank you, Emily," she responded with real gratitude, and smiled at the maid through the glass.

In truth, she thought, looking at her reflection, she did look good. Emily had piled her black hair high on her head in an elegant style that bared the nape of her neck so that it looked impossibly long and slender. Her eyes sparkled like topazes beneath the silky black wings of her brows, and her matte white skin had just the faintest blush of color as it stretched over the high cheekbones that gave her face its unusual claim to beauty.

The months of good living she had enjoyed had changed her past all recognition, she decided, noting how straight and slender her nose was above full, well shaped lips that needed no crushed rose petals rubbed over them to provide their rich mauve color. Even the black dress became her. She had chosen one of elegant striped silk today, with leg-of-mutton sleeves and demure high neckline ornamented with a simple cameo (a gift from Sebastian) at the base of her throat. In the severe dress with its tight bodice and full skirt she looked the very picture of a lady. Julia smiled tentatively at herself in the mirror. It was hard to believe that the beautiful young woman who smiled back was herself.

"Can I get you anything else, Miss Julia?" Emily stood back to survey her handiwork with obvious pride. Julia took one final look in the mirror, then stood up.

"No, thank you, Emily, that will be all," she said.

Emily dropped her a quick curtsy before leaving the room. Julia, following more slowly, marvelled at how quickly she had become accustomed to being the mistress of servants, to giving orders and being waited on. But as she descended the stairs into the great hall, nervousness drove every other thought from her head. Soon she would see Sebastian. What would he say? At the memory of what they had done together, bright color crept into her cheeks, and her eyes sparkled. What could one say after a night like that? She didn't have the least idea, but she devoutly hoped Sebastian did.

"Good morning, Johnson." She greeted him with a beaming smile as she stepped down into the hall. Then, recalling the last time she had seen Johnson and realizing the suspicions he couldn't help but have after the way Sebastian must have been discovered this morning, she felt another rush of color to her cheeks. Her eyes quickly inspected Johnson's face. His answering smile was warm and held no hint that he had any inkling of how much her world had changed since she had last spoken with him.

"Good morning, Miss Julia. A very fine morning, if I may say so."

"You certainly may." Julia couldn't seem to repress her gaiety. Soon the whole world would know that she belonged to Sebastian. Even if there was no public announcement, she would not be able to keep the shining joy out of her eyes whenever she looked at him.

"Is his lordship about yet this morning?" No matter how carefully she phrased the question, Julia still found that her cheeks were pinkening again.

"He went riding, miss. He's been gone about two hours, so he should be back soon."

"Oh."

"If you don't need anything, Miss Julia, I'll be about my work now."

"Oh, yes. I mean, no, I don't need anything, Johnson."

The butler bowed and took himself off. Julia walked slowly down the length of the hall, chewing lightly at her lower lip. She had been all keyed up for her encounter with Sebastian, and it was something of an anticlimax to find that he had gone riding on this of all mornings. It was something he did nearly every day, but somehow she had expected that today would be different.

Reaching the end of the hall, she turned back toward the stairs. Vaguely she was aware of a footman and then a maid scurrying across her path as they went about their duties, but she hardly registered them. She would go crazy if she hung about the house waiting for Sebastian's return. She was much better off in the open air herself, with something active to do. She would go for a walk, and by the time she returned he would almost certainly be back.

Julia lifted a hand to the little maid who was busy polishing the oak banister, and the girl stopped what she was doing and came across to her, dropping a curtsy and looking nervous. Julia smiled to set her at ease, then sent her in search of Emily with instructions for Emily to bring her cloak. The maid hurried off, and in no time Julia was bundled up in the warm hooded cloak of tightly woven alpaca that Miss Soames had sent over as the weather grew colder.

It was cold out, the heather was crisp beneath the little kid boots that buttoned up to her ankles. Her breath hung in the air like puffs of white smoke, and her nose was soon chilled at the tip. She wandered around the topiary garden admiring the living sculptures of beasts. It took one gardner working full time to keep the shrubs so perfectly shaped, but Julia didn't see him around anywhere today. Her eyes lifted to the rooms that made up Chloe's suite, but there was no movement at the curtained windows. After the tumultuous events of the previous night, the child was very likely still asleep.

Julia wandered around the perimeter of the north wing of the house, a frown creasing her brow as she thought about Chloe. Obviously Sebastian terrified the child. But why? Last night Sebastian had still refused to discuss the subject. Julia's face lightened briefly as she considered what they had done instead. He had certainly managed to distract her from the subject, she thought with a quick smile. But not forever. She still wanted to talk to him about Chloe, and sooner or later she would.

A curricle was standing in front of the entry, Julia saw with surprise as she rounded the edge of the north wing so that she could see the front of the house. Did that mean visitors? She hated to think so. So much had to be said between her and Sebastian, visitors would be very much in the way. Besides, who knew if they would accept her? Julia felt suddenly very uncertain. As much as she now felt like a lady, who knew if she would pass muster with outsiders? Would she be scorned, or worse, secretly laughed at? During the months she had lived practically alone with Sebastian at White Friars, the thought of confronting the world in her new guise had seemed far away, and thus had not worried her. Now she was worried. Not so much for herself but for Sebastian. Desperately she wanted him not to be ashamed of her.

She moved toward the curricle, not sure whether to go inside and greet the guests or to slink away and return later. But she could not hide forever; besides, the very idea was ridiculous. She knew the proper thing to do was to go inside and be very composed but gracious. That was what Julia Stratham would do. And she was Julia Stratham.

Julia lifted her chin and was proceeding toward the front steps when something began to niggle at the back of her mind. That curricle looked extremely familiar. She looked again. It was black and shiny with overly large wheels and a natty leather interior. A matched pair of bays was harnessed to it, and the little man who stood at their heads looked very familiar indeed. Julia had not seen much of him since she had arrived at White Friars, but she had no trouble recognizing him. It was Jenkins.

The equipage was Sebastian's. She stared, then hurried toward it just as Leister came down the stairs with a large leather valise in hand and placed it in the curricle. A footman appeared on the steps, holding the door wide while another ran down to open the door of the curricle. The footman and the valet stood waiting as Sebastian himself appeared, clad in his buff colored, many caped driving coat that swung open over tan breeches and dark blue, elegantly tailored coat. From the toes of his polished boots to the waves of silver-gilt hair, this was very much the arrogant earl. Julia watched in disbelief as he descended the steps, Johnson trailing in his wake.

"Sebastian!" He was near the bottom step when she called out to him and hurried forward. All eyes swung toward her, from the celestial blue ones she had come to know so well to Johnson's worried ones. Julia didn't care if there was an audience of thousands. She picked up her skirts and practically ran the short distance to the foot of the stairs, where she stood looking up at Sebastian. Meeting his eyes, she was suddenly wordless.

"Good morning, Julia." His voice was cool, composed, as if she were a chance-met acquaintance in whom he had no real interest. She stared up at him, eyes widening with disbelief. Was it possible that he had forgotten the momentous thing that had occurred between them in the library the night before? He had after all been drinking heavily. She studied his expression for a clue, noting the way the cold white sunlight bathed his features in a harsh glow that revealed every tiny flaw. On him the tiny lines radiating from the corners of his eyes and the faint creases bracketing the perfectly carved mouth just added character. His eyes met hers, and their very lack of expression gave her the answer. He remembered perfectly well. If he hadn't, he would never have looked at her like that.

"Are you going somewhere, Sebastian?" Her voice was thin. Something was very wrong.

He resumed descending the steps until he stood beside her. Julia was once again surprised by how tall he was as she tilted her head back to look up at him. The hood of her cloak obscured her vision and she pushed it back without a care for the elegant hairstyle that she had admired with such pleasure less than an hour before.

"I am returning to London. I have business to attend to

there." His words were clipped. Julia was burningly conscious of the listening ears of the two footmen, the valet, and Johnson, who hovered discreetly some few steps above them, despite the servants' stony stares into the distance.

"When will you be back?" She hoped she didn't sound as anxious to his ears as she did to her own.

"When I finish my business." He slapped his gloves against his palm, looking as though he were eager to be on his way. Julia suddenly felt her temper begin to heat.

"You were going without a word to me?"

His eyebrows lifted. "I wasn't aware that I had to account to you for my movements."

Julia met those icy blue eyes, and at the coldness of them her heating temper boiled over.

"You bloody swine!" The words were quiet, meant for his ears alone, but she didn't much care if the servants did overhear. Sebastian's mouth tightened.

"If you will excuse me . . ."

"No, I bloody well won't excuse you!" Despite her months of practice, a distinct Cockney accent crept into her words as she hissed them at him. "Wot do you think I am, a bloody handkerchief that you can just use and throw away when it's dirty? Well, if I'm dirty, I wasn't that way before you made me so, and you know that's the truth!"

"Watch your mouth, Julia." The words, gritted from between clenched teeth, were meant as a warning because of the servants. But Julia was beyond caring, her breasts heaving with anger as he went on. "This is no place for a private discussion. My movements are not yours to order despite whatever mistaken claims you may think you now have on me."

"Oh, is that wot's worrying you, my lord? Are you afraid that the little guttersnipe might be makin' claims now, my lord? Well, you can set your mind at rest. Lord or no bloody lord, I wouldn't have you on a silver plate with an apple between your teeth!"

Julia was practically spitting in her fury. Sebastian's mouth tightened, his eyes took on a second layer of ice, and he made her an ironic little bow.

"You relieve my mind," he murmured before turning on his heel and boarding the curricle with a single fluid bound. Julia, her fists clenching and unclenching beneath the sheltering folds of the cloak, watched with growing rage as a pokerfaced Leister climbed up beside him, the footman shut the door, Jenkins released the horses' heads and leaped up behind, and the curricle began to move away down the drive.

"I've known high tobies that were bigger bleedin' gentlemen than you!" she screamed after the departing curricle.

But if Sebastian even heard, there was no sign of it as the curricle turned onto the road and bowled out of sight.

XVII

EBASTIAN was in a black mood by the time he arrived in Grosvenor Square. His disposition was not improved by the sight of every window in his house ablaze with lights, an unmistakable sign that there was some sort of revelry taking place on the premises.

Without a word to the servants, he jumped from the curricle, leaving Jenkins to drive it around to the stables. Stalking up the steps with Leister at his heels, he found to his annoyance that the door did not swing open at his approach. Scowling, he made a mental promise to have a serious talk with the malingering servant responsible for such a lapse, and let himself in.

Fortunately (although irresponsibly) the front door was unlocked, revealing immediately the reason for such malfeasance of duty on the part of his employees. From the snatches of gay conversation that drifted to him from the direction of the dining room, it was obvious that a dinner party was in progress. Smathers, apparently having been on service in the dining room and just now becoming aware of the new arrival, came hurrying to greet him, full of apologies for not being on hand to open the door to the master. It seemed that the dowager countess had required the services of himself and all the footmen in attendance in the dining room.

Sebastian favored him with a cold stare that Smathers, shivering, thought said more than most employers' longest tirade. With an impatient gesture he waved Smathers away, and stalked up the stairs to his bedchamber. Leister, with a fatalistic shrug at Smathers, followed.

Knowing well the signs of his master in a temper, Leister did not venture to speak until the earl was undressed and ensconced in a steaming tub with one of the thin brown cigars that he favored thrust between his teeth. Then Leister dared a thin "Shall I have your dinner sent up, sir?"

The icy blue eyes turned in his direction for a pregnant moment. In all the years he had been with his lordship, Leister had weathered many a black mood, but just lately he had gotten out of practice. In the past months spent at White Friars in the company of that girl his lordship had been almost cheerful, an unheard-of condition for him. In the ten years Leister had been in his service—since my lord had ascended to the exalted position of earl—he had occasionally been pleasant, but never, never cheerful. But apparently there had been some trouble with the waif, and his master was back to his usual stern self.

"I'll be eating at my club. You may lay out my evening clothes."

"Yes, sir." Leister jumped to do his master's bidding, hastily removing evening dress of a cutaway coat and breeches in severest black along with a black and gray striped waistcoat and snowy white linen from the wardrobe.

Then he hurried over to wrap his master in a large bathsheet as he arose dripping from the tub. The earl dried himself as was his preference, and then allowed Leister to assist him into his clothes. When his lordship's neckcloth was tied to his own satisfaction (never a very lengthy procedure as the earl was a master at it), Leister assisted him into his coat and stood back, admiring as he always did the handsome figure the earl cut.

"Don't wait up for me," the earl said over his shoulder to his valet as he left the room. Leister knew that meant his lordship probably wouldn't see his own bed that night.

Sebastian was walking down the stairs when the female members of the dinner party left the males to their port and filed out into the hallway on their way to the salon. He continued to descend, making an idle survey of the company. He was in a mood for female company tonight, but none of these presently under his roof seemed at all promising. His mother was present, of course, in one of the black dresses she had affected since Edward's death seven years before. At her side was Caroline, the supposedly still grieving widow, in an ice blue satin gown that made her look younger than what he knew was her twenty-nine years. Besides those two, there were four more. He knew them all, if somewhat vaguely. Lady Curran, a plump dowdy dowager of about his mother's age, was one of the ton's highest sticklers and a great disapprover of him. Her daughter, Lady Courtland, was making a push to one day soon be as plump as her mother. The other two ladies he was less familiar with, but one was obviously a debutante in her first season, and the other was just as obviously her mother. He searched his memory, and from somewhere the name Sinclair popped up. He wasn't sure if it belonged to them, but it didn't matter either way.

He continued his descent in leisurely fashion, and as the ladies came around the stairway Caroline looked up and saw him.

"Sebastian!" Her greeting was one of restrained pleasure, and her pale blue eyes glowed suddenly as they met his.

Sebastian had known for a long time that his sister-in-law cherished a fantasy that she would one day be Lady Moorland through him instead of his brother as she had originally expected. The idea was foolish, of course, because she was his brother's widow and therefore proscribed from him by law unless granted a special dispensation. Which he supposed would not be that difficult to obtain, if he should ever wish to, but he did not anticipate that he ever would. He had no fondness for Caroline, who did not attract him in the least, and was vain and silly besides, but he bore no enmity toward her. He did not wish to embarrass her in front of her guests. Therefore he smiled slightly despite his dark mood, said "Good evening, Caroline, mother, ladies," in a civil fashion, and descended to stand amongst them.

"You should have apprised us of your return, Sebastian," his mother said, her cold blue eyes resting on him with distaste. "But, of course, we quite understand you could not be expected to trouble yourself about our convenience."

"No, I really could not," Sebastian agreed tranquilly and bowed, meaning to leave the ladies to their evening. But Caroline caught his arm, babbling in a desperate attempt to salvage the situation.

"Of course you know Lady Curran, and her daughter, Lady Courtland," Caroline was saying. "And this is Lady Sinclair and her daughter, the Honorable Miss Lucy Sinclair."

Lady Curran was regarding him with hostility, her head drawn up so that she was as near to looking down her nose at him as was possible, given he was nearly a foot taller than she. Sebastian, remembering that she had also been a dear friend of his dead wife's father, met her cold stare with an icy one of his own. The lady's obvious disapproval annoyed rather than enraged him, but lumped on top of Lady Sinclair's grasping of her daughter's arm to hold her back from him like he was the devil incarnate, and the irritating presence of his mother, to say nothing of his original foul mood, it was enough to bring a warning glitter to his eyes.

"Ah yes, Lady Curran," he said with icy sweetness. "You must forgive me. I had no idea! Of course your fame precedes you. It was you, wasn't it, who was the victim of that unfortunate carriage accident just outside Lord Childress' hunting box all those years ago when it rained so hard that it was not fit out for man or beast? Yes, I do remember now. I believe the weather, uh, trapped you there with him for the night?"

The lady's eyes grew wider and wider as she listened to this speech, and by the time Sebastian stopped to look at her with lifted brows she was practically spluttering in her haste to deny such a socially ruinous accusation.

"No, my lord, it was not all night!"

"Sebastian," moaned Caroline, flushing, while his mother regarded him with stony eyes. The other ladies looked at him with as much horror as if he were a poisonous snake.

"I beg your pardon if I was mistaken," he said with mock contrition. "I should have known better. It is both unwise and ill-bred to go around spreading rumors without ascertaining their truth, is it not?"

Lady Curran, who had with great relish been spreading rumors about Sebastian having murdered his wife for some years now, flushed an alarming shade of puce. The other ladies looked discomfited, and young Miss Sinclair clung closer than ever to her mother. Sebastian bent a deliberately lascivious look on that young lady's too plump bosom, and ended with a wolfish smile directed into her frightened eyes. As the girl turned red and her mother gasped, Sebastian bowed again, murmured that it had been a great pleasure, and turned on his heel. This time no one tried to stop him as he left.

Sebastian was scowling as his closed carriage bowled over the cobbled streets. God, how he despised women! Hell born bitches, the lot of them. From the fat matrons who were only too ready to believe evil of him to the still attractive married women who were very obviously all too ready to grace his bed while pretending to eschew his company in public to the plump little girls who thought his only desire in life was to ravish them. He grimaced. The women he had known intimately weren't any better. His mother was a rapacious, bitter woman whose limited capacity for love had been expended on her elder son. Caroline was an empty-headed widgeon with an eye on the main chance. Elizabeth—Elizabeth had been a sweet innocent girl who had been horrified to learn what was expected of her as a wife. She had cringed and wept on their wedding night, but had also been horrified to discover that he was unfaithful to her. Even Suzanne, the latest in his string of mistresses, was far fonder of his pocketbook than himself. Not that it bothered him really. Such was the way of the world.

Sitting upright and scowling ferociously, he realized he still was not able to banish the face of the one female that he despised more than all the others. That thick, lustrous black hair, those eyes as golden as a lioness', those lips as full and soft and luscious as a new rose—all of it swirled together in one haunting image of Julia.

He smiled savagely to himself. Like Frankenstein with his monster he had given life to the creature that plagued him. The scrawny, dirty, common little guttersnipe who had forced herself into his household all those months ago had not attracted him in the least. She had been a mere plaything to him, something to momentarily alleviate the boredom of his joyless existence. He would have almost instantly forgotten her if she would have let him. If she had been a meek, grateful little chit, quietly accepting food and shelter and education, he doubted that he would have ever been more than peripherally aware of her existence. But Julia was never any of that. From that first ridiculous scene in the front hall, he should have been warned. No properly humble member of the lower classes would have dared to conduct herself so in an earl's establishment. In fact, now that he thought about it, it was amazing that she had even gotten in. No one else that he knew of had ever managed to get past Smathers if Smathers wished to keep them out. Even lords and ladies of the realm bowed to the dictates of the Peyton family butler.

He should have taken warning, but he hadn't. She had forced herself on his notice; his lips twitched even now as he remembered her scratching at that awful dress, and how she had topped off that highly novel journey by expurgating the contents of her stomach on his boots! And he had let her. Perhaps he was just bored, or perhaps even he, the evil earl, as he had heard himself described, was simply lonely.

She had amused him at first, and then he had found himself intrigued by her keen intelligence—amazing in one of the lower classes!—and burgeoning beauty. He never would have guessed that first night what effect good food and a little soap and water would have. So swiftly that it had stunned him when he first noticed it, the grubby guttersnipe had turned into a regular little beauty. He had decided to take advantage of that beauty to while away a few weeks of boredom while he attended to business at White Friars. Only the chit had been too damned trusting, consuming all the wine he had pressed on her the night he had meant to seduce her, making herself too drunk for the actual seduction. Evil earl or no, even he drew the line at bedding a sixteen-year-old chit who was so drunk she couldn't even sit up.

So, furious at the evening's unexpected ending, he had carried her up to bed and in the process been struck by how lovely she really was, and how ready she was to like and even trust him. It had made him feel like a cad for what he had intended, but it had also touched some deep chord within himself that must, he decided with some irony, be hungry for affection. Starved was more the right word, if the thought of a reformed guttersnipe nurturing a fondness for him was enough to dissuade him from his evil designs on her person. But whatever the explanation, he had strictly censored himself from that night on, treating her in an avuncular manner that had amazed himself, and would certainly have flabbergasted any of his cronies or former mistresses had they seen him.

His mouth twisted. What made it all so ridiculous was that she had been chasing him the whole time. He had grown to like her, really like her, which was novel in his relationships with females. It had been a bitter blow to discover that she was no better than all the rest. If he hadn't gotten so blind drunk and so furious at her, he would in all likelihood still be at White Friars, growing fonder of her by the day. In a way, he was grateful she had taken to heaping coals of guilt on his head about Chloe. Otherwise, he would never have gone to see Chloe in her room, knowing he only aggravated her illness. He never would have gotten so damn drunk afterwards, and he never would have seen his creation in her true colors. She was a round heeled little whore, as he had expected from the first, succumbing to him without even the first hint of reluctance.

But in that she had made a huge miscalculation. Possibly she had believed him too drunk to know the difference, possibly she had tossed away her virginity so long ago that she had forgotten how virgins react to a man's animalistic advances, or possibly she was so used to a man using her body that she was starved for it by the time he had finally got around to trying his luck. That night in the music room should have warned him. She had been eager then, too, responding to his compliments and caresses like a kitten wanting to be stroked. In the library she could have easily stopped him with a slap, or even a strong "no!" He had not been so far gone that he would have raped her. But she had been eager, so eager that he had known immediately that this was nothing new to her. And then he had wanted her too badly to stop himself.

He thought of her standing on the steps at White Friars with her hooded cloak clutched about her, her golden eyes huge and falsely innocent as she stared up at him as if she were the injured party. He had wanted to put his hands around that soft slender neck and wring it. He got some little satisfaction from hearing her slip back into her gutter-snipe's cant for the first time in months. Like the mask of her innocence, the mask of her gentility was only a thin veneer hiding what she really was.

She was a lying little whore, and he was lucky he had found out that truth before he had committed the monumental folly of growing fonder of her than he should. Even as he told himself that, Sebastian became aware of an aching sensation in the pit of his stomach. He had enjoyed her company—and her body. His memory of taking it was so strangely clear . . . and it had been perfect. He felt his groin tighten just thinking about her creamy white, full breasts and tiny waist, and he swore savagely.

He would forget all that soon enough. He had not visited Suzanne in months, but he was paying for her house, her clothes, her carriage, and even the food she put in her mouth. He would visit her now, and slake the memory of that golden-eyed little bitch with the same cure that proved so effective with a hangover: the hair of the dog that had bit him.

The carriage rocked to a stop, and his outrider jumped down to open the door and let down the steps. Sebastian saw the brightly lit facade of White's, and scowled.

"I've changed my mind," he growled, glaring at the hapless servant, and gave the man the address of Suzanne's snug little house in Lisle Street.

XVIII

HE remainder of that fall passed uneventfully for Julia. After the first few weeks, when it became obvious that Sebastian had no intention of returning and explaining his actions, she clamped the lid down on her temper and refused to think of him at all. He had made her love him, taken her virginity, and then cruelly discarded her. If she thought about it, it made her furious; it also made her want to cry. So she resolutely refused to think about it.

If she was lonely without Sebastian, she told herself, no one had ever died from loneliness. She lived a pampered life in a warm house with plenty of food to eat and an army of servants to see to her every wish. She had spent her childhood dreaming she might one day live this way. When she had pictured heaven with its pearly gates and streets of solid gold, it hadn't been half so nice. She was determined to enjoy what she had, and not pine for what she didn't. In truth, what—or, more properly, who—she didn't have was not worth pining for.

She kept up with her reading, and before long had gone through nearly a quarter of Sebastian's considerable library. Shamed by her lapse into street cant on the day Sebastian had left, she practiced her speech as well, reading aloud in the library until the well-bred accent was second nature to her. Finally, she grew confident that she could hold her own conversationally in both manner of speech and subject in any company, however exalted. Mrs. Johnson, whom she had come to consider a friend, would frequently invite her to the cozy housekeeper's room to share some tea, and insights into some of the little social niceties she had picked up from a lifetime of observing the aristocracy in action.

Julia took long walks almost daily. She loved tramping over the heath in all its moods. When a light drizzle was falling, the scent of wild lavender was lovelier to her nostrils than any perfume. When the sun shone, the rolling acres of bracken seemed to sparkle and beckon. If the air was nippy, she loved the crispness of the heath beneath her feet. The activities of rabbits, birds, and chipmunks as they prepared for winter fascinated her city-bred soul. Sometimes she would sit for hours at a time on a small hill, her cloak wrapped tightly around her as she watched the comings and goings of its furry inhabitants. At other times she would perch on the banks of a stream and watch for the flashing bodies of fish or the occasional predatory bird who flew in low, looking for them.

Sebastian had only been gone a week when she first felt she was being followed on her walks. The idea of it frightened her, as she knew both Elizabeth and Sebastian's older brother Edward had been killed in these seemingly peaceful surroundings. It was on a bright September morning and Julia was not too far from the old monastery, which she had never visited again after that once. She was sitting in a little hollow watching the antics of a pair of ground squirrels who were frolicking in and around a rotting log. The roar of the Wash was a pleasantly muted accompaniment, and the air was clean and crisp as she breathed it in.

Suddenly she had looked around, certain for no reason except that she was, that someone was behind her. She saw no one, but still she could not shake the feeling that she was not alone. Immediately her overactive imagination pictured a pale gentle ghost, which just as immediately she dismissed as ridiculous. Still, she demanded sharply to know who was there. When there was no answer, and since she could see for quite some way in every direction and knew that she must be truly alone, she tried to settle back down to watching the squirrels. But they had fled, and she had no other reason to linger. She had gone straight home, but she could not shake the feeling that something, or someone, was following her the whole way. Although she kept looking uneasily over her shoulder, she saw nothing but rolling miles of deserted heath.

The next time she had felt she was being watched, she was closer to home. In fact, she was just beyond the topiary garden, where anyone could easily have been hiding behind one of the tall shrubs. She searched, but was unable to discover anyone that time either. She felt more uneasy than ever as she returned to the house.

Gradually, though, she stopped being bothered by the sensation of being watched and followed. She felt it frequently, but she could never see anyone and never came to any harm. After a while she was able to cast a single casual look over her shoulder, and go on with what she was doing with scarcely more than a shrug. If it was indeed a spirit, of Elizabeth or anyone else, she preferred to think of it as friendly. And if it was simply her overactive imagination seizing on the brooding atmosphere of the heath, then she wasn't about to allow her subconscious to undermine her pleasure in being out of doors.

She also occupied her time with trying to befriend Chloe. Two or three times a week, she would go to the nursery and spend an hour or so with the child. Chloe was wary during these sessions, remaining huddled in a chair while Julia sat on the far side of the room and read very loudly from one of the little girl's picture books. Sometimes Chloe watched from the safety of a corner as Julia undressed a flaxen haired doll that Miss Belkerson assured her was one of Chloe's favorites and pretended to tuck it into bed with a story and a kiss. Chloe never actively participated in the play, and at times appeared not to even be aware of Julia's presence. But at other times, those sky blue eyes that were so like Sebastian's would light up for a scant moment before being diverted, as if Chloe had some inner warning system that kept her from getting too interested in whatever had been taking place.

Always after such a moment those eyes would become even more unfocused, and Chloe would stare mindlessly into space until Julia left. Once, as Julia performed an especially silly bit of play-acting with the doll, she thought she caught a glimmer of a smile on Chloe's face. A screaming, kicking tantrum followed that experience, and Chloe ended up being borne away sobbing to bed. Julia, shaken by the violence Chloe displayed, nevertheless continued her visits. Despite her lack of obvious headway with the child, she felt in some obscure way that she and Chloe were becoming friends.

Mrs. Johnson was also concerned about Chloe's well-being. Occasionally as Julia played in the nursery suite, she would look up to find the housekeeper standing in the doorway, watching Chloe with a sad little smile. The child never seemed to notice the older woman's presence, just as she barely noticed Julia's. Still Mrs. Johnson expressed a fondness for the little girl, and kept coming up to check on Julia's progress in befriending her.

"Because I was that fond of her mother, you know," Mrs. Johnson explained as Julia sipped a cup of tea with her one rainy afternoon. "And of his lordship, of course. The little mite does look so like her father, doesn't she?"

There was nothing Julia wanted to discuss less than Sebastian, or Chloe's resemblance to him. So she smiled sympathetically and remained silent, hoping Mrs. Johnson wouldn't pursue the subject. Today, she wasn't so lucky.

"I've known the little one all her life, you know," Mrs. Johnson continued chattily, unaware of Julia's discomfort. "And Miss Elizabeth, milady, practically ran tame over here when they were growing up. And Miss Caroline, too, of course. Miss Caroline was the beauty, although she was only a sort of cousin to Miss Elizabeth, taken in by the Tynesdales when her own parents died. Miss Elizabeth was quite an heiress, and we all thought that Master Edward would end up wedded to her. The Peytons weren't too plump in the pocket then, you know. Most of my lord's money came to him through Miss Elizabeth. But anyway, somehow or another Master Edward wed Miss Caroline, and it was she we all thought would be my lady. When Miss Elizabeth married his lordship—the second son was all he was then—Miss Caroline seemed to get a lot of satisfaction from kind of lording it over her. I suppose Miss Caroline had had to put up with some snubs growing up, being the poor relation, like. Then Master Edward died, and right after that the old earl, who'd been an invalid for years, died too. And Master Sebastian inherited the title. Ain't it funny how things work out?" Mrs. Johnson paused to marvel at the vagaries of fate.

Julia felt her interest caught despite herself. "Their marriage—Sebastian's and Elizabeth's—was not a happy one, was it?"

Mrs. Johnson shook her head. "No, and that's something most people don't know. I suppose Emily has been talking about things that she shouldn't again. But since you're one of the family now, Miss Julia, I suppose it's all right. From the very start that marriage was rocky They weren't right for each other, though of course hindsight always shows us where we went wrong, doesn't it? Miss Elizabeth was such a quiet little mouse of a thing, you know, and Master Sebastian—well, he was always extraordinary handsome, even as a little lad. At first, I thought it was kind of funny that he should love her, but then I saw how she seemed to look up to him and I could see how he might like that. He didn't get much attention as a boy, you know. It was all Master

Edward this, and Master Edward that. He was the heir and all. And besides, Miss Elizabeth stood to inherit all that money. I'm sure that influenced Master Sebastian too. He'd have been a fool if it didn't."

The idea of Sebastian as a young man wedded to Elizabeth caused a queer little pain in the region of Julia's heart. She refused to acknowledge it, and after a moment it went away.

"Do you know what went wrong between them?"

"Who could know what all goes on between man and wife?" Mrs. Johnson asked in such a way that Julia knew the question was largely rhetorical. The housekeeper took another sip of tea and whispered conspiratorially, "I think it had something to do with milady's wifely duties, if you know what I mean. She was a lady through and through, and ladies don't always like the things that their husbands expect of them. Now me, I've got good yeoman blood in my veins, and me and Johnson never had no problems like that. But I think my lord and Miss Elizabeth did."

"But they had Chloe."

Mrs. Johnson shook her head. "My lord had to have an heir you know. He couldn't have let her alone even if he wanted to. She was his legal wife, and it was her duty to give him children. But after Miss Chloe's birth they never shared a bed again to my knowledge. Milady thought the sun rose and set on Miss Chloe, but the birth was real hard on her. I don't think she wanted to go through that again, and I don't think my lord would have forced her. If milady had lived, who knows? Maybe she would have given him his heir after all. But now there's only Miss Chloe, poor little thing. What happened to her is as much a tragedy as what happened to Miss Elizabeth. More maybe."

"Was Chloe . . . all right before her mother died?"

Mrs. Johnson nodded her head. "Fine as sixpence. A bonny little lass she was. So bright and pretty, we all petted her up something awful. Then, from the very day Miss Elizabeth was killed, Miss Chloe has been like you see her today. Like I said, it's a real tragedy."

"Has she always been so terrified of . . . her father?" Julia hesitated over the question, frightened by what the answer might be.

"Just since milady was killed. Miss Chloe started screaming like a crazed animal when my lord went up to break the news of what had happened to her right after he brought Miss Elizabeth home. She started screaming as soon as she saw him, before he said a word, so it wasn't because he told her about her mother being dead. All we can figure is she must have seen him carrying milady's body into the house from her window, and associated him with milady's death. That's all we can figure." Mrs. Johnson looked uncomfortable suddenly. "What else could it be?" The very way she said it lacked conviction, and Julia wondered how much Mrs. Johnson had speculated about whether or not Chloe had some intuitive knowledge of her father's guilt in the matter of Elizabeth's death. Even old time retainers like the Johnsons weren't proof against such gossip.

Mrs. Johnson changed the subject then, as if afraid she had said too much. She and Julia chatted about desultory things until finally they had to get ready for dinner. But long after that conversation Julia mulled over what had been said. Mrs. Johnson had provided Sebastian with at least two good motives to murder his wife, whether she knew it or not. The first was money, and the second was Elizabeth's apparent inability or unwillingness to give him a male heir. But just because Sebastian might have had cause to wish himself rid of Elizabeth didn't mean he had done the deed, Julia told herself. There was absolutely no proof that he had killed his wife, and until any was found Julia refused to convict him in her own mind. Despite the way he had treated her, she still couldn't believe him guilty of murder.

Winter came and went in much the same way as fall had. When it was finally followed by unmistakable signs of approaching spring, Julia was amazed to realize she had been at White Friars almost a year. She hardly ever remembered the old hard days in Jem's loft, and she never thought of herself as anything but Julia Stratham, a lady. In her own mind that's who she was, and she would never, ever go back.

The pleasant days with Sebastian the summer before were a scarcely thought of memory as well. She could not remember the good times without also remembering that shameful night he had taken her virginity and the even more painful morning when she had come to him full of happiness and love and he had spurned her. She supposed that she must see him again someday, as he was nominally her guardian, but until then she would not allow thoughts of him to taint her days. If at times she couldn't help it, she at least comforted herself with the hope that eventually that too beautiful face with the celestial eyes would cease to appear with such lifelike vividness in her mind.

Rainy, muddy March was halfway through when the carriage bowled up White Friars' circular drive. Julia, who had been walking, felt her heart stop when she saw it. They had had no visitors in all the months she had been in residence except for two men who had arrived within days of her own arrival. They had been closeted with Sebastian for perhaps an hour and then gone on their way again, and no outsiders had stopped since. Now the only person Julia could think might be arriving was Sebastian. Had he come back at last?

Her heartbeat returned, faster than before. Her first impulse was to run toward that carriage as fast as her feet would take her. Her second was to run in the opposite direction, to hide herself on the heath and never return. But Julia had learned quite a lot about self-possession in the weeks and months that Sebastian had been gone, and she did neither. She finished the ramble that she had just begun, and returned wind-blown to the house some forty-five minutes later. If she had secretly hoped to impress Sebastian with how unconcerned with his return she was, she had wasted her time.

Because the carriage brought not Sebastian but a message from him. She was, his note informed her tersely, to present herself in town in two weeks' time.

XIX

HE journey to London took two days in the closed carriage that Sebastian had sent for her. With only Emily for company, Julia soon felt she was going quietly mad. The country-bred girl, excited by this first venture beyond the confines of Bishop's Lynn, chattered constantly, exclaiming over nearly everything she saw.

Since she had experienced much the same thing in reverse when Sebastian had brought her into the countryside after a lifetime spent in London, Julia was sympathetic to a point. But even heartfelt sympathy could not quell the urge she felt to ask Emily to hush for just five minutes. Since kindness forbade her to do any such thing, Julia spent most of the journey praying that it would end.

But as evening fell and they entered the outskirts of London, bowling along the familiar narrow streets and crowded thoroughfares, Julia suddenly wished that the trip would go on forever. The thought of seeing Sebastian again filled her with dread.

When the carriage rocked to a stop at the address on Lisle Street, Julia made no move to alight. Instead she delayed by leaning to look out the window. Her stomach churned with what she suspected was nerves and what she insisted to herself was travel sickness. To her surprise she saw that their destination was a neat little row house that looked cozily welcoming in the glow of the torches burning at either end of the street. It was a charming dwelling, but it did not look like any place Sebastian might live. A footman opened the door and let down the carriage steps. Julia could delay no longer. Frowning, she accepted his proffered assistance and stepped from the carriage.

Her anxiety over meeting Sebastian again was now over-layed with a different unease. Upon first reading his message she had noted that the address at which she was instructed to present herself was not that of his house in Grosvenor Square. She had guessed it was a lawyer's office or some other business establishment. But this was defi-nitely someone's home with ruffled curtains and pots of big pink geraniums on either side of the door. She could not by any stretch of the imagination picture Sebastian living in this pretty little house. From her knowledge of the high and mighty Earl of Moorland, he took grand surroundings as much for granted as he did air to breathe. She made a face. Standing there wondering who owned the house was only another way of buying time. Sooner or later she would have to go in—and face Sebastian.

Was he even now inside? That was the question that drove all other considerations from her mind. She stood hesitating at the bottom of the modest set of stone steps that led up to the entrance, staring at that white painted door with the simple brass knocker as if it were the gateway to hell. There was no way to know without going in herself, of course.

Taking a deep breath to quiet the butterflies that were doing flips in her stomach, she climbed the steps, a thankfully silent Emily at her heels. The door opened as she approached it. A man stood there, but it was not Sebastian. A short, thin, cadaverous fellow in a butler's uniform was looking her over in a way she could not quite like. She stared back at him nonplussed while his eyes passed quickly over what little of her body he could see, shrouded as it was by her hooded cloak.

"Mrs. Stratham?" His voice was extremely polite. Perhaps she had just imagined the look in his eyes.

She decided to give him the benefit of the doubt, and responded with a cool affirmative to the title that was still a little strange to her. He bowed his head as she passed by him into the entry hall, which was charmingly decorated in whites and yellows but was still nothing like what she would have expected of one of the earl's residences. But, of course, it must be. There was no possibility of a mistake. The butler even knew her name.

"I am Granville, ma'am. Please call upon me for anything you may need. The staff here is rather small, just a cook-housekeeper, two maids, and myself. And now your own maid, of course."

Behind them the footmen who had accompanied Julia were carrying in her bags. Granville raised his voice to a surprising degree, shouting out, "Mary!" A plump girl responded, and Granville directed her to show Mrs. Stratham upstairs.

Julia could stand the suspense no longer. "Is my lord Moorland here?" She had to know if he was liable to appear at any moment like a demon in a puff of smoke.

Granville's face took on an expression that she couldn't quite decipher. The look was completely devoid of respect; instead she could almost have sworn he leered. But that was impossible, of course. No servant would do such a thing in response to an innocent query from a member of his master's family. It would be grounds for dismissal. She must be overly tired, and letting her imagination run away with her.

"His lordship left orders that word was to be sent around to him as soon as you arrived. No doubt he will be with you in a very short while."

The words were expressionless, but there was something there—she was sure of it. A kind of contempt? Perhaps this man somehow knew of her background? But how could that be? She was very sure that Sebastian would never tell anyone. With a cool thank you she followed the plump maid named Mary upstairs, followed by Emily, who carried her traveling case.

The house was quite small, Julia saw, though the bedroom to which Mary showed her was spacious enough. It occupied the entire front of the upper level of the house, and like the downstairs was decorated cheerily in shades of yellow and white. An enormous bed dominated the far wall, and Julia stopped as she entered, staring at it. Its headboard and footboard were of gilt, and bore carved images of naked females cavorting with chubby cupids amidst hearts and twining vines. The bed hangings were of riotous floral print whose primary color was lush pink, and pink velvet curtains which could be closed to give the bed's occupant complete privacy hung from the canopy.

All in all the bed was like nothing she had ever seen before, and she found it rather shocking. She pictured Sebastian sleeping amidst the profusion of pink velvet and flowers, and her mind boggled. It was harder and harder to believe that this house was his. Perhaps it belonged to a friend, and he was merely borrowing it so that their meeting could be private?

"Miss Julia, would you look at that? Those ladies don't have on any clothes at all!" Emily's shocked whisper from behind her told Julia that the maid also was stunned by the bed. But if the house and servants belonged to someone besides Sebastian, she did not want to inadvertently insult them by seeming to dislike their taste in furnishings.

"Shh, Emily," she whispered back, and turned to look as Mary pointed out the location of the room's conveniences in a voice that was surprisingly coarse for a maid in a gentleman's establishment.

"I'm sure you'd like to change out of your travel dirt and bathe, ma'am, so I'll leave you alone now." Mary finished, heading for the door. With one hand on the knob she stopped, and turned back as though struck by an afterthought. "Would you like me to take one of your nightdresses down t' the kitchen and press it? Travelin' is that hard on clothes."

"You can press a dress for me, Mary, thank you." She assumed the maid didn't know Sebastian planned to visit her that evening. "And bring some hot water to wash in. A full bath will have to wait until later, I'm afraid. His lordship will be arriving shortly and I would not wish to keep him waiting."

"No, ma'am." A little grin played about Mary's too full mouth. Julia, noting it, frowned a little as she turned to Emily and told her which dress to remove from one of the trunks that the footmen were even now carrying into the room. Perhaps the girl was simple, she thought, puzzled by the maid's expression. But, remembering the butler's attitude, she shook her head. Perhaps the entire staff was simple.

Emily handed over a dress of fine black silk, which was indeed sadly wrinkled, and Mary bore it away with her. Another maid appeared at the door momentarily with a can of warm water, and Julia set about making a hasty toilette. She wanted to be ready when Sebastian arrived. Knowing him, he was quite capable of entering her bedchamber without ceremony if she kept him waiting. The thought made her heart speed up. Seated at the small dressing table in her underclothes, Julia stared into the mirror with unseeing eyes as Emily brushed out and repinned her hair.

The image of Sebastian rose up to suffocate her. She had banished it with such success for all these months, but now it would no longer be denied. He had shamed and humiliated her, and she despised him. She was furious at him. She resented his cavalier way of ordering her about; the note by which he had summoned her had been terse to the point of rudeness. But the very fact that he had requested her presence, however impolitely, made her heart pound so that she feared it might beat itself to death in her chest. She hated him for the way he had treated her—but perhaps he was ready to offer her some explanation for his behavior that would ameliorate her hatred.

A tap on the door announcing the return of her dress interrupted her thoughts.

"My lord has arrived," Mary said with another of those annoying grins as she handed over the dress with a curtsy and slid back out the door.

Julia, watching the door close behind the maid, felt a queasy sensation in the pit of her stomach. She took another deep, calming breath, and allowed Emily to throw the dress over her head so that not a hair of her elegant upsweep was disturbed. Standing before the cheval glass as Emily fastened the dress up the back, her fingers were trembling. Quickly she clenched them into fists. She refused to let Sebastian see her agitated. Her pride demanded that she be as icily in command of herself as he always was. He might be the earl, but she could match him in dignity.

"You look lovely, Miss Julia," Emily said at last, standing back. Julia, smiled, thanking her, and turned away from the mirror. To tell the truth, she was so nervous that she could hardly look at her own reflection. If only her agitation would not show.

"Go have your supper now, Emily. I shouldn't be too long, but I'll ring when I need you again."

Then there was no more reason for delay. Julia, palms sweating, went down to meet Sebastian.

X X

IS first thought was that she had changed.

She opened the door to the salon and stood for a moment, her slender body backlighted by the glow of the chandelier in the hall. Good manners dictated that he rise as she entered, but the sight of her standing there, so apparently cool and collected while he was as on edge as a debutante at her first ball, annoyed him so much that he remained lounging in his chair.

She saw him then. Her eyes had been moving over the room and at last they fixed on him in the high backed chair flanking the window. He watched her discover him, watched the widening of the golden eyes that had eaten like acid into his mind, watched the faint frown on the lovely ivory face smooth out into nothing. His second thought was, God, she is a beauty. His third was unreasoning anger that that should be so.

"I see your manners are as unexceptional as ever, my lord." That cool little voice taking the offensive pricked him like the point of a sword. He felt his annoyance increase. She was not supposed to chide him for a lack of breeding, for God's sake. She might choose to pretend that she was a lady born but he knew better than anyone that she was not. She was just a little guttersnipe that he had chosen to elevate high beyond her station.

"Hello, Julia." Instead of entering into argument with her, he chose to continue lounging in the chair, his legs thrust out before him in an attitude of utter relaxation. He was sure she had learned enough to recognize the insult of his posture, since a gentleman would never sit so in the presence of a lady. His eyes moved over her, weighing the pleasing curves and hollows. His memory had not played tricks on him as he had half-hoped. She was every bit as delectable as he remembered. The fact should not annoy him as it did. After all, she was his to enjoy.

In the absence of any further comment from him, she walked into the room, closing the door behind her. She moved to the fireplace, putting her back to it. There was a momentary silence as his eyes ran over her from the top of her elegant coiffure to the toes of the kid half-boots peeking out from beneath the modishly full skirts of her black silk dress. Anyone who did not know she was not a lady born would never guess her origins by looking at her. The high cheekbones and pointed chin, the delicate straight nose and wide forehead, the enormous black-lashed golden eyes and full, sweet mouth, the lustrous sheen of her ebony hair and the slender feminine curves of her body had none of the ripeness that was the form that beauty among the lower classes tended to take. Suzanne had been breathtaking, but the very abundance of her charms, the brightness of the blond hair she had "enhanced" with God knew what preparations, the fullness of her face and even the shape of her hands and feet had been a silent testament to her low birth. But Julia had long slender bones, lovely long fingered white hands, and narrow feet. It occurred to him suddenly to wonder about her father. Her mother had been a whore; the Bow Street runners he had hired to check her story had told him that. But who had her father been? Looking at Julia, he thought that the unknown father must have been well-born. There was no other way to account for her appearance, or the ease with which she had learned to act the lady.

"Did you bring me all the way up here just to stare at me?" Her voice was testy.

It made him smile involuntarily and very briefly. Few people dared to talk to him that way. Whatever else she was, she was certainly no coward. He thought of their coming association with satisfaction. He would enjoy having a mistress with a sharp tongue. In all the time that Suzanne had enjoyed his protection, she had never disagreed by so much as a sniff with a word he had uttered.

"Do you like the house?" The question, seemingly out of the blue, surprised her, Sebastian saw. It surprised him, too. He had meant to seduce her, and then inform her of the happy change in her circumstances. He had learned by hard experience that that was the way to save himself from having to listen to a lot of coy protests. From the way Julia had responded to him that night in the library, he had no doubt that she would be delighted to take up residency in his bed. The sticking point, as with all of them, was getting her to admit it. But Julia was an intelligent young woman, certainly more intelligent than any mistress he had had before. Perhaps he would be honest with her. It would make a nice change, and anyway he did not feel like seducing her. He felt more like wringing her neck.

"The house? It's . . . it's very nice." She was looking at

him strangely.

He stood up suddenly, thrusting his hands in the pockets of his dove gray breeches. It was the only way he could think of to control the almost irresistible impulse he had to grab her by those slender shoulders and shake her until her head rattled.

"It's yours, if you want it." He could not help himself, but growled the words when he had meant to be charming. She was maddening him just by standing there looking so damned innocent when he knew she was anything but.

"This house? It's mine, if I want it?" She sounded as if she thought he had lost his mind. She was frowning as she looked at him. Then her brow cleared. "Oh, did it belong to Timothy?"

He gritted his teeth and took a step closer, cramming his hands deeper into his pockets.

"No, it did not belong to Timothy. Your inheritence from Timothy consists of some twenty thousand pounds invested in the funds. Not a fortune, but enough to keep you from starving one day if you are careful with your income. But the income will not provide you with luxuries, like this house."

"If it is not Timothy's, then whose house is it, and how could it be mine? Are you suggesting that I buy it?"

His mouth twisted into an unpleasant smile. "As the guardian of your financial affairs, I would never suggest that you squander your money on such an unnecessary purchase. No, I was not suggesting you buy it. The house is already yours if you want it. It belongs to me, and I would be more than pleased to give it to you."

"You would give it to me?" She was looking at him,

wariness plain in those huge golden eyes. He smiled at her again, not the charming smile he had thought to persuade her with, but a hard, cold baring of his teeth.

"Not only the house, but the furnishings, a carriage, and a substantial sum of money to maintain all that. Shall we say a sum of twenty thousand pounds, to equal what you will get from Timothy's estate? The combined income will be enough to keep you in comfort for the rest of your life."

He had not meant to offer so much, of course. It was pure folly. The accepted practice was for a man to support his mistress according to his pocketbook while she lived under his protection. When he tired of the arrangement, he settled a small sum on her and she was free to go on to another admirer. Never before had he offered a woman outright possession of this house, which was centrally located and convenient for him to visit and which had seen him through three mistresses. But then, never before had he wanted a woman as badly as he wanted this one. He had found, first to his dismay and then his fury, that the hair of the dog was not as effective a remedy as he had thought for the malaise that had plagued him upon his return to town. At least not the hair of any dog. What he needed, he decided, was the hair of the very dog that bit him. And he meant to have it—and her—whatever the cost.

"In return for what, Sebastian?"

He smiled that wolfish smile again. His hands, thrust into his breeches pockets, clenched into fists.

"In return for becoming my mistress," he said brutally.

There was a long moment of silence as she seemed to absorb what he had said. He watched as she whitened so much that for a moment he feared she might faint. Her eyes were huge topaz moons in that colorless face as she stared at him. One hand went out to grasp the back of a nearby chair, but that and her paleness were the only outward signs of agitation she betrayed.

"You brought me to London to set me up as your mistress?" The words were uttered through stiff lips. She sounded as if she had trouble forcing them out. Sebastian felt a surge of violence. How dare she stand there looking so—so damned stricken, when he knew and she knew that she was nothing more than a two-bit whore?

"You made yourself my mistress that night in the library at White Friars. I propose merely to formalize the arrangement." His words were cold, and in no way expressed the volcano of emotions that churned through him. He could not shake the absurd fury that had sprung to life in him all those months ago when he had discovered that his so innocent protegee was in fact no better than she should be.

She moved then, letting go of the chair back with what appeared to be an effort and walking toward him without a word. Sebastian watched her approach, his hands still thrust into his pockets. When she was directly in front of him, so that not as much as a foot of space remained between them, she stopped. He could almost feel the heat of her body even across the space that separated them. But that heat was nothing compared to the golden fire of her eyes. He started to withdraw his hands from his pockets so that he could grasp her waist, but they were still hung up in the folds of cloth when she drew back her hand and slapped him with all her might in the face.

The sharp sound of her flesh making stinging contact with his own was echoed by the even sharper indrawing of his breath. His head snapped back, not so much from the force of the blow as from the very unexpectedness of it. Recovering, feeling rage build in him like a rushing, overflowing river against a dam, he lifted a hand to his burning cheek, staring at her. She still stood before him, disdaining to run, her chin high and her golden eyes aflame.

"You insult me," she said coldly. And with that, she turned away.

X X I

insult you, do I?"

His hands clamped onto her shoulders even as he spoke. Julia hardly had time to wince at his brutality before he was spinning her about to face him. Those celestial blue eyes were now blazing with fury, she saw as she lifted her own to meet them. His face was harsh with it. If she had ever wanted to break through the icy self-control with which he faced the world, she had succeeded beyond her wildest dreams.

"I didn't think it was possible to insult a two-bit whore!"

The gutteral insult left her gasping. But before she could retaliate either physically or verbally, he yanked her against him, his arms pinning hers to her body as his head descended. Caught off guard, she just managed to turn her head aside so that his mouth found her cheek instead of her lips. The feel of those burning lips against her skin sent an agonizing shaft of longing through her. But she would not, could not give in to it. This was not Sebastian, her Sebastian of all those months ago, but the violent brutal stranger he had so bewilderingly become.

"Let go of me!" Unable to get her hands free, she could only writhe against him in her efforts to break away. As her abdomen twisted against him, she felt a sudden, horrifying change in his body that involuntarily sent her eyes flying to meet his.

That wolfish smile appeared again, transforming the beautiful face into a mask of pure masculine aggression. He was strong and she was weak and he was out to prove his power.

"Not—quite—yet," he said through his teeth, and then his mouth descended once more.

Quickly she twisted so that his lips again missed their mark, but this time one of the hands that clamped her arms to her sides snaked upwards to burrow through her hair and close over the back of her skull. Slowly, inexorably he turned her head so that she was an easy target. His single arm held her securely as his other forced her head around and held her helpless. He met her angry, frightened eyes with a smile. Then, as she twisted and struggled he slowly, oh so slowly, bent his head. Those blue eyes, ablaze now with blinding emotion, never left hers. She jerked against his iron hold, but to no avail. Then his mouth was on hers, hard and hot and demanding, and he was kissing her with a fury that stole both breath and reason with it. He was kissing her as if he hated her; and she, shameful, spineless creature that she was, loved it.

He tasted faintly of brandy and cigars, and he was warm, so warm. The sheer heat he generated had an enervating effect on her. She struggled briefly, then forgot to fight him as his tongue slid between her lips, stroking over them, flicking against the white barrier of her teeth before weakly, helplessly, she opened her mouth and let him inside. He growled then, and whether the sound was of victory or of passion she neither knew nor cared. All she knew was that he was kissing her so deeply she felt as though he would steal the very soul from her body, bending her back over his arm so that if she had been in any rational state at all she would have feared that her spine would snap. But she was not rational, her mind had fled, leaving her emotions running rampant, and she could not fight them. His kiss was making her dizzy; the room was spinning round and round in front of her dazed eyes. All she could do was close them so that she was enveloped in a warm dark void.

Her heart was pounding so loudly that it drowned out all other sounds. Her bones had turned to jelly, melting like hot liquid in his hands. She could feel the burning fire of her own surrender in her breasts and belly and thighs and especially between her legs, where it tightened and pulsed and throbbed. Then she traced the fire to him, and connected it to his hand, which was sliding over her body with abandon, fondling and possessing while with his other arm he supported her boneless weight. The thin silk covering her and flimsy underclothes beneath were no protection from the invasion of his touch. His palm found her breast again, rubbing roughly across it, tormenting her with the sudden sharp pleasure-pain of it. Then his hand traveled to her other breast, enclosing it in burning heat, and if she had not been lost before she was now.

She groaned, quivering in his arms, and lifted her hands to clutch the shoulders that were bent so ruthlessly over her before sliding her arms around his neck. She couldn't think, couldn't reason; she could only feel. His mouth was hot on hers, demanding, devouring, his tongue exploring the sweet wet hollows of her own. Her tongue moved at last, shyly, to touch his. He jerked, and stiffened in her arms. She tightened her hold on him, clinging as he kissed her with greedy passion, kissing him back now without reserve, her hands clutching in the silver-gilt silk of his hair, digging into the tense muscles at the back of his neck, running over the broad expanse of shoulders still clad in the smooth cloth of his coat. It had been so long, so long. . . .

He bent her even further over his arm, kissing her, and then his mouth left hers to slide along her throat. The faint roughness of his cheeks and chin scraped her skin as he pressed his face into her neck. Then his mouth was moving even lower, sliding over the slippery silk to find the tip of her breast. She felt the moist warmth of his mouth through her dress, and cried out. He left his mouth on her for a long moment, while the heat of it seared through to the very core of her and all her feelings concentrated on that one spot. Then abruptly he pulled his head away.

Before she could do more than whimper a protest at this abandonment, she was being lifted off her feet, and for a moment her eyes opened and reality intruded. He was carrying her out of the salon, a dark and hungry expression on his face that matched the way she was feeling inside. As he maneuvered her through the doorway and into the hall, she recovered just enough presence of mind to look swiftly around. Thankfully the hall was deserted.

"Sebastian. . . ." It was a faint protest as some semblance of sanity returned to her.

"I'll be damned if I'm going to make love to you on the floor again when there's a perfectly good bed waiting upstairs," he said roughly. Before she could martial her resources to say anything else he was climbing the stairs with her in his arms, taking them so fast that she felt dizzy and had to cling to him.

"Sebastian. . . ." She tried again to remember why she couldn't let this happen as he reached the upper hallway. But her mind wouldn't function properly with his arms all around her carrying her as if she were weightless and her body throbbing where he had touched it and the taste of him still burning on her lips.

"Don't talk. Just kiss me," he muttered, his hand already finding the knob to the bedroom door even as his mouth descended.

Her eyes helplessly fixed on that gorgeous mouth, Julia complied. She was hardly aware of being carried into the bedroom, of the click of the door closing behind them, of the softness of the bed as he lowered her into it. All she was conscious of was the loss of his warmth as he straightened away from her to blow out the bedside candle.

"Julia," he muttered as the room plunged into shadowy darkness, and then he was on the bed beside her, kissing her so deeply that he stole her breath away.

She couldn't talk, couldn't think, could only feel. His hands were everywhere, on her breasts and belly, sliding up beneath her skirt to caress her thighs, pulling her undergarments with hands that shook too much to untie knots or to unfasten the tiny buttons that did her gown up the back. Julia felt the tug at her throat, felt the resistance of the silk and then heard the soft ripping sound as the hands that couldn't manage her buttons tore her gown open from the neck. He knelt above her, pulling the ruined garment from her and then tearing the ties that held her petticoats and pantalets from their moorings. When the garments were free he slid them down her legs, following each baring of her skin with tiny biting kisses that should have hurt but instead sent her into a frenzy of passion. By the time he rolled each silk stocking down her leg, kissing carefully back up over toes and insteps and ankles and calves, trailing his tongue over the insides of her knees and then up the insides of her thighs, she was whimpering with passion, afire from the toes he had just drawn inside his mouth to her head which was writhing against the overblown roses of the still made bed. Only the loosened chemise saved her from being completely naked, and then he was drawing that over her head and pushing her roughly back into the nest of bedclothes, covering her body with his own. The textures of his coat and breeches and even the soft linen of his shirt abraded her tender skin, exciting her unbearably. He was still fully dressed, even to his boots, while she was naked and quivering with wanting him.

"Sebastian . . ." she muttered into the mouth that was devouring hers, but the taste of his tongue and the feel of his hands on her swelling breasts left her incapable of further talk. Feebly she tugged his coat in an effort to get her message across, but his mouth followed his hands down her body, fastening on her breast with a hot wetness that made her cry out and clutch his head. He bit her nipple with his teeth, hurting her and yet not hurting her, reducing her to a kind of mindless ecstasy that left her gasping as his mouth moved over to torment the other soft peak. His hands were stroking her thighs, and she tried to writhe under his weight, wanting to bring his hands to perform the wonderful magic that they had performed before. But he was too heavy, his body had her pinioned, she could hardly move—or breathe. Then he was lifting himself off of her, as he rolled to the side of the bed and stood up.

"Sebastian!" This time his name was a pitiful plea for him to return, but it died on her lips as she watched him tear the clothes from his body. Her eyes grew accustomed to the dark, and she saw him shrug out of the black superfine coat, letting it drop where it would, then strip the cravat from around his neck and tear at the buttons on his shirt with hands that she knew were trembling. He let the shirt drop, too, then sat down on the edge of the bed to tug off his boots. Julia was fascinated by the planes and angles of that lean powerful back as it curved away from her, muscles working. She wanted to touch it.

She sat up, conscious of her nakedness and her femininity as she had never been conscious of anything before in her life. Crawling toward him, she thrilled to the aching, pulsing need that made her breasts feel heavy and her secret woman-place weep. In the shadowy darkness his hair gleamed silver and his back arched as he pulled off first one boot and dropped it to the floor with a thud before tackling the other.

She touched his spine, a delicate butterfly touch, and he stiffened. He was rigid, unmoving, as she traced a path from the silky curls at the nape of his neck over the ridged indention of his spine to the edge of his breeches. The breeches frustrated her exploration, so she put both hands on his back, palms down, and slid them upwards, testing muscles and sinews, ribs and shoulder blades, then stroked broad muscular shoulders. His skin was hot, smooth, just beginning to dampen with sweat. He was very muscular, with a honed, lean kind of strength that was deceptive when he was dressed. She slid her hands downward again in a sweeping caress. Then, propelled by instincts she hadn't even known she possessed, she leaned forward to slide her arms around his waist and press her breasts against the warm moist silk of his back.

"Christ!" It was an expletive, muttered as he shot off the bed and stripped off his breeches, giving her just a glimpse of a muscular, fur-sprinkled chest above narrow hips and a flat abdomen, and the enormous jutting male part of him below it.

Then he was pressing her back into the bed, his mouth fierce on hers and his body hard, demanding, over-whelming as it bore her down. This time he was as naked as she, and she gloried in it. She felt the abrasion of his body hair against her breasts and belly and thighs, and squirmed beneath him the better to feel it. She felt the iron hardness of his back muscles under her hands and sank her nails into them, the better to test them. She felt the burning heat of his mouth against her neck, and opened her own against the salt dampness of his shoulder, the better to taste him.

His thigh slid between hers, hair-roughened and hard from years in the saddle. It was joined by its fellow, and then he lay between her legs, throbbing and pulsing and prodding, and he was kissing her deeply on the mouth and his hands were on her breasts and then . . . and then . . .

He slid inside her. She gasped as he filled her, arching, trembling and crying out his name. The sensation was exquisite, wonderful, setting her a-quiver from head to toe, stopping her breath and stilling her heart and spinning her away.

She clutched him close, her arms straining him to her, her sharp cry swallowed by his mouth even as her body was consumed by his body. He plunged inside her with a pulsing urgency that drove her over the edge, and then, as he felt her ecstasy, he was himself swept away.

Later, when they had both drifted back to earth and lay limply together, their breathing eased and their sweat drying on their bodies, Julia started thinking all the thoughts that had not managed to squeeze past her passion.

Her body was sated and her mind, while still somnolent, was beginning to function again. This man in her arms, this arrogant infuriating gorgeous male whom she hated to love and loved to hate, had brought her to London for the express purpose of making her his mistress. She, who had been a good girl all her life despite the fact that making money by selling one's body was as common a thing in her world as changing clothes was in his, had allowed him to do so. Despite her outrage at the suggestion, despite her proud denials and the ringing, richly deserved slap she had dealt him, she was now his mistress. It was funny, really. He had made her a lady only to turn her into the one thing she had vowed she would never be: a whore.

"Do you always get what you want?" Her voice was tinged with resentment. She was too tired for real anger, but she suspected that might come later.

"Ummm." His face was nuzzled against her left cheek and ear while his arm lay heavily across her waist and his sprawled leg trapped both her thighs. "Not always. Just most of the time."

He sounded sleepy, contented, and more than a little self-satisfied. Julia felt her anger prick a little more sharply.

"Such as tonight?" The sharpness came through in her voice. Against her ear she felt his breath expel in a little sigh.

"Do we have to discuss this now? I can think of more pleasant things to do."

His husky whisper would have sent a tingle down her spine if she had let it. As the realization of exactly what position he expected her to occupy in his life came home to her, her anger increased by the millisecond until in less than a minute it was full-blown rage. The suggestive nibbling of his lips on her ear did not help; neither did his hand, which slid up from her waist to cup and caress a soft breast. When he shifted, lifting his head to catch her lips with his in a deep soft kiss, she exploded. Her hand whizzed through the air to slap the side of his face with a satisfying crack and a force that made her palm throb. At the same time she jerked away from him and clambered to the opposite end of the bed, where she sat with her arms crossed over her breasts, glaring at him.

"God damn it!" He roared the words, sitting bolt upright, his hand flying to his face and his eyes sparking so furiously that she could see their bright glitter through the gloom. "What the hell ails you now, you little hellcat?"

"What ails me? You have the nerve to ask what ails me? After first you call me a whore, and then you make me one?" She was sputtering in her fury, bouncing off the bed to stand, arms akimbo, eyes flaying him. He moved too, rolling off the bed and leaning over the round table that flanked it, and she saw that he was lighting the candle.

"I apologize for calling you a whore," he said over his shoulder, the words only slightly gritted. "But I tend to get a little angry when I'm slapped. And as for making you a whore . . ." His voice trailed off suggestively as the room flickered to life.

Instantly Julia became aware of his nakedness and her own. She looked down at herself, saw the peaks and valleys of her own femininity and how his possession had branded them, and flushed a painful red. She looked across at him, got her first full-front, well lit look at a naked man, and averted her eyes. He was just as magnificent naked as he was dressed, she observed even in that brief glimpse, but as the thought registered she immediately banished it from her mind. Dragging the coverlet from the bed, she wrapped it around herself, and felt marginally safer. That is, until she saw that he was advancing on her with purposeful strides.

"You stay away from me, you dishonest swine!" she shrieked. When he kept coming she darted to the far side of the room.

"*Me* dishonest!" he growled, stopping to put his balled fists on his hips and glare at her. His total nakedness did not seem to bother him in the least. "What about you, my guttersnipe-turned-lady? Pretending to be so innocent! 'I don't like anyone to see me naked,' " he mimicked in a mincing falsetto, "while all the time you'd probably been whoring since you could walk. What's the matter," he added as she whitened, "didn't you think I'd notice? I wasn't that drunk that night, my dear."

"You think I . . ." Words failed her as she realized that the insult he had hurled at her in anger was in fact what he thought of her. She had struggled so hard against that fate almost all of her life that the accusation was the mental equivalent of waving a red flag before a bull. And that *he* should make it, who of all men should know better because she had given him incontrovertible proof. "You were blind drunk, you no good rotten filthy dirty *earl!* You were so drunk you passed out afterwards! You were so drunk you stank like a brewery and . . . and I had never, ever been with a man before, and you were so drunk you didn't even notice! You didn't even *care,* you bastard, you . . ." Words failed her. She was gibbering with fury, bouncing up and down with fury, and to drive her point home she looked wildly around for a weapon. Snatching up a delicately carved hand mirror in a silver frame, she hurled it at him. He yelped, ducking, and as he straightened she threw a brush, then a box of rice powder that sprayed its contents in a twisting arc as it flew.

"Stop that, you little bitch!" He was roaring again, his handsome face dark with fury, his eyes bright with it.

As she hurled yet another missile at him, he ducked with quick agility so that the small crystal perfume bottle bounced harmlessly off his shoulder, just splashing a little of its contents on him before dropping to roll away on the pink flowered rug beneath his feet.

While her attention was momentarily deflected by watching the perfume bottle's path, he dived for her. His arms wrapped around her waist and he tossed her over his shoulder before she was even aware he had moved, holding her like a sack of potatoes with her head dangling down his back and her legs kicking frantically for freedom while he carried her across the room. She shrieked with fury, and beat his back with the silver bud vase she had intended for her next missile. But he threw her on the bed and, as she tried to scramble away, dropped on top of her. She tried to hit him in the face with the vase, but he caught her hand and wrenched it away from her. Finally he caught both wrists in a vice, pinning them to the bed while he held her body and legs with his own. She could do nothing but glare at him and curse, which she did with fluent enjoyment and a complete absence of her hard earned ladylike accent.

"Back to being the guttersnipe, are we?" he sneered, and she glared at him with hatred for a pregnant moment. Then, deliberately, she spat full in his mocking face.

"You hell born vixen." He drew the words out, transferring both her wrists to one of his hands and using the other to wipe the spittle from his face. His eyes were glittering with temper; at such close range they would have intimidated the devil himself. Julia was conscious of their threatening glint, but she was so angry and so hurt that she just didn't care what he did to her. She was beyond feeling anything but the desperate need to wound him as he had wounded her.

"Be yer goin' ter beat me now, me lord?" The release of her spittle had served to defuse a little of her helpless fury; she was deliberately aping her own uneducated accents, wanting desperately to goad him into the same frenzy of anger she felt herself. "Ain't that wot the fine gen'lmen do to whores when they be displeased?"

Those blue eyes glinted down at her. He was close, so close that she could see every line and pore in the gorgeously masculine face. The candlelight glinted off his silver-gilt hair, turning the tousled waves into living gold. The broad naked shoulders loomed above her, leanly muscled and powerful. His mouth, even compressed with temper as it was at the moment, was elegantly carved beneath the perfectly straight line of his nose. His very beauty maddened her. It wasn't fair that he should look like that. He was nasty and insulting, a lying, deceitful, tricky dog—and he looked like one of the Lord's archangels.

"You deserve to be beaten," he said through his teeth, but as he looked down at her his expression softened slightly. "But I can think of better ways to tame the she-cat."

The hand that he had freed to wipe her spittle from his face slid between them to capture a breast.

"Take your hand off me!" she shrieked, jerking furiously as she tried to dislodge his hand. His eyes narrowed.

"Would you rather I beat you?" The question was silky. His hand on her breast continued to caress, and despite her anger and the insults he had flung at her she felt a sharp little frisson of pleasure.

"Murder's more your style, isn't it?" she flung at him out of desperation and a desire to wound. He froze, staring down at her while his face iced over.

"Sebastian, I'm sorry," she whispered, frightened by the look on his face. Of all the weapons with which to wound him, she knew she had picked the deadliest. But he seemed not to hear her apology. Even as she uttered it, he released his hold on her wrists, got to his feet and pulled his breeches on with deliberate movements. "Are you deaf? I said I'm sorry. I didn't mean it," she cried.

Why she should apologize to *him* when he thought such dreadful things about her, she didn't know, but he looked so white and cold and distant suddenly that she couldn't bear it. Scrambling into a sitting position, one hand clutching at the slipping coverlet, she stared at him helplessly.

"I don't really think you killed Elizabeth," she said desperately. "I just said that to make you angry. I'm sorry."

He finished buttoning his shirt, then picked up his coat and boots and headed for the door.

"Don't bother to apologize," he said, his voice as icy as his face as he turned to look at her with one hand on the knob. "After all, what could be a more felicitous combination? A murderer—and a whore."

Then, as a bright scarlet wash of color flooded her cheeks, he let himself out the door.

X X I I

HREE days later, when Julia had begun to think that she would never hear from Sebastian again, another of his terse notes arrived by special messenger.

This one instructed her, in as few cold words as possible, to pack her belongings and remove herself to White Friars at once. There was no polite salutation, not even the "Dear Julia" that the merest acquaintance could expect, and at the end of the curt two sentence message he signed himself "Moorland."

After reading the note for a third time, Julia crumpled it in her hand. He was dismissing her, just like that. Like she was a thing, with no feelings to take into account. She was angry, furious really, when she thought of all he had done. But remembering the still remoteness of his face as he had left that night, she was also afraid.

Some instinct told her that if she didn't do something to rectify the situation soon, it would be beyond recall. She had wounded Sebastian, really hurt him, and unlike herself—who screamed and shouted when she was hurt—Sebastian pulled back inside himself to present an icy shell to the world. If she did not somehow manage to break through that shell before it had totally hardened against her, Julia was afraid that she would never be able to break through it again. Sebastian, the real man behind the unapproachable exterior, would be lost to her forever. And she knew with a sudden flash of insight that whatever he had done, whatever he thought of her, she wouldn't be able to bear that.

She received the note at mid-morning. After reading it, she stood staring at her reflection in the cheval glass in the front hall. It occurred to her as she regarded her somber figure that her year of mourning was over. She could wear colors again. And Julia Stratham, she realized, would be lovelier still clad in the bright hues she loved. As the truth of that hit her, she realized something else: if she wanted Sebastian, she could fight for him.

She had the weapons of her beauty and her knowledge of him—and the way he wanted her. And he wanted her badly; the shaking passion in his mouth and hands and the hard driving urgency of his body had told her that. At present he thought he only wanted her for a little while. But she wanted him forever. She had known it for months really, but she had hidden from the knowledge because of the hurt he had dealt her. But now she was ready to admit it.

She wanted to be his wife. That was the secret wish she had cherished during those dreamlike months when he had been her mentor, friend, and finally her lover. Of course, she should have known better than to expect him to offer marriage; to begin with, he apparently thought she had been with many men before himself. A man of his pride would never accept a shopworn bride. But she had the incontrovertible proof of her innocence—her blood-stained nightdress—hidden in her room at White Friars. That left another obstacle, one that was more difficult to overcome: the Earl of Moorland could not ally himself with one of her birth. Despite his desire for her, she doubted that he had ever considered her as a possible wife. In the world he came from, such a union was unthinkable.

But what if she were to show him that she could fit into his world? What if she were to become Julia Stratham so thoroughly that even society's highest sticklers welcomed her into their homes? Would it make a difference? She rather thought it might. After all, he was fond of her; he had valued her company at White Friars just as she had valued his. He desired her; there could be no mistake about that. Could she make him love her? As Julia Stratham, a lady amongst all the other of the ton's ladies, she just might.

Because she loved him. Despite everything, she loved him. That was why he could hurt her so badly, that was why he could raise her, who had never before so much as allowed a man to kiss her fingers, to such heights of passion. She loved him.

"Not bad news, I hope, Mrs. Stratham?" Granville's unctuous voice behind her ordinarily would have made her jump. With her new resolve to become Julia Stratham so thoroughly that not even she remembered her origins, Julia merely looked at him coolly and shook her head.

"Not at all, Granville," she said, knowing that since he had given her Sebastian's message, he must have seen the crest with which it was sealed and be wondering what it contained. Jewel Combs would have enlightened him. The Julia that she had been earlier might have felt compelled to fob him off with some inanity. But the Julia she was now, the new Julia, would never feel obliged to tell a servant anything. *She* knew how to put an insinuating one such as Granville in his place.

"Would you summon a carriage for me, Granville?" It was an order, not a request. Of course, her tone was polite, because that was how the lady her new Julia was would speak. She would be polite to the lowliest of creatures because she was so certain of herself and her position that she could afford to be.

"A carriage, Mrs. Stratham?" Granville's raised eyebrows and doubtful question were insubordinate, but she would ignore them as if they weren't even there.

"That's right, a carriage," she replied serenely, heading for the stairs to collect her pelisse and Emily. "I'm going shopping, you see."

And shop she did, with the single-mindedness she had once put to lifting fat purses from gentlemen's pockets. By the end of the day she was the proud possessor of a complete wardrobe, courtesy of Madame de Tissaud, the most fashionable modiste in the city. She had discovered Madame courtesy of Mary, who upon being asked imparted the information that Miss Suzanne, who had used to occupy the house, was occasionally taken to shop for clothes there whenever she managed to wheedle his lordship into giving her a high treat.

Julia had started out by buying only a single afternoon dress and accessories because the prices were so dear. But upon instructing the shop girl to bill the Earl of Moorland for her purchases, she was disconcerted to find herself confronted with Madame de Tissaud herself. Madame, a sprightly little lady in what was possibly her fiftieth year, had been voluble in her assurances that she was delighted to meet another member of the earl's family. As the lady confided that both Mrs. Caroline Peyton, the earl's sister-in-law, and the dowager countess had patronized her for years, Julia relaxed. Apparently Madame de Tissaud had no difficulty in taking her just as she presented herself: as Mrs. Julia Stratham, widow of the earl's young cousin and ward.

As Julia explained the sad fact that her wardrobe was almost nonexistent because she had been in mourning for her husband for a year, Madame de Tissaud was most sympathetic. She had then whisked Julia into a back room, and draped her with a bewildering variety of fabrics. Those selected by Madame Tissaud were mostly in the bright sapphires and emeralds that Julia had always loved. In addition, there was a dull gold tissue that Julia had looked at askance until she saw herself swathed in it and even Madame had declared her to be "ravissante," which was to be made into a ball-gown for "la grande occasion."

By the end of the day Julia, with Madame's voluble advice, had selected pattern-cards from which each dress was to be made. Madame had even managed to prepare one walking dress with a matching coat in emerald wool trimmed with black braid for Julia to carry home. (The walking dress Julia had originally planned to purchase was pronounced, with a sniff, as insufficient.) The other garments were to be sent to the earl's residence in Grosvenor Square, two the next day without fail, and the others within the week. The reckoning also was to be sent to the earl. That it would be quite staggering Julia had no doubt, though after Madame de Tissaud had taken over nothing so vulgar as price had ever been discussed. But if Sebastian was upset about her expenditures, he could take the money out of that which she had inherited from Timothy, Julia told herself. She left the shop with Madame de Tissaud's voluble adieus ringing in her ears, feeling extremely pleased with herself and her purchases.

For Julia's plan to work, she had to be presented to the ton. As a member of Sebastian's family, she would have entree everywhere—provided that no one knew of her background. She was perfectly prepared to tell whatever fiction was necessary to assure her acceptance. The only difficulty was Sebastian himself, and his mother and sister-in-law, who of course were aware of the truth. But it was in none of their interests to unmask her. Sebastian himself might not care about scandal, but she would bet farthings to pounds his female relatives did.

As a member of the earl's family she had a perfect right to reside in Grosvenor Square with the rest of them, she told herself to quiet the nervous qualms that afflicted her as she climbed into a hired carriage the next morning resplendent in her new dress, with Emily at her side. If she and Sebastian had not become lovers, she rather thought that he would have introduced her to the ton at some point anyway. He had always said, with a chuckle, that he meant to. So she was not doing anything too coming by thrusting herself in. Besides, if she wanted Sebastian this was a necessary step. She had to be known as an accepted member of the earl's family, and to do that she had to reside in the most logical place, the Peyton family's London residence.

All her reasoning was not enough to calm her nerves, however, and her palms were sweating as the carriage rocked to a halt in front of Grosvenor Square. But it was too late for second thoughts, and anyway she refused to have any.

The gleaming lion's head knocker caught her eye as she ascended the steps. Remembering how it had once awed her made her smile despite her nervousness. And so she was smiling as Smathers, having apparently heard the carriage arrive, opened the door.

"Good day, Smathers," she said composedly, walking past him with Emily at her heels. He blinked at her, obviously not recognizing her as anything but a lady of quality.

"Would you be so good as to have someone bring in my bags?" she asked, turning back to him.

"You—you are visiting us, madame?" Smathers sounded all at sea. Obviously he was searching his mind to recall if any of the family had made mention of visitors, and drawing a blank.

"Did his lordship forget to mention it?" she smiled sweetly. "Yes, I am come to visit. I am Mrs. Stratham."

For a moment the butler looked blank, and then his eyes widened and ran swiftly over her again. But before he could say anything, there was another step on the stairs. Julia turned to see Sebastian descending from the breakfast room with Caroline at his heels. It was an almost uncanny replay of her previous entry into this house. As Sebastian saw her, he stopped dead for a moment, and then continued his descent. His eyes were like frosty blue ice as they fixed on her unwaveringly. Behind him Caroline looked surprised, but not more so than she would have been by any unexpected visitor. It was obvious she did not recognize Julia—yet.

"Good morning, my lord. Did you forget to tell Smathers that I would be staying with you for a while?" Julia essayed a gay tone while Emily, hovering discreetly behind her, looked as if her eyes would pop out of her head.

There was a brief silence as Sebastian gained the bottom of the stairs and gave her a hard, measuring look. For a moment Julia's heart pounded—would he send her packing with a flea in her ear?

"Apparently I did," he said in an icy drawl, and Julia breathed again. "You may have Mrs. Stratham's bags taken up to the gold room," he instructed Smathers. Turning to Caroline and offering his arm to assist her down the remaining two steps, he added, "Of course, you remember Mrs. Stratham, Caroline my dear."

"Mrs. Stratham!" Caroline's pale blue eyes looked at first bewildered, then widened with dawning horror. But with a swift look at the implacable face of the man beside her, she managed a wan smile. "Of—course I do! How do you do, er, Mrs. Stratham?"

"I am very well, thank you," Julia said with outward composure. Inwardly her heart was pounding like a kettle drum. She had not meant to encounter Sebastian so soon. He was looking at her from behind that icy mask like he hated her.

"If you will excuse us, Caroline, I have business I must discuss with Mrs. Stratham." His tone was bland, but his eyes were not as he inclined his head in the direction of his study.

Julia, taking one look at those icy blue eyes, almost lost her courage. But then she remembered that she loved him, and wanted him, and if she wanted him she would have to fight for him. So she lifted her chin, and with a slight smile at the dazed Caroline, preceded Sebastian down the hall to the study that she remembered so well.

As she went, her eye was caught by the ugly blue and white vase that she had threatened to smash all those months ago. Sebastian had since treated her to several long lectures on porcelain of that type, and she now knew it was indeed very valuable. No wonder Caroline had looked on the verge of a heart attack when she had thought it would end up in jagged shards on the floor. And the elegant gilt chair she had treated so disrespectfully was Louis XIV. Julia smiled involuntarily as she remembered the havoc she had created on her last visit to the earl's Grosvenor Square household. She hoped this time to make a better impression.

When they reached the study, Sebastian held the door for her with a punctilious courtesy that was daunting. Firmly fixing her goal in mind, Julia mustered the courage to meet his eyes with insouciance as he sat down behind the desk. Their positions were exactly the same as they had been on the first night they had met, and Julia found it rather uncanny. Everything was the same, from the hunting print on the paneled wall behind the desk to the huge leather chairs to the faint smell of cigar smoke. Sebastian was lighting one of those thin cigars now, placing it between his teeth before leaning back in the chair. As always she found the sight of the raffish looking cigar strangely at odds with Sebastian's austere beauty. The cigar should have belonged to a highwayman, or a pirate. But perhaps the real Sebastian was far more akin to those ruthless men than to the elegantly handsome gentleman he was by birth and appearance.

"With your permission, of course, Mrs. Stratham," Sebastian said with heavy irony as he caught her eyes fixed with some disapproval on the cigar. Julia nodded; she would never have dared deny him permission to smoke, especially not in his present snit with her. He eyed her up and down, the blue eyes hooded beneath lowered lids and the white swirl of smoke.

"Now suppose you tell me what the devil you're playing at?"

"I'm not playing at anything. I simply have no wish to return to White Friars right now. I plan to enjoy London. As your kinswoman I felt the correct place for me to stay was here, in your house."

He eyed her with icy remoteness. "I won't humiliate you by insisting that you leave immediately, but you will return to White Friars tomorrow. Do I make myself clear?"

Julia met his eyes without flinching. Now was the time to make it clear that the relationship between them had undergone a major change. She was no longer the adoring little guttersnipe, but his equal. "I do not take orders from you any longer, Sebastian. I will stay as long as I please. If you throw me out of your house, I will camp on the doorstep. I promise you."

He raked her with eyes that would have sent her cringing for cover a few days ago. Now she merely lifted her chin at him.

"If you think to challenge me, miss—" But she cut off his threat.

"I don't want to challenge you, Sebastian. I simply want to go shopping, for one thing. Do you like my dress? I hope so, because you'll be getting the bill for it—and a few other little purchases I made. You may take some of my money out of the funds to pay for them."

"Thank you," he replied with heavy irony. "I will do so. And you will leave for White Friars tomorrow."

Intimidation was something Sebastian was very good at, Julia remembered. He had used it before when she had displeased him, wearing her down until she had been so afraid of his displeasure that she had been ready to do anything to win her way back into his good graces. But this time she could not allow him to defeat her so easily. If she was to win the battle, and eventually the war, she would have to go on the offensive, to keep him off balance for a change.

"Do you remember the last time I was in this room, Sebastian?" The unexpected question threw him a little, Julia could see by the slight wariness that entered his eyes.

"I do indeed. You made an, uh, indelible impression. Not only on me, but on the entire household."

"You said you would make me a lady. And you did."

His eyebrows lifted as if he questioned that, but Julia ignored that silent insult and rushed on.

"You took a guttersnipe and made a lady, Sebastian. You taught me to talk like a lady, act like a lady, think like a lady. Is it so unreasonable that I should want to live like a lady?" She took a deep breath, and decided to take the bull by the horns. "I couldn't be your mistress, don't you see?"

"You were doing a fairly good job of it, as I recall." The cynical observation threatened to unleash her temper, but Julia quickly controlled herself. Getting angry at Sebastian was not part of her plan. She looked at him steadily, trying to disregard the warm rush of color that heated her cheeks as his words recalled the fiery passion they had shared.

"I thought you were the most wonderful thing on earth, Sebastian. I looked up to you, admired you, respected you. Until you came along, I'd never had a friend, you see."

There was a moment of silence. Sebastian's face could have been carved from stone as he stared at her.

"I hardly think I would call us friends." The quiet observation in the chilly voice was belied by the glowing red tip of the cigar as he took a deep drag. That icy mask he wore was slipping, just a little, she hoped, and rushed on.

"But we were friends, Sebastian. Good friends. And more than friends. I cared about you, Sebastian, and I thought you cared about me. That's why I—I let you . . ." Her voice trailed off and her face turned scarlet. For all her good intentions she found that she could just not spell out exactly what it was she had let him do in the face of those cold, unwavering blue eyes.

"You *let* me?" He made a cynical sound that was halfway between a snort and a laugh. "As I recall, you more than let me. You were all over me as soon as I touched you. Each time."

Her color was one thing she was unable to control. She wanted to crawl under the chair and hide as her face burned even hotter than before. But she did not; she kept her chin high and met his eyes with as much dignity as she could summon to her aid.

"And," he continued smoothly, but she got the sense that his muscles were tensing like those of an animal about to spring, "you'd more than let me now. I could take you, right here in this room, with the whole staff undoubtedly hovering about outside, and you would love it. That's how it is with whores. Especially good ones. And you are very, very good, my dear."

The hot color faded from her cheeks. She felt herself pale as the insult sank home. Her eyes met his, and she saw the hostility flaming beneath the ice. He was deliberately trying to hurt her, she told herself, deliberately attacking her most sensitive spot to keep her from getting too close. Because she had been close. As she had thought about it the day before, it had suddenly become clear to her that Sebastian cared for her opinion, and therefore for her, more than he was willing to admit. People had been calling him murderer for years; apparently it had never particularly bothered him before. But he had not liked hearing the accusation on her lips, and that augered well for the success of her plan. If she could just control her temper until he could be brought to a realization that he cared for her more than he knew . . .

"I don't really think you murdered Elizabeth, you know." Her quiet statement in the face of his flagrant provocation brought a fierce frown to his face. His eyes flamed, and then were quickly banked with ice.

"Do you think I gave a damn what you think?" The cold, polite tone was at variance with the savagery of the words.

"I just wanted you to know," she said simply, and smiled at him. That sweet smile seemed to madden him. He went very still for an instant, staring at her with disbelief, and then the banked flames leaped to life in his eyes and he snarled as he came out of the chair. He looked bent on violence, but Julia sat where she was, fingers curled into the leather arms of the chair in anticipation. Shaking him out of his icy armor was part of the plan, and she had to be prepared to take the consequences when she succeeded.

But before he made it more than halfway around the desk, the door to the study flew open. He stopped, lifting flaming eyes to glare at the intruder. Julia felt a mingling of relief and disappointment as she too looked toward the door.

"My God, it is her! When Caroline came and told me that you had invited her to stay, I thought she must be hallucinating. Not even you would invite a—a female of that stamp into our home. Have you no regard for our name at all?"

The Dowager Countess of Moorland stood silhouetted in the doorway. After one condemning look at Julia, her attention was all on her son. Looking at the still slender, silver-haired figure clad all in black, Julia was struck once more by how very much she resembled her son. She must have been a dazzling beauty when she was young, Julia thought with a swift glance at Sebastian. But now she was an unhappy bitter woman estranged from her only surviving child. What had happened to make her so?

"Do come in, mama," Sebastian said mildly. With one hard look at Julia he abandoned his intended assault and seated himself comfortably on the edge of his desk. One booted foot swung idly as he returned his mother's angry look with a slight mocking smile.

"Taking her in off the streets and sending her to live at White Friars was bad enough, but at least no one ever had to see her there. Here, she is bound to be discovered by all our friends. I tell you, I will not have it! She must leave this house at once!"

"Come in and close the door, mama. I have something to say to you that I am sure you would prefer was not overheard by the staff."

The dowager countess, who had ignored his previous ironic invitation to enter, stood poised for a moment longer in the doorway, giving her son a glance of such intense dislike that Julia's eyes widened. Then with a haughty lift of her head, she stepped inside the room and closed the door. Sebastian smiled at her. Julia shivered. She would not like to have that smile directed at herself.

"First of all, mama, you force me to remind you that this house is mine. I allow you to live here simply because you are my mother, however little you or I may relish that fact. Caroline too lives here strictly on my good will. If I choose to invite another member of our family to reside in this house as well, I will do so. Julia has as much right here as either you or Caroline—the right of my say-so. Remember that, if you please."

The dowager countess turned icy blue eyes on Julia. Julia's first impulse was to shrink back, but then pride took hold and she held her head high under the woman's scathing regard. "Julia! She wasn't Julia the last time she was here! I seem to recall something far more common. Ah yes, Jewel. A vulgar name for a vulgar little—"

"Mama!" Sebastian broke in sharply. "You will be civil to *Julia* at all times. Is that clear?"

The older woman's eyes swung back to her son. "I will not. I will have nothing to do with her. I cannot prevent you from lodging her in this house, for as you say it is yours and you will do as you please, just as you always do, with no thought for the pain you inflict on others, but—"

"Julia has come to town to be introduced to the ton. I expect you to perform that function."

The quiet statement made the older woman stiffen. She swung wild, hating eyes from Sebastian to Julia and back again. Julia stared at her, half afraid of what she might do. She did not look quite sane.

"*I* introduce *her* to the ton? You must be joking."

"Indeed, I am not. You, my dear mama, are one of the premiere hostesses in London. If you take Julia under your wing, there will be no question about her acceptance. I desire you to take her around just as you do Caroline. After all, Julia is a member of the family."

"That rackety Timothy! How could he do this to us? Sebastian, if you had only repudiated her from the start, we would not have come to this pass. But of course, anything you can do to disoblige me, you will do. You were always the most unnatural son."

"And you the most unnatural mother." Sebastian's eyes narrowed faintly. It was the only indication that the altercation disturbed him that Julia could perceive. She wondered what it would feel like to have one's emotions under such icy control, and shivered. It would not suit her at all. She would probably burst with the strain of it.

"Understand me, mama." Sebastian's eyes were a cold, steady blue as they impaled his mother. "You will treat Julia like a daughter. You will take her around to parties and routs and what-have-yous; you will introduce her to people as your deceased nephew's dear widow; if you are questioned about her antecedents, you will tell them that she is a connection of the Frames. Indeed, she could well be; Howard Frame's by-blows alone are sufficient to populate half of Yorkshire. Julia, are you attending to this? You are to remember as well." His eyes flicked to Julia once, then returned to fix on the dowager countess. His voice went very soft. "You will never, by the slightest look or deed, give anyone cause to think that she is other than Julia Stratham, a lady and our kinswoman. Should you fail in any of this . . ." Sebastian smiled that particularly frightening smile at his mother. "Should you fail in any of this, I will cut off the very handsome allowance which I make you, which would leave you quite dependent on the extremely inadequate widow's jointure that my father, in his infinite wisdom, chose to settle upon you. I will also require you to leave this house, for, I think, my property in Scotland. Where you will remain."

The dowager countess stared bitterly at her son for a long moment. The two pairs of icy blue eyes met and clashed; finally the dowager countess spoke.

"Giving birth to you was the worst thing I ever did in my life," she said, and she turned on her heel and left the room.

When she was gone, Sebastian's shoulders seemed to sag for a moment. Then, so swiftly that Julia might have imagined the brief lapse in his control, he recovered, swiveling to face her. The icy mask of his face tugged at her heart. To have a mother who hated one so must be the source of terrible pain.

"Sebastian. . . ." She half-rose from her chair, instinctively wanting to offer him comfort, but the cold eyes he turned on her warned her off. Like a wounded animal he could not bear to have his injuries touched. At least not yet. If she succeeded in her plan, Julia hoped to have the chance to heal them.

"I presume you are happy now. You have your wish, and more." The clipped words belonged to the Earl of Moorland, not the Sebastian she knew and loved. But Julia felt that now was not the time to press for that Sebastian's return.

"I'm sorry to be the cause of any trouble with your mother," she quietly said instead. He shrugged, and moved back around the desk to sit down in his chair.

"There is always trouble with my mother," he muttered, and his eyes were sharp on hers as if he were afraid that even that simple statement revealed too much. "She will do as I say, however. As you heard, I have the means to compel her. And Caroline as well. They are both dependent upon me for the lavishness with which they live. If by chance either of them should not treat you as you would like, you are to come to me at once. Do you understand?"

He looked tired suddenly, so tired that Julia had not the heart to argue with him that she would really prefer not to be a talebearer. So she nodded.

"Good." He picked up the cigar that was still burning in the ashtray and stubbed it out. Then those blue eyes returned to hers. "I expect you to conduct yourself with propriety at all times as well. To put it bluntly, that means no men. Not while you are living under my roof."

Julia, who had been feeling sorry for him, stiffened. She stared at him with golden eyes whose softness rapidly turned to anger. A heated denial hovered on her lips, but she bit it back, distracted by a sudden thought. Unintentionally he had given her the germ of another idea on how to break through his wall of icy reserve. He wouldn't like to see her going about with other men . . .

"Just as you say, of course," she agreed pleasantly, then stood up. "Unless you have something else of a pressing nature to say to me, I'd like to go to my room. I am expecting some deliveries this morning, and I would like to be on hand to direct Emily where to put them."

He looked at her. "You were very sure that you would be remaining, it seems."

"Yes," she said with a sideways smile. "I was."

And then she dropped him a little mock curtsy and left the room.

XXIII

PLEASE do not take the way Margaret is behaving to heart," Caroline said earnestly.

It was nearly two weeks later, and Caroline and Julia were waiting in the entryway of the house on Grosvenor Square for the dowager countess, whom Caroline called by her given name of Margaret. It was evening, and they were on their way to a small soiree.

The gathering would mark Julia's first real venture into society. She had, of course, joined Caroline and the countess when they had received callers in the afternoons, and she had accompanied Caroline in making calls. The countess had pleaded a severe headache on those latter occasions, which had been two in number, just as she had professed to have one tonight. Sebastian had been on his way to dinner at his club when Wigham, his mother's dresser, had come down to give Caroline and Julia the countess' regrets. The earl had immediately turned on his heel and gone back upstairs to confront his mother in her chamber.

The result was that Caroline and Julia were standing about in the front hallway while the countess made a hasty toilette. Sebastian had already taken himself off, apparently confident enough of whatever he had said to his mother that he did not feel the need to remain to make certain that his wishes were carried out.

Julia hated being such a bone of contention between Sebastian and his mother. The evening, which had seemed so exciting as she had donned a lustrous blue silk gown trimmed with yards of creamy lace, had already gone sadly flat. But the Countess was just one of the many obstacles that she would have to overcome to get to Sebastian, she reminded herself. Looked at in that light, the silent hostility that the older woman radiated could be tolerated if not ignored. The rest of the haute ton—at least those whom she had met—had seemed perfectly ready to take her at face value, as the widow of the dowager's nephew.

On the first occasion when she had sat in the front salon with Caroline and the countess waiting for afternoon callers, she had been so nervous of betraying herself that her knees were shaking. But when the countess had explained with a tight little smile that "dear Julia" was newly come up from the country, where she had met and married Timothy and where she had stayed during the obligatory year of mourning, there had been polite expressions of regret at Timothy's passing but that was all. No one had stood to denounce her as an upstart foisted upon the ton; no one had seemed shocked or horrified by her speech or behavior. She had been accepted, rather to her amazement, without question. As if she were truly the lady she pretended to be.

Caroline had been surprisingly friendly. Wary at first of the other's seeming readiness to accept her, Julia had gradually come to believe that there was no meanness in Caroline. She was something of an airhead—witness the way she treated Sebastian's every word as though it had come down from on high—but she was sweet-natured and Julia thought she might come to like her very much. Although Caroline was some twelve years older than Julia, she was still very lovely in the blonde, blue-eyed fashion that was so much in vogue. Julia had come to believe that one reason that Caroline was so ready to take her about with her was that they were excellent foils for one another: Caroline tall and reed slim, dressed in the soft pastels that were so becoming to her fair coloration, with Julia smaller and curvier, her ebony hair and ivory skin set off by jewel tones. Indeed, the two were a study in contrasts, as Caroline had remarked in a pensive tone one time when she had caught a glimpse of them side by side in a mirror. But whatever the reason, Caroline's friendship was very welcome. It was a pleasant antidote to Sebastian's cold politeness and his mother's outright hostility.

The countess' descent of the stairs put an end to Julia's mental wanderings. The older woman was wearing shimmering silver silk, Julia saw as she looked up, and looked wonderful despite the irritable frown that marred her still beautiful face. Sebastian would age well, too, she thought irrelevantly, and then the countess reached the bottom of the steps and swept by them without a word.

Smathers leapt to open the door before she reached it. Caroline threw an apologetic look at Julia, then the two younger women followed the countess out. Tense silence reigned in the carriage during the short drive to Lady Frayne's residence, where the soiree was to be held. Julia, growing more and more apprehensive as she sat squashed into a corner in the silent carriage, wished ridiculously for Sebastian's presence. Icily angry with her or not, she knew she could have counted on his support whatever happened. Now, when she felt like Daniel about to be thrown into the lion's den, she had only Caroline, who was sweet but weak, and the countess, who actively despised her.

Then the carriage was rocking to a halt, and before she knew it she was being ushered into Lady Frayne's salon. As the countess had made them late, a heavyset lady was already sitting before the company with her harp, ready to sing and play. Besides a smiling welcome from their hostess, and amiable nods from those among the company who were one or the other of the ladies' particular friends, they were scarcely noticed as they took their seats.

By the time the singing had ceased—the lady sang opera, which Julia found herself totally unable to appreciate—she felt considerably more comfortable. Julia was almost relaxed as she rose with the rest of the guests and adjourned to the refreshment tables. The countess and Caroline were mingling with the other guests, and Julia knew that she should join one or the other of them. But for just this moment she wanted to stand back and observe.

It was a small party by the ton's standards, with perhaps fifty people in attendance. But those who were invited were the cr me de la cr me, and as Julia watched all these splendid people laugh and flirt and chatter she felt a sudden sensation of being caught up in a dream. In her days as a homeless street waif she would never even have been able to imagine such a gathering. Never in her wildest dreams had she thought to find herself dressed in silk and lace, with hunger the farthest thing from her mind as she stood amongst a crowd of the sort of people whose purses she had used to lift. She blinked, bringing herself back to the present with determination. That part of her life was over, forgotten. She had been a different person then, one who no longer existed. Now she was Julia Stratham, and this glittering extravaganza was her world.

Julia swallowed the last crumb of a sugary macaroon without tasting it. She saw Caroline, chatting happily in a foursome that included a plump blonde in pink whom Julia vaguely remembered being introduced to during one of their at-home afternoons, a small slender gentleman with a lively laugh, and a tall older gentleman with dark hair and a kind smile. But before she could move to join them Caroline was detaching the older gentleman from the group and bringing him over to Julia.

"Julia, Lord Carlyle has asked me to make him known to you, so here you see me performing my duty as chaperone. Lord Carlyle, this is my cousin by marriage, Mrs. Julia Stratham."

"How do you do, Mrs. Stratham?"

Julia held out her hand, smiling up at him. Lord Carlyle took it, bowing over it with a slow smile that she immediately liked. Then he turned that slow smile on Caroline.

"You are far too young and lovely to be a chaperone, Mrs. Peyton. In fact, it is my wager that the two loveliest ladies in the ton this year will be widows instead of debutantes."

"You flatter me, sir." Julia offered a shy smile to this big bear of a man whom she liked immediately.

"Oh, and me!" Caroline was being excessively gay, Julia thought, noting the two bright spots of color in her cheeks and hearing the arch note in her voice. "Julia quite outshines me, you know. She is such a sweet young thing, while I—I fear I must appear old in comparison."

"You could never appear old, Mrs. Peyton," Lord Carlyle assured her gallantly, and Caroline giggled. Julia looked at her in surprise. In the two weeks she had been accompanying her so-called cousin about, she had never seen her show any interest in a man. Now here she was practically flirting with Lord Carlyle.

"I fear we should resume our seats. It appears as though the second half of the evening's entertainment is about to begin." Julia thought her own voice sounded quite wooden next to Caroline's, but then she was not trying to attract Lord Carlyle.

But that gentleman turned grave gray eyes on her, listening to her few words as if they were pearls of wisdom. Why, he is attracted to me, she thought, and felt a little frisson of pleasure. If she could attract the interest of a gentleman like Lord Carlyle, perhaps she was closer to her goal than she had thought.

"Isn't Madame Crieza in fabulous voice?" Caroline remarked in a hushed voice as they moved to resume their seats. Lord Carlyle smilingly agreed. And Julia thought again of how far she had to go to become a lady in fact as well as in name. To her the fabulous diva's singing was about as pleasing as the caterwauling of a scalded cat. But apparently the truly well-born enjoyed it.

By the time the evening was finally over, Julia had a headache. She said a civil farewell to her hostess, and those of the other guests to whom she had had occasion to speak, and a smiling one to Lord Carlyle. He was really a very nice man, she thought, then dismissed him from her mind as she followed the countess and Caroline into the carriage. One good thing about the countess' displeasure, she thought, was that at least the drive home would be silent, so her aching head could recover in peace.

But it was not to be. Caroline was full of chatter, and what was not in praise of the performance was spent extolling the virtues of Lord Carlyle.

"He is so handsome, do you not agree?" she trilled. "So truly distinguished looking, and very much the man. Exactly how I like a gentleman to be, do you not agree, Julia?"

"He seemed very nice," Julia responded in a small voice, wishing that Caroline would hush and that the carriage wheels would not bounce so lustily over the cobblestones.

"Very nice!" Caroline sounded scandalized. "Why, he is considered quite a catch, you know. He has been on the ton for years, ever since his wife died. But I've never heard of him asking for an introduction to a lady before. You must have made quite an impression on him, Julia."

"Julia does seem to make an . . . impression on widowers, does she not?" The cool voice belonged to the countess. It was devoid of any real expression, but the look in the older woman's eyes was malicious in the extreme. She could mean only one thing, of course. Just as Julia's person had attracted Lord Carlyle's notice, it had also attracted Sebastian's. Julia, feeling her cheeks begin to burn at the silent accusation, found herself suddenly grateful for Caroline's inane chatter.

"His wife was dark, like you. He must like dark women. Wouldn't it be wonderful if he should be interested in you? He would be quite a catch, you know. Besides being Lord Carlyle, which title has been in existence since practically the Norman Conquest, and being a very handsome gentleman, his purse is as deep as anyone's and he never stinted his late wife. Of course there are the children—he has three, you know—but then Sebastian mentioned that you had spent some time with Chloe, so you must be fond of children. Poor little girl, Chloe, I mean, she—"

"Would you hush your senseless chatter, Caroline?" The dowager didn't frown, but the look she bent on Caroline was taut with displeasure. Then those blue eyes, so like Sebastian's, shifted to Julia again. "Of course Julia made a show of being interested in Chloe. She would be a fool if she didn't. But you'll catch cold at trying to catch Sebastian through his daughter, my girl. Like myself, he is a most unfond parent. It must be in the blood."

"You and Sebastian are very much alike," Caroline agreed, then appeared horrified at what she had said. "Of course, not that I mean to imply that he is not fond of Chloe, because I am sure he is, or that you are not fond of him, because you know you are, Margaret, underneath everything—"

"You are a fool, Caroline," the countess said with chilling precision, her attention focusing on her daughter-in-law again. "I despise Sebastian, just as he despises that chit of his. Edward was the son of my heart. If Sebastian did not look so like me, I would swear that the midwife had slipped a changeling into my bed. He is everything that is displeasing to me: cold, arrogant, cruel. . . ."

"Very much like yourself in fact, ma'am?" Julia had not been able to listen to that icy denunciation in silence. Sebastian was not here to take his own part against this heartless woman. Therefore, she would take his part for him. She could not bear to hear him abused, and especially not by one who should love him.

Those icy eyes met Julia's heated golden ones. "You do have a tendre for him, don't you? You are more foolish than I thought. Sebastian feels nothing similar for you. It is not in his nature. I have never seen him display a fondness toward anyone. Me, his mother, he despises. He disliked his only brother, and felt contemptuous of his father, who I must admit was deserving of it. I felt the same way myself. That poor stick of a wife of his he was civil to, but no more. And as for his daughter, I laugh when I think of that wretched little mite. Sebastian married for a son, a son to carry on our name, and what he got was a girl who is not even normal but a freak! She—"

"Stop it!" Julia could not listen to any more of this woman's poison. "How dare you call her that? Chloe is not a freak, but a lovely little girl! And if Sebastian cannot show affection, whose fault is that? Yours, you nasty old woman, for never showing him any. You should be ashamed!" The faces of Chloe and Sebastian rose in her mind. Chloe, just a child who desperately needed love. Sebastian, a man grown, who needed the same thing. That this woman, who was mother to one and grandmother to the other, could say such things, could deny them the affection that was theirs by right and custom, infuriated her.

Sebastian might be too armored against emotion to denounce his mother as she deserved. But Julia had no hesitation about doing it for him.

The countess was looking at her as if she had suddenly grown two heads. Apparently she was not used to being shouted at, or spoken to as Julia had spoken to her. Sebastian was invariably icily polite to his mother, Julia recalled, even when he was threatening her. But she did not feel an instant's regret about what she had said or the manner in which she had said it. She looked the countess right in her soulless eyes and ignored Caroline's horrified sputters as she attempted to smooth over the ghastly scene.

"Stop clearing your throat, Caroline, you sound like a chicken whose neck is being wrung," the countess said coldly. Her gaze had never left Julia. Those blue eyes no longer reminded her of Sebastian's, Julia realized as she met them without an outward sign of a qualm. Sebastian's eyes had been many things in the time she had known them, but never this, never evil.

"You will regret speaking to me in such a fashion," the countess said finally.

Julia felt a shiver feather its way down her spine as the carriage thankfully rolled to a stop in front of the house.

XXIV

HE following morning a nosegay of purple and gold pansies was delivered for Julia, along with a charming note from Lord Carlyle. As she accepted the tribute from Smathers and pressed it to her nose, breathing deeply of the soft fragrance of the flowers, Sebastian came in through the front door.

He was dressed for riding in a severe black coat that emphasized the silver-gold of his hair, buff breeches, and a pair of highly polished boots. A silver-topped riding crop was in his hand, and he surrendered this and his hat to the footman who opened the door. From the disordered waves of his hair and the healthy flush of color in his cheeks, he had obviously just returned from an early morning gallop.

His eyes narrowed as they found Julia, who looked back at him with a pleasure she could not quite disguise; even frowning as he was at the moment, he was handsome enough to stop her breath. Her eyes traced the flawless lines of his forehead and chin, the straight, high-bridged nose, the stern mouth with its slightly fuller lower lip, the broad shoulders and lean hips and long muscular legs, returning to meet the celestial blue eyes. They were anything but celestial now as the dark brows met above them in a frown of irritation.

"Tributes from an admirer already?" The smoothness of his voice did not quite conceal the hint of a sneer. "I would scarcely have thought you would have had time to make any conquests as yet. You do work fast, don't you?"

"Lord Carlyle sent them. I met him last night." She sniffed the velvety blooms again, pretending not to notice his annoyance, then held them out for his inspection. "Aren't they lovely?"

"Lovely." If anything, his voice was even more curt than before. His eyes ran over her, lingering on the white swell of her flesh above the low round neckline of her pale lilac morning gown with its trimming of deeper lilac ribbons. There was a restlessness in his eyes that was not like him, and Julia rejoiced as she saw it. She disturbed him, she knew. She also knew that the fact angered him extremely.

"Have you breakfasted yet? If not, you might join me. I want to talk to you, and now seems as good a time as any." Even in issuing an invitation, his tone was clipped.

"I've had chocolate, but I can always manage to eat a little more." She twinkled at him, not one whit disturbed by his sour mood. If anything, she welcomed it. It was not like Sebastian to display anything so human as irritability.

"If you don't stop eating like you expect a famine to strike tomorrow, you'll get fat," he warned in a jaundiced tone as he gestured to her to precede him up the stairs to the breakfast room. A jaunty swishing of her full skirts in his direction was the only reply he received.

Breakfast was strictly a serve oneself affair, and the array of dishes on the sideboard was truly astonishing, especially considering the fact that Sebastian was the only member of the household who habitually rose early enough to partake of it. The countess and Caroline always remained in their rooms until noon, and Julia usually breakfasted in her chamber on the sweet chocolate and rolls for which she had developed a passion. But (strictly to be sociable, mind!) she helped herself to toast points and preserves, and a rasher of bacon. That, along with a cup of tea, and on top of the chocolate and rolls she had already consumed, would make for quite an adequate second breakfast.

"Will you have a kidney?" Sebastian asked with a hint of sarcasm, eyeing her filling plate.

Julia declined with an airy smile, watching as he helped himself to several kidneys, a substantial serving of eggs and bacon, and some toast. Julia, eyeing his meal, rather thought that, if anyone was going to grow fat, it would be Sebastian instead of herself. He could really put away an incredible amount. Strangely enough, the idea of Sebastian with jowls and a pot belly appealed to her. He was so very handsome she sometimes felt she was in love with a figment of her imagination rather than a man.

"What are you smiling at?" He looked up from his meal just in time to catch that glimmering amusement on her face.

"I was picturing you with a pot belly," she answered, and he almost choked on his bacon.

"God forbid," he said with loathing, and Julia's smile broadened.

"I think I would like it," she said, and his eyes narrowed on her.

"Well, I would not," he answered crisply. "Which brings us to the subject I wished to talk with you about."

"Does it?" she said, sounding polite though her motive was to tease him. "How interesting! You wish to talk to me about something to do with your incipient pot belly?"

He put down his fork and stared at her with such disdain that she would immediately have been chastened—if she had not known that he deliberately used that look when he wished to achieve just that effect.

"I understand that you had words with my mother last night," he said after a moment. With some difficulty Julia resisted an urge to stick out her tongue at him. It was strange how Jewel Combs seemed to pop up in her when she least expected it.

"News certainly travels fast around here, doesn't it?" Julia was still deliberately trying to get a rise out of him. He had been so distant since she had arrived in this house—and she was tired of him being distant.

"From Caroline to her maid to Leister to me," Sebastian responded. "There is no need for you to take up cudgels on my behalf. I am perfectly capable of defending myself should I feel the need."

"I cannot sit there and listen to that woman say such things about you," Julia muttered. "It makes me want to slap her. Besides, I was defending Chloe as much as you."

"I thank you for your championship on my daughter's behalf as well as my own, but in future I wish you would not. Agreed?"

"No, we are not agreed! If you wish to allow your mother to say that you are an unnatural son and father and cold and cruel and incapable of affection, then you may do so. But if she says such things in my presence, then I reserve the right to protest!"

Sebastian put down his fork and stared at her. She was delighted to see that he looked faintly exasperated.

"Does it not occur to you that my mother may be speaking nothing more than the truth, in my case at least?"

Julia took another bite of toast, chewed, swallowed, and met his eyes. "No, it does not. You are many things—including a distrusting, dishonest swine—but you are not incapable of affection. You are fond of Chloe, for one—no, don't deny it, I have seen the evidence with my own eyes. And I believe you are fond of me."

His eyes widened at this last. They gleamed very blue suddenly as they stared at her. "Do you indeed?"

The soft syllables were as much a warning as the hissing of a snake. Julia met those blue eyes dauntlessly. Faint heart did never win fair maiden, she reminded herself—or in this case fair gentleman.

"You are just afraid to admit it."

"On the contrary, I am not the least afraid to admit that I am, as you say, fond of you—at least in a particular way." The leer that he offered her in accompaniment to this last made hot color wash into Julia's face. But she refused to allow any other outward sign of embarrassment to show.

"And I am fond of you in that way, too," she said cordially, taking a sip of her tea with as much calm as if they were discussing the weather. "But I rather think that there is more to our feeling for one another than that."

He was looking at her now with the icy mask back in place so that she could not read anything in those glacial blue eyes.

"You are, of course, entitled to your opinion." With deliberate care he touched his lips with his napkin, then laid it down beside his plate before getting to his feet. "If you will excuse me, I have things to attend to." And before she could answer, he was striding from the room.

Julia reacted to this flagrant breach of good manners—a gentleman never left a lady sitting at a table—with a tiny smile. The smile widened as her eyes found his barely touched plate.

X X V

ONDON at the height of the season was a whirl of sights and activities. There was shopping, of course, as Julia found the vast wardrobe which she had bespoke from Madame de Tissaud was not nearly so vast after all. There were visits to the Pantheon Bazaar, the lending library, and the theatre. Nary a day went by when there was not a breakfast party, a picnic, a soiree or a ball.

In addition, there were the afternoon outings in Hyde Park, which were de rigueur whenever the weather permitted. Ladies in their rainbow-hued dresses, sporting fetching bonnets and kid gloves and carrying jaunty parasols, bowled through the park in their open carriages, the object being to see and be seen by as many fashionables as possible. Those with good seats were on horseback, to better show off this advantage they had over their less gifted sisters.

The gentlemen came, too, just a tad less brightly dressed than their ladies, some on horseback, some on foot hoping to be invited to ride with the lady of their choice, and some showing off sporting carriages. Even the occasional Cyprian turned out, taking the air in a carriage bestowed upon her by some lord in payment for services rendered, gaudily dressed and sassy as she waved at those of the gentlemen whom she knew. These horrified gentlemen generally pretended to be conveniently afflicted by blindness. Although the ton's ladies were aware that their men were acquainted with all manner of undesirable females, they too pretended a convenient ignorance on this subject, which the gentlemen were pleased to encourage. The park was one of the few places where the two sides of a man's life might meet. It was a horrible fact of fashionable life.

It was a warm sunny day in late April, and Julia was seated in Lord Carlyle's carriage as he guided it carefully through the park. The main thoroughfare was packed with traffic and, as Lord Carlyle had to weave his horses in and out of the laughing, calling throng, conversation between him and Julia was desultory.

Julia was very pleased with herself as she waved demurely at acquaintances. She was looking very fine, she knew, both from her mirror and because Lord Carlyle told her so. She wore a dress of sapphire blue sarcenet, styled with the new narrower skirt and topped with a cunning little jacket made of the same material. A wide, flat-crowned hat of chipped straw trimmed with flowers and ribbons in the same shade of blue was perched on her head, its three-inch wide ribbons tied in a jaunty bow beneath one ear. She was not carrying a parasol, but that was because she had no need of one. The hat served the dual purpose of framing her face charmingly while at the same time shielding it from the sun.

But her appearance was not the only reason why Julia was feeling so cheerful. There was also the fact that her plan to become part of the ton was an unqualified success. In the brief time she had been in town, the haute monde had ceased to treat her as a newcomer. She was now an accepted member of Society, and was included without question in any invitations addressed to the Peyton ladies. Lord Carlyle was paying her what Caroline assured her was determined court, and she also had a satisfactory number of other admirers who gathered around her at parties and filled her dance cards so that she had never yet suffered the ignominy of having to sit out a dance.

The only fly in her ointment was that Sebastian was apparently unaware of the scope of her success. He never attended the ton's functions, either from a sensitivity toward the Turkish treatment sure to be accorded him by some of the sticklers, or from simple distaste for the social whirl. Thus he did not witness the small crowd of gentlemen she invariably gathered around herself, or the smiles that the very ladies who would cut his acquaintance bestowed on her.

Which was funny when she thought about it. Here was she, the former Jewel Combs (although she hardly ever allowed herself to remember it), now an accepted member of Society. And all the while he, the earl born and a gentleman to his fingertips, was to all intents and purposes an outcast from the society to which he belonged by birth.

"The park is very crowded today." This observation was the first that Lord Carlyle had offered in quite a few minutes. Julia smiled at him. He was not a talkative gentleman, but she liked him, a liking that was not harmed by her knowledge that it was considered quite a feather in her cap to have attached him. And besides, he was a very attractive man, himself.

"Yes, indeed it is." Julia responded with a smile. "I don't know how you manage to keep us on the road. There is scarcely any room at all. With any other gentleman I would quite fear being overturned."

"You need have no fear of that when you are with me. I would never overturn one so lovely as you. Why, think of the affront to your dignity! Every feeling is offended."

"And besides that, I would undoubtedly land in the mud, and my beautiful dress would be quite ruined." The mournful tone of this last made him burst out laughing.

"That is quite why I like you, you know," he said with a sideways smile at her. "You are the most totally unaffected female it has ever been my privilege to meet! Your parents must have been most unusual to have raised such a daughter. Tell me, what were they like?"

She had already told him that both parents were dead. Now he was pressing for details, and she had none to give him. The story she had concocted, and which had been agreed upon icily by the dowager countess and with much frowning memorization by Caroline, came with difficulty to her lips. She did not like to lie to Lord Carlyle. She liked him too much.

"My mother was a very kind, warm person. My father I don't remember at all. As you know, he died when I was very young."

"What was his name?"

Julia's eyes rolled around desperately as she searched for some way to end the conversation.

"Howard. Howard Frame." Frame was a very common name in England, Julia had learned, its members scattered across the country and occupying every walk of life.

"One of the Yorkshire Frames?" Lord Carlyle was quietly persistent. Julia gave up. She hated to lie, so she turned the tables on him.

"You are very interested in my antecedents, my lord," she said with what she hoped was a gay smile.

He smiled back at her. "Indeed I am. I had not meant to speak of this so soon, but it is my hope that one day your antecedents will be joined with mine through posterity."

Julia's brow knitted as she unraveled that. The only way that that could happen was if they had children together. At the realization her eyes rounded, and leaped out to meet his. He was still smiling at her, the swine.

"I wish you will take me home now, my lord." Sebastian's examples of arctic rage stood her in good stead now. She wanted to denounce Lord Carlyle furiously, but Hyde Park was no place for such a display. Her hands clenched in her lap as she glared at him, letting her eyes say all that her lips could not.

"I have offended you? Mrs. Stratham, I apologize." He sounded bewildered. "I realize that we have not been acquainted long, and indeed I had not meant to speak so soon, but I thought you must surely have some glimmer of how I felt."

"If I had had such a glimmer, my lord, you may rest assured that I would not now be sitting in your carriage!" This furious mutter brought a frown to Lord Carlyle's face.

"You are angry with me," he said, sounding surprised. Julia glared at him in silent confirmation. She had never, ever thought to be insulted so as Julia Stratham, lady. Perhaps he sensed something about her, perhaps Jewel Combs showed through despite all the care to eradicate her.

"I know I should have spoken to your guardian first," Lord Carlyle said rapidly. "But I have never been intimate with Lord Moorland and given, uh, his circumstances, I have felt awkward about approaching him. Not that you are in any way to blame for that rackety fellow, of course. One cannot help one's relatives, after all."

"You were going to approach Seb—, Lord Moorland, with this?" Julia's mind boggled at the thought. Sebastian's reaction to such a proposal did not bear thinking of given his present state of mind.

Lord Carlyle looked surprised. "It is the proper thing to do, after all."

The proper thing to do . . . Julia's mind reeled. Then the

tiniest glimmer of realization began to shine through.

"If I had realized that you were so averse to the very idea," he said, his voice as stiff as his face, "I would never have broached the subject. I hope we may still be friends, even if you will not be my wife?"

"You are asking me to marry you?" Her stunned tone brought his head, which had been averted, swinging around. She looked up into that broad, darkly-complected face with the soft gray eyes and felt a kind of shame. Of course, he was asking her to be his wife. A gentleman such as Lord Carlyle would never, ever insult a lady by suggesting that she become his mistress.

Lord Carlyle looked down at her with lifted brows. "Well, of course I am asking you to marry me. What else have we been talking about these last few minutes?"

Julia smiled suddenly, brilliantly. She had gotten the situation entirely wrong. Instead of insulting her, he was doing her the ultimate honor. He was asking her, Julia Stratham, to be his wife. He had not even suspected Jewel Combs' existence

In response to her directive to be taken home, he was turning the carriage out of the press of traffic toward the gates. This maneuver was not accomplished without a near brush of the wheels with a high-perch phaeton, and an exchange of glares with its driver, a dashingly dressed young gentleman in a spotted neckcloth. By the time Lord Carlyle had his carriage bowling toward the gates, Julia had recovered from her astonishment. She laid a gentle hand on his gray superfine clad arm, and when he bent an inquiring glance upon her, she smiled guilelessly.

"I must apologize for my intemperate reaction to your

proposal, my lord," she murmured with an air of embarrassed modesty. "To tell the truth, it was not until we reached the end of the conversation that I realized what it was you had asked. I'm ashamed to have to confess that I was wool gathering at the start of it."

Lord Carlyle grinned, looking suddenly very much younger than what Julia guessed were his forty years. "You did not realize that you were being proposed to?"

Julia shook her head. "No, my lord, I fear I did not. must apologize."

"And I thought it was my children," he muttered, shaking his head. "Or my person. Or. . . ."

"It was none of those things, my lord," Julia interrupted gently. "I have no objection to your children. At least, I don't think I do, though never having met them I can't say for certain. And as for your person," she cast down her eyes modestly, in a way that would have made Sebastian shout with cynical laughter, "I find it—not displeasing."

"Am I to take it then, that you are not rejecting my suit out of hand?"

"N-no." Julia had plans of her own where Lord Carlyle was concerned, but she liked him and did not want to hurt him. Encouraging him with the object of enraging Sebastian was one thing. Actually accepting a proposal of marriage from him was something else. The phrase Mrs. Thomas had drummed into her head popped up on the tip of her tongue, and she uttered it with relief. The strict rules governing the actions and utterances of those in Society had their advantages, she thought, when they provided one with something so pat to say.

"It is just that this is all so sudden, my lord." Her eyes

fluttered up to look at him, and she was surprised to see a sudden flare of passion in them. It was quickly banked, but she was slightly shaken by it. Managing Lord Carlyle might be more difficult than she had anticipated. For a moment he had looked very much as if he would have liked to kiss her.

"But I may hope?" His well modulated voice was a note deeper than usual.

Julia looked up to meet kind gray eyes and felt a warming toward him. She really did like this man. Marrying him would be the most sensible thing she had ever done in her life. As Lady Carlyle there would never be any uncertainty about where she belonged in life. Then, unbidden, Sebastian's too beautiful face appeared in her mind's eye. He was unprincipled, mean tempered, cold, and insulting, but she loved him, and while there was breath in her body or his she knew she could never give herself to another man.

"One may always hope." Accompanied as it was by a demure smile, this statement satisfied Lord Carlyle as a coy affirmative. And she was not actually lying, Julia consoled her conscience. After all, who knew what twists and turns life might take?

"Now that we are friends again, do you still wish me to take you home? It is quite early yet." The carriage was about to pull out of the Park Lane into Piccadilly. The road was, as usual, packed with traffic while the sidewalks teemed with pedestrians and vendors pushing hand carts.

"Perhaps you'd better," Julia said with a smile. "If we are to attend the theatre this evening, I shall have to rest beforehand or I fear I shall look quite haggard."

He laughed. "You could never look haggard, Mrs. Stratham. Your youthful beauty is such that would defy the most sleepless night."

"Why, thank you, Lord Carlyle."

Such badinage as this was the staple of the interaction between the sexes in the polite world. To Julia it was almost second nature now. She dimpled as she said the words, her eyes already fixed on the press of carriages as Lord Carlyle expertly maneuvered his rig out to join them.

She was just about to say something else when her eye was caught by a gleaming black curricle with overlarge wheels and a natty leather interior just ahead of them. It was Sebastian's vehicle with Jenkins up behind. As Lord Carlyle's equipage drew nearly abreast of it, she saw that Sebastian, looking lean and powerful and incredibly handsome in a coat of pale blue bathcloth, was handling the reins. But even as the sun gleaming off his silver-gilt hair caught her eye and distracted her, she saw that he was not alone.

Beside him was a lady in an almost indecently low cut dress of palest pink, with a deep flounce across the bodice, baring her shoulders and much of her generous bosom. If one was attracted to avaricious blondes in full bloom, then Julia supposed that the lady must be considered quite beautiful, although personally she did not admire the lady's style. In fact, the longer she looked the clearer it became that this was no lady, but what the polite world termed "a fashionable impure."

Julia, nearly reverting to Jewel in her mounting anger, could think of several more descriptive terms, but she refused to allow them to form in her mind. Instead she stared glassily at the oblivious pair as they laughed and chatted in the carriage ahead. As she watched, the lady squealed, and jumped to her feet to throw her arms around Sebastian's neck in an obvious ecstasy of excited pleasure. Julia felt her muscles stiffen in outrage, and then her eyes grew huge with golden fire as Sebastian lowered his head to plant a quick kiss on the lady's too full pink mouth. Spiraling anger fortunately strangled her, or she would have given vent to the curses that were in the heat of the moment forming themselves in her brain. But before she could say anything, another vehicle maneuvered between Sebastian's carriage and their own. Strain as she might to see what happened next, she could not even catch so much as a glimpse.

"Damned rum-un," muttered Lord Carlyle with loathing.

Julia, eyes glittering, glared at him for a second without really realizing who it was she was looking at. Then it dawned on her that he must have witnessed the same thing she had.

"A shame you had to see that," he continued, apologizing as though it were somehow his fault that Sebastian had no more sense of what was proper than to make love to a harlot on a public thoroughfare. "It's a crime, if you'll forgive me for saying so, that a sweet young lady like yourself should be under the protection of one that I can only describe with repugnance as a cursed loose-screw. If you would only give me the right, I would see to it that you were removed from his influence as soon as may be. As my wife, you need never—"

"I will," Julia said abruptly, still glaring. She was completely unaware of the militant expression on her face, or the way her hands were clenched into twin fists in her lap. Lord Carlyle stopped in mid-speech, looking shocked.

"I beg your pardon, Mrs. Stratham?"

"I said I will marry you," she practically spat. "As soon as it may be arranged."

Lord Carlyle still looked stunned, but as what she had said registered he began to smile. He said something about how she had made him the happiest of men, but Julia scarcely heard him. She was busy glaring at the weaving traffic ahead of them, searching for another glimpse of a gleaming black curricle.

X X V I

OU *what?*"

The following morning Julia sat in Sebastian's study and with great relish watched the celestial blue eyes darken stormily as he absorbed the news of her coming nuptuals.

"Don't be absurd," he continued, lighting one of his everlasting cigars and leaning back in his chair to stare at her over its curling smoke. "Of course you are not going to marry Carlyle. If you think I'm enough of a flat to swallow that faradiddle—"

"I tell you, he asked me to marry him, and I said I would. He is coming to see you tomorrow to ask your permission, which I assured him was a mere formality, and to talk over settlements and whatever it is that gentlemen talk over at such a time."

Julia took pleasure in investing the words with as much icy dignity as possible. Doing so required considerable restraint on her part. What she really wanted to do was scream at Sebastian, slap his maddeningly handsome face and rend his cheeks with her nails. She could still see him kissing that overblown trollop!

But, of course, he had no idea that she had witnessed that disgusting little scene, and she certainly wasn't going to enlighten him. With his monstrous conceit he might very well assume her engagement was motivated by *jealousy.*

"You are asking me to believe that Carlyle sincerely wishes to marry you? You were not even acquainted with him until scarcely more than a month ago."

Julia smiled sweetly, although underneath she was gritting her teeth with temper. She would not lose her dignity—with him she always seemed to revert to Jewel Combs. But never again, she vowed, never again.

"Do you have difficulty believing that a gentleman might wish to marry me?"

Sebastian's eyes glinted with a sudden flash of deep blue light as he stared at her over the curling smoke of his cigar.

"You are serious, aren't you? You've somehow got the prosy boor to propose to you."

Julia's lips tightened. "The prosy boor considers you a—a dashed loose-screw, for your information, my lord. And for your further information, Lord Carlyle is in love with me. He considers that I do him honor in consenting to be his wife."

Sebastian snorted. "Carlyle fancies himself in love with Julia Stratham, my own. What are you going to do when he finds out about Jewel Combs?"

Julia glared at him. "How could he? I have put that part of my life very much behind me."

Sebastian smiled slowly. It was not a nice smile. "Have you indeed? I can see traces of the guttersnipe in you very clearly—particularly at certain times. In bed, my love, you are no lady."

Julia's eyes flashed, and she half started out of her chair. "And you are no gentleman at any time!"

"Sit down." Sebastian never raised his voice, but the cold authority which he could invoke whenever he chose had her sinking back into her seat before she realized what she was doing. It was not until she saw the satisfaction that glinted momentarily in his eyes that she realized that she had once again obeyed him like a scolded child. The thought incensed her, and she leapt to her feet, her eyes shooting golden sparks at him.

"I will not sit down!" she shouted, throwing dignity to the wind as she stood with arms akimbo glaring at him. Then, more moderately she added, "I am not a child you can order at your whim."

His eyes measured her. She was dressed in a very becoming morning gown of cherry striped muslin with a wide silk sash in the same shade of cherry around her waist. With her flashing golden eyes and the angry flush tinting her cheeks to almost the same color as her dress, she looked both annoyingly beautiful and tempestuous. He despised tempestuous women, he told himself. The ebony haired little firebrand before him needed a few more lessons in the conduct becoming a lady.

"No, you are not a child," he agreed dispassionately, still surveying her with that hooded expression she found so disconcerting. "And you are not marrying Carlyle either." His voice was very quiet, but there was no mistaking the cold certainty of his words.

"You can't stop me. I shall marry Lord Carlyle if I wish."

"I can stop you, believe me." His lips twisted in a chilling half-smile. His next words were very soft. "I have only to tell Carlyle the truth about your background—or to tell him that you've been my mistress."

As the words penetrated, Julia's temper exploded. Her face contorted with rage, and she leapt to grab something, anything that she could hurl at him. Her fingers closed on the glass paperweight on his desk—but he was quicker than she. His hands closed around hers, squeezing until they hurt and she was forced to drop her missile. But she was beside herself, clawing at his hands, hurling curses learned from a lifetime in the gutter at him. In her fury Julia Stratham was no more. It was Jewel Combs who screeched at him, Jewel Combs who writhed and kicked and spat as he yanked her around his desk and fell back into his chair with her, so that she was sitting in his lap with his arms locked around her waist, holding her so that her hands were useless. It was Jewel Combs who looked up into his face with loathing and saw it twisted with amusement, and it was Jewel Combs who twisted around to sink her teeth into his neck.

"You poisonous little bitch!" He yelled, jerking away—but still she wouldn't quit, couldn't quit, and her teeth went for his ear this time. He caught her jaw just in time, his fingers cruel as they bit into the soft flesh of her cheeks, his eyes alight with an anger to match her own as he glared down at her.

"Filthy bastard, no good—" She hissed at him, but before she could continue with the litany of abuse his fingers tightened on her jaw until she was gasping with pain. Still, she stared at him, eyes bright with hatred and defiance.

"Shut up," he said brutally, then crushed her mouth with

his. It was a kiss designed to hurt her, to insult her, and she fought against it, struggling in his arms, refusing to open her mouth until he forced her to by the pressure of his fingers digging into her cheeks. Still, she refused to respond to the heated kiss as his tongue conquered her mouth with ferocious intensity. He kissed her with such force that her lower lip split and she tasted blood on her tongue, kissed her until she was whimpering with pain and limp in his arms. He kissed her until at last she could no longer fight the raging needs of her own body, kissed her until her arms were twining around his neck and her mouth was opening to his in a mindless passion that incinerated her anger and humiliation with the heat of its blaze.

He felt her sudden uncontrollable response, and for an instant his grip gentled. Then abruptly he jerked his head away. She lay quivering in his arms, looking up at him with her heart and her passion in her eyes. He returned that look for a long moment, his eyes brightly blue and burning, his mouth set in a taut line. Then even as she watched, his eyes froze over and his lips twisted into a sneer.

"You're no more a lady than I am," he said with contempt, and pushed her off his lap so that she fell in a heap on the floor.

She sat there for an instant amidst a cascade of cherry striped skirts and lacy white petticoats, her legs in their white stockings exposed from her knees to the toes of her small black slippers, her breasts heaving above the low cut neckline of her gown. Her eyes were bewildered as they met his; the cold insult and the cruelty she saw in his eyes left her stunned and shaken.

Slowly she gathered the tattered remnants of her pride

about her and got to her feet. All her anger had drained from her now. She felt icy cold inside—as cold as his blue eyes. She looked down at him without expression as he lounged back in his chair, staring up at her as she stood, hands and knees shaking, beside him.

"You tell Carlyle that you're not going to marry him," Sebastian instructed harshly. "Or I will. And if I do it, I'll take great pleasure in telling him the rest."

Julia stared down at that beautiful face, at the silver-gilt hair and celestial blue eyes that weren't angelic at all but cruel, at the perfectly carved mouth that was set in a hard bitter line, and felt anger such as she had never known boil up inside her. He was always so sure of himself, so in control. Even now he thought that all he had to do was threaten her, and she would meekly bow to his dictates.

Well, he was wrong. At her core was still the fighter that she had been all her life, the hungry unloved street urchin who had survived more deprivation and abuse than he would ever know. He had brought that fact home to her again, and suddenly she was no longer quite so ashamed of her origins. For all its lack, the way she had grown up had not left her more of an icy shell than a human being. She could laugh and cry and love while all he could do was hate. So who was the poorer really?

She had never actually meant to marry Lord Carlyle, and she had known it from the instant she had accepted his proposal. She had only wanted to use him to get back at Sebastian. But now Sebastian was looking at her in that dismissive way that told her that he considered the matter settled, that she would do as she was bid and that was all there was to it. Only this time he was wrong. She had knuckled down to him time after time, overawed by his autocratic manner and icy eyes, but not this time. It was blindingly clear to her now that Sebastian considered her rather in the nature of a prettily painted but not intrinsically valuable objet d'art— something that was nice to own but was not deemed costly enough to show off to one's friends. To him she would always be the guttersnipe. While to Lord Carlyle she was a lady. And she liked being a lady, enjoyed being treated with gentleness and consideration and respect. Why, Lord Carlyle had never so much as kissed her cheek. While Sebastian had treated her as what he thought she was: a whore.

Her spine stiffened, and her knees quit shaking. With slow dignity she turned her back on him, and walked carefully to the door without a word. Then she turned to look at him.

He still lounged in his chair, his booted legs stretched out beside the desk, his broad shoulders resting comfortably back against the tufted leather while the thin brown cigar in his hand sent smoke curling around his perfectly sculpted head.

"You are as cold and cruel and unfeeling as your mother says, Sebastian," she said quietly, looking him full in the eyes. "I feel sorry for you."

She saw his white teeth clamp on the cigar, but before he could say a word, she turned on her heel and left him.

XXVII

SHE was going to marry Lord Carlyle—or, rather, Oliver, as he had told her to call him, just as he now called her Julia. She might not be in love with him, but then love was not a requirement for a successful marriage. He might not engender in her the soul searing passion that Sebastian managed to arouse with his slightest touch, but then that kind of passion was nothing on which to base a lifetime commitment.

Oliver was a kind, steady man who would take care of her; he was rich and well-born and could give her a good life. And, most of all, he respected her. At least he respected Julia Stratham. How he would feel if he found out about who she really was, she couldn't begin to guess. Should she tell him? Her every instinct screamed no—except her instinct for fair play. And she determinedly squashed that. Would Sebastian tell him? That was another question entirely. He might very well—but then he, as well as his mother and Caroline, would be put in the interesting position of having foisted a fraud on Society. And Society was not likely to be very forgiving of a thing like that.

Fortunately she had time to think it all through before anything irrevocable happened. Sebastian had left London early on the morning after their confrontation, accompanied only by the long suffering Leister and bound for his estates in Suffolk where urgent business required his presence. He had been in a tightlipped rage when he left, according to Smathers. Julia was both relieved and strangely disappointed to hear of his going. Coward, she mentally castigated Sebastian. Running again, just as he had when she had frightened him by getting too close when he had first become her lover in the library at White Friars. Julia was beginning to suspect that this was the way he avoided having to deal with his emotions—he simply ran from them. Apparently her parting shot of the day before had had some effect. She hoped so. He had made her love him during those months at White Friars, she who had been more starved for affection than she had been for food. He had been like a great shining sun suddenly arising on the horizon of the dark sky that was her life, lighting up her world with a heat and intensity that had penetrated to her very soul. He had felt it, too, she knew he had. And it had scared him back into his icy shell.

But one day he was going to have to stop running and face himself. And his feelings. But by then it would be too late to regain what he had lost. She had loved him, truly loved him, but she was not fool enough to spend her life mooning over a man who underneath the fondness and passion and friendship secretly held her in contempt. It would kill her to be his mistress until he tired of her. Getting him to marry her was about as likely as having a carriage horse win at Ascot. She saw that now. In his mind he would forever be the lordly earl and she the nameless guttersnipe. A cat could look at a king, but a guttersnipe could never become a countess.

Sebastian had left with only one valise, which most likely meant that he would not be gone for more than a week or so. But, then, he had only taken one valise with him when he had first taken her to White Friars, and he had ended up staying for months. But those circumstances had been unusual. Julia rather expected to see him back in London before two weeks at the outside had passed. Which didn't give her much time to decide what to do.

Apparently Sebastian was so confident of her obedience to him that he had not considered that she might not break her engagement to Lord Carlyle. But Sebastian's word was no longer law to her and she *was* going to marry Lord Car-lyle—Oliver!— if for no other reason than to spite Sebastian. How he would hate seeing her as a real lady of the ton and another man's wife! She hoped he would hate it. She wanted him to hate it. She wanted him to squirm every time he thought of it.

But to put him in that satisfying position, she first had to get Lord—Oliver!—to the altar. Unless Sebastian hated the idea of scandal more than he hated the idea of her becoming Lady Carlyle, that might be difficult to do. Julia did not fool herself in thinking that Oliver would marry her if he knew all that Sebastian threatened to reveal. Her lack of birth was a nearly insurmountable obstacle, and if Sebastian were to throw in the fact that she had been his mistress to boot—no, Oliver would not marry her. And Sebastian would have the last laugh.

The thought of Sebastian laughing goaded Julia as nothing else. He would not have the pleasure of seeing her rejected and humiliated! She would become Lady Carlyle, and as she thought about it she saw just how to do it. All she had to do was to persuade Oliver to marry her out-of-hand. If the deed were done before Sebastian returned to town, it would be too late to do anything about it. In all likelihood Sebastian would not even make good on his threat once he saw that it was too late to prevent the marriage. And if he did tell Oliver—well, she would be Lady Carlyle by then, and Oliver would not be able to do a thing about it without bringing down on himself the type of scandal that she instinctively knew he would go to any lengths to avoid. The difficulty was going to be getting him to agree to an over-the-anvil marriage. Oliver was very much a stickler for convention. . . .

"Come, Julia, I know you are only funning, but I wish you would not do so about such a delicate subject. We will of course be married in St. James at the end of the proper three month period. Since you are not a girl but a widow, of course, the affair will be relatively quiet. But still, we will manage to do things up splendidly, you'll see."

Oliver's whisper was audible only to Julia over the commotion of the farce that was taking place on the stage below. She stared down at the gaudily dressed players with unseeing eyes, so annoyed with Oliver's insistence on propriety and so anxious that Sebastian might turn up again before she had talked him around to her way of thinking that she could hardly sit still.

In the five days since Sebastian's departure, she had brought up the subject as many times as she had seen Oliver. Each time he treated her hints as to how romantic she would find a runaway wedding like they were a not particularly tasteful joke. Now he was actually sounding irritated with her. Julia chewed on a fingernail and stared out over the darkened theatre while her mind worked furiously. If she truly wished to become Lady Carlyle, she was going to have to think of some way to move this thickheaded lump of a man around to her way of thinking. And fast!

With them in the box were Caroline and her escort, Lord Rowland, a tall thin man of perhaps forty-five with a charming smile. The other members of the party, which had been gotten up at nearly the last minute, were Lord and Lady Courtland. Lord Courtland was small and slight, and he spoke with a hint of a lisp that made him seem slightly afraid of his more forceful wife. Lady Courtland was one of Caroline's bosom bows. She was a plump woman who had the poor judgment to try to squeeze her too large frame into the most daring of the latest fashions, and the result was not beautiful. But she was most amiable, at least when she was not issuing silky orders to her husband while her eyes flayed him like twin whips.

The play seemed to last forever, so anxious was she to get Oliver out to a place where she could talk to him. Finally she could wait no longer. The heroine of the dramatic piece following the farce had just announced her intention of killing herself if her lover didn't return to her when Julia leaned over to Oliver and whispered that she had a headache.

Immediately he was all solicitude, offering to take her home at once, and she smiled her thanks at him. With a quick word to Caroline, who nodded and appeared not to have the least objection to Julia going off alone at night in a closed carriage with a man who was not a close relative— something that was considered to be questionable behavior by the ton's high sticklers. But Julia was not one to look a gift horse in the mouth, and she quickly gathered up her evening cloak and reticule and allowed Oliver to lead her from the box. But by the time they reached the lighted lobby and had ordered the carriage to be brought around, Oliver himself was beginning to have second thoughts.

"Perhaps we should have asked Mrs. Peyton to accompany us," Oliver said thoughtfully as he draped her cream silk cloak around her bare shoulders. "I know that you would not wish to give the least appearance of impropriety, my dear Julia, and it is not quite the done thing for us to leave the theatre alone together. Though such a thing might not occur to you—you are such an unworldly innocent! I feel that it is my responsibility to consider such repercussions for us both."

"Dear Oliver," Julia said, smiling up at him, though it was something of an effort to assume an expression of proper affection. In reality she wanted to shake him. He was always so, so proper! "It could not be right to disturb Caroline and her friends. They are enjoying the play, and I would feel quite low if they had to leave without seeing the end on my account. Grosvenor Square is only fifteen minutes from the theatre, after all."

"Still," Oliver said darkly, "there may be those who will take note of the impropriety. We are not officially engaged yet, you know, and I do not want anyone saying that we are to marry because . . . because it is necessary. Yes, the more I consider the matter the more I feel that we must ask Mrs. Peyton to accompany us."

Julia counted to ten before she replied. As she counted, she made a little business of fastening the silver frogs that closed her cloak up the front. Worn over a full skirted, tightly bodiced dress of the same cream silk embellished with silver lace, it was an elegant and highly becoming ensemble. She looked all the crack, as the wags would say, and she was surprised that she did not enjoy the knowledge more. Earlier this evening, when she had first put on the dress and stood looking at herself in the glass, the beautiful picture she made had elicited hardly more than a shrug from her. What good was looking beautiful if there was no one to see? Despite her best efforts to make him do so,

Oliver simply didn't count. Neither did Caroline and her friends, nor the rest of the theatre. The audience she wanted to dazzle was Sebastian and Sebastian only. Without him to witness and be moved by her beauty, it was meaningless. The realization annoyed her past bearing, but she could not blind herself to the truth.

"I shall send a note in to Mrs. Peyton." Oliver was still mumbling, and Julia could no longer contain her irritation.

"Don't be a goose, Oliver," she said crisply, turning to face him. Seeing his eyes widen in affront, she hastily smiled and put her hand on his arm. She did not want to alienate him, after all.

"I'm sorry, Oliver, I spoke without thinking. But you see, you really mustn't send for Caroline. I don't have a headache at all, I only used it as an excuse. The truth is, I wish to talk to you alone. I have something to say that is very important for you to know, and I must tell you at once. I had hoped to keep the truth from you, but I find I cannot so deceive you. So if you will humor me?"

Oliver stared down at her. Before he could say anything, the link boy called that the carriage was waiting. Julia, breathing a sigh of relief, immediately moved toward where the footmen were waiting to assist her inside. Oliver had no choice but to follow.

"What is it that is so important for you to tell me?" he demanded testily once they were inside and the door was closed.

Seen in the light from the streetlamps which poured through the window, he looked old suddenly. The lines on his face were shadowed into deep creases, and webbed circles surrounded his eyes. His jowls were heavier and his nose was longer and thicker. Instead of the vigorous man in the prime of life that Julia had thought him, he seemed old enough to be her father.

"Oliver, it saddens me to have to tell you this, but I feel I must," Julia began, looking down at her hands in an attitude of virtuous sorrow as the carriage jerked into motion. "There is an impediment to our marriage of which you are unaware. I fear that unless we wed secretly within the next few days, we will be torn from each other forever."

That was very well done, Julia congratulated herself. She silently thanked Mrs. Radcliffe's novels, which were full of lovers being torn asunder by cruel guardians, and from which she had culled her idea. Given the way Oliver felt about Sebastian, he would have no reason to doubt her story, which was, she defended herself to herself, almost true in a way.

"What kind of impediment?" Oliver was staring at her. Through the shifting patterns of light cast as the carriage passed through the streets, Julia could see that his expression was very stern.

"I—I hate to have to say this. Indeed, I hoped I would not! But I have turned the matter over and over in my head, and I can hit on no other solution. Oh, Oliver, you must tell me what we should do! Sebastian—Lord Moorland!—will never allow me to wed you. You see, he wants me for himself."

"Moorland wishes to marry you?"

Julia managed a blush and an anguished look up at Oliver before casting her eyes back down to her clasped hands.

"I am afraid it is worse, much worse than that," she said

mournfully, in a voice so tiny as to suggest she could hardly speak at all. "I am almost ashamed to tell you, but Lord Moorland made it quite, quite clear that he . . . he was not offering marriage."

"That bas—, your pardon, Julia. That blackguard had the insufferable cheek to offer you a slip on the shoulder?" Oliver looked outraged. Julia, casting a swift look up at him, had to suppress a smile of pure satisfaction. Her confession was certainly having all the effect she had hoped for.

"I—I am so ashamed," she whispered.

"Oh, my dear," he said in quite a different voice, reaching out to take her hand. Julia allowed her hand to be swallowed up by his larger, warmer one, and even turned hers over so that her fingers were clinging to his as though for support. "There is no shame attached to you. It is Moorland who should be ashamed. For years the ton has whispered of his depravity, even before the tale went round that he had murdered his wife. But that he should have offered such an insult to you! He shall meet me for this."

This last was said with fierce determination. Julia, who had not anticipated such a violent eventuality, gasped. Oliver could never be allowed to call Sebastian out! She did not know, but she suspected that Sebastian might accept even a groundless challenge. He had no liking for Oliver either. And Sebastian might kill Oliver—or, nightmare of nightmares, Oliver might actually succeed in killing Sebastian!

"No, no, you must not do that!" Julia hurried into speech with a conviction borne of true horror. "Only—only think of what a—a slur that would be on my reputation! For there could be no other reason for you to quarrel with my guardian, and all the world must know it! Besides, you could be killed!"

She threw that in because it sounded like something a loving fiancée would say, and looked up at him with trepidation. He appeared much struck by what she had said, and she hurried on.

"What we should do—I've thought about this, you see, through many a sleepless night—is be married out of hand. It would not have to be a havey cavey affair at all. Is there not such a thing as a special license? We could be married right here in London, in a perfectly proper fashion, before Lord Moorland even returns to town. Then—then he could have no further hold over me, and could not undo what had been done."

Oliver was silent for a long moment, running his fingers absently over the soft skin on the back of her hand. Julia, impatient with his touch, nevertheless allowed it. Anything to persuade him to her way of thinking!

"You may be in the right of it. I will have to think about it," he said slowly just as the carriage pulled to a halt in front of the house in Grosvenor Square. "If you will permit me, I will call upon you tomorrow to let you know what I decide."

Such lack of a definitive answer did not sit well with Julia, but there was nothing she could do but smile tremulously at him as he pressed his lips to her hand just as the footman swung open the door.

XXVIII

wo evenings later Julia was preparing for Lady Jersey's ball. One of the highlights of the Season, it was a grand affair which nearly everyone who was anyone would attend. All across fashionable London, ladies were dressing in their finest ballgowns and bringing out their most valuable jewelry. A tangible sense of excitement lay over the haute monde.

Julia was in her bedchamber, oblivious to its comforts as she sat before the mirror watching Emily do her hair. Caroline, who had treated her as a bosom bow since Julia had confided that she was engaged to Oliver, had offered the services of her dresser, Miss Hanks, on the grounds that Emily had not the expertise to turn one out "complete to a shade" as was necessary for Lady Jersey's ball. But Julia had declined the offer with thanks, and now as she sat looking at herself in the glass she saw no reason to regret her decision. Emily had done a beautiful job of twirling her hair into an intricate knot on top of her head, and then coaxing curling tendrils down from the upsweep to frame her face.

"A little rice powder, Miss Julia?" With Julia's hair complete Emily turned her attention to the collection of cosmetics on the dressing table. Julia usually wore only the barest minimum of cosmetics, but rice powder was unexceptionable—everyone with the smallest pretensions to beauty wore it. She nodded, and Emily passed the paper over her face, leaving it milky white without the least hint of shine. Fortunately her lashes were naturally inky black like her hair, so she had no need to resort to stoking them with the burnt ends of matches as some of the fairer ladies did.

"Some color, Miss Julia?" Emily was already reaching for the rouge pot before Julia nodded. With a whisk of a rabbit's foot across her cheekbones and lips, she bloomed with subtle color. No one but Emily and herself would know that it was not a real blush.

Then Emily removed the towel that she had placed around Julia's neck to prevent any cosmetics from getting on her throat or bosom and Julia stood up to be eased into her dress. In honor of the occasion, she was laced so tightly that she could scarcely breathe. Above the lacing her breasts threatened to pop from her chemise. Below it four lacy petticoats billowed, ending in layers of flounces just above her slender silk encased ankles and narrow black dancing slippers. Emily lifted the dress from the bed, and threw it over Julia's head with a deftness that disturbed not a hair. Then Julia stood before the cheval glass in the corner of the room, staring at her reflection as Emily did the dozens of tiny pearl buttons up the back.

The dress was made up of dull gold tissue over an under-dress of gold satin. It was designed with tiny off the shoulder sleeves that made the most of her neck and shoulders and arms. The neckline was low and heart shaped, dipping to form a vee in the valley between her breasts, where it was held in place with a tiny gold satin rose. The bodice clung closely to her shape, outlining her proud high breasts and slender rib cage before flaring out into the enormous circle of her skirt. A wide gold satin sash wrapped her tiny waist, ending in an enormous bow with trailing satin streamers at the rear. The overskirt of tissue was caught up in scallops all around the hem and secured with tiny gold satin roses like the one at her bosom, revealing the gold satin underdress. A necklace of topazes loaned by Caroline was around her neck, a gold satin rose was pinned to a matching satin ribbon around one wrist, and another tiny gold satin rose was perched in her hair. The color made her eyes gleam even brighter than the topazes, and emphasized the creamy whiteness of her skin and the ebony blackness of her hair. It was a dream dress, and in it she looked like a dream.

Emily finished with the buttons, and stepped back. Taking a long look at Julia in the mirror, she shook her head and sighed.

"You surely do look a picture, Miss Julia. You'll be the most beautiful lady at the ball."

"Thank you, Emily." Julia smiled at the girl with real affection. Emily had seen her through some of the most difficult days of her life, and she thought of the girl as a friend as well as a servant. Never by word or look did Emily treat her as anything other than a lady, though she knew as well as anyone the arduous process that had gone into producing the fashionable damsel who stood before her tonight.

"You're welcome, Miss Julia." Emily smiled back at her, the round face lightening into impish prettiness. She turned away to pick up a fan with an intricately painted scene in gold and creme, and Julia's shawl, which was of gold lace and which was designed to droop negligently from the elbows. Just then a knock sounded at the door.

"Lord Carlyle is below, Miss Julia," a voice called. Then footsteps hurried away, presumably to so inform Caroline and the countess. It was close on ten o'clock, and the ball had started at half past nine. Of course, no one who was anyone would dream of arriving on time, but it was not good manners to be too late. Forty-five minutes to an hour was about right. And Oliver, of course, was punctilious about matters of that sort.

It was foolish to let something so praiseworthy irritate her, Julia told herself as she scooped up her reticule and told Emily with a smile not to wait up for her. Oliver was to be her husband—in three days' time, to be exact—and reliability was an excellent quality in a husband. If he dictated to her (such as by telling her, when he took her driving the afternoon after their aborted theatre visit, that they would be married in his London townhouse in four days' time, when she would have preferred a far shorter wait for fear Sebastian would return and dash their plans), then she had best get used to it. Husbands had the absolute ordering of their wives' lives, and the price she would have to pay for being Lady Carlyle, with all that that entailed, was being Oliver's chattel. He was from all indications a kind and generous man, and she did not fear that he would abuse her. So surely putting up with his occasionally pedantic ways should not be too great a hardship. If she could just quit comparing his deliberate weighing of everything with Sebastian's careless confidence. She would not compare him to Sebastian, she would *not.*

Oliver was looking very distinguished, she saw, in black evening clothes with a tall black top hat which he carried in one hand and an ebony cane. The silver streaks in his dark hair gave him a look of importance. Clearly he was a gentleman of influence, and she should be proud to be his fiancée.

"You are looking very nice, Oliver," she called gaily down to him. He looked swiftly up at her as she came down the stairs, her golden skirts swirling around her feet. His eyes widened with appreciation, then he smiled his slow kind smile.

"And you are looking dazzling," he responded, his eyes moving over her. He looked as if he would say more, but then his eyes traveled beyond her and his smile changed to the merely polite.

"You look very lovely too, Countess," he said. "And you too, as always, Mrs. Peyton."

Julia reached the bottom of the stairs and looked up to see the countess, out of black for the occasion, clad in an elegantly severe gown of silver brocade. Beside her stood Caroline, dressed in a floaty organza in her favorite shade of pale blue. The countess smiled coolly at Oliver, of whom she approved, while her eyes passed over Julia with scarcely veiled malice in their depths. Julia had never forgotten the countess' threat to make her regret speaking out in Sebastian's defense, and that look made her shiver. The moment quickly passed as Smathers handed the ladies their cloaks, and Caroline and Julia exclaimed over each other's gowns. Then they were off to the ball.

After fighting their way through the street that was thronged with carriages all on their way to Lady Jersey's, Julia's party was a good hour and a half late. But other late arrivals still streamed in the door, where they were relieved of their cloaks by liveried servants and pressed on up the wide staircase that led to the reception rooms on the first story. At the head of the stairs stood the receiving line, consisting of Lady Jersey and her seldom seen husband, her married daughter and the daughter's husband, and Lady Soames, who Julia knew was a good friend of Lady Jersey's, and her husband. She passed down the line as in a dream, murmuring polite phrases as the august ladies beamed at her.

The rumors about her forthcoming marriage to Oliver had been flying thick and fast through the ton in recent days; Julia suspected she had Caroline's loose tongue to thank for that. Their effect was so beneficial that she could not regret her secret's loss of secrecy. The wife of so influential a man as Lord Carlyle would be a person to be reckoned with in Society, and these ladies were prepared to take her to their bosoms. Once the marriage actually took place, she would be part of the crème de la crème of the ton.

The ballroom was long and narrow and burningly hot already, though tall windows at the rear had been opened onto the terrace and a light breeze stirred the tied back curtains. The orchestra was in place, and the strains of a lively country dance filled the air. Couples skipped merrily to the music in the center of the room, laughing and calling to one another as the movements of the dance gave them no opportunity for private talk.

More people milled around the edges of the floor, where the debutantes waited until they should be asked to dance and the dowagers sat as chaperones. It was incorrect to permit a gentleman who was not one's husband or fianc to claim more than two dances in one evening, but still the popular ladies were always surrounded while the less popular ones languished.

As the gentlemen who usually paid court to her perceived Julia's arrival, she was immediately surrounded. Oliver frowned a little at all the compliments the gentlemen showered on her as they bantered good-naturedly over her dance card, but as he was not officially her fiancé there was little he could do besides putting his name down for the maximum two dances and for supper. As his first dance was not until right before supper—served at the fashionable hour of midnight—he was forced to relinquish her to Viscount Darby, who had put his name down for the first dance. Julia smiled an apology at Oliver as the thin young man led her away, and was rewarded by his reluctant smile. Oliver, it seemed, was not the type to be overly jealous.

Julia danced every dance, laughing and flirting with her partners and calling out to those of the ladies who had become her particular friends. Caroline spent more time than was proper in the arms of Lord Rowland, leading Julia to hope for a romance there. The dowager countess didn't dance, but instead sat amongst her cronies at the edge of the floor, looking like an icicle in a room full of spring flowers. Julia felt those cold blue eyes on her once or twice, but she deliberately ignored the shivery sensation they caused. She would not let that horrid old woman intimidate her.

Supper was marvelous, and Julia thoroughly enjoyed herself gorging on chilled salmon mousse and lobster patties, roast goose and Cr me Bruille. But by the time it was over and she had danced a couple more dances, her hair had started to fall from its pins and her feet had started to hurt. She began to find her partners' chatter silly, and when the honorable Mr. John Somerset trod on a trailing flounce of her gown and ripped it, the magic of the evening disappeared completely.

She had to go to an antechamber and pin the flounce up. When she returned to the dance floor, she stood for a moment looking about her. She had lost her dance card sometime after supper, so except for Oliver, who had claimed the last dance, she had no idea who her partners for the rest of the evening would be. She looked over the crush of people talking and laughing, trying to divine who might have a claim on her for the dance that was just striking up. She spotted Tim Rathburn, looking forlorn on the other side of the room as he scanned the crowd, and she seemed to remember that he had signed her card. So she made her way toward him, weaving through the throng. He saw her coming at last, and his thin dark face lit up with relief. Quickly he pushed toward her until he was at her side.

"I'd thought you'd gone and forgotten our dance, Mrs. Stratham," he said, smiling down at her as he took her elbow.

"Certainly not, Mr. Rathburn," she replied, now having to force the gaiety that had come so easily to her at the beginning of the evening.

He pulled her into his arms, chatting about inconsequentials as Julia mentally sank into the movements of the waltz. She loved this dance, probably because it always reminded her of Sebastian and how he had danced her down the long gallery at White Friars.

"By Jove," Rathburn said, sounding odd as he looked at something over her head. Julia, turning around, saw that everyone else on the dance floor was, one by one, doing the same thing. As heads turned and steps faltered, she too craned to see what was causing so much commotion. Then she did see, and caught her breath. It was Sebastian.

He was clad in impeccable black evening clothes that molded his broad shoulders and long muscular legs, and contrasted spectacularly with the gleaming silver-gilt of his hair. He appeared completely at his ease, and seemed impervious to the attention he was attracting. To Julia's knowledge he had not attended a ton party since Elizabeth had died, and she doubted that he had been invited to this one. He was very much the social pariah, and people, particularly the ladies, were drawing back from him on all sides as he passed among them.

But if he noticed the silent hissing, he gave no sign of it. He looked remote and confident as though he were the only aristocrat amongst a roomful of peasants. His air of cold hauteur, combined with the dazzling good looks that made Julia's heart speed up and completely eclipsed every other man in the room, set him apart quite as effectively as the silent withdrawal of the others.

Julia saw the dowager countess sit up a little straighter as she became aware of her son and the treatment he was receiving, but other than that she made no sign that she was even acquainted with him as he stood there, quite alone at the edge of the dance floor, surveying the awkwardly turning couples.

Then he saw Julia. She saw those blue eyes fix steadily upon her, and she felt suddenly, fiercely glad that he had come. Despite everything. . . . She smiled at him brilliantly, defying the shocked stares of the curious and her partner's sudden intake of breath. Sebastian saw that smile and looked at her for a long moment, his blue eyes blazing into her gold ones with an intensity that sliced through the heavy, largely silent air that had fallen over the crowded room. He started walking toward her, and the other dancers parted like the Red Sea before Moses. She watched him come and her heart swelled. She had wished for him, oh, she had wished for him. . . .

"Excuse me, but I believe this is my dance," Sebastian said politely to Rathburn as he came to a stop beside them.

Rathburn looked indignant, and his hand clutched Julia's tighter, but she freed herself from him impatiently. Not even looking at him, she left Rathburn standing alone on the dance floor as she turned into Sebastian's arms.

Sebastian looked down at her, a faint smile playing about his chiseled mouth, his blue eyes gleaming. He swung her around into the crush of couples who were staring and dancing at the same time to the haunting melody of the Blue Danube Waltz.

And, for Julia, the magic was back in the evening.

X X I X

E waltzed expertly, as he did everything else. Julia felt the hardness of his broad, black-clad shoulders beneath her fingers, felt the strength of his hand grasping hers in the correct posture for the waltz, felt the muscular length of his legs brush against her skirts as he whirled her around in the movements of the dance, and thought that if her heart beat any faster she would surely die of it right there on Lady Jersey's dance floor.

"Does that brilliant smile you sent me mean you've recovered your temper since last we met? Or do I have to be on guard against a swift kick in the shins?" Sebastian's voice was so close to her ear that she could feel the warmth of his breath. His words were whimsical, but there was something odd about his tone.

Julia dared another look up at him. She was so conscious of her own reaction to him that she feared that it must blaze as plain as daylight in her eyes. He was looking down at her with a faint, twisted smile, and she felt her heart give a queer little jerk as she was caught and held by that almost tender expression.

"What are you doing here?" She almost whispered the question that she was afraid to ask, mindful of the straining ears of the twirling couples all around them. Sebastian appeared completely oblivious to the sensation he was causing as he smiled down into her upturned face.

"I've come to fetch you," he said as the teasing glint deepened. "Will you come away with me?"

Julia did not trust that mocking gleam. She felt her heart slow a little bit with disappointment. "Be serious, if you please."

"I am very serious. Never doubt it."

Julia looked up at him uncertainly. Her head did not reach far past his shoulder, and she had to tilt her head back to see his eyes. They were gleaming with amusement and something else. Something that made her heartbeat speed up again.

"You're teasing me," she accused, then caught her breath as the blue eyes suddenly heated to the bright blaze of sapphires as he shook his head.

"I just got into town an hour ago after riding hard all day to get here. When Smathers told me where you were, I was even willing to brave the wrath of the august ladies of the ton who so despise me to come to you here. Does that sound like I'm teasing?"

He was smiling still, but beneath the glittering blue his eyes were not. They were hungry as they met hers and curiously vulnerable.

"Why did you want to see me so urgently, Sebastian?" she managed, feeling as if the rest of the world had vanished and she was alone with him in a great whirling void. Her heart was knocking in her rib cage. Was he trying to tell her in this roundabout, maddening way, that he had realized that he cared for her? That he loved her? Her lips parted in breathless hope as she waited for the declaration that was surely coming. But suddenly he laughed, and cast a quick look around the crowded ballroom.

"Oh no," he said, "not here. If you want to finish this very interesting conversation, you'll have to come with me. I have a carriage waiting outside. I told you I'd come to fetch you away."

Julia stared up at him as if mesmerized as he swept her around the floor toward the open French windows that led outside. He took her silence for the consent it was. She was still staring at him as he waltzed her out onto the stone terrace. And she was still staring at him, her eyes locked to his, as he stopped dancing and lowered his head.

Her arms went around his neck before his mouth ever touched hers, and then she was on tiptoe, straining against him, locking him to her forever as she kissed him with a passion that was all the stronger because of the weeks she had tried to deny it. He kissed her too with shaking intensity, his lips and his tongue making promises that he had never put into words. The kiss seemed to last forever, and Julia was lost in it as all the while the scent of the sweet roses that grew in the garden beyond the terrace wafted about them and the lilting strains of the waltz that was still being played inside drifted through the air. At last Sebastian lifted his head, and Julia slowly, reluctantly let him go. Her hands slid down from his shoulders to rest against the solid warmth of his chest. She could feel his heart beating against her palms even through the thickness of his shirt and coat.

"I love you," she said, clearly, and even through the moonshot darkness she could see his eyes gleam.

"I know," he answered, and bent his head to kiss her again. This time it was a brief, hard claiming of her lips, and then his hand was on her arm, turning her about to lead her along the terrace away from the house. He walked close by her side, and Julia was so aware of him that the scandalized stares of the other couples who had also sought the privacy of the garden did not cause her to turn so much as a hair. She was with Sebastian, and suddenly her whole life had meaning again. She saw now, as she hadn't before, that she belonged with him forever. Oliver was a nice man, a kind man, but he wasn't the man for her. For better or worse, as wife or even mistress, forever and ever, she belonged to Sebastian and he belonged to her. Had he finally realized it? She thought that he had first gotten an inkling that he might be growing fonder of her than he wished on the morning after he had first made love to her at White Friars. The knowledge had frightened him into running from her. It was only now that she realized just how telling his flight had been. The very fact that he had run from her shouted that he cared so much that it scared him, and his subsequent coldness was his way of fighting the way she made him feel. But now—now it seemed very much as if he had stopped running. As if he was ready to admit to himself and to her that he cared.

"Where are you taking me?" She didn't really care; she would have gone with him to hell itself tonight if he had asked her. But she wanted to hear his voice, to reassure herself that he was really beside her, her arm tucked into his as he led her toward the tall iron gates at one side of the walled garden. It had rained that morning, and the roses that brushed against her skirts were dewy. Their heady scent filled the air. Overhead scudding clouds passed before the moon, casting silvery dark shadows everywhere. Curious eyes followed their progress, but Julia no longer even felt them. She had room in her heart and mind for nothing but Sebastian.

"I find I have this overwhelming urge to make love to you, my own. Will you trust me as to where?"

"I would trust you with anything, Sebastian," she murmured softly, not one whit disconcerted by his avowed intention to love her. It was what she wanted, too.

She looked up at him with her heart in her eyes. His breathing seemed to stop for a moment; then he bent and kissed her again, another brief, hard possession. Then they were through the garden gate.

On the other side of the narrow cobbled street waited the same closed carriage that had conveyed her to town all those weeks ago. A driver whom Julia could not recognize because of the tall collared greatcoat that muffled him sat stoically on the box while Jenkins jumped down from the rear to open the door as he saw them approach.

The street was riddled with puddles from the recent rain, and Julia was picking her way between them when suddenly Sebastian swooped her up in his arms and carried her the rest of the way. After her momentary surprise she smiled at him, and wrapped her arms around his neck.

"This would be a hell of an inconvenient time for you to get your feet wet and come down with a chill," he muttered in her ear. She laughed and hugged him. Jenkins didn't blink an eye as his master deposited his burden inside the carriage, then jumped in behind her. The door closed with a soft click, the carriage swayed as Jenkins jumped up behind, and then they were moving, the horses' hooves clip-clopping over the cobbles as they drove away.

Inside the carriage the claret velvet curtains were drawn over the windows and the lamp was lit, enclosing them in a cozy cocoon. Sebastian lounged in the seat opposite her, and Julia looked over at him with her heart in her eyes. He was so very handsome with his silver-gilt hair gleaming in the lamplight, his long powerful body clad in the elegant black evening clothes and his eyes burning out at her from that impossibly beautiful face.

"I've missed you," she said softly. His eyes darkened on her face.

"It must be true what they say about absence making the heart grow fonder because I've missed you too. Damnably."

The admission, in a low, almost expressionless voice, made Julia's eyes glow with soft radiance. It was the closest he had ever come to admitting that he cared. Would a declaration follow? The very thought of Sebastian admitting to something as warm and human as love made her go weak at the knees.

"Well?" she said when he showed no disposition to say

anything else.

"Well?" He lifted his eyebrow at her, a slight smile curving his lips, and she understood that he was not quite ready to state his piece yet.

"Why are you sitting way over there?" Her voice was throaty with invitation, and her eyes were flirtatious as they met his. She was teasing him a little, but she meant it, too.

"Because if I come any closer, my own, I'll take you right here in this exceedingly cramped carriage. I'm sure that you would prefer that I wait."

"Are you? Sure, I mean?" She batted her eyelashes at him in mock flirtation. The reaction she got both surprised and excited her. His eyes burst into bright blue flames, and his hands clenched where he had jammed them in the pockets of his breeches.

"You're asking for trouble." The gritty warning was delivered between clenched teeth. Julia eyed him with satisfaction. Here was her so handsome lord brought low from wanting her.

"Maybe I want trouble," she purred, and before he could say anything more she moved with a rustle of skirts to sit beside him.

He eyed her askance for a moment, his hands still jammed in his pockets, while her hands stroked the lapels of his coat. Suddenly his mouth twisted into a wry smile, and his hands came out of his pockets to close over her upper arms and pull her into his lap.

"On your own head be it then," he muttered, and as Julia smiled into his eyes he kissed her.

Her arms slid up around his neck as she opened her lips for him, and then his tongue was in her mouth, exploring all the dark wet surfaces that he had claimed before. She kissed him back with a fierce sweetness that ignited a fire in them both. His arms quivered as they strained her to him, and Julia felt that quiver and reveled in it. He wanted her as badly as she wanted him.

"Enough," he muttered suddenly, pushing her off his lap so that she was once again sitting on the velvet seat. His mouth was compressed into a hard straight line, and his eyes were glittering so brightly that Julia thought that at any moment they might burst into flames. His hands were clenched into fists again and jammed into the pockets of his breeches as if he did not trust himself to keep them off her.

This evidence of the control he was exerting over his needs lit a blazing conflagration of desire in Julia. She smiled at him, a slow, tantalizing smile, and leaned deliberately closer so that he could not fail to appreciate the deep decolletage of her dress. His eyes did indeed dip to admire her as she had intended. He jerked them up, and when they met hers again he glowered at her.

"Listen, you little minx, I'm too old to be making love in carriages—especially when we'll be arriving at our destination in about fifteen minutes. I have no desire to be caught flagrante delicto by my own servants. So behave yourself, if you please."

"But I don't please," she whispered wickedly, and as he glared at her she smiled again. Her eyes ran over him, luxuriating in the sheer pleasure of being able to look her fill at him, loving the lean powerful contours of his body as much as she admired the sculpted planes of his face.

His fists were still balled in his breeches pockets, she saw, and as her eyes followed the line of the material as it stretched from one clenched fist to the other she saw something else as well: the swollen, unmistakable bulge of his manhood straining against the tight fitting black cloth. She stared at that telltale shape, and then, before she even knew she meant to do so, her hand stretched out to touch it. She ran her fingers lightly over the bulge, marvelling at its hardness and the heat she could feel radiating from it even through his breeches. He gasped and went rigid as she touched him, and she looked up at him in mild surprise.

"Don't you like that?" Her query was all innocence. Violence seemed to explode in his eyes. His face hardened, set into rock-like immobility.

"I like it too damned much," he said through clenched teeth. His hands came out of his pockets to catch her wrists and lift her hands away from him. "I said, *behave.*"

"I don't take orders from you anymore, my lord," she breathed as she leaned closer to plant a soft kiss on his mouth. His hands tightened on her wrists, and then he seemed to forget about his prisoners as her kiss deepened and became more persuasive. Her hands once again free, they fluttered like butterflies to settle on him again. He groaned as she traced the shape of him through the cloth, then groaned again as her hand tried to close over the tensile hardness. But the tightness of his breeches prevented her from giving him more than a slight squeeze. She frowned even while still doing her best to distract him with kisses, and her fingers probed the swelling again. But this time she was searching for buttons.

She found them beneath a flap of material, and slowly, cunningly slipped first one and then another from its hole. There were five in all, and when they were freed it was an easy matter to adjust his underclothing so that his manhood burst from its confines, glorying in its freedom.

"What the hell do you think you're doing?" He spoke with difficulty into her mouth, while the hands that had been stroking the bare skin of her neck and shoulders and arms moved to capture her wrists again. Since distracting him with kisses had proved only partially successful, she lifted her mouth from his with a final regretful kiss and smiled up into his eyes.

"I want to please you," she whispered, her hands twisting so that they could stroke the hands that imprisoned them. "I know there are ways women please men, but I don't know how. Teach me."

The words were a siren song, accompanied by a witchy look out of eyes of molten gold. Sebastian stared at her, and Julia saw by the blind heat that glazed his eyes that she had won.

Easing her hands out of his slackened grasp, she reached down again to touch him, and this time there was no cloth between their flesh. Her fingers curled around him, testing the strength of him, and he groaned suddenly, his eyes in flames as he watched her hand on him. Julia looked, too, and the sight of her slender white fingers wrapped around the heated proof of his desire awakened a harsh, empty aching between her legs. She wanted him to love her, but first she wanted to brand him, to put her mark on him so that he would never be able to do this with anyone else. She wanted him to burn with desire.

"Teach me how to please you, Sebastian." The words were the merest breath of sound, but he heard because his hand was on hers and he was showing her the motion, showing her how to stroke and caress and tease and she was doing it until his head was thrown back on the velvet roll of the seat and his eyes were closed and he was groaning. . . .

He was so hot and heavy in her hands, so turgidly male as he pulsated with desire. Julia stared down at the thing she held with awed fascination. His body was so different from her own, so excitingly different. In order to better watch herself pleasing him, she slipped from the seat to kneel between his spread knees, her gold skirts swirling around and enveloping his feet and calves in their glossy black Hessians. She stroked him again, slowly, slowly, up and down, and saw his teeth clamp hard on his bottom lip. Then, compelled by an instinct that she couldn't explain, she leaned forward and pressed her lips to him in a soft, sweet kiss. He gasped, and jackknifed into an upright sitting position to stare down at her with eyes that were drugged with passion. They flickered into blazing life as he saw her there between his legs, her black hair working loose from its elegant upsweep so that tendrils curled down to feather against her white neck and tangle tantalizingly with the nest of dark body hair that she had exposed. Her golden eyes were molten with excitement as she looked up at him, and her soft, rose pink lips were only inches from that part of him that they had just caressed.

"Christ, Julia, where did you learn *that?*" The harsh croak of a demand would have angered her at any other time, but tonight she was too caught up in the magic she had generated, too lost in the heat and pulsating excitement she had created.

"I—I just wanted to do it. You liked it, you know you did." Her husky defense as her fingers still enwrapped him and her mouth hovered that tantalizing few inches above his flesh left him unable to form words. While he stared down at her, trying to cudgel his overheated brain into some kind of working order, she leaned forward again and pressed her lips to him while he watched. His mouth went dry, and his breath rattled in his throat like a dying man's.

"See?" she whispered, and he was lost. His hands moved to cup and hold her head, and wordlessly he showed her how she could pleasure him in this way. Under his guiding hands her lips and tongue and fingers learned everything there was to know about him, about the taste of him, the smell of him, the feel of him. When at last he went rigid and his hands pulled her away from him, she watched the physical proof of the peak he had reached with smoldering eyes. His shaking excitement stoked her own. . . .

The carriage rocked to a halt, jerking on its superb springs as the horses were reined in and Jenkins jumped down. They had arrived at their destination. Julia got to her feet on shaky legs, and leaned over to blow out the lamp in order to afford Sebastian an extra measure of privacy while he repaired the mayhem she had wrought on his person.

When Jenkins opened the door and let down the steps, she stepped into the pool of light cast by the streetlamps looking no more disheveled than she would have been if she and Sebastian had exchanged a mere few kisses. But as for him—she threw a quick look back over her shoulder as he stepped down behind her. He looked as coolly elegant as he always did. Not a hair on his head was disordered. If she hadn't known in what an intimate position he had been not three minutes before, she would never have believed it even if a witness had sworn to it on a stack of Bibles. He caught her eye on him then, and the blaze that leaped to life in those heavenly blue eyes was all the proof she needed that the past few minutes had been no dream.

"Before you lose that ungovernable temper of yours, let me assure you that my motives in bringing you here again are very different than they were the last time. It's just that I needed privacy to say what I want to say to you, and I do own this house after all. It seems a shame to waste it, though we can of course go to an inn if you wish."

Until Sebastian uttered this hasty speech in her ear, Julia had not realized that they were standing before the cheerful little house where he kept his mistresses. For a moment she stiffened under the restraining hands that rested on her bare shoulders. The look she threw over her shoulder at him must have been a sizzler because he smiled in an utterly charming, conciliatory fashion that soothed her despite herself. After all, she wanted to be alone with him, too—and not just to talk! This house would certainly afford them far more privacy than a public inn. Her expression must have mirrored her acquiescence because his fingers tightened in a quick squeeze.

"And, of course, it does have that nice big bed upstairs," he added in a whispered addendum. As her eyes shot quick suspicious sparks at him he chuckled. Before she could decide whether or not she ought to get angry, he was beside her, drawing her hand into the crook of his arm as he led her up the stairs. Julia went with him unresisting as the carriage rattled away behind them. Granville was there, looking as if he had hastily pulled on his coat at the sound of the carriage, swinging the door open for them with a subservient bow that Julia knew owed everything to the presence of the man beside her.

"Good evening, my lord, madam," he said deferentially, closing the door behind them. "Can I get you some supper, or—"

"Nothing, thank you," Sebastian said crisply, hardly looking at the obsequious butler. "You may go."

With another deep bow Granville vanished. Julia stood looking up at Sebastian, whose face was tinted with gold from the flames of the three branched candelabra that sat on a small table near the door and appeared to be the only light in the house.

"I should have had him light some candles," Sebastian said ruefully as he took in the darkness that surrounded them on all sides.

"We can do it—or at least I can. Does my lord Earl even know how to light candles?"

"Barely." He was smiling at her. Julia thought that she could live forever on the warmth of that smile. She went up on tiptoe suddenly to press a quick kiss on his mouth. His eyes flamed, and he reached for her, but she snatched up the candle and dodged away from him toward the stairs, laughing. She felt suddenly very happy.

"Your teasing is liable to get you into trouble one of these days, minx," he warned.

"I certainly hope so," she replied with a shameless grin, and he laughed and followed her up the stairs. At the door to the bedroom she hesitated, feeling suddenly a little shy. She was being very bold tonight—perhaps he did not like bold females?

But he was behind her before she could even try to retreat, his arm coming around her as he opened the door, then pushed her gently through it. Closing it behind them, he took the candelabra from her and set it on the table at the side of the bed.

"You look very nervous all of a sudden," he said with a quick grin, and walked toward her.

"I . . ." She took a step backward. It was suddenly very important that she hear what he had to say. Back in this room with the gilded cupids and naked maidens, she felt like a straw damsel. If all Sebastian wanted of her was for her to be his mistress, then she would take what she could have of him and be thankful. But she had to know. She could not wait any longer.

"I won't hurt you, little girl," he said with a wicked leer, reaching out to catch her by the upper arms.

Julia had to smile at the lascivious smile he had adopted, but she put a hand up to his chest to hold him off. He looked down at her with raised eyebrows. She shook her head.

"No, Sebastian." Her voice was faint but firm. "First we talk."

X X X

INALLY he nodded. "As you wish."

Julia waited a moment, but apparently that was all he was going to say. He still held her upper arms, his fingers moving sensuously over her soft flesh, causing responsive goosepimples to quiver up and down her spine. She shook off the distracting frissons of feeling, and looked at him severely. The hand she had planted against his chest tapped him sharply.

"Perhaps I should have said, first *you* talk."

He grinned a little at that, but his eyes were faintly wary. "You're turning into a very demanding female, did you know that?" he muttered, squeezing her arms once before releasing them and turning away. Three jerky steps took him to the window, and he stood with his back to her, pushing aside the ruffled curtains so that he could look out into the street.

"Sebastian. . . ." She had turned to watch that lean powerful back framed so incongruously by tiers of rose pink ruffles, but she made no move to follow him. He had to say what he had to say with no coercion from her or anyone else.

"I've been doing a lot of thinking this last week," he said to the window, his voice sounding uncharacteristically stiff. "It rained every damned day, so there was precious little else to do." He paused for what seemed like an eternity. Julia resisted the urge to say something. He would proceed when he was ready, she hoped.

"While I was trapped in the house looking out at all the rain, I realized something." He turned to look at her then, leaning back against the window frame while his hands clutched the sill on either side of his muscular thighs as though for support. His eyes were very blue as they met hers—and very remote. Even his voice was distant, she thought, and realized that it was in self-defense.

"I realized I was lonely," he said after a moment. "That I've been lonely most of my life. My parents—my father was a good man but weak, too weak for my mother. He was invalided when I was six, and never had much time for me after that. I loved him, and I think he loved me, but he never had the courage to stand up for me to my mother. Until I was old enough to be packed off to school, she left me to a series of nannies—I was no angel, and I went through quite a few. But when she did notice me—sometimes I tried to make her notice, as often as not by some bit of mischief that I knew would drive her mad—it was almost invariably to reprimand me in that cold way of hers.

"She preferred Edward. Edward was as different from her as the sky from the moon, but she loved him. She never loved me, for some reason that I have never to this day discovered. Not that it matters any more, of course, but when I was a boy it hurt. It hurt to see her so besotted over my brother, who was no better than myself as far as I could see. It hurt to spend holidays at school because my mother did not want to be bothered with a grubby schoolboy—this grubby schoolboy. Edward, of course, was a different matter. It hurt to have no one at White Friars but the servants in the summers because she was taking Edward to Paris or Spain or somewhere. And Edward—he was my brother, but I never really knew him. Four years is a lot between youngsters. If he'd lived, who knows, we might have grown closer. But we were as far apart as ever when he was killed."

He paused again, and Julia had to resist the urge to go to him, to put her arms around him and hug him and make up for all the affection he had never had as a child. But she resisted, knowing that if she did not hear all he had to say now he might never feel compelled to say it again. After a brief hesitation he went on.

"Then I was the earl. Suddenly the nonentity became a person of considerable importance. I was the head of my family, and I could control everyone—Caroline, Timothy, who was a pug-nosed schoolboy at Harrow, even my mother. Because I controlled the purse strings. Except for her widow's jointure, which is relatively modest, my mother became dependent on me for everything. How that must gall her! And it must worry her, too. I could have cut her off without a farthing. But I didn't. I suppose I had some foolish hope that maybe with Edward gone I could make her care for me. But she was no fonder of me as Earl than she was of the grubby schoolboy.

"And of course there was Elizabeth. We'd only been married six months when my father died, and I suppose I still had hopes for our marriage. Elizabeth was gentle and sweet, the exact opposite of my mother, I thought. She was of good birth and I had known her forever, and she was rich as Croesus besides. That summer before I inherited the title I fell top over tail in what I thought was love. We married, and I got the shock of my life. Beneath that soft loving exterior she was just as cold as my mother, only in a different way. She was horrified by the physical act of making love. I tried everything. I was patient. I told her I loved her and respected her. Hell, I even begged her. And still she cried every time I went near her. But I was an earl, and I had to have an heir. So I kept going to her, and she hated it more and more, but at last she got with child. I don't know who was more relieved at her pregnancy, Elizabeth or I. I never touched her again after that night when Chloe was conceived.

"So there I was, all of twenty-four years old, with a pregnant wife who couldn't stand for me to touch her. I reacted as any young man would react—there are lots of women in the world, and I took advantage of the fact. For all her dislike of marriage, Elizabeth chose to enact for me a Cheltenham tragedy when she found out I had a mistress. This was after more than four years of being kept out of my wife's bed, mind. What a farce! When I refused to go down on my knees and apologize, she went crying to her papa. Old man Tynesdale had wanted his daughter to marry an earl, but now he was beside himself. Knowing Elizabeth and how she felt about making love, there is no telling what she told him I'd done to her besides being unfaithful. He called me on the carpet and read me a regular bear garden jaw for mistreating his daughter, and we had words. Then about a month later, Elizabeth was killed. And you know what? I was relieved mostly. Relieved because I wouldn't have to spend the rest of my life tied up with a woman I was beginning to actively dislike.

"Then, of course, the rumors started. I had murdered Elizabeth. I hadn't, but not many people chose to believe me. By that time I didn't even care particularly. If people wanted to brand me a murderer, that was fine with me. I didn't need any of them. Except Chloe. My God, in all my life, what happened with Chloe was probably the worst of it.

"Elizabeth had kept her from me mostly. She always acted like my vile presence would contaminate her precious baby. But I loved the child. And I would swear she loved me. She seemed to. She was just a tiny thing, four when Elizabeth died, but she always seemed glad to see me. I would bring her presents sometimes, and she would put her little plump arms around my neck and kiss me and whisper in her lisping little voice. And then . . . and then . . ." He broke off to draw a deep, steadying breath. Julia saw a betraying hint of moisture in his eyes, and despite all her good intentions could not keep from going to him.

Her skirts rustled as she crossed quickly to his side. He was stiff and resisting at first as her arms went around his waist, but as she pressed against him in a wordless gesture of comfort his arms came around her. He held her close, his voice not quite steady as he bent his head to finish with a near whisper in her ear.

"When you showed up in my hallway that day, looking like a cross between a third-rate Cyprian and a drowned rat, I thought I didn't need anyone. I was totally self-sufficient and I liked it that way. Oh, I had friends, of course, as everyone does, but they were really just acquaintances. In all the world there was not a single soul who really gave a damn if I lived or died. And then you came.

"If my mother hadn't come into my study that day, I probably would have had you thrown back out into the streets. Those marriage lines you showed me were not worth very much when it came right down to it. You would have had the devil's own time claiming anything with them. But I didn't have you thrown out. I took you down to White Friars with me because I couldn't think of anything else to do with you—I was already regretting the impulse that had caused me to let you stay. But you were a funny little thing, and I ended up quite liking you. And then you turned into a raving beauty. . . . I should have seen my Waterloo coming. In fact, I probably did. I just refused to recognize it. You were a virgin that night and I knew it, and I wouldn't admit it even to myself. I told myself that I had to be wrong about the physical signs because no virgin could have responded the way you did. You were all fire, my own, and you set me aflame, too. My reaction terrified me. I wanted more, much more. So I ran, and I've been running ever since. Until yesterday, when I realized that I was all alone in a cold gray world, and I was tired of being alone. I wanted to warm myself at a fire—and that fire was you. I wanted to hold you and kiss you and never let you go as long as either of us lived. I wanted you to love me, and I wanted to love you."

As he finished his voice got lower and lower until at the end it was barely audible. But Julia heard. She heard, and wept inwardly at every syllable. Her proud Sebastian, always needing love and never finding it, had gotten so he feared the very thing he craved. He had treated her as he had because he had been emotionally scalded too many times. Even now he sounded as if he were afraid to risk his heart again.

"I do love you, Julia," he muttered into her hair, and Julia felt her heart swell and ache with the sweet pain of it. Her arms tightened around him, hugging him to her, and she turned her head so that her face nuzzled into the warm sandpaper skin of his neck just below his ear.

"And I love you, my darling," she whispered, pressing her lips into the soft place where his vein pulsed with telltale urgency. His arms enwrapped her so tightly that she feared he might crush her, and then his head was turning and his mouth was seeking hers.

This time when they made love, there was a feverish urgency to their passion. He took and she gave, and she took and he gave. Their bodies clung to each other with fierce tenderness, and when they came shuddering back to earth together they barely had time to catch their breath before the need that drove them reared its head again. They made love again and again until at last dawn was lighting the sky with pink streaks and the first faint stirrings of a new day were heard in the street outside the window.

Sated, they lay together in the huge bed, their naked bodies pressed together beneath the single sheet that was the only covering they could bear, their hearts finally slowing to something resembling a normal rhythm. Julia, sleepy-eyed and heavy limbed, lay with her head on Sebastian's shoulder and one hand pressed into the nest of fur on his chest. Sebastian was flat on his back, one arm beneath his head and the other around Julia. His hair was ruffled, and the dark beginnings of a beard shadowed his cheeks and jaw. He looked gorgeously raffish, Julia thought as she looked up at him, and could not forbear pressing a soft kiss into the sandpapered underside of his jaw.

"You are insatiable, woman." He turned his head to smile down at her as he spoke.

"Mmmm." It was a purring, contented agreement. Beneath the sheet Julia's hand moved lazily down the hard muscled contours she had come to know so well during the long and tumultuous night. The flat muscles of his abdomen contracted as she stroked them, and even as her fingers lazily circled his belly button she could feel the rising tautness that spoke as no words could have of his hunger for her.

"So are you," she added with a glimmering upward slant of her eyes. He pulled her hand away and brought it to his mouth, kissing it lightly before pressing it back to his chest.

"I hate to disappoint you, my own, but we have to get up."

"Do we?" The provocative whisper was accompanied by

her fingers heading off an another foray into newly charted territory. They were firmly recaptured, and this time held.

"Yes, we do." His voice left no room for argument.

Julia nipped his neck with her teeth in punishment. He yelped, and rolled so that she was pressed down into the bed and he was looming over her. The possibilities inherent in the position pleased her, and she smiled at him with promises in her eyes.

"None of that, now. We've got to get you back to Grosvenor Square before there's more of a scandal than there's bound to be already. There'll be talk about the way I spirited you off as it is, but we can always say that I came to fetch you on urgent family business."

"I don't care about scandal." She moved against him with sensuous enticement. His muscles tightened in answer and a half-smile played about his lips, but he shook his head.

"I do. I won't have the entire ton gossiping about the future Countess of Moorland more than I can help."

Julia went very still suddenly, her golden eyes huge as they stared up into his.

"Sebastian," she said faintly after a moment. "Are you asking me to marry you?"

He looked down at her, a frown gathering on his brow.

"Hell, no." The blunt words were like blows to her heart. Then he smiled, a sweet and charming smile such as she had rarely seen on his face. Despite the disordered hair and stubbled cheeks, or perhaps because of them, he looked so breathtakingly handsome in that moment that she felt her breath catch. "I thought I took care of that last night."

Julia, feeling dazed and not quite sure she was hearing

what she thought she was hearing, shook her head. "No."

The smile died from his lips, but his eyes were very tender as they looked down into hers. "What did you think last night was all about then?"

"I didn't know." The words were scarcely more than a whisper. Then, from the fountain of her love for him and the knowledge of the lack of birth that made her ineligible to be his wife sprang the courage to deny herself what she wanted most in life. "You don't have to do this, you know, Sebastian. You don't have to marry me. I'll be your mistress if you like, for as long as you like."

He scowled at her, his blue eyes turning menacing. "What kind of nonsense are you talking now? I thought you said you loved me!"

"I do! You know I do. But—but, Sebastian, we both know that Julia Stratham is just someone you made up. I'm not her, not really. You're an earl, a member of the nobility, and I know you have a duty to your name. I'm—a mongrel. My mother was an actress, and my father could have been anyone as far as I know. I—"

"Shut up." His voice was fierce. "If what you're trying to say is that you're not good enough for me, then I'm ashamed of you. Where's the spitfire who used to look down her nose at me, and call me names? Is she gone completely, forced out by the *lady* we've created between us? If so, then I'm sorry. I liked that chit, and I won't have you apologizing for her. Do you understand me?"

Julia felt suitably abashed at the savageness of his tone.

"I'm sorry, Sebastian," she said in a small voice.

His frown lessened, but he still looked severe. "And so you should be. Offer to be my mistress indeed! You've a sad lack of morals, my girl, and you should be thankful I don't beat you."

"But, Sebastian, are you sure you want to marry me?" Her voice was tiny. But she had to say it, despite his displeasure. Now that she was on the verge of achieving her dream, she realized that the tactics she had resorted to to fix his interest had backfired on her. She wanted, oh she wanted, to believe that he genuinely loved her enough to overlook her background and hundreds of years of prejudice to marry her. But it was fatally easy to wonder if she had merely caught him by the masterly use of feminine wiles. Oliver's proposal might well have acted as the final spur.

"Oliver!" she squeaked the name. From the moment she had seen Sebastian at the ball until this instant she had not given Oliver a thought. Now she did, and she was horrified. She had promised to wed him in two days—no, one day, now—she thought feverishly. And instead she had run out on him at the ball the night before. He would be furious and rightly so. She would have to explain—what? That now she would be marrying Sebastian instead?

"Oliver!" Sebastian stiffened and sat up on the edge of the bed, scowling down at her out of storm-darkened eyes. "I'm making you an offer, and you're thinking of Oliver?" The terrible mockery in his voice as he said the other man's name told her how near he was to losing his temper. Unlike Oliver, Julia remembered, Sebastian was prone to jealousy. In fact, if the glower on his face was anything to go by, he was extremely prone to it.

"I just remembered that he had his name down for the last dance last night. He—he must have wondered what on earth had become of me." The excuse rang lame even in her own ears. Sebastian's scowl did not lessen by so much as a single degree.

"So?" The brutal syllable warned her that if she could not smooth him down, an explosion was imminent. The knowledge that he loved her enough to be so fiercely jealous was warming, but she did not want to deal with a furious Sebastian, especially over so paltry a cause. Oliver meant less to her than Sebastian's little finger.

"So nothing," she answered meekly. "He—he just happened to pop into my head, that's all."

"See that he doesn't again." It was an order.

Julia bowed her head in contrite acquiescence. No need to trouble Sebastian with the details of her plans for Oliver which were all over now, of course. All she had to do was tell Oliver.

"You did tell him that you were not going to marry him, I presume?" The rapier question, uttered in a tone of extreme displeasure, rattled Julia. She wet her lips, saw his eyes following the telltale movement, and hurried into speech.

"Of course I did."

He eyed her for a moment before his frown slowly relaxed. His expression was still stern, but he no longer looked on the verge of doing someone a violence.

"Good. I don't want to hear his name on your lips again, is that clear?"

Despite her newly found meekness, that dictate brought a little of her own temper rushing to the fore.

"You don't own me, you know, Sebastian." A touch of rebellion glimmered in her eyes. Despite her love for him, if he thought she was just going to lie down and play doormat for him to walk on for the rest of their lives he had another think coming.

He turned suddenly, catching her wrists in his hands and looming over her so that she was pinned to the bed. The sheet had been pulled away from her breasts by his sudden movement, and she lay bare to the waist, her long black hair loose and tousled by their exertions of the night. Her straight black brows met in a forbidding frown over those golden eyes, and her soft rose pink lips were compressed above her obstinate little chin.

His eyes roved over her, moving from her face to the smooth white column of her throat to the narrow shoulders with their prominent collarbones, then slid down to rest on the strawberry tipped mounds of her breasts standing out above the delicate rib cage and narrow waist before coming back up to meet her eyes.

"Oh, yes," he said low, his eyes fixing her with a burning possessiveness that shook her with its intensity. "You're mine now. Never mistake it. You're mine, and I'll drag you down into hell with me before I'll ever let you go."

She stared up at him, not sure she liked being the object of such savage passion. Those blue eyes bore into hers relentlessly, pinning her just as his hands pinned her wrists to the bed. She felt anger start to gather inside her like clouds before a storm, then suddenly she thought of the lonely little boy he had been once. In all his life he had never really had anyone to love, and now he loved her. Of course he was jealous, of course he was possessive. If she wanted him—and she did, oh, how she did!—this was a part of him she would have to accept. Until perhaps one day he felt sure enough of her love not to have to guard it so fiercely.

"I love you," she whispered. He glared at her for a moment longer before the fierce look slowly began to fade. "And I'll marry you whenever you say—if you'll just let go of my wrists." She added the last with a wry smile.

He looked surprised, as if he hadn't known he was holding them, and then smiled sheepishly himself, as he released his harsh grip. Julia sat up, not minding a bit about her nakedness as she rubbed her wrists and gave him an admonishing look at the same time.

"You hurt me, you know."

"I'm sorry." He picked up each wrist in turn and pressed a gentle kiss on it at the point where the fine blue veins traced through her milky skin. "You should have told me. I would never intentionally hurt you."

"I know." She smiled at him, stretched out her arms to encircle his neck and pull his head closer. He came to her willingly, and returned her soft kiss with interest.

"We don't have to go this minute, do we?" she whispered. And, with more kisses, he agreed that they didn't.

X X X I

HE rest of the day passed in a glow of happiness for Julia. She couldn't believe that Sebastian loved her, or that he wanted her to be his wife—but he did. She hugged the knowledge to her like a child with a lovey.

Sebastian sneaked her back into the house on Grosvenor Square with none of the servants the wiser. He opened the door with his own key, and they crept through the hall and up the stairs like wayward children. Everything went smoothly, except that Julia had difficulty holding back a nervous attack of the giggles. She had just made it to her room and managed to get out of the gold balldress (which Sebastian, who had acted as lady's maid when they dressed, had left partly unfastened so that she could get out of it alone), put on her nightrail and get into bed before Emily entered with her morning meal of chocolate and rolls. Julia felt absurdly guilty at first, but Emily seemed to notice nothing amiss, just clucking to herself over the state of the gorgeous ballgown that Julia in her haste had dropped to the floor as she stepped out of it.

"You should have rung for me when you got home, Miss Julia," Emily said with mild reproach, shaking out the dress and restoring it lovingly to the tall mahogany wardrobe.

"It was very late, and I didn't want to disturb you," Julia said with perfect truth as she sipped her chocolate. Considering that she had had no sleep at all, she felt surprisingly, wide awake and glowing with energy. Amazing what an effect love had on her, she thought with an inward giggle. She wondered then if Sebastian felt as marvelous as she did, or if he had collapsed on his bed and was even now sound asleep.

"Are you ready for your bath now, Miss Julia?" Emily asked, bringing her back to reality. Julia nodded, not one whit sorry to be brought back. After all, she no longer had to dream of Sebastian because he was hers, hers! And thus started another day.

It was nearing the noon hour before Julia finally came downstairs. She had dawdled over her toilette, partly because it had occurred to her as she was dressing that there might be an awkward scene with the dowager countess and, to a lesser extent, Caroline. Those two ladies had seen Sebastian spirit her away and would know perfectly well that the fiction they had decided to tell anyone else who inquired—that he had brought her bad news from a relative—patently untrue. But they had to be faced sometime, as did Oliver. She would have to inform him of her change of heart and plans without Sebastian being any the wiser. Sebastian would undoubtedly fly into a rage if he were to discover just how very far advanced were the arrangements to make her Lady Carlyle.

Hiding away in her room would serve no purpose. She had to go downstairs and face the music, and at the same time contrive a way to meet with Oliver without Sebastian's knowledge. Which might, if Sebastian chose to be possessive, prove difficult. But she felt she owed Oliver more than to acquaint him with such news at a public gathering. Perhaps she could send him a note? No, she couldn't do that either. She owed it to Oliver to break off their engagement face to face.

There were numerous servants scurrying about the first and ground floors, polishing and sweeping and moving furniture about with a great deal of muffled noise. Julia checked in her descent of the stairs, staring down at all this unaccustomed activity. Then she remembered that evening Caroline was holding a rout. What awkward timing, Julia thought before realizing it was probably better to get it over with. She would have to face the curious and malicious out to make what scandal they could from last night sometime, and where better to do it than in her own home? If she just held her head up and presented a composed front to those who might question her, the whole incident would soon be forgotten.

"Miss Julia, his lordship left a message for you." Smathers was following two footmen laden with enormous arrangements of hothouse flowers. Upon seeing Julia on the stairs, he fumbled in his pocket and came up with a folded scrap of paper. Julia accepted it from him with a smile and a thank you, then took it into the morning room to read.

"I had urgent business to attend to this morning, so I will not see you until later on today. I have informed my mother of our plans, so you need feel no awkwardness with her. Behave yourself. Sebastian."

This brief message sent a shaft of pure happiness shooting through Julia. Not that it was at all loverlike. Julia had to grin at the idea of cool, controlled Sebastian penning a love letter. But to her, who knew him so well, it said more than the most glibly composed love letter ever had. It said that he had thought of her, that he loved her enough to explain his whereabouts to her, that he had thought to spare her an unpleasant confrontation by breaking their news to his mother without her presence. Julia thought about how that lady was probably taking the intelligence that her son was marrying a trumped-up guttersnipe, and shivered. The harridan would be out for blood—her blood. For one of the few times in her life, Julia decided to turn tail and run. If Sebastian would be out most of the afternoon, so would she. His absence gave her the perfect opportunity to call on Oliver and explain. She could always say she was going shopping. There was some shopping that she needed to do anyway, so it would not be a lie.

"Good morning, Julia." Caroline's voice made her start. Julia looked up to see the other woman coming toward her with a gentle smile.

"I understand we are to be sisters now," Caroline added, coming up to where Julia stood by the window and brushing a quick kiss on her cheek. "I must say I was nearly floored when Sebastian gave me the news. I thought you were about to announce your engagement to Lord Carlyle, so you may imagine how very surprised I was. But of course I am glad for you."

"Thank you. And I know you will understand when I say that Oliver was . . . a mistake." Julia smiled back at the taller woman, who nodded sympathetically.

Dressed today in a gown of palest jonquil crepe, Caroline did not look anything near her twenty-nine years. Her flaxen hair was drawn back into a smooth, stylish chignon at the nape of her neck, and the skin of her face and throat was soft and pale. Her slim figure displayed to advantage in the elegant morning robe added to the impression she gave of youth, and Julia thought that an observer might have guessed that the two were much of an age if it had not been for the dark smudges that ringed Caroline's gentle blue eyes. Perhaps like herself Caroline had experienced a sleepless night. Julia's eyes twinkled as she considered the possibility that Lord Rowland had borne the proper Caroline off to a love nest until dawn streaked the sky. No, that was clearly impossible. She did not know about Lord Rowland, but she did know that Caroline would be shocked at the very idea.

"I am sorry to say that Margaret is not taking the news at all well." Caroline's tone was faintly regretful. "But I imagine you must have guessed that. And the way Sebastian chose to tell her—can you imagine, he got her out of bed at some ungodly hour because he said he had business to take care of and couldn't hang about for hours waiting for her to come downstairs? Well, that didn't help matters as you can imagine. Her maid tells me that she is laid down upon her bed with the migraine. But she will come around, never fear. In the meantime you must tell me your and Sebastian's plans. Do you mean to be married at once?"

"I really don't know," Julia said, her cheeks pinkening with pleasure at actually discussing her forthcoming marriage. It was all so wonderful, so impossible to believe. Like a dream. "I believe I must just leave all that to Sebastian. Whatever he decides is fine with me."

"You love him very much, don't you?" There was a curious note in Caroline's voice. Julia looked at her carefully, and saw the faint shadows at the backs of Caroline's eyes. She must be remembering her own love for Sebastian's brother, Julia guessed, and the memory must still after all these years cause her pain. Of course it would. Even if Sebastian had been dead ten years, or twenty, or a hundred, as long as her heart still went on beating she would mourn him. She felt a rush of sympathy for Caroline.

"Yes, I do."

"And he loves you?"

"I, yes. Yes, he does."

"I thought so. I, none of us have ever seen him make such a display of himself as he did last night. There was a great deal of talk as you may imagine. I had no idea what to say to people, and neither, I am sure, did Margaret. But Sebastian tells us that we are to say that he brought you news of an ill relative, and since you two are to be married any scandal will be quickly squashed. But Julia, there is one thing I feel I must point out to you. It pains me to say it, but you know that Sebastian is not generally received. You have achieved a not inconsiderable success, which I know is important to you as well it should be, considering—well, never mind. But have you thought that if you wed Sebastian you must share his onus? The parties and balls you have enjoyed will be largely a thing of the past."

"I don't mind. I'd rather be married to Sebastian than attend a thousand parties." The soft glow in Julia's eyes as she spoke of her marriage to Sebastian was reflected in her voice. Caroline's face changed, just a little, suddenly looking almost furtive.

"Julia, there is one more thing. I—I feel I would not be a true friend to you if I did not just mention it. You—you do know what happened to Elizabeth? Sebastian's wife?" The words were said quickly in a hushed tone, as if Caroline feared being overheard. Julia stiffened.

"Yes, I am aware of how she died, but I don't see that it has anything to do with me. Surely you don't think I believe that Sebastian killed her? And surely you don't believe such a thing yourself?"

"No, no, of course I do not. I—I just felt that I, that someone should make you aware of what has been said. But if you do not mind, then of course that is the end of it."

"I do mind," Julia answered quietly. "For Sebastian, not myself. He has been dreadfully wronged. But such a slander would not deter anyone who truly loves him, as I do."

The haunted look vanished from Caroline's eyes, Julia was relieved to see. "That's wonderful," Caroline said briskly, once again her usual composed self. "I trust you will inform the family before the ceremony actually takes place? I, for one, would very much like to be in attendance."

"Certainly we will. At least I think so. Unless Sebastian—" Julia broke off, as it occurred to her that she would willingly fall in with whatever arrangements Sebastian preferred. She would gladly marry him over the anvil in Scotland if that was what he wished. She only wanted to be his wife, and the means did not matter in the least.

Caroline smiled. "Ah yes, of course, the decision must be Sebastian's. Well, I will talk to him. But now you must excuse me. I have much to do for tonight's party."

"And I think I will do a little shopping."

"Running sly from the afternoon's callers, are you?" Caroline eyed her with a roguish little twinkle. "You need not, you know. Since we are having a party tonight, we are officially not at home today. So you need not fear to meet anyone before you are ready."

Julia responded to that twinkle with a smile of her own. "I own, the thought did occur to me, and I thank you for the reassurance. But I think I will go shopping anyway. I feel a trifle restless."

"As you wish, of course." Caroline smiled again, and left the room.

Julia stood for a moment, staring out the window into the square. There were a few people coming and going along the street, vendors and servants mostly, with a single fashionable carriage pulling to a stop outside number 57. Julia watched an obese old man alight with much assistance from two footmen and a valet. It was funny to reflect that all these people, from the obese old man to the grubby urchin lurking at the edges of the park to the bun vendor pushing his cart down the street, all had their own separate interests and their own separate lives. None of them, she was willing to wager, were even a tenth as happy as she was at the moment. With a warm smile, she went to summon the carriage. She then went upstairs to get her cloak and Emily before the carriage was at the door.

It was not the done thing for a lady to call on a gentleman at his residence, but Julia could see no other way of meeting Oliver without Sebastian's knowledge. She had the carriage drop her and Emily in Bond Street; it was to return for them in some three hours. She then hired a hackney to convey them to Oliver's residence.

On the way there it occurred to Julia that the best thing might just be to send Emily to the door with a note for Oliver requesting him to join her in the carriage. That would leave little chance of anyone ever finding out that she had called on him, and telling Sebastian. Sebastian would be livid if he knew.

But Emily, who swore eternal secrecy, clambered back into the hackney with the news that the stuffy butler had informed her that Oliver was not at home. Nonplussed, Julia thought for a moment, then scribbled another note asking Oliver to call on her without delay. She had Emily deliver that to the disapproving butler, then shrugged fatalistically. If Oliver did not receive her message in time to call on her before the rout, she would just have to tell him when she saw him there. It would be awkward, but not as awkward as it would have been if Sebastian were in the habit of attending parties. Surely she could manage a moment or two alone with Oliver; it was his own fault if she had to give him such news at a party. She had tried her best to do the honorable thing, but she was not prepared to risk any more.

Accordingly she had the hackney return to Bond Street, and resolved to put the niggling little worry that was Oliver out of her mind. After all, breaking such a private engagement was a relatively minor thing. She would simply tell him that she had changed her mind. Oliver, being the gentleman that he was, would take his congé with good grace. He would not fly into a rage as Sebastian might under the circumstances. . . . Sebastian. The dazzlingly handsome face rose in her mind's eye, and she smiled. She was going to marry Sebastian. It seemed impossible, but it was true. Every time she thought of herself as his wife the day took on a rosy glow. So she banished Oliver from her mind for the time being, and concentrated on her shopping. It was almost six o'clock before they finished and returned home.

As luck would have it, she was almost upstairs, with Emily and a footman behind her carrying her purchases, when she came face to face with the dowager countess, who was on her way down. Julia hesitated, and the older woman, immaculately turned out as always, fixed her with a look that would have frozen a steaming cup of coffee in an instant.

Julia lifted her chin despite the craven pitching of her stomach, and said good evening in a cool but perfectly civil voice. The countess did not even bother to respond. She swept on down the stairs as if Julia didn't exist, leaving only the memory of her eyes that were so like Sebastian's glowing with hatred to follow Julia as she continued on up the stairs.

XXXII

ULIA was of two minds about attending the rout. If Sebastian wasn't going to be there, and she seriously doubted that he would be, she didn't care to attend either. But it would give her a chance to talk to Oliver, and to face down those of the ton who might question her disappearance from Lady Jersey's ball.

Besides that, it would take her mind off Sebastian's whereabouts. According to Emily, whom she had sent down to inquire, he had not yet returned from whatever business it was that had taken him off so early that morning. The thought had occurred to Julia that he might once again have taken fright at the prospect of too much emotional intimacy and bolted, but she was able to dismiss that idea with scarcely a qualm. Last night she had sensed that he had stopped running from her at last. No, he was simply late. Rather than sitting around thinking about him she would be better occupied attending the party and tying up the few loose ends left in her life.

The dress she chose for the evening—actually Emily chose it, but Julia agreed it was a good choice—was of garnet red silk trimmed with yards of silver lace. The ruched bodice was fitted with a heart shaped neckline and a waistline that dropped slightly below her natural waist to end at a point just above her navel. The sleeves were puffed and cut short at the elbow, where they ended in points of silver lace. The skirt was shirred and full, but caught in just above the hem with a banding of silver lace so that its silhouette was narrow. Around her neck she wore a silver ribbon to which her cameo was pinned. Her hair was arranged in a twist high at the back of her head from which two long curls—the product of curling tongs and much coaxing on the part of Emily—descended to trail over one white shoulder. Looking at herself in the mirror, Julia was more than satisfied. She looked lovely, she thought, but, even more important, she looked every inch the lady. In appearance at least, she would not disgrace Sebastian.

She was late going downstairs, so most of the guests were already assembled. Still Caroline and the dowager countess stood by the door to the drawing room, receiving latecomers, and Julia had perforce to join them.

Caroline gave her a smile that was only faintly reproachful because of her lateness, but the dowager countess' look could have chilled hell itself. But a false smile was pasted on her lips only seconds later as she replied to a crony's teasing remark.

Most of the arriving guests were too well-bred to reveal if they were avidly curious about Julia's abrupt departure from Lady Jersey's ball, although as she shook hands and made polite remarks she was aware of a few speculative looks passed over her person. But she held her head high and acted as if she were totally unaware that there might even be grounds for speculation. She congratulated herself on a job well done when finally she was released from the line without so much as a single impertinent question being asked.

Caroline, in an aside, informed her that only Lady Carruthers had displayed enough ill-bred curiosity to actually ask about what everyone must secretly want to know, so Caroline had told her what they had agreed. No doubt it was already spreading around the room like wildfire, so if Julia just behaved as if nothing at all out of the ordinary had occurred they should brush through the evening tolerably well. Just as long as Sebastian didn't make another impromptu appearance to spirit her off. Julia smiled at this, secretly rather wishing he would, and was still smiling when Mr. Rathburn came up to her.

"Good evening, Mrs. Stratham. You're looking as lovely as the rose that dress makes you resemble."

"Why, thank you very much, Mr. Rathburn. But I fear you flatter me."

"That would be impossible," he replied gallantly, offering her his arm. "May I take you to the refreshment tables?"

"You may, sir." Julia smiled, placing her hand on his arm and walking with him toward where the long tables were set up in the dining rooms. "I am ashamed to admit it, but I am famished."

"I, too," he murmured, but from where his eyes rested it was obvious that he was not referring to food.

Julia appeared oblivious to his meaning, but she did not like it. As the evening went on, she liked what was happening even less. It became increasingly obvious that there had been a subtle but telling change in the attitudes of the gentlemen toward herself. Where before they were as respectful as a maiden aunt could have wished, now their remarks were occasionally just a shade too personal, their compliments too fulsome, their eyes too bold. In short, they treated her very much as if she were well on her way to becoming haymarket ware. Julia, deeply ashamed and even more deeply offended, still did her best to ignore all but the worst offenders. The best way to scotch such behavior, she reasoned, was to treat it as if it didn't exist.

The ladies were a little better, but not much. None turned a condemning shoulder to her or cut her acquaintance outright, but some, particularly the very old ladies and a few of the very attractive young matrons, were noticeably cool. Julia could understand the elders, and she tried to redeem herself in their eyes by behaving with the utmost propriety. But the young matrons had her in something of a puzzle until she overheard an exchange that enlightened her.

"You know they say he murdered his wife." The speaker was Lady Westland, a full figured brunette of perhaps thirty or thereabouts attired in a demi-robe of peach brocade.

"I don't care if he murdered three wives," replied the Honorable Mrs. Mayhew, a willowy redhead who was perhaps a little younger than her friend. "He is simply gorgeous! I could have died when he walked into Lady Jersey's house like that, without so much as a by-your-leave, and waltzed out with that Stratham chit. It was so romantic! Why does nothing like that ever happen to *me?*"

"You may thank your lucky stars that it doesn't. Would you like to end up like poor Elizabeth Tynesdale?"

Mrs. Mayhew made a charming pout. "Pooh! I never said I wanted to *marry* him, did I? And I very much doubt that marriage is what he has in mind with his little—what is she, his cousin? A brief affaire is more his style, I'm sure. And mine, as well."

Lady Westland crowed with laughter, and smacked her

friend sharply on the arm with a fan. "Naughty, Irena! What would dear Wesley say?"

"Why, nothing, for he will never hear of it. Besides. Wesley is boring. Did I tell you that he . . ."

Julia didn't hear any more because the two ladies moved on. She had been sipping a glass of ratafia, waiting for Mr. Rathburn to return to her from replenishing his plate at the buffet. They were to go together to watch the whist players in the card room Caroline had set up. A potted palm had shielded her from the speakers' view during this exchange, but she had heard every word perfectly and it enlightened her considerably. Of course, a number of the younger women envied her! Naturally Sebastian was not a prime catch on the marriage mart; the suspicion that he had murdered his wife and his subsequent semi-ostracism from society was enough to ensure that, but as a lover . . . These correct ladies wanted her man in their beds, and the knowledge both pleased and annoyed Julia. It was fine as long as they kept their claws to themselves and Sebastian kept himself out of their way. But if he were to succumb to one of the ladies' lures, it would be quite a different story. Julia was surprised to find that the very thought had caused her hands to clench around the cup she held. It was enlightening to discover that she could be just as fiercely possessive as Sebastian.

"There you are!"

The voice was Oliver's, and Julia jumped like she had been shot. Ratafia splashed all down the front of her dress, and she let out a dismayed exclamation. The dark red silk was absorbing the stain without too much damage, but still she set the cup down on a nearby table and dabbed at the wet spot with her napkin before looking up at Oliver, who was standing over her with a glower. He was very late; she had almost begun to believe he was not coming.

"I want to talk to you, Julia. In private." He looked very stern, his eyes hard, his mouth implacably set. His arms were folded across his chest, for all the world as if he were a schoolmaster and she a small boy to be chastized.

"I want to talk to you, too, Oliver, but please keep your voice down. There is no need to make the entire room aware of our personal affairs."

"Affaire is the word for it, isn't it?" he said bitterly. "For your relationship with Moorland, I mean. Or are you going to deny it? I heard from three separate sources that he was seen kissing you on the Jerseys' terrace. After that disgraceful display in the ballroom!"

Julia sighed. This was going to be worse than she had expected. The civilized gentleman that Oliver had always appeared to her to be had vanished with his anger. Ordinarily she would have grown angry with him in turn, but this time she felt she deserved every insult he could fling at her head. She had played him false, in a way, by leading him to believe that she could marry him when her heart had long been irretrievably lost to Sebastian.

"If you are going to rake me down, Oliver—and I concede you some right to do so!—at least have the decency to do it in private. Come with me to the study, if you please."

Oliver clamped his lips together and bowed, obviously too angry to trust himself to speak.

Aware of the nudges and avid stares that were turning in their direction, Julia smiled at him for the sake of appearances. When he did not offer his arm she walked beside him, silently directing him to Sebastian's private sanctum, which was the only room on the lower two levels left undisturbed by the party. When Julia indicated the entrance, Oliver stood back to let her precede him inside, then closed the door after him.

His eyes were hard as agates as he leaned back against the closed door and surveyed her as though she were a particularly distasteful bit of trash he had found in his path. Julia did not enjoy being looked at in such a fashion, and her chin came up. But after all, she reminded herself, he did have a right to be angry, so she resigned herself to enduring a blistering condemnation of her character and morals for a quarter of an hour before she sent him on his way.

"You owe me an explanation, I believe," he said furiously after a long moment. "Am I right in believing that you are having an affaire with Moorland? Did he force you to it at last? If he did, I'll—"

"Sebastian has asked me to marry him," Julia interposed quietly, her hands clasped in front of her as she broke the news to Oliver in the least painful way she knew. "And I have said that I will do so."

Oliver stared at her, a deep red slowly rising over his throat to mottle his face. "You certainly have a knack for collecting proposals, don't you? This time last evening, you were engaged to be married to me. Or at least so I thought. What made you choose Moorland, I wonder? I'm by far the better catch, you know. I'm a wealthier man than he, and Moorland isn't even received. And I've certainly never been suspected of murdering my wife. Or is that it? Do you like violence in a man? Have I been too gentle with you? I assure you, I'm not so gentle in bed!"

"I'm so sorry, Oliver, I . . ." Julia began, ignoring this furious speech in favor of placating him, only to be interrupted by a snarl.

"Sorry! You're *sorry.* By God, I'll make you sorry! No one makes a fool of me!"

He was across the room before Julia was even aware that he had moved, catching her in a cruel grip and dragging her into an embrace. His mouth came down to catch her lips, and his hands were roving over her in an intimate way that made her want to squirm with distaste. But he was strong, and he held her in such a way that she couldn't move. His tongue entered her mouth, and she considered for an instant clamping her teeth down on it, but this was Oliver after all, and she had wronged him already. But then he picked her clear up off her feet and carried her to the tufted settee that sat on the opposite end of the room from Sebastian's desk. Depositing her on it, he threw himself down beside her, imprisoning her with the weight of his upper body while he knelt on the floor at her side.

"Stop it, Oliver!" she said severely, as if she were addressing a naughty schoolboy. His gray eyes blazed, and then hands that were clutching her upper arms tightened so much that they hurt.

"I'll wager you don't say that to Moorland," he growled with loathing. "I'll wager you let him do whatever he likes to you. I saw you looking at him on the dance floor last night, you slut! You wanted him. . . . I wouldn't marry you now if you begged me, but I'm going to take you. Just like he has. And he doesn't even have the excuse of being your fiancé. At least, he hadn't. And once I've had you, he won't."

"Oliver, stop it! Let me up!" Julia was getting alarmed. Oliver looked crazed with temper, his gray eyes flashing with it, his well formed mouth tight. It frightened Julia to realize that she was completely at his mercy. He was very strong, and it would be impossible for her to get away from him by brute force. She could scream—Julia shuddered as she pictured the scandal that would cause. And the worst part of it was that Sebastian would inevitably find out.

"Kiss me, you slut!"

Julia had been evading his demanding mouth, seeking desperately for some kind of solution that would not involve herself in a major scandal, but none came to mind. His hands clamped down on either side of her head, and he crushed his mouth onto hers. In the process he freed her hands, and she was just about to rake them across his face when a better idea occurred to her. If she pretended to go along with him, for just long enough to put him off his guard, she might then have a chance to escape with no one but the two of them the wiser about what had occurred in this room. Sebastian wouldn't have to know a thing.

"Oh, Oliver," she murmured into his mouth, and opened hers just a little, allowing him to kiss her as her arms came up around his neck and her fingers twined in his thick, coarse hair. Angry as he was, he was hurting her mouth, but still kissing him wasn't completely distasteful. It simply failed to arouse any of the wild longings that surged through her at Sebastian's slightest touch.

His hand was on her breast, sliding down beneath the neckline of her gown, hard and rough as it closed around her softness. Julia jumped, and tried to pull away. She hadn't bargained on letting things go as far as this. Her hands were curling into fists as she prepared to let him have a roundhouse punch to the nose, when the study door swung back on its hinges with a load crash. Julia started, and Oliver did too, both of them looking around with surprise. As she saw who was standing there, Julia's eyes went wide with horror.

It was Sebastian. Behind him stood his mother, a satisfied smile playing about her lips. Julia had no doubt at all about how Sebastian had known where to find her.

He was furiously angry, Julia knew that at first glance. She shoved desperately at Oliver's shoulders in a futile attempt to move him so that she could sit up. But the dolt didn't seem to realize the danger he was in because he continued to kneel on the floor beside the settee, his head dangerously close to hers, and his hand still on her breast! Julia gasped as she realized that, and hastily grabbed at the offending hand and dragged it from her before she realized that to do so must only call Sebastian's attention to how Oliver had been touching her.

She looked back at Sebastian with horror, praying that somehow he had not seen. But in a glance she saw that her prayers were in vain. He was staring at her like a man who has seen hell, while murder exploded in blue flames from his eyes.

"Get off your bloody knees, Carlyle."

The icy, growling syllables made Julia tremble. There was an edge of roughness to that smooth voice that Julia had never heard before. Sebastian was ripe for murder, and Oliver was only the first victim he had in mind.

"Sebastian darling, it's not what you think—"

"Shut up." The look he sent her was soul shriveling.

Then he turned back to Oliver. "And you, you bastard, get up. Unless you want me to beat the hell out of you before you even get on your feet."

"You've got no right bursting in here like this and threatening me!" Oliver was blustering, Julia realized. In the face of Sebastian's icy menace Oliver's very real anger had been tempered by fear. Not that she blamed him. He must have seen, as she had, that Sebastian in his present state of mind was more than capable of some ferocious act of violence. To her horror, she heard Oliver say, "Julia is my affianced wife. We are to be wed tomorrow, and as such our behavior has nothing to do with you!"

"Oliver!" Julia gasped in horror, glaring at him before turning her attention back to Sebastian, who was looking at her with the fires of hell burning behind the icy surface of his eyes. "Sebastian, it's not true!"

Oliver was still on one knee beside her, and she practically shoved him over so that she could go to Sebastian. Sebastian who was standing there looking beautiful and terrible in his blue coat with the white waistcoat and linen and black pantaloons, his silver-gilt hair elegantly brushed and fury leaping out of those blue, blue eyes . . .

"Isn't it? I have the special license in my pocket to prove it. Julia and I are to be wed tomorrow. And I also have a note that she personally brought to my house this afternoon, asking me to call on her here today. To discuss the arrangements for our wedding, I have no doubt."

"No!" Julia moaned, scrambling off the couch and running to Sebastian's side. She clutched at his arm, which he promptly jerked away with a fierceness that sent her reeling back. She stumbled against his desk and would have fallen except for its support. Clinging to the rolled edge with both hands, she stared at Sebastian with anguished dismay. He was not even looking at her. He was glaring at Oliver, who returned his look with one of loathing. The two men bristled at each other like furious fighting cocks.

"Show me the license, and the note." Sebastian's words were forced from behind clenched teeth.

Oliver, with a glint of satisfaction, got to his feet and reached into the pocket of his coat, pulling forth a folded sheet of white paper and another crumpled piece that Julia recognized with horror was indeed the note she had written him earlier in the day. Oliver took two steps forward and held the incriminating papers out to Sebastian, who accepted them stiffly and read the words printed thereon.

"It was Julia's idea to wed by special license, you know. She told me she wanted to get the whole business concluded while you were out of town. She said you would try to stop her because you wanted her for yourself, but I thought she was exaggerating the danger as females are prone to do. I apologize, Julia, for my lack of understanding, and for the harsh things I said to you in this room earlier. I understand now what you were up to in Lady Jersey's ballroom last night. You were merely trying to throw Moorland off the scent until you could be safely wed to me. You should have trusted me to protect you, my dear. He has no hold on you, whatever he says. With that license we can be wed tomorrow just as we had planned, and there is not a thing in this world he can do to stop us." Oliver's voice as he directed it to Julia was cooler now, and laced with spurious sympathy and concern as he saw a way to revenge himself on both Sebastian and Julia.

Julia, listening to this exchange with mounting horror, could do nothing to save herself. She felt as if she were frozen in place by the waves of icy fury emanating from Sebastian's stiff body.

"Is any of this true, Julia?" The carefully measured, remote syllables sent icy chills skating along her spine. Julia could only stare at him with horrified, pleading eyes as she shook her head.

"No," she whispered, her eyes locked to Sebastian's in a gaze that shut out everyone else.

Oliver gave an angry laugh. "Come now, Julia, are you still afraid of the man? Can you deny that we were planning to wed tomorrow? Without Moorland's knowledge? Or that you told me he was trying to force you into an affaire and that marrying me out of hand was the only way to prevent him?"

Julia looked into Sebastian's eyes, and found she could not lie to him. "Oh, Sebastian, what he says is true, but . . ." she whispered miserably, determined to make a clean breast of the whole story. Oliver interrupted with a satisfied smirk.

"You see, Moorland? Whatever she may have told you, it was done merely to put you off the scent. Her intention has been to wed me all along."

"Sebastian, no! I—" He silenced her with a single look. She watched wide-eyed as he slowly, deliberately ripped the special license and the note to shreds, which he then let fall to the floor. Could he possibly, by some miracle, overcome the distrust bred in him by years of being unloved long enough to trust her in this instance?

"You will never wed her, Carlyle, and not just because I

will not allow it." Sebastian's voice was calm—too calm. Julia felt a terrible disquiet as he turned his eyes from Oliver to fix hers. "You will never wed my dear cousin by marriage Julia Stratham because she doesn't exist. Her real name is a very common one—Jewel Combs, wasn't it, Julia?—and she has lived most of her life in London's gutters. She became my kinswoman by the act of participating in a robbery that eventually took the life of my cousin. Ah, yes, you didn't think I knew that, did you, my own? But I am not quite the fool you continually take me for. I had the runners on your trail before you had been in my house an hour, and they had the whole story for me soon after we arrived at White Friars. But to continue, Carlyle, Jewel Combs then coerced my cousin into marrying her on his deathbed, and finally had the gall to present herself to me as his grieving widow. I took her in—look at her, and you will see why—and agreed to educate her as a lady. She has been my mistress for some months. Now, Carlyle, do you still wish to make her your wife?"

Sebastian's eyes had never left Julia's as he spoke. She in turn stared back at him, mesmerized by the magnitude of the humiliation he was visiting on her. She was scarcely aware of Oliver's horrified gaze on her or of the concerted gasps and fascinated stares of the crowd that had by now gathered around the dowager countess just outside the study door.

"Julia?" Oliver's face was a study in conflicting emotions. Julia had no inclination to sort them out as she continued to look steadily at Sebastian. To be stripped bare like this before them all . . . she couldn't bear it. She wanted to wilt, to melt away into a little puddle on the floor, but she refused to give Sebastian the satisfaction of seeing just how devastating was the blow he had dealt her. Instead she lifted her chin and straightened her spine, standing away from the support of the desk to face Sebastian squarely on her own two feet.

"Most of what he just said is true." Her words were icily clear, and ostensibly directed to Oliver. But her eyes never left Sebastian's. "He has a few minor details wrong, but I won't bother to correct them now. I am sorry that I deceived you—all." This last word was tacked on in reference to the gaping onlookers in the doorway. Sebastian, his set face as white as his linen while his eyes burned out of it like fiery jewels, stared at her as she walked steadily toward him.

"Excuse me," she said with perfect calm, and he moved out of her way like a man in a trance. She was walking by him, and the crowd was already parting to let her through. He turned to her, his eyes glittering with some emotion she couldn't name.

"Julia . . ." His voice as he said her name was a hoarse croak.

Julia paused for a moment, her head turning on the white stem of her neck as she looked at him with contempt in her eyes.

"You are a fool, Sebastian," she said clearly, and then she was walking away, bearding the avid stares of the onlookers with the regal calm of a queen of the blood on her way to the block. Most of the faces with their shocked eyes and gaping mouths were a blur. Only the dowager countess' face with its eyes that were so like Sebastian's penetrated the fog that surrounded her. There was hatred in those blue eyes and triumph.

Julia lifted her chin a little higher in response, and then the onlookers were turning to watch her as she walked steadily along the hall and down the stairs. A surprised footman leaped to open the door for her when he saw that her intention was to leave, and then Julia was walking into the cool dampness of a late spring night.

Despite the delicate silk dress that left much of her arms and bosom bare, she never even felt the faint chill that brought goosebumps to her skin. Her mind was mercifully blank as she walked and walked, walked without thinking for what seemed like hours. She moved along the crowded thoroughfare that was Piccadilly, down through Haymarket and Whitehall, oblivious to the thinning crowds or their changing character, as well as the catcalls and lascivious looks to which a young woman alone on the streets at night was prey when she had neither cloak nor shawl to conceal her décolletage and the obvious quality of her dress.

Finally, without even knowing how she had arrived there, she was back in the slums of Whitechapel amongst the winos and trollops that had been her everyday companions before. But she was not even aware of them. She was in a state of shock through which nothing penetrated. Not until she felt a hand close on her arm, its fingers squeezing her soft flesh with enough force to hurt her. The pain penetrated her daze, and she looked around to see a broad pockmarked face smiling evilly at her from beneath a shock of greasy black hair.

" 'Ello, Jool, me dear. You ain't gone and forgot ol' Mick, now 'ave you? 'Cause I sure ain't forgot you," he said. And then Julia came out of her trance, but it was too late.

suppose you realize that you have ruined us all over that little slut?"

It was a little more than two hours after the guests had left in a flurry, ordered out in no uncertain terms by Sebastian. The babble of shocked questions and exclamations that had followed Julia's exit had been silenced temporarily by his icy command, but when he had closeted himself in his study the uproar had resumed as the house had quickly emptied. Now his mother spoke to him from the door she had unceremoniously opened, and Sebastian stared back at her with cold eyes.

"I am sure you will understand if I tell you that it is a matter of the most supreme indifference to me."

The dowager countess, still in the pale lavender brocade that she had worn to the rout, stepped inside the room and crossed to the leather chair on the opposite side of the desk from her son. He was lounging back in his chair, his coat and cravat discarded. His booted feet were crossed at the ankles and propped on the edge of the desk, and he held a cheroot in his mouth and a glass in his hand.

"You look disgusting," she said.

"I feel disgusting," he answered levelly, removing the cheroot from his mouth to take a gulp of the fine Scotch whiskey in his glass. "So I would suggest you leave me to it."

The dowager expelled her breath in an audible hiss. "Good God, Sebastian, you're not pining over that slut already, are you? After the way she behaved with Carlyle—

the way she betrayed you?"

"Which you were very careful to bring to my attention, mama. Now I'm starting to ask myself, why?"

"Obviously I felt you should know the kind of female she is. Any man of sense would have already assumed her lack of virtue from her background, but then you have never been a man of sense as we both know. I should think you would feel grateful to me for having saved you from the consequences of your own folly."

"Do you know, mama, I do not. I also believe that you acted out of malice—for me and for Julia."

"You're not blaming me!"

Sebastian's eyes glinted. "Yes, mama, I am blaming you. I'm blaming you for a great deal. Not entirely for this fiasco tonight, but certainly for the years and years of your neglect and indifference toward me. Now I'm finally giving you a chance to explain yourself. Why?"

The dowager countess hesitated, her still lovely face creasing with fine lines as she frowned down at her son. The cold smile with which he was so familiar lifted the corners of her lips, and the blue eyes that were so like his own gleamed at him.

"So you want to know why I've never liked you, Sebastian? Very well, I'll tell you. If you do not like what you hear, you have only yourself to blame."

The smile vanished as her face contorted with bitterness. Staring up at her, Sebastian thought that for the first time in his life he found his mother almost ugly.

"The father that you thought was so wonderful was a monster to me. Edward was conceived within weeks of our wedding, and by the time I found out that I was with child

I was never so thankful of anything in my life. I did my duty. I gave him his heir. I never wanted another child after that, but he did. He raped me time after time to get you, and I've never been able to look at you since without remembering the violence with which you were conceived. Now there you have the story. Are you pleased?"

Sebastian stared at his mother, stared into the cold blue eyes and wondered with a sense of shock if she could be telling the truth. Certainly he could never remember his father mistreating his mother, but then his father had been an invalid since his sixth birthday. If it were true, it put a different complexion on things—on a whole spectrum of things. Perhaps his mother had some justification for her aversion to him. Sebastian also thought of himself with Elizabeth. It sounded very much as if he and his father had faced a similar situation in regards to their wives, but they had responded to it very differently. If Elizabeth had lived, Sebastian wondered, would he too have eventually resorted to rape? And would the whole of his miserable childhood have been played out again with his own second child?

"I'm sorry, mama. I didn't know." Sebastian's voice was quiet, and his eyes were very blue as he met his mother's glittering gaze.

She stared at him for a moment, her eyes hostile and her mouth tight. Then she seemed to crumple, and sat down in the chair across the desk from him.

"You didn't know." Her voice was harsh as she threw the words at him. Her eyes gleamed wildly beneath a sheen of moisture, and her mouth was shaking. "Of course you didn't know. How could you? You couldn't help the cir- cumstances of your birth. I used to tell myself that when you were an infant, but it didn't make any difference then—and it doesn't now. From the very first moments when I felt you moving inside me, all I could think of was that you were a child *he* had forced on me. I hated him for it, but he didn't care if I hated him. So I hated you." The countess looked up at him, her mouth compressing in an effort to still the trembling at the corners. Her voice was barely audible as she continued. "I could hardly even bear to look at you. My own son. And I hated him for that as well."

Sebastian stared at his mother for a long moment. He had suffered from her maltreatment all these years, but it seemed that she had suffered, too. He had always thought that maybe there was some flaw in himself that only his mother could see, some flaw that rendered him impossible to love. But now he realized that he had been viewing himself as through a distorted mirror from the very earliest moments of his childhood—and that mirror had just shattered into a million pieces. It was not him that his mother hated at all. . . .

But the revelation had come too late to change anything much. He no longer needed his mother nor her love. He was a man now, and the lonely, heartsick little boy who had lived for so long inside him could at last be laid to rest. For that if nothing else, he had to be grateful. His feet dropped to the floor and he sat up, stubbing out his cheroot and setting the glass with a little clink on the desk.

"I'm very sorry for all you've suffered, mama," he said quietly.

For the first time in his life he was able to look at her without feeling the corrosive bitterness that had colored his every thought of her for as long as he could remember. He was suddenly aware of how small and frail she was—and how old. With all her material possessions, her title, and social position, what had she really? Her husband had died bitterly estranged from her; the son of her heart was dead, too. She was left with him, a son whom she had spurned and despised from birth, and who had learned to despise her in turn. She was simply an unhappy old woman, who, whether she would admit it or not, needed him far more than he needed her.

And she was his mother. Whatever else she might do or be, there was that inviolable bond of blood tying him to her. And, he realized, he might be looking at himself as he would be in his latter years, alone and unloved. He shuddered inwardly, and from this revelation came the strength to ignore all that lay between them and reach out to her.

"Maybe we should give ourselves a second chance, mama."

Those eyes that were so like his own filled with tears as she stared at him. Her hand lifted, and for a moment he thought that she would touch his arm that rested on the desk. But the habit of years prevailed, and her hand dropped back into her lap. She blinked once to clear the tears away, then lifted her head in the familiar prideful way.

"I'm afraid it's far, far too late for that," she said. Even as Sebastian stared at her impatiently he saw her withdrawing behind her veil of ice.

A knock sounded on the half-opened door. At Sebastian's brusque "What is it?" the door opened fully. Sebastian lifted his eyes from his mother's controlled face to see Smathers, as immaculate as ever despite the lateness of the hour and the excitement the evening had generated. He looked apologetic at the interruption, but Sebastian gestured to him to speak.

"There is a man here to see you, my lord. A Mr. Bates, he gave his name as."

"Bates!" It was the name of one of the Bow Street runners Sebastian had set after the man or men who had murdered Timothy. Sebastian wasn't entirely certain, but he rather thought that Bates was the heavyset one of the pair who had driven down to White Friars all those months ago with the information about Julia's involvement in the robbery that had ended in Timothy's death. Bates had also told him about how she had nursed his cousin on his deathbed, just as she had claimed. That information, in Sebastian's mind coupled with the liking he had already begun to feel for the chit, had outweighed the other, particularly since Bates had been quite certain that the murder was the result of panic of one of the other participants and not planned at all.

"Where is he?"

"I have left him in the hall, my lord."

Without another word Sebastian strode out to meet the man. Bates was indeed the man he remembered. He waited uneasily amongst the Meissen porcelain and Louis XIV chairs that Julia had once threatened. Thinking of Julia hurt, so he tried to banish her image from his mind. But it was impossible not to remember how she had betrayed him, or that she was even now out there alone in the dark on the streets of London. Sebastian set his teeth. Whatever this fellow wanted, he would give him short shrift.

"You wanted to see me, Bates?" His tone was abrupt, his eyes cool. Whatever the man had to say, he did not want to hear it. Not now. It could make no difference, with Julia lost to him.

"It's about that gentry-mort you set me to find out about, yer worship."

Gentry-mort meaning female in the man's rough cant, Sebastian deduced, and his eyes took on an icy hauteur that made the other man look apprehensive.

"I have learned all I wish to know about the, er, 'gentry-mort,' thank you." Sebastian's eyes narrowed as he thought of something. "By the by, isn't it a trifle late to be making business calls?"

Bates nodded, his jowly face lugubrious. "Aye, yer worship, it is that, but I jest clapped me peepers on the gentry-mort and it looked like she was in a peck o' trouble. So I jest thought to meself, I thought, Will, old boy, you'd better go on around o' that earl's house and tell someone what you seen. Jest in case you shouldn't want the gentry-mort to come to harm, yer worship."

"What did you see?" Sebastian's voice was hoarse. Bates shook his head sorrowfully.

"That cove wot pulled the toothpick on your kin has the gentry-mort, and if I were him and worried about scraggin' I'd be wishful of makin' sure she didn't peach on me. O' course, since she's such a pretty little thing, it'll likely take him a while to get around to that part o' it. So we've likely got some time, yer worship."

Sebastian felt his heart race as he absorbed from this that Julia was in extreme danger from the man who had killed Timothy because he feared hanging if she should identify him. The lout would probably kill her with as little compunction as he would swat a fly—but first he would pleasure himself with her body.

Sebastian felt a stabbing pain unlike anything he had ever felt before slice through his heart. If she died, he would not want to go on living. If one hair on her head was harmed, he would with great pleasure kill the swine responsible.

But of course, the one with the ultimate responsibility would be himself. Because he had not trusted her enough to let her explain about Carlyle. And he was sure suddenly that there would be an explanation. He had allowed himself to be poisoned by his own jealousy and his mother's whispered spite. Only now, when Julia's very life was in danger, was he beginning to think clearly again. She loved him; it had not been a trick, and he had come very close to throwing it all away. He had in truth been the fool she had called him. But there was no time for recriminations. All that could come later. What mattered was that he get Julia safe.

"Smathers, wake George and Rudy and arm them with whatever you can find. And have the carriage brought around. On the instant, do you understand?"

"Yes, my lord!"

Sebastian was already vanishing into his study again, to emerge moments later with a pair of duelling pistols which he thrust into the waistband of his pantaloons.

"Where are you going with those?" His mother was standing in the hall staring at him, an indecipherable expression on her face. He looked at her without really seeing her at all.

"I'm going to fetch Julia, of course. Get out of my way, mother. Come on, Bates."

XXXIV

KEEP away from me, Mick!"

Julia's voice was hoarse as she backed away across the garbage-strewn floor of the cellar. She held Mick at bay with a broken whiskey bottle, which she had grabbed as soon as he released her wrist after dragging her into the dark room. As she moved away from him, the bottle clutched in her hand her only weapon, he watched her with a lustful smile that turned her stomach.

"My, Jool, ya sure do talk pretty now! Almost as pretty as ya look. Ya know, I'm sorta glad I never 'ad ya when you was one of us. It wouldna been nearly so much fun as this is gonna be."

"What about Jem, Mick? He'll be very angry if you hurt me."

Mick folded his arms over his chest, making no move to come after her. He was right, she thought sickly, there was no hurry. Here in this filthy cellar she was at his mercy. She was under no illusions that even a broken bottle would hold him off for long. She would be lucky to even cut him, but she would try. She would die trying because he would kill her if she didn't succeed. After he raped her. The very thought made her sick.

"Yer off there, Jool. A lot's been 'appenin' since you were with us. Ol' Jem, he's got a 'ole new gang o' prigs. 'E won't care a farthin's worth wot I do ter ya. 'Fact, 'e'll probably be fair glad. 'E's been mortal 'urt that ya peached on us, your friends like."

"I never peached!" That accusation got through to the

Jewel she had once been, and made her straighten with righteous indignation.

Mick shook his head at her. "Ain't no use ter lie, Jool. We knows ya peached, 'cause who else set the runners on our tail? They came down on us like rats on cheese right after ya ran off. Who else coulda tole 'em wot we done?"

"If I told them, why weren't you arrested? Why wouldn't I have given them your names and where to find you, you dolt?"

"Don't ya be callin' me names now, missy," he warned with an ugly look that made Julia step back another pace. She would have retreated even further, but her back was pressed against the moldy stone of the cellar wall as it was.

"I don' know why we wasn't taken up. Maybe ya didn't peach all the way—jest tole 'em sommit of wot 'appened. Sommit that made you look awful good, by my reckonin'. But that don't matter now. If ya ain't peached yet, there's no tellin' when ya might. That's what I tole Jem when I set that boy to watchin' that fancy 'ouse where you was livin'—oh, yes, I been knowin' where ya were fer about a month now, ain't much that 'appens in London-town that gets by ole Mick. I knew'd that sooners or laters I'd get a chance to shut ya up permanent. So when the boy comes ter me ternight and sez yer out runnin' the streets alone, I knew the time 'ad come. O' course, I didn' know yer'd make it easy for me by comin' back to the ol' neighborhood. I thanks ya for that."

"Mick," Julia said desperately, looking around at the windowless cellar, "I have some money now. I'll—I'll give it to you, if you let me go."

That caught his attention, and he seemed to weigh it.

Then he shook his head regretfully.

"Nah. I couldn' trust yer, once yer got out o' ere. Besides, yer could still peach."

"I promise I won't peach!"

Mick shook his head again. "Nah."

His arms dropped to his sides, and hung long and ape-like while his fingers flexed. He took off his tattered stained greatcoat and the scarf looped around his neck deliberately, as if to frighten her. The gesture succeeded in making Julia shake with fear. No one knew where she was, or, she thought bitterly, would even care. Sebastian had watched her walk out of his life without lifting a hand to stop her.

"Are yer goin' ter come over 'ere, or are yer goin' to make me come and get ya?" This leering question put an end to any thoughts except for immediate survival. The fighter that Jewel Combs had once been surfaced again in this moment of danger. Julia found herself instinctively leaning forward a little, balancing on her toes as she swung the bottle back and forth in a slow arc in front of her body.

"Come and get me, then. If you think you can."

With a loud roar Mick dove for her. Julia, frightened by the yell, nevertheless managed to leap aside, swinging the bottle down in a vicious arc that ended as it smashed into Mick's cheek. Glass shattered and blood spurted—but Mick, with a howl, straightened. He was apparently materially unharmed, and put a questing hand to his cheek. When his fingers came away red with blood, he looked at Julia in a way that made her blood turn cold. Murder was in his eyes now, where only lust had been before.

"Yer goin' ter regret that, Jool, me girl." Then he dove at her again, and this time she wasn't quick enough to leap out of the way. She stabbed at him with the remains of the bottle, but the jagged edges only just penetrated his shoulder, drawing blood and curses but not seeming to do him any real harm. He grabbed her wrist, twisting it viciously until she cried out and her numb fingers dropped the bottle. Still he kept twisting her arm until she fell to her knees in front of him, tears starting from her eyes. In another minute he would break her arm. He leaned over her, smirking down into her pain contorted face.

"Ain't so sassy now, are ya?" he grinned, as blood from the gash she had opened on his cheek ran down over his dark pitted skin to drip from the fleshy, stubbled jaw. While Julia's eyes followed fearfully, he drew back his hand to slap her as hard as he could across the face, releasing her wrist at the same time. She cried out as the force of the blow sent her toppling backward. Before she could scramble up, he was straddling her, chuckling maliciously at her struggles, not even trying to control them as the solid weight of his body held her down.

"Ya shouldna cut me, Jool," he said softly, as he drew his arm back, and slowly clenched his broad hand into a meaty fist. She cowered, trying to shield her face with her arms as he slammed his fist into her averted cheek, but the very first blow broke through that weak barrier. She screamed siren loud, and then continued to scream and scream as his fist hammered into her face and throat and breasts. Blood spurted from her nose and mouth, and her eyes were already swelling shut as he continued to beat her. Her screaming quieted to a dull keening, and finally even that stopped as he pummeled her with vicious blows like a pugilist with raw meat. What little she could see of the cellar through her swollen eyes was swimming crazily and she no longer even felt the pain of his continuing blows. Was he going to beat her to death? she wondered groggily. But some distant, still cognizant part of her mind heard him rip her silk dress. Then his hands were on her breasts, hard and hurtful as they squeezed. She couldn't struggle, couldn't even care as he ripped her clothes from her body until she was naked, then settled himself over her quiescent form. Hardly conscious of it, she felt his knees parting her thighs.

There was a tremendous crash, and then another. Through the haze she realized the door had splintered on its hinges. Then Mick was jumping to his feet and trying to run as a veritable army burst through the shattered door. There was a brief scuffle, and then Mick cried out as his hands were wrenched behind his back and he was forced to the floor.

Her dazed brain reeled as it tried to sort out why Smathers should be there, armed with what appeared to be a cricket bat, or why two of Sebastian's footmen should be brandishing butcher knives. A burly stranger was calling out for them to hold Mick securely. And then she saw Sebastian himself, with a silver barreled pistol in his fist, looking toward where she lay naked and bloody on the stone floor with a frightening pain in his eyes.

"Sebastian," she moaned, but she couldn't seem to focus her eyes. Besides, she remembered vaguely that he didn't want her, didn't love her. . . . Tears formed in her eyes, trickling from their corners as he knelt beside her and covered her with his coat.

"Oh, my God. Julia," he whispered. "Don't cry, my

love." She was vaguely aware of him leaning over her, of him tenderly wrapping his coat around her, of him removing the snowy cravat from around his neck and using it to wipe some blood from her face. He had called her his love—was he no longer angry with her then? She tried to smile at him, although it was difficult to focus her eyes. The agony she saw in his face made her peer up at him with befuddlement.

"Don't be angry with me, Sebastian," she managed on a reedy breath, and suddenly his face contorted with such pain that she shivered at the sight of it. He must have felt her shudder because his expression quickly changed to an expressionless mask that showed nothing but a suspicious glitter in his eyes.

"I'm not angry with you, my own. Shhh, don't try to talk now. Just be still, and we'll get you out of here. There's nothing for you to be afraid of anymore," he murmured soothingly, gathering her up in his arms with infinite care as he stood. For a moment he cradled her against his chest like a hurt child, while pain and grief and a terrible anger all showed for an instant on his face.

"Everything's going to be all right, my love," he whispered softly. He carried her to where the other men huddled in a group guarding the blubbering Mick. Then he gently handed her over to one of the footmen.

"Take her out to the carriage, and stay with her," he directed. She wanted to reach for Sebastian because only in his arms did she feel truly safe, but found she didn't have the strength.

George (she thought it was George) was carrying her carefully up the narrow dirty stairs when she heard Sebastian say, in quite a different voice from that which he had used with her, "You lowlife bastard!"

She heard a dull thunk that sounded much like a blow, then another, and another. Finally, just as George got her outside and lifted her into the closed carriage, she heard the silvery echo of a pistol shot.

Moments later, Sebastian climbed into the carriage beside her. A moonbeam glinted off the pistols that he had returned to the waistband of his pantaloons. She frowned as she tried to remember what disturbed her about their presence.

"What . . . Mick . . . ?" she tried to say, but found that she could not even manage to focus her thoughts. Besides, her mouth ached dreadfully when she tried to form words. But he must have sensed her unspoken question because he came to kneel on the floor beside her as she lay on her side on the seat, her bare arms huddled over her breasts beneath the enveloping comfort of his coat and her bare legs curled up into its sheltering skirts.

"He won't bother you ever again, I promise," Sebastian said softly, his hand coming up to smooth a tangle of hair away from her swollen left eye. Julia winced, and his mouth tightened. He turned away from her, leaning out the carriage door, and said something to George who still waited outside.

Then there was a jolt and the crack of a whip, and the carriage was moving. But Julia never knew when they reached the house in Grosvenor Square. By then she had lost consciousness, and did not regain it for three days.

XXXV

IT'S going to be touch and go, my lord. The fact that she has been unconscious for so long is not a good sign."

"Damn it, man, there must be something you can do! You're supposed to be the best bloody sawbones in the City!"

Sebastian's angry voice was the first sound that penetrated the layers of fog that enclosed Julia. She tried to speak, to open her eyes at least to see who he was talking to, and why he sounded so distraught, but found she could not. She was sinking back into the fog. . . .

"I regret, my lord, that some things are in God's hands only. The beating she took was most severe. As you can see, there is a great deal of damage about the head."

Warm hands touched her temple gently, and Julia shuddered at the pain the slight pressure caused. She tried again to let them know that she was conscious, but her body seemed incapable of following her brain's directions.

"You can't just let her die!" The desperate voice was Sebastian's. The doctor said something in reply, but she couldn't quite understand his words. A buzzing noise began to build in her ears, sounding almost like the rushing of the tide on the rocks below the Wash. Julia had a sudden sensation of falling down into a thick black fog, and then she heard no more.

When next she awoke, the room was pitch dark. She was alone, she thought, and yet she did not feel alone. It was as if someone was there, but she could not quite see who it was through the darkness. She stared into the inky black, trying to see . . . The room was cold, so cold. Someone had let the fire go out . . . She shivered, and then she heard a faint sound tickling at the edges of her consciousness. It seemed to be a whisper, a hoarse whisper. At first she thought it was the roaring in her ears again, but the whisper took on words and form, like a chant. It was repeated over and over, but still she couldn't make out the words. Until at last she picked up one here, and another there. . . .

"Elizabeth died. So will you. Elizabeth died. So will you." The whisper grew louder and louder, building to a harsh chorus that rang in her ears. Julia's eyes grew wide with horror as she listened. Cold chills raced up and down her body. This could not be happening—it had to be a terrible dream.

There was a scratching noise, and then a ghostly white glow appeared at the far end of the room. Julia stared mesmerized at the thing, realizing that the chant was originating from it. There was a swirl of white as the thing turned around, and Julia found herself staring at a white cowled figure holding a candle as it chanted. Where its face should have been she saw nothing but a void as black as death.

Julia screamed. She was still screaming when the thing disappeared. She was still screaming when the door to her room crashed open with a bang, and Sebastian appeared, silhouetted in the open doorway. Sebastian . . .

She tried to call to him, but she could not. Her hands lifted toward him in a gesture of supplication even as the darkness rose again to swirl her away.

The next thing she was aware of was the sound of someone sobbing. It was such a heartbroken sound that it tugged her from the darkness. She listened to the muffled cries for a moment or two, feeling a great pity well up within her for anyone who was suffering such distress.

With great difficulty she lifted her lids. They felt abominably heavy, and as they parted the light hurt her eyes. It was not much light, only the gentle orange glow of a fire blazing in the hearth near the bed. Other than that one source of illumination the room was shrouded in darkness. She blinked, fighting the urge to let her lids fall and merciful darkness take her. Then her eyes focused on the tousled, silver-gilt head of a man as it was cradled in his arms on the edge of her bed.

The keening sounds were coming from Sebastian. Her hands were resting on top of the downy cream duvet that covered the bed, and her right one was not too far from that bent head. She listened to the gasping sounds he made, watched the broad shoulders heave, and felt an almost maternal urge to comfort him. Staring at that bent head, she willed her hand to move. For a moment she thought that it would not . . . but then it did. She rested her fingers lightly on the rough silk of his hair.

His shoulders stiffened, and then his head came up and he was staring into her eyes. He looked a mess, she thought, unshaven and disheveled with red-rimmed eyes that glittered with tears.

Tears. He was crying. Her cold, proud Sebastian was crying. Over her.

"Julia. . . ." His voice was hoarse. His eyes were wild with hope as they stared into hers. "Oh, God, Julia, you're awake!"

"Don't cry, Sebastian." It was a mere breath of sound.

But he heard it. He caught up the slim white hand that had touched his hair and pressed his lips to it. The feeling of his warm, dry lips was a pleasant antidote to the almost unearthly cold of her skin.

"You're not to die!" The words were fierce, an order. That was more like her arrogant Sebastian. A faint smile trembled and then died on her lips.

"No," she agreed, her eyes smiling groggily at him. A faint memory tugged at her, and she frowned. The very act of frowning hurt her, and her eyes drooped shut. Why did the mere mention of dying disturb her so?

"The White Friar," she whispered, and he looked at her as if he feared she was losing her mind. The apparition came back to her in all its horrible detail, and she shuddered, closing her eyes.

"Julia!" Sebastian sounded panicked. Julia opened her eyes again to blink at him. Why was he so frightened?

"I hurt," she whispered, and he visibly flinched.

"I know you do, my own, but you'll be better, much better, soon."

"What happened?" She couldn't quite remember, although something was niggling at the edges of her consciousness. Something painful. . . .

"You were beaten. You'll be all right." The syllables were clipped, the glittering eyes fierce as they bore into hers. His very vehemence told Julia that he had some doubts about it—was she going to die? The White Friar had come for her. She shuddered. But that was only a bad dream. She wouldn't frighten Sebastian more by telling him about it.

"Mick," she whispered, remembering. Her eyelids

drooped as her body instinctively tried to block out the remembered horror with darkness.

"Don't you dare leave me again! Julia, do you hear me?"

The fear in Sebastian's voice brought her eyelids fluttering open. His face was so dear to her, she thought as her eyes focused lovingly on him. Even unshaven and dirty and tear stained, he was still the most handsome man she had ever seen. And he was hers—or he had been.

"Are you still angry with me, Sebastian?" The sad little whisper made him flinch. He blinked once, twice, as though to hold back the tears that made his eyes glitter like diamonds in the flickering light. His hand tightened around her fingers and he brought them to his lips again.

"That you could ask me that . . ." His voice broke, and for a moment he couldn't continue. Then he seemed to get a grip on his emotions, for he went on in a low, husky rush. "No, Julia, I'm not angry with you. I never should have been angry with you. When my mother told me you had sneaked off into my study to be alone with Carlyle and I found you there kissing him, letting him touch you, I went a little crazy. I didn't stop to think that the Julia I loved was incapable of the kind of convoluted deceit I'd spent most of my life watching. I was so jealous I didn't stop to think anything at all. I just wanted to kill Carlyle—and hurt you as much as I was hurting. And I did. I did hurt you. I hurt you mentally, and I hurt you physically. But if it's any consolation to you, you hurt me as much. Every time I close my eyes I can see your white face as you stared down the vultures of society that I had turned loose on you. You were every inch a lady, my own. I was never so proud of you as when I saw you walking toward that crowd with your head high and your back straight. And I can see you too, lying on that cellar floor, hurt and crying because I had made you run from me. . . . Christ, Julia, I'm sorry. If I could redo it I would—but I can't. I can only ask you to forgive me. Please."

He whispered the last word, and his eyes clung to hers, pleading with her. She looked at him for a long moment, her eyes tender as they touched on every plane and angle of that beautiful face. Then the hand he was holding turned in his, and her fingers wrapped his warmly.

"I love you, Sebastian. There's nothing to forgive."

He closed his eyes briefly, and a single tear trickled down the lean hard cheek. Julia felt her heart ache as she looked at him. He was so beautiful—like one of the Lord's archangels, she had thought when she had first set eyes on him. Now she knew that if he was an angel at all, it was a very tattered and shabby one, halo severely dented by numerous falls from grace. But his flaws were part of the man and she loved him. More than anything in her life, more than her life itself. It seemed like she always had, and she knew that she always would. Despite anything and everything.

"I'll make it up to you, my own, I swear it." His eyes had the fierce zeal of the confessional as they bore into hers. "I'll be so good to you. You'll have everything you ever wanted. Clothes, carriages, servants, anything."

The only affection he had had in the past had been the kind he had had to buy, she remembered. To him material things were the currency of love. But she would teach him better, if it took her the rest of her life. And his.

"I only want you, Sebastian. Nothing else. I love you."

She said the words patiently, as if she knew she would be repeating them many, many times over the years. Then she blinked as his face seemed to recede and then draw closer again. The buzzing was suddenly back in her ears.

"Sebastian," she said faintly, clutching his hand. She was afraid to give in to the darkness again, afraid of what might await her in it. But even his warm grip could not keep her from the swirling void that opened up to claim her.

"Julia!" She heard him calling her with fear in his voice, missed the warmth of his hand as it abruptly disengaged from hers, heard the bang of her door crashing on its hinges and Sebastian's voice bellowing. "Wake that damned sawbones and get him in here!"

And then the darkness caught her again and she heard nothing more.

X X X V I

ow are you feeling this morning, my love?"

It was nearly three weeks later. Julia, clad in a demure blue sprigged white nightgown with a little frill of lace around the neck, was propped up in the four poster bed in her room at White Friars. Despite Sebastian's fears she had made a fairly rapid recovery since her first brief return to consciousness. The next day she had woken to sip a little broth, and when she had closed her eyes again it had been to sleep. Since then she had been growing stronger each day.

As soon as she had been fit to travel, Sebastian had brought her into the country to recuperate. She would do better in the fresh air of Norfolk, he told her, and she agreed. London was a bad memory to put behind her; White Friars beckoned like home.

Sebastian accompanied her, riding in the closed carriage with her throughout the two-day trip when she knew he would have preferred by far to drive himself or ride astride. She was blissfully happy despite the injuries that made her wince at every jolt. He loved her, and he showed it with every look and gesture, and that was all that mattered to her.

Since arriving at White Friars, he had pampered and cosseted her, insisting that she remain in bed. She did so to please him, even though she was feeling much better every day. She smiled to herself as she watched him through the day—dismissing Emily in the mornings to bring her chocolate and rolls himself, spending the afternoons reading newspapers aloud to her when she knew that he must be going crazy from so much inactivity. At White Friars he was accustomed to spending much of the time out-of-doors, and the early June weather was glorious. Julia found this evidence of his devotion both touching and secretly amusing. Knowing Sebastian, she was sure that such solicitude could not last too much longer.

"I'm fine, Sebastian. Really." She smiled at him as he carefully deposited the breakfast tray across her knees. He bent to drop a gentle kiss on the side of her mouth, then straightened to look down at her critically.

"You look a little better," he admitted. "At least you don't still have huge purple and black rings around both eyes. They've faded to kind of a yellowish gray. Very becoming."

"Thank you, kind sir." Though her voice was wry, she dimpled at him, trying not to wince as the smile made her bruised cheeks ache. Every evidence of her pain hurt him more than it did herself, she knew. She patted the bed beside her, and he sat down where she indicated, accepting a roll she proffered. She watched him fondly as he munched, marveling as she always did at his good looks. Today, dressed in baggy tweed coat and suede pantaloons that on any other man would have merely looked comfortably sloppy, he was the very picture of the elegant aristocrat in the country. It would be interesting to see over the course of the next thirty or so years if there were any circumstances under which he could look less than handsome. She was inclined to doubt that there were.

"What are you thinking about, my own?" He downed the last of the roll as he spoke, and helped himself to a sip of her chocolate.

"How handsome you are," she said, smiling at him. He looked startled, then grinned back at her as he replaced the cup.

"You're wasting your time," he advised her. "Flattery will not lure me into your bed. Nothing will, until you've fully recovered."

"I wasn't trying—" Julia began indignantly, glowering at him, only to laugh as she realized that he was teasing her. "Conceited beast!" she chastized him without heat, watching him with open pleasure as he came to his feet beside the bed, and stretched with lazy grace.

"I have a present for you," he said. When she looked at him inquiringly he reached into his coat pocket and brought out a small box. Julia's eyes widened at the sight of it. Even without opening it, she knew it must contain a ring.

And what a ring it was! Its huge central diamond was

surrounded by marquise topazes set in yellow gold. Julia stared at it speechlessly, then looked up at him. He was frowning down at her, his lean body slightly tense. Her long silence had apparently made him uneasy.

"I had it sent down from London. If you don't like it, we can get something else." His diffident tone was so unlike him that Julia smiled.

"I love it." Her soft assurance must have been utterly convincing because he dropped down to sit on the bed beside her again, taking the box from her. She watched the long fingered hands as he removed the ring from its box, then caught her left hand and slid the ring onto her third finger. He pressed a kiss to the knuckle just above the ring before releasing it.

"How do you feel about short engagements?" he asked, watching her as she turned her hand this way and that, admiring the stones as they sparkled in the light streaming in through the long windows.

"How short?"

"Say, a month from today?"

That caught her attention. She looked at him, her eyes the exact color of the stones in the ring.

"Oh yes, Sebastian," she breathed, and for once unaware of her injuries she threw herself at him, flinging her arms around his neck and pressing her lips to his willing mouth. He kissed her thoroughly before he freed her, and she enjoyed the experience so much that she didn't even mind the twinges that prickled over her cheeks from her bruised mouth, or the aching of her still sore body where it pressed close to him.

"I hurt you," he said, concerned. He caught her upper

arms in a firm yet gentle grip and held her away from him while looking down into her face.

"No, you didn't," she insisted, but he knew better. He put an admonishing finger over the lips he had just kissed, and frowned severely at her.

"No more of that, now. The doctor said you needed the most tender care for the next few weeks, and I mean to see that you get it. So quit tempting me, you baggage. I mean to save myself for our wedding night."

She smiled at him, a slow sleepy smile that made tiny flickers of fire leap to life in the backs of those blue eyes.

"Am I tempting you, Sebastian?" The question was a husky, provocative murmur. He stared hard at her for a long moment, then released her arms and stood up.

"You know you are."

"Good. Because you're tempting me, too."

With that, flickers in the backs of his eyes flamed to vivid life and for a moment she thought he was going to come back down on the bed beside her. But his hands clenched into fists at his sides, and he almost glared at her.

"I find that I need some exercise. If you don't object, I think I'll go riding. I'll be back before luncheon, of course."

Julia smiled at him and sank back upon her mound of pillows. It was pleasant to think that he wanted her so much that he had to leave the house to control his impulses—and equally pleasant to imagine him getting back into his normal routine. Their relationship would come to grief if he continued to treat her like a hothouse flower forever.

"I don't object at all. Just don't break your neck. Or anything else," she added with a naughty smile and a downward flick of her eyes. This surprised an unwilling smile from him, and he bent down to drop another quick kiss on her mouth, straightening before she could catch and hold him.

"Just wait until after the wedding," he threatened in a growling undertone.

"If I have to," she pouted, peeping up at him from beneath sooty lashes. He grinned, told her that she did indeed have to wait, flicked her nose with a finger, and exited. Julia sank deeper into her pillows as she listened to the sound of his boots retreating down the hallway, feeling very content.

XXXVII

HE twentieth day of July in the year of our lord eighteen hundred and forty-two was Julia's wedding day. The ceremony was to take place at two in the afternoon in the great hall at White Friars. By noon she was completely dressed except for her veil. She wanted to have time to stop by the nursery and show Chloe her wedding finery—the little girl would love to see it, she knew.

Julia smiled as she thought of Chloe. Miss Belkerson had first brought Chloe to visit her while she was still confined to bed, and something about seeing her so battered must have touched the little girl's heart. Twice more before Julia was allowed to get up, Chloe had come on her own to visit, peeping shyly around the doorway until Julia saw her and bade her come in.

Chloe never did—she always ran at that point—but Julia could not help but feel that the little girl considered her a friend. Perhaps the child had missed her in the months she had been absent from White Friars, she thought. Certainly Chloe remembered who she was, and seemed pleased to see her again.

Once Sebastian allowed her to get out of bed, she made a practice of visiting the little girl in her rooms every day. Sometimes she would sit and talk to Chloe through her doll. While the child never responded, she did seem to listen intently to Julia's nonsense. At other times she would accompany Chloe and Miss Belkerson outdoors for their afternoon walk. Chloe was always quiet and well behaved on these occasions, but once in a while, as a bushy tailed squirrel scurried across their path, for instance, the little girl would stiffen and point, displaying a silent excitement and interest that gave Julia hope that she might one day be a normal child again.

As the days passed, Julia felt a flowering of affection along with a keen sense of responsibility for the child. Almost as much as she wanted to marry Sebastian, she wanted to bring Chloe into the magic circle of their love. Love was what the child needed, Julia thought, although she fought so hard against accepting it. It hurt to think of the little girl leading such a separate, unnatural life when she and Sebastian were so happy. But even if Chloe could eventually be coaxed out of her shell, it was something that could not be rushed. It would have to be done one small step at a time.

Mindful of the fiasco that had resulted the last time she had interfered, Julia had not suggested that Sebastian again attempt to befriend his daughter. And he had not tried it on his own. But she kept him informed, in the most casual way she could contrive, of her own progress with the child. She was hopeful that as time passed and Chloe grew to accept her more and more, she might eventually be able to persuade her to accept Sebastian, too. But even if that never happened, she herself intended to treat Chloe as her child. She would love the little girl, and they would see what love could do.

The consensus was that actual attendance at the wedding might prove too much for Chloe. Julia had not even discussed the matter with Sebastian, but she had talked to Miss Belkerson and Mrs. Johnson. They all agreed that unless they wanted to risk subjecting Sebastian to a nasty scene, it would be wiser to keep the child away.

Julia did mean to include her in as much of the celebration as was possible under the circumstances. She had already told Chloe, with the help of her doll, that she would be staying at White Friars with her and her papa forever. She had also explained that after the very special ceremony that would take place on this day, she hoped that Chloe would come to like her as much as she, Julia, had come to like Chloe.

Chloe had said nothing, but Julia had thought that she understood. Now she meant to go to the nursery to show the little girl her beautiful dress; she had already learned that the child loved clothes, and indeed any pretty thing. She had a gift for Chloe, too: a small replica of her wedding bouquet of creamy white roses and baby's breath. Chloe would like that, Julia thought as Emily carefully threw the lace veil over her hair and anchored it with the circlet of creamy roses that matched the ones in her bouquet.

"Oh, Miss Julia, you do look a picture." Emily sighed as she stood back to survey her handiwork.

Julia, looking at herself in the cheval glass, had to agree. Her wedding dress was of white lace over satin, with the satin underdress cut away in a modest scoop above her breasts so that only the filmy lace covered her neck and arms. Seed pearls painstakingly sewn by Miss Soames to accentuate the delicate pattern of the lace swirled over the slim bodice and the full, graceful lines of the skirt. With the demi-train in the back and the floor length lace veil, her bridal outfit was a dream come true. Indeed, in those long ago days she had never even dared to dream of such a dress, or imagined that one so exquisite could exist. But now she was the very embodiment of a bride, a vision in white. Even her skin was velvety pale. The only touches of color about her were the ebony of her upswept hair and winged eyebrows, the gleaming gold of her eyes, and the soft rose of her mouth. Julia imagined Sebastian's reaction as he watched her come down the stairs to him. The blue of his eyes would deepen, and he would smile. . . .

A knock sounded on the door, effectively banishing her daydreams. It would not be him, she knew. Everyone from Mrs. Johnson to Johnson to Leister to Emily to the footmen and parlor maids had insisted that it was bad luck for a groom to see his bride on their wedding day before the actual ceremony. He had laughingly agreed to stay out of her way. He was probably in his rooms now, Julia thought, picturing him donning the morning clothes that he had decided were most suitable for the solemnity of the occasion.

"You're looking very beautiful, Julia. Sebastian will be pleased."

The cool, quiet voice was Caroline's. Julia, lost in her

imaginings, had not even realized that Emily had admitted her soon to be sister-in-law. She smiled affectionately at the other woman, who was looking very lovely herself in a powder blue silk dress. Caroline had insisted on coming down for the ceremony, to provide family support, she said, and would be standing with them. Julia deeply appreciated Caroline's show of loyalty after the scandal they had brought down on her head. Julia would have welcomed her without reservation if she had not brought the dowager countess with her. But Sebastian's mother had come as well, and would be present, she said, at the ceremony. Julia was inclined to view this seeming olive branch with grave suspicion, but it seemed to please Sebastian, so she said nothing of her numerous reservations. If it made Sebastian happy to have his mother with them on their wedding day, then she would bear the woman with good grace. Unless she said something typically nasty about Sebastian, or Chloe.

"And dreamy," Caroline added with a hint of humor as Julia was slow to respond to her remark. Julia's smile widened as she acknowledged the truth of that—she could not seem to keep her mind on anything today—and returned Caroline's compliment with utmost sincerity.

"Thank you. Well, we are quite the mutual admiration society, but that is not why I have come to you at this moment. I ran into Miss Belkerson in the hall, and she tells me that she has not seen Chloe all morning. She bade me ask you if the child was with you, but," Caroline finished, her eyes sweeping the chamber, "obviously she is not."

"No, I haven't seen her," Julia said, frowning. "Has Miss Belkerson been looking for her long?"

"For about three-quarters of an hour, I gather. Perhaps the best thing to do, as the child is not with you, would be to have some of the menservants look around the grounds. Ordinarily I would not worry, but . . ."

"But?"

Caroline looked oddly hesitant for a moment. Then with a quick shake of her head, she said, "She may be upset about the wedding. It's hard to tell, of course, with her. But last night when I visited her I thought she seemed a little more . . . brittle, I suppose, than usual."

"Yes." Julia frowned abstractedly. Chloe had not, to her knowledge, disappeared since her own return to White Friars. From what Miss Belkerson had said, it was something she only did when she was upset. Had she understood more about the wedding than Julia had realized, and had the knowledge upset her? Julia had carefully avoided telling her that she would be her new mother, but perhaps she had overheard some of the servants gossiping. Instinctively Julia knew that Chloe would find the idea of a new mother wildly upsetting.

"I believe I know where she may have gone," Julia said slowly. "There is a place she sometimes goes when she is upset. Emily, unfasten this dress, if you please. I am going for a quick walk, I believe."

"Julia! You can't go anywhere! You're marrying Sebastian in two hours!" Caroline sounded aghast.

"I should be back in half that with Chloe, if I'm right. Come, Emily, do as I say."

"Yes, Miss Julia." Emily sounded extremely disapproving as she did as she was bid. The veil and dress were reverently laid aside, and Julia, at her direction, was buttoned into a daydress of white sprigged, pale yellow muslin. Her satin slippers were replaced with sturdy walking shoes, and she was ready.

"At least tell me where you're going, so that I may tell Sebastian if you should happen to leave him standing there at the altar with no bride in sight." Caroline's normally placid voice was faintly tart.

Julia smiled. "I would never in my life leave Sebastian standing at the altar! He wouldn't like that one bit. And if you must know, I am going to the old monastery where I discovered Chloe one day when she ran away from her governess before."

"The old monastery," Caroline said slowly, her eyes clouding. "Chloe goes there? Do you think you should go there alone, Julia?"

"Because of what happened to Elizabeth, do you mean? I don't believe in ghosts, Caroline—and I think that is where Chloe will be."

"Would you like me to come with you?"

Julia smiled at her affectionately. She could sense Caroline's distaste for the place where her cousin had died, and yet she was enough of a friend to offer to accompany Julia there.

"Thank you, but no. I think this is something that Chloe and I can best work out alone."

"As you wish," Caroline said quietly, her eloquent shrug telling Julia that her friend thought her crazy, even if she wouldn't argue with her anymore.

"I'll be back as soon as I possibly can. Which will be in plenty of time, I promise, so don't look so disapproving, the pair of you!" With this half-laughing, half-exasperated remark, Julia left the room.

Caroline looked after her with clouded eyes, while Emily, who was lovingly smoothing nonexistent wrinkles from the bridal dress, signified her opinion of such carryings-on on one's wedding day with a loud sniff.

The walk over the heath would have been very pleasant at any other time. The sky was a gorgeous bright blue that reminded her irresistibly of the color of Sebastian's eyes, and the tiny leaves of the sturdy green shrubs were a vibrant green. Birds and small animals fluttered and scurried about their business, while the heady scent of the heath itself rose to curl about Julia's nostrils. But she barely noticed the spicy scent; her thoughts were all centered on the small girl who was in all likelihood crying her eyes out in the bell tower of the ruined monastery that was even now visible to her as she topped the small rise.

She stood for a moment, shading her eyes as she looked at the magnificent ruin silhouetted against the halcyon sky. But Chloe was nowhere in sight. Julia sighed. She estimated that she had been gone for nearly twenty minutes already, which didn't leave much time to extract Chloe from the tower, return with her to White Friars, and then get into her bridal regalia again. But the passage of time was not the only reason for her rising uneasiness, she realized; she was conscious suddenly of a strange reluctance to approach the place where Elizabeth had met her death. Only the thought of Chloe's small figure as she had seen her before, huddled and crying heartbrokenly in the place where her mother had spent her last minutes on earth, kept her from turning back.

It was all imagination, of course, but as Julia approached the monastery she felt she was not alone. It was the same feeling that had plagued her during her walks about the heath the previous summer. Now, as then, she could see no one else around. If it was a human being who was responsible for the eerie feeling. . . . She was being ridiculous, Julia told herself firmly as she clambered over the fallen rocks that blocked the monastery's entrance. Of course Elizabeth's ghost was not following her about. How absurd could one get?

Still, when she stood inside the little chapel, and felt the sudden chill caused by coming inside the ancient stone walls after just having been in the warm summer sun, Julia could not repress a shiver—and it was not from the chill. The sun was shining through the broken window just as it had been the one previous time she had been here, only this time the red glow beamed down on the arched entryway to the tower. Julia walked slowly toward it. Her reluctance was growing ever stronger. Again she had to fight the urge to turn tail and run.

She compromised, standing at the foot of the stairs and calling out.

"Chloe! Chloe, dear, come down, please! It's Julia!"

But of course Chloe did not appear on the stairs, as Julia had known she would not. The child would probably not answer a summons like that at the best of times. And today, as upset as she must be, she would likely not even hear it.

The feeling that all was not right grew stronger, but Julia told herself firmly that she was simply allowing her imagination to run away with her. Of course she had nothing to fear merely by being in this place. Even if Elizabeth did haunt the place, she would have no reason to harm her unless of course she was jealous that Sebastian meant to replace her and . . . But she was being ridiculous, she told herself firmly as she picked up her skirts in both hands and began a careful ascent of the slippery stone stairs. There were no such things as ghosts.

It seemed to take forever to reach the top of the stairs. Julia felt as if she were climbing through air that grew ever thicker, intentionally impeding her progress. But of course that was just her imagination, too, and her imagination that caused her heart to pound when she saw a golden glow suffuse the open trap door that led into the aperture where the bell had once been.

Taking her common sense firmly in hand, Julia climbed the two steps remaining and pulled herself up into the small room. She saw at once that it was empty, and that the golden glow was caused by the bright summer sunlight streaming in through the open archway. No ghost at all, of course.

But also no Chloe. Her walk and her worry had been in vain. But where could the child have gotten to? Struck by a dreadful thought, Julia crossed to the knee-high stone wall across the open archway through which the bell had swung. Placing her hand carefully on the wall beside her for support, Julia peered down.

Two hundred feet below, past the blackened walls of the monastery and the craggy stone cliffs with their outcroppings of heath, lay the Wash. Spray darkened rocks stood stolidly while creaming waves washed over them, retreated, and washed over them again. The salty smell of the sea was faint so high above it, as was the muted roar of the breakers. Far louder were the cries of the seagulls and terns as they circled and wheeled not far from where Julia stood.

Of course there was no small figure smashed on the rocks below, and Julia shook her head at her own fancies. Yet she couldn't shake the feeling that something was wrong.

Then she saw it. In the tiny graveyard. The white cowled figure with the face of death, looking up toward where she stood.

Julia wheeled away from the arched opening through which Elizabeth had fallen to her death, her hands pressed to her heart which was pounding wildly in her chest. Her eyes were huge with horror. This was the vision she had seen in her dream; this was what the villagers saw when one of the Peyton family was facing death. Good God, had it been the last sight Elizabeth had seen on earth? Was it the last sight *she* would ever see?

She had to get out of the tower—now. Just as instinctively as a rabbit knows to run from a fox, Julia knew that her life depended on getting out of that bell tower as quickly as possible. But her limbs, nearly frozen with terror, seemed strangely reluctant to move.

She was stumbling toward the trap door when a head emerged through it. Her heart stopped, then started again as the sunlight glinted off gleaming fair hair.

Sebastian? No. Even with the golden sunlight half-blinding her and terror at what she had just seen befuddling her senses, she knew this was not Sebastian. She backed away from the figure even as it pulled itself through the trap door. As it came to its feet the long white robes in which it was enveloped opened to reveal the glittering sharp blade of a butcher knife. Her eyes fastened on that knife for a long, horror-struck moment, then lifted to the face of the figure beneath the cowl.

For a moment, with the sun shining so brightly all around, she again thought she was looking at the faceless figure of death. Then the hood was thrown back.

"Caroline!" Julia gasped. She stared into the serene blue eyes that looked exactly as they had in her bedroom less than an hour earlier, and felt hysterical laughter bubble up in her throat. *Caroline* was not a murderer. Sweet gentle Caroline? It was impossible.

Caroline smiled at her, looking as unruffled as if they were meeting in the drawing room at White Friars, and Julia felt an icy chill race down her spine. Something about that gentle smile told her that Caroline was utterly, totally mad.

"I'm so sorry, Julia," Caroline said regretfully as if she were declining an invitation to tea. "I really am."

"Did you come to help me look for Chloe, Caroline?" Julia said carefully, her mind working with lightning speed as she tried to come up with a way to save herself. Instinctively she tried to be calm, as if nothing out of the ordinary were happening. Showing fear was the worst thing she could do, she sensed.

"No." Caroline shook her head, looking momentarily puzzled, as if she couldn't remember why she was there. Julia took advantage of the moment to risk edging a step closer to the trap door. With Caroline situated as she was, it would be nearly impossible to get around her without giving the other woman the opportunity to stab her several times—if Caroline really would stab her.

"Don't come any closer, Julia," Caroline warned in a suddenly harsh voice. The blue eyes glinted as she made a threatening gesture with the knife. Then Julia knew that Caroline would use the weapon if she had to. Though undoubtedly she would prefer that Julia go over the edge of the bell tower without a betraying wound, as had Elizabeth, to be dashed to death on the rocks by the sea.

"Don't make me hurt you, Julia. I don't want to. I just want you to walk over there to the wall and . . . disappear."

Caroline sounded almost pleading. Julia, staring at her with growing horror, wondered if it would be possible to rush her and get the knife. Caroline was taller than she, but her years on the streets had made her tough.

"You don't want to do this, Caroline," Julia said soothingly, keeping her back flat against the wall and her eyes on Caroline at all times. A mounting tide of terror was making it difficult to think, but she forced it back, knowing she had to keep a clear head. She decided in an instant that she would rush Caroline only as a last resort. Talk would be her first line of defense. Emily knew where she was, Julia remembered with a surge of hope. If she could keep Caroline standing here talking long enough, Sebastian would come. Emily would tell him where she was when she didn't return in time to meet him at the altar.

"No, I don't want to," Caroline said with real regret. "But you shouldn't be marrying Sebastian. I tried to warn you, you know. I dressed up like this that night in your room when you were ill, and I told you what would happen if you didn't give up Sebastian. Elizabeth died, and you will too, I said. But you didn't listen, so this is your own fault. I am supposed to be the Countess of Moorland, not you—or Elizabeth. It's why I married Edward. *He* died, but that's all right. I like Sebastian much better anyway. Sebastian is so handsome. When he marries me, I'll be Lady Moorland, just as I ought."

"Is that why you killed Elizabeth, Caroline?" Julia's voice was soft.

"She should never have been Lady Moorland," Caroline said as if it were the most obvious thing in the world. "I was supposed to be that. When Edward died, and then the old lord, she took my place. Everyone started calling her by my name. You can understand why I didn't like that. At first I couldn't think of any way to stop it, though. Then it occurred to me that I could still be Lady Moorland if I were married to Sebastian. He didn't much like that simpering wife of his anyway, and I am far more beautiful. Sebastian used to smile at me—he liked me, he's always like me. He would have married me by now—if not for you." She directed a baleful look at Julia, who shrank back against the wall.

"Even if you kill me, Caroline, there's no guarantee that Sebastian will marry you," Julia said reasonably, praying that the showdown would not come yet.

Caroline smiled. "Who else will he marry? Everyone thinks he killed Elizabeth anyway. I didn't intend that, but it's worked out very well. And when you die, no female in the country would have him. Except for me, of course. I'll stand by him no matter what. And one day he'll start wanting children, normal children. He'll have to marry me."

Caroline's plan had a mad sort of logic to it, Julia thought. She could conceive of just the scenario Caroline described. With her death, and all that had come before it, Sebastian would be a pariah in England. He could go abroad, of course, but there was Chloe. She didn't think he'd abandon Chloe, or his estates. At least not forever. He would come back, and be lonely, and there would be Caroline.

"You don't want to do this, Caroline. And you don't have to. We can get help for you." Julia's voice was hoarse as she realized that Caroline's eyes were glazing over. The end was coming and help was nowhere in sight. The instincts of danger that had warned her against coming near the old monastery had been right, she realized. And she realized too that perhaps the eerie feeling that had plagued her earlier was a premonition she might die here.

"I don't want help. I want to be the Countess of Moorland." Caroline's voice was as calmly reasonable as before, but before Julia could think of anything else to say she took a step forward, brandishing the knife. The long silver blade glinted wickedly in the brilliant sunlight.

"Step back, Julia." The calm voice was at odds with the mad glitter of her eyes. Julia swallowed, eyeing Caroline and the knife. If help didn't come soon, she would have to jump her, and fight her for possession of the knife. But she had a few more minutes. Please, God . . .

Julia took a step back, still pressing flat against the cold stone wall.

"That's very good. You're being very sensible. Not like that crybaby Elizabeth. She cried and cried, even though I explained things to her. Finally I quite lost my patience. She wouldn't just disappear as she was supposed to. I had to push her. Step back again, Julia."

Julia knew that she was very near the low wall that opened out over the drop she had been staring down at earlier. She didn't dare take too many more steps back. Too close to the wall, and a rush from Caroline might easily send her over. Which must have been, she realized, what had happened to Elizabeth.

She took a tiny step back. Caroline looked displeased.

"I hope you're not going to be difficult about this. Stand away from that wall, if you please."

Julia had to stifle a hysterical giggle. Caroline sounded so normal; this could not be happening. It could not, but it was. And if help did not come very, very soon, she realized, she would have to grapple for the knife.

But it was too late for any kind of plan. With a furious cry and the upraised knife glittering murderously in the sun, Caroline rushed forward. Julia was almost surprised into leaping backwards out of the way—and to her death. Instead she managed to throw herself to one side just as Caroline's body slammed into hers, forcing it hard against the solid stone wall. The hand holding the knife slashed down, and Julia screamed, trying to dodge away even as her hands came up to ward off the knife. She felt the cold slice of metal through the soft flesh of her bare arm, saw the rush of warm, red blood, and saw too the knife as it was raised for another strike.

"No!" howled a voice from the direction of the trap door.

Before Julia could even grasp the identity of her rescuer, there was a rush of movement as a body flung itself across the bell tower and into Caroline. At the impact Caroline staggered backward. What happened next was over before Julia could do anything but watch in horror.

Caroline tottered against the low wall and lost her balance. She hung poised over the edge for what seemed an eternity, eyes widening and arms flailing wildly, silhouetted against the bright blue of the summer sky. Then with an ear-splitting scream she fell.

It was some minutes before Julia could turn away from the empty arch of blue sky where Caroline had been. Outside it appeared as though nothing at all had happened to change the tenor of the beautiful summer day. The seagulls and terns still wheeled and cried, the sky was still a gorgeous blue, and the sun still shone. Yet the horror had happened and was over, thanks to a small warm body pressed even now against Julia's skirts.

"Chloe!" Julia gasped weakly as the awesome fact of the child's act hit home for the first time. Feeling the child's body shake as it pressed against her legs, Julia sank to her knees and drew the trembling little girl into her arms. Blood ran from the shallow gash in her upper arm to drip onto the stone floor, but Julia was beyond feeling pain.

"Chloe, darling, you saved my life."

The small face that was so like Sebastian's lifted for a moment to look into hers with those celestial blue eyes.

"Mummy!" Chloe said clearly, and buried her face again in Julia's shoulder. Sobs shook her small frame. Julia bent over the child, crooning to her in wordless comfort as she rocked her back and forth in her arms. The two of them clung together for what seemed a long time. Finally another bright head emerged through the trap door, and Sebastian appeared beside them. Julia had not heard his approach, and neither, it seemed, had Chloe.

"My God, are you all right? Julia? Chloe? What in hell

happened to your arm?"

He was dressed in his wedding finery, and his face was as white as his shirt. His voice was hoarse as he saw the blood running down Julia's arm to stain her dress and drip on the floor. Julia shook her head at him.

"Caroline . . . had a knife. She . . . tried to kill me." She didn't want to say any more, or make a fuss about what had happened in Chloe's hearing. Sebastian, sensing the reason for her reticence, stared down at her, then sank to one knee and knotted his handkerchief firmly over the wound without speaking. He stood up, moving to the arch to look down at where Caroline's body lay on the rocks below. He stared silently for a moment, then turned back to look at his daughter and the woman he loved as they clung together on the cold stone floor.

"Chloe?" he said huskily, looking down at the child Julia still cradled in her arms.

"She's all right. She saved my life."

"Christ. I . . ." He broke off as Chloe's head came up, and she looked around at him. For a moment the small mouth trembled and the blue eyes were wide as she stared up at Sebastian's tall form towering over them both. Julia held her breath. Would the child dissolve into one of the screaming fits that Sebastian's presence always brought on?

Then, "Papa," Chloe said clearly, as big tears rolled down her cheeks. These were not the tears of hysteria but of grief, and Sebastian dropped to his knees beside his child, wrapping his arms around her and Julia both.

"Baby," Sebastian said, his own tears clear in his voice. The three of them rocked together for a long time before making their way back to White Friars.

EPILOGUE

O N a bright summer day nearly two years later, Julia was leaning back against the trunk of a huge oak tree not far outside the village of Bishop's Lynn. Sebastian was lying with his head in her lap, his eyes closed as he napped away the afternoon.

They had driven out from White Friars with a huge picnic lunch, most of which had already been comfortably demolished. The remains had been tidily packed away into the basket, which sat near them. Chloe, her bright hair arranged into a single thick plait, was busy shepherding her black haired baby sister through her first steps. Clare and her twin brother, Charles, who was at that moment asleep on a blanket near Julia's feet, were nearly a year old, and their energy was practically inexhaustible. Chloe thought they were the most marvelous beings on earth with their huge blue eyes and mops of black curls, and Julia was pleased at the almost maternal affection she showered on her two rowdy siblings.

Now, watching fondly as Chloe tried to interest Clare in a pretty yellow butterfly, Julia felt a rush of contentment. She had Sebastian, and Chloe, and Clare, and Charles, and in six months time would have another child. A family such as she could never have imagined all that time ago when she had been a homeless street waif starved for love. Now she had all the love she could ever have dreamed of, and she considered herself truly blessed. Her cup was overflowing.

The change in Chloe over the past two years was remarkable. Julia had feared that what had happened with Caroline would leave its mark on the child forever, but instead it had seemed to act as a kind of catharsis. Chloe had at last come out of the silent world she had retreated to, little by little at first and then finally with a huge rush of words that so far showed no signs of abating. She seemed to feel she had a proprietary claim on Julia and the babies, and she adored her father. Julia had never asked her, not wanting to bring back bad memories, but she guessed that the servants' speculation had been right. Chloe had probably seen Sebastian carrying Elizabeth's body into the house that dreadful day, and thereafter had not been able to look at her father without associating him with her mother's death. But after Chloe had saved Julia from the same tragic end, she had never had another screaming spell, for which Julia was thankful.

One thing Julia had discovered was that Chloe had been responsible for the eerie feeling of being followed she had so often had when she had walked out-of-doors at White Friars. Chloe had slipped away from Miss Belkerson frequently that fall to follow Julia, her small size enabling her to hide in places that would have been impossible for an adult. Apparently Chloe had associated Julia with her mother from the time Julia had found her crying in the bell tower, and ever afterwards had feared that Julia might meet Elizabeth's fate. She had acted as a pintsized bodyguard, even on that terrible day when her quick action had saved Julia's life. From what Julia had been able to piece together, Chloe had been on her way back to the house from an expedition to gather flowers as a wedding gift for Julia when she had seen Caroline following her toward the monastery.

Chloe had followed—and been on hand to save Julia's life.

The wedding had been held two weeks after it was originally scheduled, and this time Chloe had attended. She had stood with her grandmother in front of the crowd of servants and had watched as Julia and Sebastian became man and wife. Julia had been prepared to claw the dowager countess' eyes out the minute the older woman said or did anything to upset either Sebastian or Chloe, but in the end her new mother-in-law had been very well behaved. She visited them at White Friars once or twice a year, and her relationship with both Sebastian and Chloe was much improved. She didn't seem to know quite what to make of Clare—the baby seemed to take a positive delight in having temperamental fits whenever confronted with her grandmother. But she adored Charles—the heir, Julia thought ironically. But Julia, largely for Sebastian's sake, tried her best to get along with Sebastian's mother, and to her surprise succeeded tolerably well. As for the new baby . . .

"Clare, no! Stop! Julia!"

"Waaah! Ma—ma!"

Chloe's yell followed by Clare's piercing wail brought Julia leaping to her feet with scant regard for Sebastian's cozily nestled head.

"What the hell?" He sat up, looking grumpy as Julia ran to disentangle Clare from the rose bush into which she had toddled.

"Julia, I'm sorry, I couldn't stop her in time—"

"Ma—ma, bad bush! Hurt!"

Julia soothed both her daughters as she freed Clare's dress from the thorns and carried her a safe distance away. Chloe followed, looking anxious. She took her responsibilities as big sister very seriously.

"I'll watch her really carefully this time, Julia, I promise."

"I know you will, darling. You're such a big help to me, I don't know what I would do without you." Julia smiled warmly at Chloe as she set Clare back on her feet. The baby immediately staggered away, with Chloe in hot pursuit.

Julia then retraced her steps to where Sebastian now sat with his back propped against the oak tree, watching the proceedings with a faintly bemused look. Julia dropped down beside him, one eagle eye on Charles to make sure he still slept. Sebastian slid an arm around her and pulled her against his side. She looked up at the breathtaking face beneath the glinting silver-gilt hair, and smiled.

"Sorry I had to drop you like that."

"That's all right, I'm getting used to interruptions." The arm that was around her waist slid down until the flat of his hand rested against the slight swell of her stomach. "You don't mind about the new baby, do you? I know it's a bit soon after Clare and Charles. When I married you, I didn't mean to saddle you with a baby every year. Much less two."

Julia grinned, and reached up to plant a soft kiss on the smooth shaven cheek nearest her. "I plan to spend the rest of my life having your babies, my love."

He smiled too as he looked down at her, his blue eyes as dazzlingly bright as the summer sky. "And I," he said softly his arm tightening around her as he dropped a brief hard kiss on her mouth, "plan to spend the rest of my life loving you."

Center Point Publishing
600 Brooks Road ● PO Box 1
Thorndike ME 04986-0001 USA

(207) 568-3717

US & Canada:
1 800 929-9108